The Bowl of Souls: Book Five

MOTHER OF THE MOONRAT

BY: TREVOR H. COOLEY

Trevor H. Cooley

THE BOWL OF SOULS SERIES

The Moonrat Saga:

BOOK ONE: EYE OF THE MOONRAT
BOOK 1.5: HILT'S PRIDE
BOOK TWO: MESSENGER OF THE DARK
        PROPHET
BOOK THREE: HUNT OF THE BANDHAM
BOOK FOUR: THE WAR OF STARDEON
BOOK FIVE: MOTHER OF THE MOONRAT

Upcoming:

TARAH WOODBLADE

Dedication

As with my first book, I dedicate this book to my wife. Without her I never could have finished the series. She is not only my first true love, she's first in everything. She is the first one to hear any idea; the first one to read any chapter. She's my editor and my collaborator. She is the first to tell me if an idea is great or if I should throw it away. She is also my first true reader and biggest fan.

This is for you, Jeannette. I love you.

Acknowledgements

Thank you to my father, who is the second one to read any of my chapters and my brother, Keith, who read along right with him at the end.

Also thanks to Michael Patty, John Williams, Ben and Katrina Pickett, Matt Yeates, Jeff Bailey and all the others who helped with development of the Bowl of Souls Game.

And to Corky Coker, thank you for fourteen years of helping me support my family.

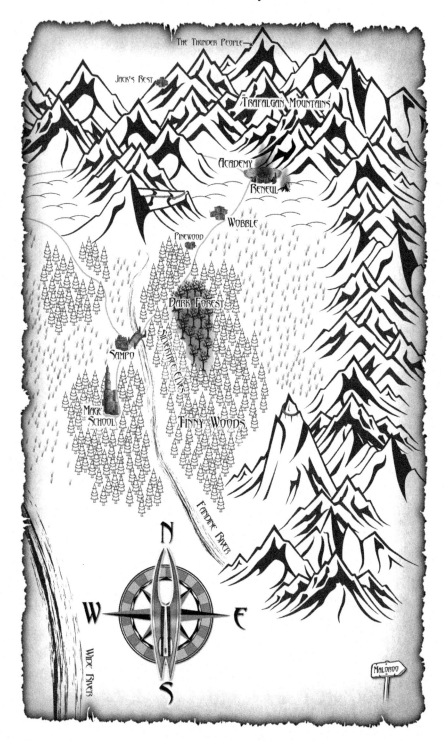

Table of Contents

Prologue

"One . . . Two . . . Now!" Sir Hilt said. Together the four of them pulled the lodestone amulets from their places in the back wall of the cave.

Deathclaw watched as the portal vanished. His link with Justan faded until the only thing that remained was a knowledge of the human's general direction. For some reason that Deathclaw couldn't fathom, that loss of communication with Justan's mind made him uneasy.

"They're coming again," Beth said, her brow furrowed in concentration. "The witch is angry and she's hurting. What we did today wounded her greatly. I think it would be best if we got away before she got her strength back."

Deathclaw could hear the screech of trolls and roars of large beasts coming from beyond the cave mouth. The effects of Darlan's devastating spell were fading away. The molten hill outside had solidified and the ground around the mouth of the cave was nearly cool enough for the creatures to walk on.

"This way," Hilt said and led them to the far left side of the cave where the rear wall bulged outward. "Master Latva told me it was over here."

The rear exit to the cave was cleverly hidden. It wasn't visible until they reached the corner and saw the downward sloping tunnel.

Charz frowned. "Don't know if I can fit down there."

"I scouted it earlier," Deathclaw said in his best attempt at an assuring tone. He had found the rear passage and explored it earlier that day, making sure no enemies were hiding within. There would be room. "The giant will . . ." *Fit through.* He wanted to say 'fit', but he couldn't. Instead he said, "Go through.

. . Just."

The giant looked at him askance. "I'll go last anyway, just in case."

"Good idea," Beth said with a smirk. "If you get stuck, they might just think you're a rock and the rest of us can get away."

"Just go," the giant grumbled.

Hilt went in first with Beth close behind. Deathclaw followed, feeling that heavy feeling that came over him any time he was in an enclosed space. He hadn't liked it the first time he had gone through either. It was dark and echoed down there. His eyes had adjusted, but raptoids were not meant to be in caves.

Charz squeezed after him, slowly edging his way down the passage, having to contort awkwardly several times to make it through the natural twists of the rocky walls. The crystal pendant that hung from the iron chain around his neck sparked as it scraped against the rock.

The passage opened up into a rocky cavern below. When Hilt reached the end of the passage, he took a white orb out from his pack. He tapped it a few times. The orb flickered, then glowed with just enough light to illuminate their surroundings.

The cavern was wide enough to fit perhaps thirty humans inside and the ceiling was perhaps as high as the giant's head. Deathclaw estimated the there were only perhaps ten feet or so of rock between them and the grassy ground above.

"Stupid . . . rock!" Charz grunted as he pushed himself through the final squeeze and stumbled out of the opening. "I could hear 'em in the cave above. They'll find the way down to us soon."

"Yes, one of the witch's moonrats is in the cave above," Beth agreed. "It has other creatures with it, but I can't quite make out their nature."

Hilt was running his hands along the uneven surface of the chamber wall. "There is supposed to be a lever here somewhere that closes off the passageway."

Deathclaw cocked his head and scanned the area himself. He found it fascinating all the ways humans found to lock the danger out. Hamford had tried to evade him many times that way. It hadn't worked, but Deathclaw had gained a respect for human ingenuity.

"I don't see anything," Charz said.

"Shh!" Deathclaw said in a forced whisper. "They will hear you."

"No," Beth said. "I am muting their sense of hearing."

"Will the witch not notice?" Deathclaw asked. The moonrats were her eyes and ears after all.

"She's more than a bit distracted right now, and I'm trying to do this subtly," she said, her teeth clenched in concentration. Sweat beaded on her forehead. "It's not easy to do."

"Wait-wait," Hilt said. The warrior shoved his hand into a dark crevice in the wall. "I think I found it!"

"They're coming," Beth said and a screech echoed down the passage. She sighed and shook her head. "Still haven't figured out how to deaden their sense of smell."

"There!" Hilt jerked his arm back. A rumbling sound of rock scraping against rock came from somewhere within the wall, followed by a heavy thud. A cloud of dust came out of the passage. "Did we stop them?"

"No," Deathclaw hissed. Something was still coming. He could hear it. It must have started down the passage before Hilt had found the lever. Its approach was slow. "It is . . ." *Big.* He wanted to say 'big'. "Large."

"It's a troll," Charz said. He slammed his fist into his palm. "I can smell it."

Hilt drew his swords and Deathclaw caught the odor the giant spoke of. It was pungent and . . . hungry. But it was jumbled, almost as if there were-.

"Two!" Beth said and rummaged around in her pack for something.

Deathclaw considered drawing his own sword, but hesitated because of the narrow confines of their surroundings. He had not fought a troll before, but Fist had shared his memories of fighting them through the bond. He knew that they would be tall and thin and trail a flammable slime behind them. And they would heal very fast.

The first troll lumbered out of the passage. It didn't look like the trolls in the ogre's memories. It wasn't thin at all. In fact, it was almost as muscular as Fist was. It opened its cavernous mouth and let out a hideous screech.

Charz's ended its screech by swinging his heavy fist into its mouth. Teeth and slime flew. It stumbled back but did not seem to feel the pain. It bit down on the giant's fist and lashed out with its claws, scoring his rocky skin.

Deathclaw left the giant to grapple with it and slid up next to the opening, his back against the wall. The next troll came out of the passage and headed right for Sir Hilt. The human was in battle stance, waiting for it. Deathclaw slashed the back of the troll's legs, tearing muscle and tendons, and it stumbled right into the named warrior's attack.

Hilt swung his swords in a downward slash and Deathclaw saw twin cuts open in the troll's back, starting from either side of its neck, and running all the way down its spine, cutting through ribs and muscle, ending at its hips. The troll's arms and shoulders peeled away from its spine and it collapsed to the ground in front of Hilt, its torso nearly sliced in three pieces.

Deathclaw hissed in amazement. The attack was impossible. Hilt's blades hadn't even passed all the way through its body. There must have been magic involved.

Charz had taken his troll to the ground and straddled it. Ignoring its clawing hands, he pounded its head with swings of his chiseled fists. Finally there was a crunch and its face crumpled in.

"Huh," said the giant, standing up. Long slashing wounds covered his torso. "Those were stronger than regular trolls, but they went down pretty fast."

Deathclaw frowned and pointed to the troll's head. "Look!"

Its face was swelling outward as its skull quickly reformed underneath. The troll let out a screech and Charz silenced it with a stomp of his foot, crushing its skull again. "That's a nuisance."

The troll at Hilt's feet was healing quickly too, its arms were being pulled back towards its body as the slices in its torso closed.

"This isn't good," Hilt said. There was a thick thunk as

he stabbed the tip of one sword down through the back of the troll's head. The other wounds continued to heal, but he left the sword in its brain, assuring that it wouldn't get back up. "Blast it, they'll chase right after us if we try to leave."

"Yeah and now the witch knows where we are," Charz said bitterly.

"I don't think so. They don't have moonrat eyes inside them," Beth said. "The mother of the moonrats may have noticed that these two disappeared, but she doesn't know what's happened to them." She pulled a small wooden tube from her pack. As Beth removed a leather cap from the end, there was a short flash of sparks. "We can't let those things come after us, though. Toss me a stick or something that I can start on fire."

"Don't use fire down here, woman!" Charz said, stomping the creature's head again. His torso was covered in troll slime. "It's a closed space. You could end up lighting yourself up."

"He's right," Hilt said. "Remember last time you lit a trail of troll slime?"

"There was a lot more slime back then," she said with a roll of her eyes. She gestured at the two convulsing monsters on the floor. "We have to do something. They are healing far too quickly."

"It will not work anyway," Deathclaw said in realization. They weren't just trolls. Justan had told him about these things. They had been changed in some way by the wizard's power. "These are not . . . regular trolls. We need . . ."

Pepper! Deathclaw hissed and clenched his fists until his claws pierced the skin of his palms. He wanted to say 'pepper'! But he had no lips to say it with and there was no other word he could use instead. Without lips, he couldn't speak words with a P, M, F, B, or V in them which made the human language a constant frustration. Communication with Justan was so much easier.

"You know something important," Beth said. She came up to Deathclaw and pulled him close, placing her head on his chest.

He flinched. Why was she doing this to him again? Then he heard her voice in his mind. *Tell me what you know. What are they and what do we need to do?*

You can hear me? he asked in surprise.

I can if I listen very hard. Your bond makes you open, but for now this communication will only work if I am this close, she responded.

Pepper, he said. *We need pepper.* He gathered all the information Justan had taught him about these trolls and pushed it through to her mind. *They have been changed by the wizard Vrill. They are resistant to fire, but pepper will make them unable to heal.*

Beth's eyes widened and she stepped back. "Deathclaw says that these trolls are special and their slime is not flammable. They will only die if cooked through, but he says that the academy recently found that trolls have a reaction to pepper that makes them unable to regenerate."

"He said all that?" Hilt asked, twisting his sword in the troll's skull as it tried to get up.

"He is an excellent communicator," Beth replied and Hilt raised an eyebrow in disbelief.

"Well I don't have any pepper. Do you?" Charz said and frowned. He stomped the troll's head again and there was a loud crack. "Stupid thing."

"No pepper really, but . . ." Hilt shrugged and pointed. "Beth, in my pack there is that dried beef we brought from the dwarves caverns. I remember it being quite spicy."

Charz snorted. "We gonna stuff dried beef into their wounds?"

"Can't think of a better idea," Hilt said and forced his sword back down into its skull. The troll was healing so quickly it kept pushing the blade out.

"I could kill it. At night," Deathclaw said, fingering his sword hilt. He rarely had the opportunity to use Star's powers in the night when they were most powerful.

Hilt gave him a questioning look but said nothing as Beth returned to him, a long piece of dried beef in her hands.

"I'd call this peppery," Beth said. The beef was practically bristling with peppercorns. Even though Deathclaw didn't like the thought of eating meat that wasn't raw, the smell of it made his mouth water.

14

Hilt tore the beef in half, wrenched his sword to crack the troll's head open and shoved the meat inside. He then removed the sword and took a step back to see what happened. The troll continued to jitter on the ground and at first the wound began to close as fast as before, but this time it stopped just short of closing completely.

Hilt shook his head. "Well I'll be. Pepper of all things. Wait until I tell the Roo-Tan about this."

Hilt tossed the other half of the beef to Charz and the giant stomped his troll's head again, then bent and pried the broken pieces of skull apart to shove the meat inside. "Stupid thing's trying to heal around my fingers!" he grumbled, then stood back up, his task complete. His troll too couldn't heal completely and lay convulsing on the cave floor.

They stared at the two quivering monsters for a moment before Beth finally said, "What do we do now?"

"That's weird. First time I've ever seen you hesitating," Charz said. The sarcasm in his voice was thick. "Don't you have any impressions, Beth? Any spirit magic visions telling you what we should do?"

"I've told you before, I don't control when that happens. They just come to me," she responded, giving the giant a tight glare. "I can tell you that the mother of the moonrats has this place surrounded. I can feel her eyes all around the hill. There are a dozen of them just pacing back and forth as if waiting for something. That moonrat is still in the cave out front with . . ." She squinted in concentration. "I think, more trolls. But it's hard to tell. Their signature is so strange."

"She can't get to us through the passage," Hilt said. "But that moonrat knows two trolls came in this way and didn't come out."

Beth shook her head slightly, "I don't know how much that moonrat really knows. There is hardly any individual mind left in them. They are just conduits for the witch's will and like I was saying before, the question is with her in so much pain, did she notice the disappearance of two trolls?"

"Either way we must be careful," Hilt said, his eyes filled with concern. "If her creatures find the exit to this cavern . . ."

"I went through it earlier," Deathclaw said. "It is well

hidden."

"Fine," said Charz. The giant sat down and leaned back against the cave wall with his hands behind his head. The wounds the troll had given him were nearly closed already. "We'll wait 'em out, then. Take off when they leave."

"But what if they do find the rear entrance? She'll have us pinned in here," Hilt pointed out. "The witch will keep sending creatures until she knows we're dead."

Deathclaw watched their faces. Each one of them looked so unsure; so doubtful. The seconds stretched out and finally he sighed.

"I will go and lead the creatures away," he volunteered. He felt uncomfortable in the cave anyway, all that rock over his head. The human way of locking out the danger didn't work for him. He would rather choose the raptoid way and run from the wizard's beasts under the open sky.

Deathclaw noticed Beth eyeing him thoughtfully, but she said nothing.

"Are you sure about that?" Hilt asked, looking dubious. "Some of those beasts are very fast."

"They are not as quick as I," Deathclaw responded. Besides, Talon was out there somewhere. He had promised Justan her death.

"I think it's a great plan," Charz said, letting out a yawn and Deathclaw wondered what had happened to the bloodthirsty giant Justan had told him about. Why wasn't he excited to get out there and fight Ewzad Vriil's creations? The giant closed his eyes. "But then what? Are we gonna just wait in here, or are we gonna go and scout around like the wizards want us to?"

"We should leave as soon as the witch's eyes have left the area," Hilt said, but he was still watching Deathclaw. "How will you find us again once you have evaded your pursuers?"

Deathclaw shrugged. He wasn't sure he was going to. They really didn't need him. The rock giant had a bonding wizard back at the Mage School. If he went off on his own he could sneak into places a group couldn't and give Justan information the others wouldn't have. "I can track you."

"You think so?" Charz smiled.

"I am pretty good at covering our tracks," Hilt said. "And

covered head-to-toe in dried orc blood, and whom, just a few short moments ago, had been known as Tamboor the Fearless, ex-master of the Academy Berserker's Guild.

Justan forced his thoughts away from the oddity of the situation and focused on the prophet's announcement. The story of Stardeon and his wife? He hadn't known Stardeon had a wife. Neither Coal or Samson had mentioned anyone named Mellinda when they had told him about the creation of the rogue horses. He asked Gwyrtha through the bond, *Did you know?*

No, she replied. *Father had no woman. There was just Father and Sam.*

"The story I have to tell you is a long one," the prophet said. He gave them a kind smile as his eyes swept across their battle weary bodies. "Unfortunately, this Hall of Majesty was designed for ceremony, not for comfort and you have all had a long day. Why don't you collect some chairs from the other rooms down the hall and bring them in here so that we can sit while I talk?"

"Why don't we simply have the conversation elsewhere?" Master Latva asked, watching with concern as Fist, Zambon, and Jhonate walked out of the hallway to do as asked.

Alfred gave the wizard an amused smile and explained, "Latva is worried that the other council members will give him grief about moving a bunch of chairs into the Hall of Majesty."

"Well . . . mainly Wizard Auger," Latva said, giving the gnome a slight glare for calling him out. It was evident to Justan that the two had been keeping their bond a secret for so long that Latva was still getting used to Alfred speaking his mind aloud.

"More of this wizard silliness," the prophet said with a dismissive chuckle. "Why should we move? The bowl doesn't mind. Besides, Tolivar and his bonded are lying here quite comfortably on that plush rug. This story is for them to hear as well and I see no need to drag them down the hallway."

"But . . . they're asleep, ain't they?" Lenny asked, kneeling at Bettie's head. He hadn't left her side since finding out she was carrying his child.

"In a sense," the prophet replied. "They are deep within the bond, learning how to deal with a new bonding wizard. The magic has a lot of adjustments to make to each of them so that the bond will work properly."

A crash echoed from a room outside the hall and Latva winced. Alfred laughed. "I suppose I should go and show them where to look." The gnome jogged out of the hall to join the others.

Justan opened his spirit sight and looked down at the man whose name had once been Tamboor. The silvery crown-like ring of the bond that the prophet had laid on the warrior's head had moved down his body and settled within his chest. The thick ropes of spirit magic that connected Tolivar to Coal's former bonded pulsed as if not yet stable. Justan thought back to the severe pain he had gone through following his bonding with Deathclaw and didn't envy the man.

The prophet continued, "So to answer your question, Lenui, while they will likely not remember the telling of the tale, the words I say will remain imprinted in their minds."

"Oh," Lenny said thoughtfully. He tenderly moved a few strands of curly black hair off of the half-orc's face, tucking them behind her slightly green tinted ear. He leaned forward and whispered something to her.

The doors to the hall swung open again and the others returned, carrying chairs.

Fist came back with two large and heavily padded chairs that Justan was pretty sure weren't meant to be moved. The ogre dropped them down next to Justan and their stout legs hit the marble floor with a loud crack. Fist eased his large frame into one of them. The chair creaked in protest, but it was just big enough to support him. Fist let out an audible sigh and moaned, "Ohh that is nice. Squirrel, come and see how soft it is!"

Squirrel climbed out of his pouch and sat on one of the plush armrests. He felt around and nodded appreciatively, then began shelling a nut. The animal's appearance was yet another oddity in this place but to Justan's relief, no one batted an eye.

Justan sat in the other chair and he had to agree with Fist. Though it was much larger than necessary, it was so comfortable that he almost let out a moan himself.

Jhonate walked up carrying two ornate chairs with padded seats. She handed one to Locksher and placed hers next to Justan. She eyed the chair Fist had given him. "Is that chair

"Well . . . I don't see why we would. At this point Dann Doudy is dead and we don't need to convince the Mage School of anything," Justan said. "Please, John. We would like it destroyed."

John reached down deep into the pack and when he withdrew his hand, he held a cloth wrapped bundle. To Justan's spirit sight, the prophet's hands glowed with a soft white light, while the bundled object blazed forth with blackness. The prophet unwrapped the dagger and when he saw it his face twisted with disgust.

"This is Tulos, the ruby dagger; one of six daggers the Dark Prophet had made and bound to his soul. In the height of his power, the Dark Prophet was worshipped like a god and the high priests used to sacrifice innocents to him with these blades." The prophet held the dagger with the tips of his fingers and turned it so that they could all see the way the rubies glinted evilly in the light. "When someone is killed with this dagger, their spirit is torn and a small portion of their essence is transferred to him."

The metal itself was black and yet the blade was brown as if caked with dried blood. Justan shuddered at the thought that they had been carrying such a thing with them all this time.

John continued, "Once he had gained enough power, he changed the nature of the daggers to an even more insidious purpose. It became a way for someone to bind their own soul to the Dark Prophet.

"To become one of his true servants and gain the powers such a position held, a person had to sacrifice someone dear to them using one of these daggers. If the person killed was dear enough, say an old friend, a spouse, or a family member. The dagger would bind the soul of the sacrificer to the Dark Prophet. From that time on, he had a conduit directly into the sacrificer's mind.

"The blood of those sacrificed clings to this blade. Their souls cry out to me even now." The prophet's eyes narrowed and his hands blazed white. The darkness that blazed from the dagger began to fade and the metal glowed with a dull heat as he spoke. "Of the six daggers made, only three are left. I destroyed Pelos, the pearl dagger and Felos, the onyx dagger myself. A good friend of mine died while destroying Dalos, the turquoise dagger.

"Now this will take some effort, so please bear with me just a moment . . ." John grit his teeth in concentration and the white energy around his hands flared. The darkness recoiled from his fingertips and wrapped itself in tendrils around the blade as if trying to shield itself. The glow dimmed for a moment, but the prophet's attack was unrelenting.

The black tendrils thinned and the dagger's glow intensified. Finally the tendrils unwrapped themselves from the blade and began lashing out at the prophet's hands. Their attack was fierce, tearing at him, but they couldn't penetrate his magic. The blade began to glow with a white heat and shone with such a bright light that Justan had to put up one hand to shield his face.

Then the light and heat faded. Justan put his arm down and saw that the dagger that once radiated blackness, now glowed with a soft light. The metal had turned to a pure white and the rubies in the hilt gleamed with a sparkling brilliance.

The prophet blew on the blade and smiled. "There! Now only two of those foul things remain."

"What'd you do to it?" Lenny asked, gazing at the white dagger with wonder. "I ain't never seen metal like that before. It's dag-gum beautiful."

"Yes." The prophet nodded. "Yes it is. Or, it may yet be. It still needs some work, but if it could be repurposed that would really sting him. Thank you for bringing it to me." He tucked the blade away in his robes and Lenny frowned in disappointment. "So. Does anyone have questions before I begin?"

Justan had several but he was hesitant to speak up. Were they worth delaying the tale further? Questioning the methods of the prophet seemed presumptive to say the least. What if he offended the man?

"I have a question, John," Locksher said, one eyebrow raised in curiosity. "With a story as important as you say this one is, why did you chose to tell it to us? I look around this hall and other than Master Latva, there are no other leaders here. Why not other members of the High Council or the Battle Academy Council or perhaps a representative of the elves?"

"That is a fair question, Wizard Locksher," John said. "As I told you earlier, the Dark Prophet has gathered his champions and I have come here to the Mage School to gather my own. The bonding wizards have ever been my champions. It is necessary that you learn what you are up against."

"But not all of us are bonded, Prophet, Sir," Jhonate said with a frown. "Why are the rest of us here?"

John smiled. "I asked the rest of you here because I had a feeling that you needed to be here. I did not know what the reasons were at the time, but some of them have become evident. Zambon had the sword that was meant for his father. Lenui had the knowledge that Tolivar needed to make his decision to accept the bond and he also carried the dagger, which I must say caught me quite by surprise. As for you and Locksher, well . . . I believe this tale will affect the two of you most directly."

"How interesting," Locksher said, leaning so far forward in his chair that Justan wondered if he would fall.

Jhonate looked troubled by the prophet's answer and Justan reached out to take her hand in his. She blinked and gave him a slight smile, then squeezed his hand in return. Neither of them let go and, as the prophet told his tale, they listened hand in hand.

"Now, first things first. In order for you to truly understand the importance of this story, there is something you should know. Stardeon's wife, Mellinda, is the woman who eventually became the creature you know as the mother of the moonrats," John said and waited a moment for the revelation to sink in.

Justan blinked in surprise. "But . . . if Stardeon's wife is the witch . . ."

"Then she's been 'round a dag-blamed long time!" Lenny said. "How come we ain't heard of her before?"

"I have never read of this woman in the histories," Alfred said.

"This will all be explained as I tell you the tale," John said. He looked around at each of them and he could tell he had their full attention.

"I first met Stardeon when he was a boy. His bonding magic came on him suddenly and quite ferociously on the day his mother died. It was actually his first display of magic. Spirit magic awakenings are rare, but for some reason he was chosen

27

early. In that burst of magic, he had bonded to his childhood friend Sam, his dog, and three small birds, all at once. As you can imagine, that was a difficult trial for a boy so young.

"Stardeon was frightened by his powers. He was afraid that his father would think him crazy if he told him that he had bonded to his friend and the family dog. So he and Sam decided to keep their bond secret. They got away with it for quite a while too, but I felt a strong impression one day while passing by the town and decided to investigate.

"When I first saw him, Stardeon was cradling the body of a little bird in his hands and weeping. The poor boy had bonded to such fragile things. One of the neighbor's cats had caught the bird and injured it and he hadn't known enough about his magic to heal it.

"The bird wasn't even his first bonded to die. His dog had been old and riddled with the diseases that come to dogs in later years. Even the portion of Stardeon's youth passed along to it by the bond hadn't been enough to save it. Most children learn to deal with loss gradually over the years. The eleven-year-old boy I met that day had already lost his mother and two bonded in just a few short months."

Justan couldn't imagine what that would have been like. He glanced over at Squirrel in concern. It sat there listening to the prophet's tale, eating perhaps its third or fourth nut. How old was it anyway? How long did squirrels live and just how long would its bond with Fist extend its life? More importantly, how would the ogre handle it when Squirrel died? Justan felt a sudden urge to give Fist a hug.

Are you alright? Fist asked. *You feel sad.*

It's a sad story, he replied and hoped Fist wouldn't probe his emotions too deeply. The ogre patted his shoulder and to Justan's relief, didn't press the issue.

"I comforted the boy as best I could, then took him and his bonded off to the Mage School so that they could learn the uses of their magic," John said. "Back in those days, spirit magic was as plentiful as elemental magic. Bonding, binding, blessing, and bewitching were all taught here at the school."

"Bonding magic can be taught?" Justan asked.

"Well . . . To a degree," the prophet replied. "Spirit magic is much like elemental magic in that people are born stronger in some areas than others. Certain aspects of bonding magic can be taught to those with the talent, but no one can be taught to bond. The act of bonding itself is a gift given to a chosen few. There were, however, bonding wizards at the school who taught those with bonds how to use them. In the days of Stardeon, bonding wizards were much more common than they are now."

"Such a different world," Latva said, his youthful blue eyes looking sad in his ancient face. "To think what we've been missing all these years."

"We can change that now," Alfred said, gripping Latva's shoulder. "Now that the ban on spirit magic is over, we can bring those times back to the school."

"I hope that's the case, Alfred," John said with a sad smile. "But the heights of spirit magic in those days may never fully be realized again. In fact, I am not so sure they should be. So much depends on what happens in this war."

"Yes, hopefully we're all still around to find out what happens," Zambon said.

"Quite true," John said. "To return to my tale, Stardeon became somewhat of a sensation at the school. He was a prodigy; talented in nearly every aspect of magic that could be taught, and he was fiercely smart. He became an apprentice at age twelve. He was a mage at age fourteen and was named at age fifteen. By the time he graduated as a full wizard, he was just eighteen and already widely regarded as the wizard most likely to lead the school as the next Head Wizard."

"Amazing," said Alfred and to Justan's surprise, the gnome gave his long drooping nose a tug. Justan had only seen Vincent do that. "He was talented in all aspects of magic and yet the histories have so little to say about him."

"That is my fault," the prophet said. "When I outlawed the teaching of spirit magic at the Mage School, many of the histories from Stardeon's time were . . . edited."

"Edited?" Master Latva said, staring at the prophet in shock. "All that history lost?"

John raised a calming hand. "Not at all. The complete editions still exist. I have them locked away in my section of the tower. I fully plan to release them back to the library shortly.

"Now, as I was saying, Stardeon was a shining star at the school and he was content to stay here and continue his research, aiming for the office of Wizard of Mysteries. I, however, felt that staying at the school was stunting his growth. At that point he only had two bonded: his friend Sam and a horse from the stables that he had bonded with when he was a mage. I spoke with the council and encouraged them to send Stardeon abroad for a time and give him a chance to explore the outside world for a while. He could return in a few years if that was what he wished to do. They reluctantly took my advice and sent Stardeon on an assignment to gather and study new spirit magic techniques from different parts of the known lands. It went well at first. He bonded twice within the first year and learned a great many new applications of his power.

"Then when he was in Malaroo, he met his first wife, Shelda. She was a sweet woman and Stardeon loved her. They even had a child together; a daughter. But Shelda grew jealous of the bond. She realized that Stardeon's bonded knew him in a way she never could. After a few short years, she decided that she couldn't stand the fact that Stardeon couldn't love her in the same way he loved them and Shelda left him and took their baby with her."

Jhonate squeezed Justan's hand slightly and he glanced over at her, but her eyes were focused on the prophet. He realized that he hadn't given thought to the possibility that his bond with the others could interfere with their relationship. Was Jhonate going to have a problem with his connection to his bonded? Her facial expression revealed nothing.

"Stardeon returned to the school shortly thereafter, a little stronger and a little wiser. He accelerated his research and became the school's foremost authority on binding magic and magical constructs. He was given a seat on the High Council as the lead spirit wizard.

"All seemed well for Stardeon, but I grew concerned. The few times I saw him, he was despondent and distracted. He began to delve into the deep mysteries, skirting the edges of dark magic. He told the other council members that he was simply trying to understand the way that the Dark Prophet's servants worked so that he could better learn how to defeat them. I perceived a different problem.

"Stardeon was lonely. On the surface, that might seem a strange thing for a bonding wizard to be. After all, he had four minds connected to his; four people that cared for him deeply. But Stardeon tried to isolate them from his inner thoughts. He dove into his research and went long stretches of time without conversing with them at all.

"The next time I visited the school, Sam approached me. He told me what Stardeon was getting into. In his opinion, what Stardeon really missed was the connection he had with his wife. He needed a person that he could confide in that loved him without being bonded to him. I spoke with Stardeon and came to understand that Sam was right. Stardeon needed a new wife. But even more than that, he needed a wife that understood what it was like to be bonded."

John paused and let out a sad sigh. "That was when I decided to introduce him to Mellinda."

Chapter Two

"You introduced them yourself?" Jhonate asked.

The prophet steepled his fingers. "I perceive that many of you are wondering why I chose to take such a direct part in Stardeon's life."

Several of the others nodded and Justan had to admit he had been wondering the same thing. The prophet was a busy man. He traveled all over the known lands influencing events. Why had he been so focused on Stardeon?

"Well, first of all, I introduced them," John said. "I didn't say, 'Stardeon, marry this woman.' But you are right. I did focus on him. He was a bonding wizard and as I said earlier, bonding wizards are my champions. So I focus more of my attentions on them, which is one of the reasons I feel somewhat to blame for our current situation."

"So, you are . . . in charge of us, Big John?" Fist asked.

The prophet pursed his lips. "Most of you should have noticed by now that I have . . . nudged the events around you throughout your lives. I do that with the major players. It's one of my responsibilities. Usually, I'm not so direct about it as I was with Stardeon. For the most part I just give a gentle push here and there; like introducing two people that need to know each other."

Everyone knew that the prophet did things like that, but Justan hadn't expected to hear him talk about it so openly. The purposeful way he went about it was somewhat disturbing. From the expressions around the room, Justan wasn't the only one to feel that way.

The prophet laughed. "Oh, don't look at me like that. Several people in this room wouldn't have been born otherwise."

"We know how it is, John," Lenny said with a frown. "Yer the prophet. Yer always goin' 'round controllin' what folks do."

"Not at all. I never take away someone's freedom to choose. I don't even force people to make decisions except in extreme circumstances," John said firmly. "That is the Dark Prophet's way. I might give positive advice from time to time, but for the most part I influence events mainly by making people aware there is a choice to be made. In fact, I usually don't know what the consequences of my actions will be. I feel a prompting and follow the directions I think best.

"For instance, Sir Edge, I stopped by Wobble one day and felt inspired to order a dagger from Lenui's brother. When he asked me what I wanted it to look like, the idea came to me that it should have two separate blades and I sketched it out as I saw it in my mind. I never returned, and it wasn't until much later when I learned of the circumstances of your naming that I understood why."

"So yer the one that ordered that gall-durn dagger," Lenny said. His eyes narrowed. "Never paid for it, neither."

"If he had, you wouldn't have finished it, Lenny," Justan said in understanding. "Chuck would have finished it himself and held onto it and you wouldn't have given it to me that morning when we parted ways in Sampo."

The dwarf frowned again. "I guess yer right."

"Wizard Locksher," John said, holding up a finger. "I know you have a question and I'm pretty sure what it is, but I am not going to answer it just yet." Locksher grunted. His eyebrow was raised as high as it could be and his face was nearly red from holding his question in. "I'm sorry, but I need to redirect us from this tangent. I need to shift the focus of my tale to Mellinda now.

"When I introduced her to Stardeon, the poor woman was in almost as sad a state as he was. She was a bonding wizard as well, but Mellinda's life had taken a very different path than Stardeon's. She wasn't from Dremaldria, you see. She was born to a people known as the Roo."

Jhonate's hand gripped Justan's tightly and he saw that her eyes had widened in recognition at the name. "What is it?" Justan asked, but she frowned and shushed him before returning her eyes to the prophet.

"The Roo were a proud warrior people steeped in traditions of spirit magic. In those days, they populated most of southeastern Malaroo. They were a people that shunned the use of elemental magic. In their minds, the elements were the realm of the gods and for a human to use such magic was blasphemy. Those found with the talent were banished from their lands and those found using it secretly were dealt with even more harshly.

"Mellinda's elemental magic was discovered when she was a teenager. The day of her awakening, her parents knew what was going to happen to her and contacted the Mage School in Alberri. The wizards were there to meet her when she was left at the border.

"Once at the school, Mellinda learned that she was quite weak in elemental magic, but when it came to spirit magic, she was gifted. She was especially strong in bewitching and blessing. Her bonding magic was not as strong. It didn't manifest itself until just before she became a mage, when she bonded to a gnome librarian by the name of Dixie.

"As soon as Mellinda achieved the rank of mage, she left Alberri and traveled back to her people, eager to learn more about the spirit magic that they practiced. She had convinced herself that once they found out about her spiritual gifts, they would welcome her back with open arms."

"She was wrong," Jhonate said with a firm shake of her head. "The Roo would have seen any amount of elemental magic ability as a taint whether she used it or not."

"Correct," said the prophet with a smile. He gestured to the others. "Jhonate's people are descended from the Roo. They still cling to some of the same sensibilities today."

"Wait, how long ago was this?" Zambon asked and Justan realized that, of all of them, Zambon probably knew the least about the history of Stardeon.

"Just over a thousand years ago," John replied. The guard blinked in surprise, but said nothing more and John continued, "Mellinda returned to her family lands to seek out her parents. She thought that since her parents had been so kind as to arrange for her passage to the Mage School, they would take her in with open arms. Instead, they summoned the guard. The local priestess had her expelled by force. She and Dixie were taken to the border and dumped in an unfamiliar land that would eventually become Dremaldria.

"Now there is something you must know about Mellinda. She was a very proud woman and fiercely intelligent, but this was the first time she had traveled the wilderness by foot. She had always either had her parents with her or traveled by carriage. As a result, she was . . . let's just say somewhat of a priss.

"Unfortunately, Dixie was the same way and neither of them were prepared to take care of themselves out in the wilds. The two of them had a very rough couple of weeks, only surviving because she was able to use her bewitching magic to drive away wild beasts and lure in food.

"They then stumbled upon a group of treasure hunters and she bonded for the second time. Her new bond was to a half-elf by the name of Gregory. He was an excellent warrior and a survivor, which was exactly what she needed at the time. Gregory guided Mellinda and Dixie back to Alberri, where she intended to continue the path to becoming a Wizardess. Unfortunately something happened along the way. Gregory fell in love with Mellinda. To make things even more uncomfortable, he lusted after her.

"You see, Mellinda was a rare beauty. She had thick lustrous black hair, a figure that drew eyes, and a face that made men weak in the knees. She had learned this at a young age, too, and though she didn't always know she was doing it, she had become adept at using flirtation to get what she wanted. One wink of her striking green eyes or one pouting lip could get her a lower price from a merchant or a better seat on a carriage. All her life she had seen her beauty as a blessing, but now it was a curse.

"Gregory wanted her and he couldn't hide it. She could feel his emotions through the bond every moment of the day. Now Gregory's love for her was true and he was too good a person to take advantage. He never tried. But that didn't stop him from looking, and thinking, and dreaming."

Justan shivered at the thought. He remembered what it had felt like having Deathclaw watch him day and night, sometimes with anger, sometimes with curiosity, sometimes trying his best to hide his emotions, but always there. He couldn't imagine what it must have been like for Mellinda to have that intimate of an emotion focused on her.

"What did she think of him?" Alfred asked.

"Mellinda did not return his affections. Things would have been different if she had. It's happened before, bonded marrying each other, and they have been some of the best relationships I've seen, but those two got off to a bad start.

"Gregory had lived a hard life. He had a rough attitude and sense of humor that grated upon her sensibilities. In addition, though he was still relatively young for a half-elf, he showed the wear and tear of the life of an adventurer. He had a pronounced limp from a badly healed knee and his face was marred by burns and battle scars.

"I think she would have been able to overcome those bad first impressions given time. After all, they were both good people and once she got to know him, she did love him much like a sister would love her impish brother. But his desire for her was very much unwanted and just as he could not hide his lust, she could not hide her disgust, and those emotions festered between them like an open wound."

"How horrible," Fist said. The whole thing made the ogre feel queasy and Justan agreed. The bond was too intimate a connection for such emotions.

"What did she do about it?" Jhonate asked.

"She tried to mute the feelings between them as best she could, but you can't truly hide from the bond. They spoke to each other about it and agreed to try and stop feeling the way they did, but that didn't change anything. The resident bonding wizards in Alberri were of no help. Some of them found it amusing, others were simply repulsed. Finally she decided to seek me out and headed towards this, the original Mage School where she had heard I often visited.

"Now I had not met Mellinda before the day she sought me out. There were far too many bonding wizards in those days for me to be involved with all of them. If I had only known of her problems sooner I might have helped in a different way, but the day she arrived at the Mage School, Stardeon's needs were very much on my mind.

"Mellinda begged me to help and I could see the depth of their pain. My solution was to suggest that she and Gregory needed some time apart from each other. I suggested that she continue on the path to becoming a wizardess here at this school, while sending Gregory away for a while. He didn't like the idea, but he left at Mellinda's request. He escorted Dixie on a visit to the gnome homeland in Khalpany, knowing that it would be a full six months before he could return to her."

"You sent both her bonded away?" Latva said in surprise.

"I merely hinted at the possibility. It was Mellinda's idea to send both of them. Sometimes distance is the only way to heal a rift between bonded as you and Alfred should know," John said.

Justan knew he was referring to Alfred's bond with Charz. They had been separated for a century.

"At any rate, shortly afterward, I introduced Mellinda to Stardeon. The two of them got along right away. She was one of very few wizards that could understand Stardeon's research, and even though she didn't have his talent in elemental magic, she was his match in spirit magic. They began to spend every waking moment together.

"They were married within a month." The prophet chuckled. "They were so happy together. Stardeon veered away from the dangerous path he was on and for a time it seemed as if everything was going to work out splendidly. The only sour spot in the whole affair was when I found out that she hadn't told Gregory about it."

"But how could he not have known?" Justan asked.

"You've never been separated from your bonded before, have you?" Alfred asked.

"Well, no," Justan admitted. "Not until today." He thought of Deathclaw. The raptoid was still somewhere to the north and east in the direction of the academy. He knew where he was, but couldn't sense his thoughts or feelings.

The gnome nodded. "Well, when you are separated by great distances, speaking with each other is very difficult, and depending on how far away you are, the things you can communicate are limited. It would have been quite easy for her to hide her marriage."

"She hadn't even told Dixie about it, for fear that she would tell Gregory," John said. "I told Mellinda that hiding something this important from her bonded could not be a good thing. She assured me that she would tell both of them. In truth, she wanted to wait until they were far enough away that Gregory wouldn't try to race back to her side.

"I think she was hoping that he would fall in love with a woman in Khalpany, or better yet with Dixie. I must admit to praying for a similar result myself. The gnome had developed an unfathomable crush on the man."

Lenny snorted. "Gnomes."

Master Latva laughed and Alfred adjusted his spectacles in consternation. "And what is that supposed to mean?"

"Sorry, forgot you was a gnome," Lenny said with a shrug. "Thing is, I cain't tell you how many dag-burned times I've had to lie low in town 'cause some moon-eyed gangly gnome girl started followin' me 'round."

"I have not observed this phenomenon myself, good dwarf," said Alfred and Latva laughed again.

"Maybe it's just you, Lenny," Fist said and Justan sensed his amusement through the bond. "Maybe they like your mustache."

The dwarf nodded thoughtfully. "Could be . . ."

"Ugh, romantic entanglements," said Locksher in return, shaking his head glumly. He shot Justan a dull glare. "I say we'd all be better off without them."

Justan's cheeks reddened with guilt. When he had chosen Jhonate over Vannya, Locksher had been the only one available to console the mage. Qyxal's funeral had made things even worse and it was obvious to everyone that the wizard was ill equipped for such duties. At least now they were back at the Mage School. He could turn her over to her father.

"The prophet was telling us a tale," Jhonate said, giving them all a scowl.

Yes! agreed Gwyrtha, stomping her foot. *Tell John to tell the story!*

Jhonate leaned forward fixing her eyes on the prophet. "What happened, Sir? When did she tell him?"

John had been watching their interaction with

amusement. "Well . . . I didn't find out what happened until much later. As often happens, I was forced away on a series of important errands and while I was gone, some unfortunate decisions were made.

"Stardeon and Mellinda left the school together before Mellinda became a full wizardess. Stardeon bought some land in the foothills of the Trafalgan Mountains, far from any city. They hired in some laborers and started building their own wizard's keep. It was a beautiful location, though hard to find if you didn't know where to look.

"Then Gregory and Dixie began their return trip. The closer they came, the more it seemed Gregory sensed something was amiss. On top of that, Dixie seemed quite anxious. Mellinda began to panic. Stardeon begged her to tell her bonded what had happened before her secret damaged their relationship irreparably. Finally, when they were only about a week out, she came clean to them. "

Jhonate gasped, "How did Gregory react?"

"Gregory was heartbroken. And furious," said John. "His rage was so intense that Mellinda feared he would try to kill Stardeon. He refused to speak to her, closing off the bond whenever she tried. Instead, he picked up the pace of their travel. Dixie was a gibbering mess because he refused to speak with her as well. When Mellinda pressed her for details, all she would say was that Gregory had changed.

"When the day of their return arrived, Stardeon and Mellinda waited for them together, Stardeon's bonded staying just out of sight in case they were needed. Gregory continued to keep the bond closed tightly as he could, but Mellinda still felt his rage seething. When their horses came up the path towards the keep, he was wearing a heavy cloak with a hood that hid his features.

"Gregory dismounted and strode towards them. He stopped in front of them, shaking with rage. He threw off his cloak and the man that stood before her looked very little like the Gregory she had bonded to. Gone were the scars that had ravaged his face. Gone was the hideously flattened nose from his years of brawling. In their place was the face he would have had if his life had been different. The face Gregory now wore was even more handsome than Stardeon's."

Jhonate gasped, one hand flying to her mouth.

"Dag-gum idjit had his blood boiled, didn't he?" Lenny said with a shake of his head.

"Ah! That makes sense! He was a half-elf after all," Locksher said, his eyes wide in understanding. "It was a hideous process, from what I've read."

"What are you talking about?" Justan said. As far as he knew, what the prophet had described was hard to do, even for a master healer. Elemental magic could repair almost any nonfatal wound, but scarring and old badly healed injuries were more problematic.

"Centuries ago, there was a group of dark wizards known as the Khalpan Blood Mages," Locksher said. "They were based somewhere near the capitol city of Khalpany and it was said that they could provide any spell or enchantment. But they demanded payment in blood magic. They were the only people in all my research that had discovered a way to extract the blood magic from a half-breed."

"Disgustin' bunch of blasted foot-lickers!" Lenny spat. "My grandpappy was part of the group that destroyed 'em years 'fore I was born."

"You are correct," John said. "Gregory had been desperate to find a way to change Mellinda's feelings and while he was in the gnome homeland, he heard about the Blood Mages. Poor Dixie was so in love with him that she helped him seek them out. In exchange for repairing his scarred body and fixing his leg, Gregory let them tear the magic from his blood.

"By doing so, Gregory gave away decades of his life. But it was worse than that. His elf side was fairly weak. The mages didn't think the magic in his blood was enough, so Dixie sold some of her own." The prophet noted Alfred's wince. "Yes, she would have been completely ostracized if the gnomish community found out. As it was, she hated herself for doing it. When the Blood Mages finished their work she stayed in their compound and refused to leave Gregory's side until he recovered.

"While Gregory stood before Mellinda, Dixie explained what had happened through the bond. Mellinda begged for their forgiveness and explained the reasons why she hadn't told them. When Gregory felt the depth of her feelings for Stardeon, he climbed back on his horse and left. He didn't go far, just to the nearest town where he holed up in an inn for quite some time. When he returned, Gregory sought out Stardeon. He told Stardeon that he could no longer live being bonded to Mellinda. The only way that either of them could have peace was if the bond was broken."

"Why did they not do that earlier?" Jhonate asked.

"The bond is permanent," Justan explained. "It can't be broken."

"This is what Stardeon told him. The only things a bonded can do to avoid their wizard are leave and keep their distance. But that wasn't good enough for Gregory. No matter how far he ran, he would feel Mellinda there in the corner of his mind and know that she was with another man." John shook his head sadly.

"When I returned from my journey, they were at the Mage School waiting for me. They begged me to release Gregory from the bond. I was saddened by their tale, but I told them that I couldn't do it. I didn't have the authority."

"Alright, I can't hold this question in any longer," Locksher said. The wizard was sweating.

The prophet sighed. "All right, Wizard Locksher. I might as well get this over with. Go ahead. Ask your question."

"Thank you." Locksher took a deep breath. "All my life I've heard tales of the prophet. We all have. And I've done my research. I've looked up everything our library has on you. The theories on your origin differ but nowhere in the histories do scholars refer to you as being beholden to anyone.

"From the moment you brought us in here, you have been qualifying things by what you are and are not allowed to do. Allowed by whom? Who is above you? You just said that you didn't have the authority to break the bond. Well if you don't have the authority, who does?"

The hall was silent as everyone waited for the prophet's answer.

"I understand your confusion," John said. "Keep in mind that the histories are rarely written by those who experienced the events. The descriptions in those books are usually based on second and third hand information mixed with excerpts from poorly written or degraded journals. To be honest, most of what you read in so-called scholarly work is rubbish."

He hesitated, glancing around at each of them as if gauging their reactions. "I have never hidden my limitations and I have never skirted around the fact that I am beholden to a higher power. However, I am limited as to what I can reveal about my master. I . . . Just a moment, please."

The prophet closed his eyes and pressed his palms together. He rested his forehead on the tips of his fingers for a few seconds, his brow furrowed in a slight frown. Finally, he leaned back in his chair, his face lined with regret.

"The last time I revealed this information was the day Mellinda and Stardeon asked me to break Gregory's bond. My master warned me not to tell them, but I did so anyway. I felt that they needed to understand the bond better so that they would know what they were really asking. It was but one of many mistakes on my part.

"This time, however, my master allows it. Please understand that what I am about to tell you isn't secret, but it is sacred. So, though I will not forbid you to speak of these things to others, I would ask for your discretion. Most of this world is not yet ready to hear this particular message."

John leaned forward.

Justan felt a tingle under his skin and a slight buzzing in his ears. It seemed as if the prophet was looking directly into his eyes and yet, at the same time, he knew that the others felt the prophet's eyes locked onto theirs as well. "My master is The Creator. And the bond is under his sole direction."

"The Creator?" Alfred's eyes were wide.

The prophet noted their confused expressions. "When I told this to Mellinda and Stardeon, they didn't understand at first either. The magic of a bonding wizard is different from other spirit magic in that it is split into two parts. Half of the bond belongs to you and the other half belongs to my master.

"The first part is the talent you are born with. It determines how many bonded you may have or perhaps how powerful the things you are bonded to will be. Once you are bonded, you can use this part of your magic to manipulate the bond.

"The Creator's side of your bonding magic is an active thing that moves of its own will. It knows your needs and your weaknesses and it explores the people around you looking for a match that fulfills that need. When it finds a match, my master decides if it is a good one. When he declares the bond, he does so knowing all the possible ramifications of his decision. He knows the effects the bond will have on you and your bonded and he believes in your ability to handle them."

"So this Creator of yers," Lenny said, speaking what all of them were thinking. "What is he? Some sort of god?"

"Don't be ridiculous, Lenui," Locksher said with a snort. "There are no true gods."

"That's cow turds! I done met one myself!" Lenny snapped.

Justan didn't know what to think. His parents hadn't believed in worshipping any gods, but many cultures did. The prophet was the closest thing to a deity that Justan had ever believed in.

John raised a hand. "All I will say is that there is no higher authority in this world. I am sorry, but I am constrained from revealing any more than I have."

"So the only one who can break the bond is your master?" Latva asked.

"My master would never do so," John said. "He doesn't make a bond between two people that is unfixable. I told Stardeon and Mellinda this.

"They left me frustrated that I could not solve their problem, but my explanation of the way the bond worked got Stardeon thinking. He became sure that if he could somehow separate The Creator's part of the bond from Mellinda's part, she could control it."

"That sounds like a very bad idea," Justan said.

"When they arrived back at their keep, Stardeon and Mellinda dove into experimentation with the bond. For months they tried different techniques, each time failing. Finally Stardeon came across an obscure reference in an old tome and left to investigate.

"Mellinda and her bonded waited for his return. He was away for weeks and things got worse. Gregory couldn't stop looking at her and thinking about her and with his new appearance, she began to find his attentions flattering. As much as Stardeon loved her, he was a man very focused on his work and he never made Mellinda feel as desired as Gregory did.

"It wore on her until she decided that she couldn't wait for Stardeon's return. She came up with a plan of her own. She decided to seek her answers from the Dark Bowl."

Chapter Three

"The Dark Bowl is real?" asked Zambon, voicing aloud what Justan was wondering.

"Of course it's real, dag-nab it!" Lenny said. "Everythin's real."

"It is a matter of history, Zambon," Locksher said.

"I ain't just talkin 'bout the Dark Bowl," Lenny said. "I'm talkin' 'bout everythin'. It's all real. Every dag-gum legend you heard. Every dag-gum story yer momma told you when puttin' you to bed. If'n there's one thing I learnt in my life, it's that it's all real. Every time you doubt somethin' exists, there's a good chance yer gonna turn 'round and run yer face right into it!"

"Don't be ridiculous, Lenui," Locksher said. "Why there are many-."

"What about ghost trolls?" Fist asked, leaning forward in his chair, "Crag always said there were ghost trolls in the mountains. If you went to the very top they would talk in your head!"

"True, then!" Lenny said with a firm nod.

"Oh please," Locksher said with a roll of his eyes.

"Big John, are there ghost trolls in the mountains?" Fist asked.

The prophet frowned. "Well . . . I think that's a misunderstanding. They're not trolls, not really."

"See!" Lenny said. "All true."

"That's not what he said." Locksher replied.

"If they're not trolls, they're somethin' and if ghost trolls don't exist on the mountain, con-found it, they exist somewhere. I'm tellin' you. Everythin' does." Lenny said.

"Come on, Lenui. I-." Locksher began.

"Silence!" Jhonate glared at the wizard until he shut his mouth. Then she turned her glare on Lenny. Once she was satisfied that he wasn't going to blurt out something else, she gave the prophet an earnest look. "Sir, what is the Dark Bowl? I had not heard of it before now."

John raised one eyebrow in amusement at the flustered look on Locksher's face. He cleared his throat. "The Dark Bowl, my dear, is a creation of the Dark Prophet. He patterned it after The Bowl of Souls, likely to cause confusion. But they are nothing alike. The foul thing he created very much follows his sensibilities.

"You see, The Bowl of Souls sees a person's potential and judges them accordingly. The Dark Bowl forces a person into the mold it sees fit by giving them the knowledge and abilities it requires. It is the tool by which the Dark Prophet tries to create foes to combat those named by The Bowl of Souls.

"How does it do that?" Fist asked.

"To explain how it works, it would perhaps be best if I continued Mellinda's tale," John said. "Mellinda's decision to seek the Dark Bowl did not come lightly. She knew that it was a creation of the Dark Prophet and she knew that it was used for foul purposes, but she was desperate. She needed information that I was not going to give her, and she knew that the Dark Bowl could give her the kind of knowledge that was forbidden anywhere else.

"Her bonded balked at the idea. Dixie was terrified of going anywhere near the Dark Prophet's palace and Gregory was worried that Mellinda would be corrupted and turned into the Dark Prophet's pawn. She convinced them and herself that she had a clever plan. She would sneak into the palace, use the Dark Bowl to gain the information she needed to break the bond, and leave without the Dark Prophet knowing she had come."

"The fool!" Jhonate snapped, her face twisted with derision.

"Surely she knew better than that," Master Latva said.

"The willing mind fools itself," John replied. "But it wasn't so difficult a thing to imagine back then. In those days, the Dark Prophet and I were known to be fallible. Both of us had made some very public mistakes. She believed her spirit magic powerful enough to get them past any obstacles the Dark Prophet might set in front of them.

"They set off on their journey and planned their approach as they went. It was a difficult time for all of them. During their journey there was no way for her to hide from Gregory's gaze and he had changed in more ways than just his appearance. He had learned the things about his personality that had so repulsed her in the beginning and had altered his behavior accordingly. In addition, he treated Dixie with respect and kindness, something that he hadn't done in the past. The way he acted broke down the walls Mellinda had erected to protect herself.

"By the time they reached the Dark Prophet's dominion, she was beginning to feel yearnings of her own. Gregory felt those feelings within her and it only served to embolden him. They would have succumbed to their passions if not for Dixie. The gnome stayed at Mellinda's side at all times, never leaving her and Gregory alone."

The prophet's words poured into Justan's mind and he became entranced by the story. The strange buzzing feeling returned and the surroundings of the Hall of Majesty melted away around him, new scenery rising up to replace them. John was somehow feeding these images to him as clearly as memories sent through the bond. Justan could see Mellinda and her bonded struggling along rough terrain as if they were right in front of him. Distantly, he was aware that Fist and Gwyrtha were seeing the same thing.

The vision was perfectly detailed and the character's actions added to the depth of the prophet's tale. The gnome Dixie was tall and willowy, with long curly red hair. Justan thought she was pretty, even with her long nose and drooping ears. Gregory was muscular and remarkably handsome, with a permanent smirk on his face and a ready grace that told Justan he knew how to fight.

Mellinda's appearance was the most striking to Justan. Her hair was black as ink and her eyes a vivid green. Her features looked so much like Jhonate's at first glance that it startled him. But then she smiled and he saw the differences. Her lips were full and luscious, her jaw wider, and as the vision moved around them, he saw that her figure was every bit as voluptuous as Vannya's. It was no wonder that Gregory felt the way he did.

Despite the intensity of the vision, Justan could still hear the prophet's words. His deep voice propelled the action forward.

"In order to stay undetected, they kept off the roads, traveling the treacherous mountain terrain on foot. They had difficulty staying undetected by the Dark Prophet's minions. Dixie was not a stealthy person. Her every step seemed to knock over a rock or snap a twig. Mellinda's strength in bewitching magic was the only thing that kept them from being discovered. As it was, Gregory had to slay several beasts along the way. It became evident to Mellinda that she would not be able to sneak inside with the gnome at her side.

"Soon the spires of the Dark Prophet's palace loomed ahead. Gregory scouted the area around the palace and they waited for the Dark Prophet to leave. They knew it was only a matter of time. The Dark Prophet often left his palace to patrol his dominion.

"It took a week. A long week of waiting in the cold mountain air, huddling together for warmth at night; huddling together in body and mind with a level of intimacy that only stirred up their emotions more. Again Dixie's presence saved them, but they both began to resent her interference.

"Finally the Dark Prophet left in his carriage, bringing his entourage of servants with him. Mellinda and Gregory left Dixie in a cave where she would be safe from discovery, then set off on their approach. Mellinda reached out with her magic, setting the guards at ease and they snuck in and found servants' garb.

"It went more smoothly than either of them had dared believe. No one questioned them. They were able to find their way down the opulent hallways to the bowl's chamber. A few of the Dark Prophet's priests were inside praying, so Gregory created a distraction that caused them to leave the room. Once alone, Mellinda snuck up to the bowl and plunged her knife inside."

Justan gasped as the scene froze before his eyes. The room was wide and circular. The floor sunk down in the center, curved like a great bowl. In the middle was a marble pedestal with a silver bowl perched atop. It looked very much like The Bowl of Souls until Justan looked closer and saw that the underside of the bowl was carved with tortured faces.

Mellinda stood in front of the pedestal, her striking green eyes open wide and her teeth grit together in a grimace as the blade of her knife pierced the still water of the bowl. A lance of blackness had shot upwards from the waters of the bowl and was paused a mere inch from piercing her forehead.

"Now there were things about the Dark Bowl that Mellinda did not understand. She thought it would give her the information she needed and let her walk away unscathed. But the Dark Bowl is an object of binding magic. It has pieces of thousands of souls trapped within."

Justan winced as the scene jumped a half-second forward and paused again. The lance of blackness had pierced through Mellinda's skull and her eyes were rolled back, her mouth open as if frozen mid-chant.

"When she plunged her weapon into the bowl, its magic searched her heart, taking measure of her much like the true bowl does. Then it searched itself and found the other shreds of tattered soul trapped within its depths that matched what it wanted from her. It bound them to her, in essence giving her the knowledge and memories of three of its past victims. You see, she wasn't the first bonding wizard to seek its power. She was the fourth.

"In exchange for this knowledge, the Dark Bowl bound her thoughts and memories to it. This guaranteed that when she died, a portion of her soul would be torn free and trapped inside it with the others.

"When it was finished, it granted her a new name; a name known only to the Dark Prophet's other servants. Then, much like The Bowl of Souls would have done, it left her and her weapon marked with a rune. But this was a rune that could only be seen by those with a special type of spirit sight.

"Dark runes appear opposite of naming runes. For wizards, the dark rune appears on the palm of their right hand. For warriors, it appears on the back of their left."

Justan felt the prophet's voice speaking directly to him.

"Take note of this. As bonded, you have the gift to see these markings. Use your spirit sight. As you were able to see the dark magic of the ruby dagger, you can see this proof of the Dark Prophet's servants."

Mellinda slumped to the ground next to the pedestal, her right hand shaking as she stared at the black rune on her palm. She blinked, her eyes darting back and forth, and Justan could see her mind working as she processed the new information she had gained. Her face was grim as she stood and met Gregory at the room's exit.

"They escaped the palace the way they came, relieved that no guards cried out in alarm. Gregory was thrilled that his plan had worked, but Mellinda was quiet. They climbed the mountainside and began making their way back to Dixie. Gregory asked Mellinda what she had learned from the bowl, but she would not reply. She had closed the bond so tightly that he could not hear her thoughts.

"When they were half way back to Dixie's hiding place, Mellinda stopped and tied off their connection to the gnome so she could not hear what she had to say. She told Gregory that she had not learned the secret she had hoped. She could not break the bond on her own. However, she had learned how to do something else.

"She could enter his mind through the bond and use her bewitching magic to take away his desire for her. To do so, she would have to strip out his memories of wanting her. It would be uncomfortable, but their problem would be solved. When she was done, he would love her only as a sister.

"In her mind, this was a much better solution. They wouldn't have to part forever. They could stay bonded and return home together. What's more, she wanted to do it then, before returning to Dixie, knowing that the gnome would try to talk them out of it."

Justan's skin crawled at the thought of her solution. Going into her bonded's mind and tearing out his memories? What if she took away something important accidentally? What if she did irreparable damage?

He watched the two of them standing close together between two large boulders on a rocky mountainside, their eyes boring into each other's. Mellinda's full lips trembled and Gregory's eyes were red-rimmed as he swallowed and gave her a brief nod.

"Gregory agreed to her plan, but made one request. 'One kiss,' he said. 'Please. Just one kiss before you take this away from me.'

"Mellinda let her guard down and agreed to his condition. She kissed him, but it didn't stop there. All the tension that had been building between them finally broke. Mellinda and Gregory gave in to their passions there on the mountainside in the Dark Prophet's domain.

"When it was over, Gregory was happy. He had finally been with the woman he loved. Suddenly he didn't want to be free of his desire for her. But Mellinda was filled with horror at what she had done. She had betrayed both her husband and Dixie and the thought of them finding out what had happened was too hard to bear. She told Gregory to ready himself for her to enter his thoughts, but he refused. He didn't want his love taken away anymore. He pleaded with her to leave Stardeon and stay with him.

"They argued and as Mellinda raged, the new voices in her mind, the ones with the dark knowledge, spoke to her for the first time. These previous bonding wizards told her that she did not need Gregory's permission. She had the power to take the memories whenever she wanted. When she was finished, he would never know what she had done.

"Mellinda resisted their suggestions at first, but as her argument with Gregory grew more heated, she told herself that he had agreed beforehand. He had no right to change his mind. Finally he tried to kiss her again and with a cry of anger, she entered his mind forcefully, smashing aside his mental defenses."

Justan saw their argument unfold, saw Gregory freeze and collapse, while Mellinda stood over him, her face grim.

"She did as her new knowledge instructed, combing through his memories and muting his feelings for her, tearing out any strong incidents she could not suppress. But she didn't stop there. After all, how could she? What if his feelings grew again?

Mellinda thought of poor Dixie and her unrequited love for him and went into Gregory's memories of the gnome. She

51

took his feelings of fondness for Dixie and stoked them to urges of passion. Mellinda was inexperienced at this kind of work and it showed in the bluntness of her efforts.

"When Gregory awoke, he smiled at her like he would a friend, his memories of their affair erased. He seemed fine and Mellinda was relieved. She took him back to the cave where they had left Dixie.

"The gnome had been waiting for them patiently, monitoring them through the bond. She had felt the intensity of emotion from Mellinda when she had encountered the Dark Bowl and was alarmed when she noticed the sinister thoughts entwined with Mellinda's afterwards. When Mellinda had cut Dixie's thoughts off from her own, Dixie knew that something had gone wrong.

"She was overjoyed when they arrived back at the cave safely, but something was amiss. The look in Gregory's eyes when he saw her was not what she expected. When she asked Mellinda what she had done to him, Mellinda told her through the bond that the bowl had taught her how to change Gregory's feelings and that when she had, his feelings for Dixie had surfaced. She told Dixie that Gregory had loved her all along.

"When she said these words, Gregory approached Dixie with longing in his eyes and reached for her. The gnome didn't react as Mellinda had expected. She pushed Gregory away in horror and yelled at Mellinda, demanding that she change him back. Gregory was confused by her outburst. He clutched at Dixie, professing his love for her."

Justan shuddered at the disturbing scene. Gregory on his knees, crying out with a scrap of Dixie's torn dress in his hand. Dixie had backed up against the wall and was shaking her head. Both of them were in tears.

"Melinda didn't know what to do. Her efforts had gone horribly wrong. Finally she froze them both and dove into their minds to fix the damage she had done. She took the advice of the new voices in her mind and lowered the intensity of Gregory's passions, then erased Dixie's memory of the incident, leaving the impression that everything was as it should be. She made Dixie feel as though Gregory love for her was the expected result of their mission. They had been successful. All had gone to plan.

"This time when her bonded awoke, it was better. They were both happy with the outcome. The started on their journey back home. Mellinda was pleased. Her bonded were giddy, walking hand in hand and giggling like young lovers. It was as though the unpleasantness hadn't happened.

"But Mellinda couldn't erase her own memories. Guilt for her actions plagued her and worse, her feelings for Gregory didn't go away. Despite her better judgment, she missed his desire and began to resent his feelings for Dixie.

"The voices in her head reminded her that she had the power to make her bonded act however she wished. She was their wizard, after all; their master. Mellinda pushed the suggestions away at first, but her resentment grew. She began to flirt with Gregory, but he didn't acknowledge her attempts.

"Then one night in a fit of anger, she seized their minds and made Gregory want her again. She caused Dixie to sleep and had her way with him. When Mellinda was through, she was once again wracked with guilt. She erased his memory of the incident and changed him back. Her bonded continued on, unaware that anything had happened but Mellinda was sickened by her behavior. She began to despise the bond.

"She vowed never to abuse her power again, but it wasn't too long until the temptation was too great. She began changing their minds at will. The more she did so, the easier it got. But Dixie and Gregory knew something was wrong. Their memories were jumbled and incomplete.

"The day they exited the Dark Prophet's dominion, the situation boiled over. They felt her guilt and turned on Mellinda, asking her what she had done to them. When she finally broke down and confessed what had happened, the two of them were repulsed. Mellinda couldn't bear her bonded feeling that way about her. She rendered them both unconscious again."

Justan watched Mellinda collapse next to the unmoving forms of her bonded, sobbing uncontrollably. He pitied her at that moment. The things she had done were vile and contemptible, but she had not intended for this result.

As he watched, a shadow rose from behind her. She scrambled to her feet in alarm and saw a man watching them. He was tall, muscular and handsome, with a charming smile. His eyes were light blue and his hair a blond mane. The clothes he wore looked comfortable but expensive, all white silk and gold trim.

"The Dark Prophet appeared before her at that moment. He sympathized with her pain and told her that the bond was an unjust way to force people together. He had a means to remove the Creator's part of the bond from hers. Once he was done, she would have complete control over who she bonded to and for how long. She could free herself of the burden of guilt and cut Gregory and Dixie loose to live a new life away from her."

Justan shook his head. *Don't do it*! he pleaded.

Of course Mellinda didn't hear. She looked down upon her bonded, her eyes filled with sadness. The smiling man laid a comforting hand on her shoulder and she nodded,

"She went into their minds one last time and eased their thoughts. She removed their memories of her and replaced them with a new story. The two of them had met each other on the road. Gregory had protected Dixie as they traveled to the gnome homeland, where they fell in love. She added intricate details explaining Gregory's transformation at the hands of the Blood Mages and their journey to this place where they would wake.

"When she finished, Mellinda agreed to the Dark Prophet's proposal. She handed him her knife with the dark naming rune and he used it in a ritual to cut away the Creator's connection to the bond. Mellinda now had full control and she used that power to set her bonded free.

"When Gregory and Dixie awoke, Mellinda and the Dark Prophet were gone. They felt a strange sadness, but they had no memories of why they should feel that way. They left that spot together, hand-in-hand, and never saw Mellinda again."

Chapter Four

The vision faded away and Justan found himself once more sitting in the oversized chair in the Hall of Majesty, Jhonate holding his hand. From the saddened and repulsed looks of the others it was evident that they had all experienced the same vision.

"Such a sad tale," Jhonate said with a shiver. Her green eyes were troubled. "What she did . . ."

"I'm glad I'm bonded to Justan, Big John." Fist said, his cheeks stained with tears.

Me too, Gwyrtha agreed.

"As am I," The prophet said with a kind smile.

"How'd you do that?" Lenny asked, his eyes wide with wonder.

"Spirit magic has its advantages, Lenui." John said with a shrug. "One is teaching. I was able to show you all in a few short minutes what it might have taken me an hour to tell otherwise, especially with all the interruptions."

"But magic don't normally work on me," Lenny said incredulously. "It was so real. I swear I could've reached out and slapped that idjit of a woman upside the head!"

"Your heritage does make you resistant, yes," John replied. "But certain types of spirit magic can get through even a dwarf's defenses."

"But the detail you showed us was astounding!" Locksher said, both eyebrows raised. "How did you know what took place?"

"That's a good question," Alfred said. "You weren't there at the time."

The prophet gave them a sad smile. "Years later, when

Mellinda had reached the height of her atrocities, I searched for clues to what had happened. I found Gregory and Dixie living together in a gnome village in Khalpany. They were happy with their life there. Gregory was head of the village guard and Dixie was one of the local teachers.

"Neither of them had any recollection of what had happened, or even that they had met me, but with their permission, I searched their minds and found the memories Mellinda had suppressed. The other small details came to me much later on the day I gave Mellinda one last chance to change." His countenance darkened. "But I don't have time to tell that part just yet."

"Did you help them remember?" Fist asked.

John shook his head. "That would have only been cruel. I had no doubt that opening their minds would have only sent them on a journey to find her. Mellinda had left them alone so far, but the creature that Mellinda had become at that point wouldn't have hesitated to kill them if they tried to interfere."

"The witch," Jhonate said with a glower.

"Uh, Jhonate?" Justan winced. She was squeezing his hand so hard his knuckle bones rubbed together. "Um . . . my hand."

"Sorry," she said, giving him an apologetic glance. She let go and gripped her staff instead. She turned her gaze on the prophet. "So what sort of deal did Mellinda make with the Dark Prophet?"

"We'll get back to that. I need to shift the focus of the tale back to Stardeon. I will try to finish the story quickly. Some of us are needed elsewhere and I'm sure that you must all be famished."

Justan realized that the prophet was right. He hadn't eaten since early that morning before the battle began. None of them had.

"In fact if you would like, we can adjourn for now and meet back for the rest of the story at a later date," the prophet suggested.

"But I want to hear the rest, Big John," Fist said, eager even though his stomach was aching.

"I agree with the ogre," Jhonate said.

Me too! sent Gwyrtha

"As do I," Justan said.

"Do we have any disagreements?" John asked and when no one did, he said, "Then I will tell you Stardeon's side of this tale for the short time we have left. I do have a feeling, however, that some of this will need to wait."

He cleared his throat. "While Mellinda had been off in search of the Dark Bowl, Stardeon had thought of another way to break the bond. He sought out one of the monsters of legend; a beast known as a Great Wyrm.

"Stardeon's research had uncovered the rumor that one of these beasts had been found, and he wanted it for its power. Like the other monsters of legend, a Great Wyrm is actually a rare magic anomaly. It is one of a race of snake-like dragons that live deep underground. The thing that makes the Great Wyrm different from the others is that it's born with spirit magic. It has the ability to tear away the thoughts and abilities of other beasts and store them in gemstones, leaving its mindless victims to be eaten or used as slaves.

"Stardeon knew that he had a way to defeat this monster. His bonded were immune to its attack. You see, as long as a bonding wizard is fighting against it, no other form of spirit magic can overcome the bond.

"Now, regarding Stardeon's bonded. I told you about Sam and his horse, Vaughn, but I did not mention the others. He had two more. The first was a kobald by the name of Lex. He was strong and tough. The other was Slythe. He was a red dragon; a medium-sized fire breather. He had grown quite smart through his bond with Stardeon and he was fast."

"Damn," said Lenny, his moustache tilted in disgust. "Bonded to a dag-blamed kobald?"

Justan had never seen a kobald before. All he knew was that they appeared in a lot of Lenny's curse-filled rants. The prophet closed his eyes and a vision appeared in Justan's mind of a reptilian-looking humanoid, short like a dwarf and powerfully built with large rocky scales. It stood next to the dragon. Slythe was fearsome, with long wicked teeth and wide wings. His body was covered with shiny red scales.

"Think what you will, but they were an excellent group

of bonded. Powerful and loyal. They believed in Stardeon and trusted his intelligence to see them through any situation. The strength of that belief is part of what makes their tale so sad.

"Stardeon and his bonded searched for months before they tracked down the Great Wyrm's lair. It was in a cavern deep under the Trafalgan Mountains. They left Vaughn outside and entered through a kobald surface tunnel. It took a week of underground travel before they came across the right connecting tunnel.

"The Great Wyrm had chosen a huge cavern that had belonged to a large tribe of goblins. It had stolen their minds and used them as slaves and cattle, doing its bidding as it slumbered."

This time the prophet's voice faded as the scene unfolded in Justan's mind.

He saw the yawning cavern large enough to fit a small town inside. Scattered across the floor were goblin huts and small fires. Vacant-eyed goblins walked slowly about, barely intelligent enough to do the wyrm's bidding.

In the rear of the cavern, coiled up like an enormous viper, was the Great Wyrm. Its head rested atop a pile of coils three stories high. Its alligator-like mouth was closed, its enormous lantern eyes half-lidded and drowsy.

Stardeon stayed just outside the chamber and cast a spell. A dark mist rolled in from a back passageway, obscuring the goblins and their huts and fires. The Great Wyrm didn't notice right away and the goblins were too dull to raise an alarm. The mist rose up until half the Great Wyrm's form was obscured. Then its head rose sleepily, blinking in confusion as something moved towards it in the mist, the swiftness of its approach creating waves on the cloud-like surface.

Slythe burst up from the mist directly in front of the wyrm, his head rearing back, his mouth opening. The Great Wyrm's eyes widened in alarm as Slythe let loose with a torrent of dragonfire. The wyrm's head was engulfed in flame and it roared in agony.

Lex chose that moment to leap from Slythe's back and soar towards the wyrm's uppermost coils. The kobald's pickaxe blazed with earth magic as he swung with a two-handed blow.

The pickaxe burst through the Great Wyrm's hard scales, penetrating deep in its flesh. Where he struck, the flesh turned to stone.

The Great Wyrm uncoiled in a sudden strike, its jaws open wide as it darted out from the plume of fire. Slythe slid to the side, barely avoiding its bite. Lex was hurled from the wyrm's back and disappeared into the mist.

The Great Wyrm thrashed in the mist, roaring in pain and fury, crushing its slaves and their huts under its bulk. Then the mist grew still. Its head, blackened and smoldering, rose from the mist on its long neck like a solitary tower. One eye was melted shut and fluid oozed down to drip from its lower jaw, but the other eye was open and angry and blazed with spirit magic. A white beam swept the cavern as it searched for its attackers.

A shout rang out and its head swiveled to look upon a stalagmite that jutted up from the mist behind it. Standing on the tip of the stalagmite was a man with a bow. Justan recognized him at once. It was Coal's first bonded, Sam. Samson's face grinned out above a human body armored in leather that shone bright with golden magic. The bow that he had drawn back blazed red.

The Great Wyrm focused its beam-like spirit attack on Sam's body. But the magic could not overwhelm Stardeon's hold on the bond. Sam fired an arrow that shone dark as night. As it left the bow, whirling wreathes of fire wrapped around it, causing the arrow to ignite. The arrow pierced the Great Wyrm's nostril and erupted in a shower of molten rock.

The Great Wyrm reared back and roared just as Slythe dropped Lex from far above its head. The kobald swung his pickaxe down in a mighty blow that struck between the wyrm's eyes. A laticework of cracks spread outward from the wound as flesh and bone and brain alike turned to stone and shattered.

The legendary monster crashed to the mist below, dead.

Stardeon dismissed the mist quickly and strode into the cavern. He was tall and had the regal bearing of a man confident of his power and position. His hair was brown with just a few streaks of white at the temples, but Justan knew he was much older than he looked. How much time had passed from when he married his first wife and the prophet introduced him to

Mellinda?

Stardeon approached the head of the dead monster and stood before it with a satisfied nod. He reached out his hands and the Great Wyrm's enormous eye popped free of its skull and rolled towards him. He pulled a knife from his belt and cut open the large nerve at the back of the eye. A stream of gemstones poured out of the nerve, each one uniquely colored and beautiful.

The scene shimmered and shifted as the prophet's voice once again filled Justan's mind. "These gemstones were a treasure rare and priceless, for they contained the thoughts and abilities the Great Wyrm had stolen over the years. This power was converted to pure energy and crystallized. To a wizard that knew what they were doing these stones would be a magnificent power amplifier, but to Stardeon they were even more. They were the Great Wyrm's most prized possession and a powerful tie to its soul.

"He took ten of the smallest gemstones and set them into a two sets of five rings he had prepared for just this use."

Justan saw the rings being made. They were definitely the same rings that Ewzad Vriil wore. Each ring was linked to the others by a string of golden chain. Stardeon bathed the rings in the Great Wyrm's blood and ate some of its flesh.

"Once he had his creation ready, he reached into the ether and called for the soul of the Great Wyrm. Its soul was drawn to him by the power of the gemstones. It was huge and powerful and angry at being torn from its mortal coil."

Justan saw Stardeon sitting cross legged with the rings in the palms of his hands, still glistening with the Great Wyrm's blood. His bonded stood behind him, their eyes wary. With spirit sight, they could see its spirit towering above them.

"Stardeon made a pact with the spirit of the monster. If it would agree to serve him, it would not have to pass on to the afterlife, but could stay bound to the gemstones it prized so much. For some creatures, this sort of condition would be enough, but not the Great Wyrm. It wanted more. It wanted to harm those who had killed it. It added another condition. It agreed to serve him, but only if he allowed it to tear the powers of his bonded away and store them in the stones.

"Stardeon gave it a counter offer. It would leave his

bonded alone. He would allow it to strip his powers away instead. You see, he had designed the rings so that while he was wearing them, he would have full control over any powers stored in the stones. The wyrm agreed to his conditions eagerly. Too eagerly. And that's when things went wrong. Stardeon was a binding expert, but he had never bound a creature this intelligent and powerful before. It had decided to make him suffer."

Justan watched Stardeon grin as the spirit of the Great Wyrm entered the rings and allowed him to bind it to them with powerful flows of both elemental and spirit magic. Then he put the rings on. The Great Wyrm's hunger was palpable.

Stardeon began sweating and grimaced with pain. His bonded rushed to his side. There was a horrible ripping sound and Justan saw the multicolored glow of Stardeon's elemental magic sucked away into the stones. The white glow of his spirit magic started tearing next.

Lex stiffened and cried out. As the kobald crumpled to the ground, Slythe shuddered and let out a great roar. The dragon fell and Sam's eyes grew wide as he realized he was next.

"The Great Wyrm tore the bond so violently that the very souls of Stardeon's bonded were ripped partially free from their bodies. Stardeon felt the lives of his bonded fading and panicked. He struck back, using the power of the Great Wyrm's own magic against it. He assaulted its intelligence, tearing its thoughts asunder. It stopped its assault, but the damage was done.

"Stardeon may have been able to save Lex and Slythe had the Great Wyrm not damaged his bonding magic so severely. He could not touch their minds. He could connect with their bodies, but the damage was not physical.

"He watched helplessly as they died. In sorrow, he and Sam buried their bodies and returned to the surface to look for Vaughn, but he had been left unable to feel his horse at all. He never did find him. Stardeon's bond to Sam was the only one he had left."

The scene faded away. Justan felt sick to his stomach and sensed that Fist and Gwyrtha felt the same. He had known this part of the tale already, but to see Stardeon's bonded and observe their courage with his own eyes, only to see them die because of their wizard's pride . . .

"It's a dag-gum shame," Lenny said, shaking his head.

"I do not understand," Jhonate said, her eyes red-rimmed. "Why would he submit to have his powers torn away? What did he hope to gain with such foolishness?"

John sighed. "Stardeon believed that the Great Wyrm would tear his side of the bond free from the Creator's. Then with the wyrm's power stored in the rings, he would be free to use it to help Mellinda do the same. It was a ridiculous and dangerous thing to attempt, but Stardeon was so prideful and confident in his abilities that it didn't occur to him that he could fail."

"It was a terrible tragedy, but . . . ." Locksher didn't look up, but kept his eyes focused on the ground in front of his chair. "Was he successful?"

"Partially," the prophet said, giving the wizard an appraising look. "The bond was torn free from the Creator's control. Stardeon was able to connect his mind to the body of another and see it from the inside as a bonding sees his wizard. But the link was temporary and it was physical only. He couldn't hear the thoughts of those he connected to in that manner.

"In addition, he would never be able to truly bond again. Not that he ever believed that. I don't think Stardeon truly understood just how much damage he had done until the end of his life. I believe that part of his reason for creating the rogue horses was the hope that he would one day make a creature so perfect that his bond would trigger despite the damage.

"His best chance to bond again actually came the day he returned to his keep. Mellinda was there alone waiting for him. Both of them knew something was wrong right away. Mellinda saw that Stardeon's magic looked strange and Stardeon noticed that both her bonds were gone.

"They shared their stories. Stardeon held nothing back, but Mellinda was too ashamed to tell him how far things has gone with Gregory. When they finished their tales, both of them felt hollow inside. Mellinda tried to bond with him then and there, but she couldn't. There was not enough of his power left to latch onto. It had all been bound into the rings."

"But what happened to Mellinda between the time she left her bonded and the time she returned home?" Master Latva asked. "What did the Dark Prophet ask of her? How did she get away from him?"

"I can only tell you what she told Stardeon, but I believe it to be true. The Dark Prophet asked nothing of her. He offered to teach her how to use her unfettered bonding magic and told her that he could help her become more powerful than she had ever imagined. When she refused, he let her leave."

"He let her go that easily?" Justan asked in surprise.

John snorted. "The Dark Prophet never lets a powerful prospect go; not really. As far as he was concerned, she was his servant already. He knew she would return to him again and when she did, he would make his conditions known.

"In the meantime, Mellinda was free to delude herself into thinking that she had gotten away from him without conditions. Still she missed her bonded terribly. She felt alone in a way she had never thought possible."

"Why didn't she just bond to something else then?" Zambon asked. "She had the power to bond herself to whatever she wanted, right?"

"Sure, but bond herself to what?" Justan asked. "That would be a hard choice. With the way her other bonds ended, she had to have been terrified of making a mistake with whomever she bonded to next."

"Precisely," John said. "Stardeon was the only choice she had been sure of and that didn't work. She was too afraid to take another bonded.

"When Stardeon saw how miserable she was, he had an idea. He would use his new powers to create a bonded for her; one that would never disappoint. When he told Mellinda his idea, she became excited. They planned it together, thinking of all the aspects that would be desirable in their perfect bonded.

"But as they got further into the process it soon became evident to Mellinda that there was something amiss. She couldn't understand many of the concepts Stardeon was talking about. Then one day it hit her. The intelligence she had gained through her bond with Dixie had faded away.

"Stardeon suspected the same, but he didn't say anything. Mellinda began to withdraw into herself more and more. When they made their first attempt to create a rogue horse, the result was a mess. It lived for only a few hours before falling apart. Stardeon was encouraged, but Mellinda was repulsed. She was sure that it was all her fault.

"Stardeon became so focused on his work that he didn't notice how hard she was taking each subsequent failure. Finally it became too much for her. One morning Stardeon awoke to find that she was gone. Her only explanation was in a note she left behind stating that she was going to do some research in Alberri.

"Did he go after her?" Fist asked.

"It didn't occur to him that she could be gone for good. Besides, he hoped she would find another gnome to bond to. Then perhaps she would come back more like the Mellinda he married," the prophet explained.

"So where did she go?" Jhonate asked.

"She returned to the Dark Prophet," John said. "I don't know if that was her intention the day she left, but whatever her intentions were, she ended up at his side. Stardeon didn't see her again until many years later and when he did, she was nothing like the woman he married."

A loud knock echoed through the hall and everyone's eyes moved to the doors.

"You had better go see to them, Sir Edge," the prophet said.

Justan blinked in surprise. "It's for me?"

The doors creaked open and Wizard Valtrek poked his head in. "I hope I'm not intruding."

"Not at all, Valtrek," John said. "Sir Edge will be right with you."

"But what about the story?" Justan asked.

John smiled. "Don't worry, the rest of the tale I am telling tonight deals with Stardeon and the rogue horses. I believe you know what happens."

"Oh . . . okay, I guess." Justan said, though he was disappointed. There were several gaps in the tale that he had been hoping the prophet would fill in.

"I'll tell you what you missed later, Justan," Fist promised.

Me too, said Gwyrtha.

Justan nodded and gave Jhonate a smile, then walked to

the doors and stepped into the hallway where Valtrek was waiting.

The wizard looked just as Justan remembered. His long white hair hung thick about his shoulders in stark contrast to his dark eyebrows and neatly trimmed beard. He was wearing the white ambassador's robes that Justan had seen him wear in the academy council room nearly two years prior.

Valtrek smiled and shook his hand. "So good to see you, Sir Edge!"

"It is good to see you too, Master," Justan replied. The words felt strange coming out of his mouth, but it was true. Any trace of bitterness he felt towards the man in the past had faded away. Whatever his tactics, Valtrek had been looking out for him all along.

He opened his mouth to ask what the wizard wanted of him, but his breath stuck in his throat. Someone else was in the hallway with them.

Vannya stood a short distance away, leaning against the wall between two large portraits of named wizards from the distant past. She had her arms folded and her plump lips clenched tight together. She was staring straight ahead, not looking in his direction.

Valtrek glanced over at her and his smile faded. "Please come with me, Sir Edge. We need to have a talk."

Chapter Five

Justan followed behind Valtrek as he walked away from the Hall of Majesty, acutely aware that Vannya was just a few paces back, her eyes boring into him. He looked back and her eyes darted away as if she hadn't been watching him at all.

"So, uh. Where are we heading, Master?" Justan asked. It grated him a bit to call the wizard by that title. Technically Justan was still Valtrek's apprentice and that was the proper way to say it, but in his mind, Coal would always be his master.

Valtrek opened the door to the stairwell. "My offices. They are here in the Rune Tower."

"Oh," Justan headed down the spiral staircase after him. "What is it that we need to speak about?"

"I would rather not go over specifics until we get there," Valtrek replied. "There are things I wish to say in a private setting. We have been apart for a long time and I would like a progress report."

"I understand." Justan said, suddenly hopeful that this wasn't about Vannya at all. Still, it brought another concern to his mind. "About Master Coal-."

"Just wait until we arrive, Edge," the wizard said a tad sharply, surprising Justan with his tone.

"Father is concerned about something, Edge," Vannya said from a few steps behind him. "I'm not sure what it is, but he has been tight-lipped from the moment I arrived back."

"That's enough, Mage Vannya," Valtrek snapped.

She grunted in irritation and Justan's eyebrows rose. He couldn't remember the wizard speaking to his daughter that way in the past. What was making Valtrek so cautious? What did he have to say that could not be discussed inside the Rune Tower?

They descended the rest of the stairs in silence and walked out into the high-ceilinged hallway where the portal to the academy had been not long ago. But whereas the hallway had been packed with people when Justan first came through, it was now quite empty. Justan looked through the narrow window on the wall in front of them and saw that it was dark outside.

"What time is it?" he asked. Just how long had they been in the Hall of Majesty with the prophet?

"It is just after the eight o'clock bell," Valtrek said out of hand. "Don't worry. I heard that none of you had eaten so I had some food brought to my offices,"

"Oh thanks," Justan said, though the thought of eating while his bonded were sitting hungry in the hall above made him feel guilty. "What about the others? Shouldn't we-?"

"I hadn't forgotten them," Valtrek replied and no sooner had the words left the wizard's mouth, a group of kitchen workers passed by carrying plates, a basket of bread and a large covered platter.

Justan watched them enter the curving stairwell and his sensitive nose caught the smell of something rich and beefy; most likely covered in gravy. His mouth watered and suddenly he found himself looking forward to arriving at Valtrek's offices. "But what about Gwyrtha? She-."

Another man followed after them, a glum look on his face as he carried a large roll of hay and a bag of oats slung over his shoulder.

"He couldn't have timed that better." Vannya snorted and rolled her eyes. "You loved that, didn't you, father? He always loves it when that sort of thing happens."

"Timing is everything." Valtrek continued on without looking back at them but Justan could hear the smile in his voice. "There is no better way to punctuate your words than perfectly timed proof of their veracity."

Justan blinked. Providing food for the group was a pretty minor point to be proud of. He had come to learn that Valtrek was more than just a manipulative schemer, but the man's satisfaction at making himself look good reminded Justan of why he had resented him for so long.

"Where is your office, Master?" he asked.

"Oh, it's just a short distance away," Valtrek replied. "On a lower floor."

Once more Justan was surprised. In his past experience, the faculty of the Mage School kept their personal spaces on higher floors of the Rune Tower. Below ground level was where they kept their prisoners and stores and . . . Justan wasn't quite sure what all else was down there. In fact, he wasn't sure how far down the Rune Tower went.

The histories were quite vague about the Rune Tower's vertical dimensions in either direction actually. It was one of those irritating Mage School mysteries that Justan found especially frustrating because it was so pointless. Why not just come out and say how big the tower was?

Vannya giggled. Justan turned to look at her and saw that she was now walking right next to him, a knowing smile plastered on her face.

"What?" he asked.

"It's that look on your face." She shook her head, but the smile didn't leave her mouth. "It reminds me of the way you always looked when I'd see you in the library. You get so irritated when you don't understand something."

"That's true." Justan found himself returning her smile. This felt like the Vannya he remembered. It was the first time she had sounded like herself since she had kissed him. "I can't stand not knowing something."

Her smile faltered and she looked away, clearing her throat. "Father keeps his offices on the lower levels because there's less foot traffic there."

"Oh. I see," he said, though it still didn't explain why that was important. Vannya crossed her arms and her brow furrowed again. The familiar moment had passed. Had he said something wrong? "Why is that so important to him?"

"You'll see shortly," Valtrek answered, looking back over his shoulder to shoot Vannya a warning glare. "We go down here."

The wizard stopped at an unassuming doorway and opened it inward. He entered, heading down some stairs. Justan followed behind him a bit puzzled. Wizards in the Rune Tower rarely let a doorway go undecorated. Yet the door was unpolished wood and the stairwell within was made of plain stone, a fact more odd than the door itself. Even the work closets Justan had used when cleaning the library as a cadet had marble floors.

They descended two flights of stairs before Valtrek came to another door, this one looking old and weathered. The hallway beyond was dimly lit and dusty, as if visits here were rare. There were only a few sets of tracks in the dust and they looked fairly recent. Justan began to wonder if he was being led here by some false pretense. What if they weren't heading to Valtrek's offices at all?

"Um, Master? Why is it so . . . dirty down here?" he asked.

"You are wondering why I would choose to stay in such a place, aren't you?" Valtrek said with a chuckle. "This area is warded against prying ears so I shall tell you. The dust lets me know if someone has been through the area. I smooth it out behind me every time I leave."

Justan frowned, but before he said anything Valtrek added, "I also have this hallway warded so that I will know if someone else uses magic to cover their tracks. The footprints you see now are from the kitchen workers that brought your dinner."

"I don't understand. Why go through so much trouble? Why the secrecy?" Justan asked. "We are inside the Rune Tower after all. What is there to fear?"

"I can never be too careful. Even the other council members often have agendas that oppose my own." Valtrek stopped outside a door as weathered as the last. He paused with his hand on the door handle. "But I must admit that I am not usually as cautious as this. Lately there have been some . . . unfortunate breaches of security."

The wizard opened the door and stepped inside, motioning for them to follow. Valtrek's office wasn't nearly as opulent as the other wizard's rooms he had seen, but it was spacious and clean. There were several desks with orderly stacks of papers on them, several padded chairs, and the floor was covered in clay tiles that radiated warmth. In truth, it seemed all rather cozy to Justan.

At one table sat a large covered platter that drew his eyes

immediately. Justan's mouth watered. He could sense that Fist and Gwyrtha were eating already. The ogre's happiness oozed through the bond.

Is it good? he asked while heading over to the platter.

They didn't give me meat, Gwyrtha said with a grump, but the hay and oats were of high quality and there wasn't any edge to her discontent.

It isn't spicy, Fist said and Justan knew he wore a wide grin. They hadn't had much other than Lenny's cooking for weeks and the ogre was so enjoying his meal that Justan could almost taste the mouthful of gravy covered bread Fist was chewing.

"Go on," Valtrek said, seeing the hunger on his face. "We can talk while you eat."

Justan lifted the cover, releasing a small cloud of heavenly steam. He had been right about the scent in the hallway above. Tender chunks of stewed beef and carrots in deep brown gravy were covering cubes of fried potatoes. He pulled up a chair and scooped a large spoonful into his mouth. Justan let out a small moan. He had forgotten how wonderful the food at the Mage School could be.

As he ate, Vannya and Valtrek sat across from him. Once the immediacy of his hunger had faded, Justan looked up at the two of them. The wizard was peering at him thoughtfully while Vannya just stared at the tabletop in front of her, picking at a small round knot in the wood with her fingernail.

Justan swallowed and picked up a hand towel to wipe his chin. "Sorry. Please forgive my manners."

"Why apologize to us?" Valtrek said. "It's not as if we haven't been hungry before. Why just an hour ago Vannya was stuffing her face just as loudly as you."

"Was I really that loud?" Justan asked.

"Father!" Vannya said, her face red.

Valtrek's eyes didn't leave Justan. "I must say, Edge, you really do look quite different from the day you left the school. You've grown."

"Bonding with an ogre can do that to you," Justan said. He glanced down at the broad musculature that filled out his shirt. "I gained a lot of this from Fist."

"Yes, I heard about your ogre from Master Coal," Valtrek said. The mention of his dead master's name gave Justan's heart a sudden lurch.

"About Master Coal," Justan said. "He . . ."

"I know, Edge," Valtrek said sadly. "He and I weren't exactly close, but I liked him. I hope his bonded are okay."

"They should be," Justan said. He told the wizard about Tamboor's naming and the passing of the bond.

"Fascinating," Valtrek said. "And you say that when he was named, he wore a wizard rune? Tamboor the Fearless? The berserker?"

Justan shrugged. "I don't understand it myself. But that's what happened. The prophet seemed to take it all in stride."

"I see," Valtrek replied and Justan could see the wizard's mind working on the matter. "And what else did the prophet do?"

"Well, he started to tell us a tale . . ." Justan paused. John hadn't told them to keep the truth of Stardeon and Mellinda a secret, but he had only invited their small group. "I'm not sure what I can and cannot share. Do you mind if I ask the prophet first?"

Valtrek paused as if considering whether or not to press the issue.

"It shouldn't take but a second," Justan said. *Fist, will you ask John if I need to keep the story secret?* A moment later he had his answer. He cleared his throat. "The prophet says that he trusts my judgment as far as who to tell the tale."

The wizard's brow furrowed in confusion at first, but then his eyes widened. "Ah, I see. You asked your bonded and they relayed your message. Good. So will you tell me what he had to say?"

"Well, I don't know if this information would be of any use to you," Justan said, hesitating.

The wizard pursed his lips and chose his next words carefully. "You realize that I could use my position as your master to make you tell me if I so chose."

"Father!" Vannya said in dismay.

"But I don't want to do that, Edge," the wizard continued, ignoring her outburst. "I hope you understand that I need every bit of information I can get with the situation we are in now."

Justan felt the old familiar dislike for Valtrek rise within him and frowned. He had thought he was over those feelings. Why did the man find it necessary to be so manipulative? "Alright, but before I say more, I must ask. What's happened here at the school while I was gone? Why have you been acting so secretive from the moment I arrived?"

The wizard's brow furrowed and for a moment Justan thought he would blow the question off. Then Valtrek gave a slight shrug. "Being secretive is part of my job, Edge."

"Your job?" Justan said. Valtrek was on the High Council and was in charge of overseeing recruitment. Justan knew that 'recruitment' was just the school's fancy term for gathering up all children that could use magic and forcing them to learn how to use it, but everyone knew that. It was an unfortunate necessity.

"Well, it's not truly a secret, I suppose. At least not among the people who know me, but I would ask you to be discreet about discussing this with others," Valtrek said. Justan felt the hum of magic and switched to mage sight. He watched the wizard reach out with his magic and touch the nearly invisible listening wards which lined the walls of the office. Valtrek must have been satisfied with what he found because he nodded. "Edge, as part of my role as recruiter, I am also the school spymaster."

"Oh," Justan said and gave a slight nod. It made sense. As Mage School recruiter, Valtrek would have contacts all over the known lands.

Valtrek smiled. "That's why I try to be discreet in my dealings and it's also why I keep my offices where I do. It sets people off guard. When people are sent to visit me, and see these surroundings, they can't help but underestimate me and that is an advantage."

"Yeah, but once people know your position, it's kind of obvious that's what you're hoping for, isn't it?" Justan asked. "I mean this place is so plain it sticks out."

Valtrek smiled. "Well, you have a good point. But think on this. There aren't many people that think like you. However, those that do make that connection still let their guard down just a little if only because they think they have me figured out.

Believe me, I have put this strategy to good use many times."

"Okay, Master," Justan said. "I believe you. But what about the way you were acting on the walk down here? I don't recall you being this careful in the past."

Valtrek sighed. "Yes, well there have been some changes since you left. Especially after the incident with Piledon and Arcon."

Justan frowned. He still felt guilty about Piledon's death. "Was Arcon ever found?"

"As a matter of fact, he has shown up," Valtrek said. "At Ewzad Vriil's side."

Justan's brow furrowed. "What's he doing with Vriil?"

"My source says that Arcon is connected with the moonrat mother in some way. She led him to the dark wizard partially, I think, to keep an eye on Vriil's doings. Arcon hasn't shared all that happened with my source, but we know that he had been in contact with the moonrat mother for some time before he killed Piledon. Even worse, we know that there were others with moonrat eyes that remained behind in the school after he left."

"You didn't tell me that," Vannya said with a glare. "Who are they? Workers? Students? Wizards?"

"You have been gone a long while, Vannya," Valtrek explained. "This information is relatively new. Our source at the Royal Palace has only been reporting in for about a month. As for who exactly the moonrat mother's spies are, our source does not know. All we know is that the moonrat mother gives Ewzad Vriil detailed information from within the school with some regularity."

"If you don't know who her spies are, then how did you keep our plans to break the siege and escape here a secret?" Justan asked.

"Master Latva and I had to plan it all very carefully. It was a struggle, but when your friend Sir Hilt's wife showed up, it became much easier. The prophet told us of her abilities and I discreetly took a few of the people we trusted the most aside and had her, 'listen to them' as she called it. Once we had enough people to enact our plans, we made sure that all the preparations were done discreetly. We kept every person who came through that portal hidden until we knew it didn't matter anymore." He gave a chuckle. "You can imagine the uproar in the school just a few short hours ago when thousands of refugees began streaming out of the Rune Tower."

"Did Beth find any spies, father?" Vannya asked.

The wizard's eyes darkened. "Two. And both of them were heavy blows. We had to lock them away. Keeping their disappearance undiscovered has been harder than any of the other secrets we had to keep."

"Who are they?" Justan asked. "Are they people I know?"

Valtrek raised a hand. "We can discuss them later. I need you focused on our meeting here and now. Are you finished eating?"

Justan looked down at the mostly empty platter before him and though he wasn't exactly full, it no longer looked appetizing. The unknown identity of the two spies was leaving a sense of unease in his stomach. "I suppose I am."

"Alright. Good," the wizard said with a smile. He stood and walked over to the largest of the desks in the room. He pulled out several pieces of parchment and an odd looking quill with a long red feather and sat down in a high backed chair behind the desk. Valtrek gestured to two padded chairs that were planted in front of the desk facing him. "Well, come over here then."

"So this visit is about me telling you what the prophet told us, then?" Justan asked resignedly.

"Well it's likely information that I should know. Anything that helps us understand our enemies would be helpful," Valtrek said. "But that's not why I brought you down here. If that's all I wanted, it would have been better for me to wait until he was finished."

Justan's brow furrowed. "They why did you bring me out of the meeting?"

"I wanted to see you when you first came through the portal, but the prophet asked me to wait until after dark to come and get you," the wizard explained.

"Then why threaten to force me to talk about it?" Justan asked in irritation.

Valtrek paused and Vannya said, "He's right, Professor. That was an unnecessary move."

The wizard chose to ignore their complaints. "The reason I wanted you here is so that I could go over the things that have happened to you in the time we spent apart."

"I thought Master Coal had kept you up to date on everything that happened," Justan said.

"He sent me regular correspondence, yes, but there is much that I don't know. I would like to talk to you more about your bonds. I would like to find out what you learned about your powers. If fact, I would like you to tell me everything that happened while you were away."

Justan had a feeling that he was going to have to tell that tale a lot over the next few days. His mother and Professor Beehn at least would want to hear it. "Where do I start?"

"Have a seat and start from the night you left the school," Valtrek said, leaning forward and gesturing to the chair across from him. "Leave nothing out. Tell me anything that prickles your mind about the events, no matter how small. Any bit of information could be important and from what I have heard, you have been places that none of my other sources have."

Justan moved over and sat down where Valtrek directed, wondering what the wizard would learn from his tale. Vannya followed him but paused before sitting.

"Father, do you really need me here for this part?" She glanced at Justan and looked embarrassedly away.

The wizard raised an eyebrow. "Come, dear, I know that what happened between the two of you was painful, but I need you to put that aside for now. You will understand why I wanted you here soon enough."

Justan watched as she sighed and sat down, slumping in the chair next to him. He swallowed. It sounded like she had told Valtrek everything. So far the wizard hadn't said anything to him about it but Justan felt sure that he was going to bring it up sooner or later.

Valtrek smiled at her and turned his eyes back to Justan. "Go on, then."

Justan told his story. He did his best to provide any details he felt that Valtrek would find relevant, while glossing

over anything of a personal nature, but the wizard
was sly and could tell when Justan wasn't telling him everything.
Valtrek would often stop him and ask targeted questions,
invariably ferreting out the parts Justan tried to hide.

By the time he finished his tale, Justan felt worn out. The
only thing he'd been able to keep secret was his betrothal to
Jhonate. That part had felt important to keep quiet if only
because Vannya was sitting right next to him. Besides, he was
pretty sure Jhonate would kill him if word got out.

The other two were quiet. Valtrek was looking at him
thoughtfully while Vannya stared down at her lap. "What?"
Justan asked her.

She didn't look up. "Well, it's just . . . I didn't know all
the things you'd been through since you left the school. It's . . . a
lot."

"Well, I didn't get much time to talk to you about it after
the way you . . . well, with the way things happened," he said
and swallowed. That kiss had derailed their friendship. The
feeling of her lips pressed against his was still fresh in his mind.
"Locksher did tell me all the things you went through on my
behalf though, searching for Piledon's killer and all. I never did
get the chance to thank you. So . . . thank you very much,
Vannya."

She managed a half smile. "You are my friend after all. I
wanted to help."

Justan smiled back at her and for the first time in a while
he was hopeful that she could forgive him for choosing Jhonate
over her. Maybe things could get back to the way they had been
between them.

"Well, good," said Valtrek, clapping his hands together.
"I'm glad the two of you have patched things up, because I want
you to work together."

"Wait, what?" Justan and Vannya said in unison.

"I can't keep spending all my time ferreting out the
moonrat mother's spies. They are suspicious that I am onto them
already. So you two are going to do it for me." The wizard
leaned back in his chair. "Edge, you know how to use spirit sight
to see moonrat eyes. I want you to be on the watch for them
everywhere you go. Vannya, on the other hand, knows the

students and staff of this school as well as anyone. If anyone is acting differently than normal she will be able to tell. I want you to get together fairly often to compare notes."

Vannya's face had turned red. "I don't know that I can handle that right now-."

"You can do it," Valtrek insisted.

"But Father!" she said and Justan realized from the tone of her voice that they still had a way to go before Vannya felt comfortable around him.

"You will do it," the wizard said firmly.

Vannya pursed her lips and stood from her chair. "May I be excused now?"

"You may," Valtrek said.

She turned on her heels and walked swiftly to the door. She opened it, grasping the handle with a white knuckled grip. She paused a moment while walking through and Justan could tell she was using a lot of restraint not to slam the door behind her. Instead she let go of the handle and strode out into the hallway, leaving it hanging open.

Valtrek used a gust of wind to shut the door after her and slumped back in his chair. "Oh sometimes I swear that girl was born to fray my nerves."

We're done, Justan. Fist sent and Justan caught a quick mental glimpse of everyone filing out of the Hall of Majesty while wizards came in to take the unconscious forms of Tolivar and his bonded away. *Big John wants me to tell you everything you missed.*

Me too! said Gwyrtha.

Good. I will join you soon and you can tell me all about it, Justan replied. He looked at Valtrek. "The prophet just finished his tale. The others are being shown to their quarters."

"You can join them soon," the wizard said. "But we still have some items to discuss first."

"I suppose you want me to tell you the prophet's tale, now?" Justan said wearily. He was tired and he really wanted to check in on Deathclaw. The raptoid had barely moved as far as he could tell at this distance, but all he really knew was that Deathclaw was still alive. "Can it wait until tomorrow? It has been an exhausting day and I still need to check on Deathclaw. I know that he is still to the north in the direction of the academy, but that is all I can tell from this distance."

The wizard pursed his lips, but nodded, "I suppose it can wait until morning. But since we are on the subject, we do need to discuss the matter of your bonded. What are you going to do with them while you are here at the school?"

Justan frowned. "I suppose I haven't had much time to think about it. I assumed that there would be a possibility of some uncomfortable moments until people got used to them, but-." Justan frowned. "Is this about Gwyrtha? Do you think she will be in danger here? Even now that it isn't a secret who she is to me?"

"No, not at all. The rogue horse . . . Gwyrtha, will be taken care of. Master Latva and I have already arranged for it to be made known that no one is to experiment on her, and the elves are eager to see her again." Valtrek assured him, but Justan couldn't help but feel uneasy all the same. "No, it is Fist I am concerned about."

"Fist?" Justan asked. "Well, I suppose it will take a while for people to get used to seeing him around, but as soon as they get to know him things will be fine. People seem to find it quite impossible not to like him."

"I am not speaking about his being accepted by the students and faculty here. I am talking about his schooling," Valtrek said

"Schooling?"

"Of course," the wizard said, looking surprised. "He is a bonding wizard, is he not? Haven't you tested him for elemental magic ability?"

"I, uh . . . I guess not," Justan admitted. "But why would he have any?"

"It is a known fact that in some rare occasions ogres or giants or even orcs can show some small ability in magic. Usually it isn't enough to matter much to us, but there have been times in history when a rather powerful magic user has come up in the ranks and caused the world quite a bit of trouble," Valtrek explained. "You should at least have him checked for talent and if he has it, by all means he must be taught."

"But . . ." It was a crazy idea on the surface. The Mage

School wanted anyone with magic talent to come and learn, but there were a few notable exceptions. Their refusal to admit half-orcs had been a gripe of his mother's. "Are you sure the rest of the council would let Fist be taught here?"

"It would perhaps be . . . unprecedented to have one of the dark races allowed entrance, but as the prophet has been reminding us, times are changing," Valtrek said, giving him what Justan was sure was supposed to be a comforting smile. "Besides, most of us find ogres with elemental magic a fascinating subject and I think I can use that along with his relationship to you as an angle to get him admitted. I am in charge of recruitment after all."

"Well, I suppose I can discuss it with him tonight, see if he's willing." In fact Justan was positive he'd be willing. Fist would love the opportunity to learn magic.

"Very good! I will expect you here right after breakfast then, Edge," Valtrek said.

"Alright. Good evening, Master," Justan said and stood to leave.

"One other thing," the wizard added in an offhand manner. "When you come in, I should like to hear your side of what happened with my daughter. Also, along those lines, I expect to hear an explanation of the nature of your relationship with the daughter of Xedrion. Her father is a very important man and his reaction could affect the Mage School's interests in Malaroo."

Justan swallowed and nodded. As he headed out the door and into the dusty hallway beyond, he wondered if he wouldn't rather be fighting Ewzad's monsters instead.

Chapter Six

And does Fist wish to learn this magic? Deathclaw asked from his position high in the fir tree. Despite how far away Justan was, Deathclaw could hear his thoughts clearly as long as he was willing to dim his other senses and focus.

Oh, he loves the idea. He's telling Squirrel and Gwyrtha all about it right now. Justan didn't sound like he approved.

This is good for us. Fist could become even more useful to the pack, since your magic skills are basically useless. Deathclaw was thinking of the power of the man Justan knew as Professor Beehn. Earlier that day he had seen the man hurl a large beast into the air so high that it was but a speck. If Fist could do that . . .

Deathclaw, said a fainter voice that was not Justan's, but he ignored it.

Justan hadn't heard the voice. *What do you mean about my magic being useless? We're talking right now, aren't we, and we're a week's ride apart.*

Deathclaw realized that the man's feelings had been hurt. He didn't understand the way humans were so sensitive to words and thoughts. If something was true, why take offense? To add to his point he said, *Yes, we can speak, but what of your other magic? Other wizards can cause lightnings or hurl fire or throw an enemy with the very air around them. Would it not be good if the ogre could do such things?*

I'm not disagreeing with that. It would be good for us if Fist could do those things, but it's not likely his magic will be strong if he has any at all. Ogres tend to have a low magical talent. Don't act like my elemental magic isn't useful, though. I can heal you and bring up shields against magic attack. Justan gave a mental sigh. *I just can't use it to attack our enemies.*

Why is that? Deathclaw asked.

I don't know, it's just the way my magic is. No one can explain it. I-.

Deathclaw, can you hear me? The other voice called out again and Deathclaw's nostrils flared in irritation at the interruption.

Justan paused. *What was that sound? I swear I heard a voice.*

You heard her? Deathclaw asked in surprise.

Please respond to me, the faint voice said.

Is that Beth? Justan asked. *Did they find you?*

It is her, he admitted. Justan had not been happy that he had chosen not to return to the others, but Deathclaw had other priorities to see to. *But they are not here. They are still a ways to the east. She has been trying to speak with me for some time.*

She can reach your mind at that kind of distance?

She gave me an . . . object, Deathclaw reached up to touch the thin piece of wood on the cord around his neck. Though the night was cool, it felt warm to the touch. He had thought about throwing it away several times, but for some reason he hadn't. He didn't know why. She wouldn't be able to bother him then.

What kind of object? Justan asked.

Wood. Deathclaw sent him his memories of the way Beth had broken the piece of wood off her knife and molded it in to the item that hung around his neck.

Deathclaw, that whistle around your neck is made of Jharro wood, Justan replied. He seemed quite excited. *I don't know how she broke a piece off like that, but that whistle she gave you is very valuable.*

Deathclaw frowned in confusion. *Then why would she break it?*

I don't know. But whatever her reasoning, she must have felt it was important to give it to you. Justan's next thoughts were very deliberate. *I don't understand how Beth's powers work, but from what I've gathered, she sees the importance of things. She would not have given you a piece of that dagger if she didn't think it was important that you return to them. You should go.*

Deathclaw glowered. He didn't wish to return to the others. He didn't feel at ease with them. *I may return at some point, but I have not found Talon yet.*

I see, Justan said and Deathclaw knew that he understood. They shared the desire to see Talon's existence ended. Justan wanted her dead more than ever since she had killed the wizard Coal. *Did you find any sign of her?*

I did. Deathclaw showed Justan what he had found. It had been dangerous with all of the creatures still wandering about, but he had retraced the steps of the fleeing humans and found the site of their terrible battle along the road. Among the melted remains of Ewzad Vriil's creations he had found the bodies of several fallen humans and finally the spot where Fist had struck Talon down. The scent of her blood had trailed off into the tall grass before disappearing all together.

I knew it was too much to hope she was dead. Justan sent and Deathclaw knew that back in the Mage School where he lay, the human's hands were clenched into fists. *Do you know where she went?*

No. Her scent had not reappeared and she had left no other trace of her passing. She had gone somewhere to heal, Deathclaw was sure. But after that, he didn't know what she would do.

Perhaps she is returning to her master, Justan suggested.

Perhaps, Deathclaw replied. He hoped not. He didn't want to be forced to track her that far.

Beth's voice interrupted them again. *Deathclaw, I know you can hear me. I can feel you listening. Just hold the whistle and respond.* To his surprise, after all the time he ignored her, she didn't sound frustrated, just . . . patient.

I heard most of what she said that time, Justan sent. *Please, do as she asks. I want to see if she can hear me.*

Deathclaw hesitated. He really didn't want to, but could find no good reason to refuse his pack leader's request. He gripped the small piece of wood in his hand. *I hear you, Beth.*

Good. I was starting to wonder if you actually could, she said, but Deathclaw knew she was lying. She knew full well that he had been ignoring her. *And is Sir Edge listening?*

I am, Justan responded. *Can you hear me?*

I can, she replied.

This is amazing, Justan said in excitement. *How did you do it? I mean first of all, just communicating with my bonded and then that trick with the Jharro dagger? How is that possible?*

I can listen with the use of my own bonding magic, she replied. *It isn't a permanent bond like those you bonding wizards have, but I have learned to communicate to the spirits of others as long as I am touching them. As far as the Jharro wood 'trick', Yntri taught it to me.*

Can you tell me how to do those things? Justan asked.

It isn't that simple, I'm afraid. I checked your spirit magic talent when I first met you and I am afraid that as powerful as your bonding magic is, it is limited to your connection with your bonded. As for the use of Jharro wood, perhaps your betrothed can tell you. She is far more talented with Jharro wood than I.

Oh, said Justan, disappointed.

And what do you have to be disappointed about? Beth asked, sensing his mood right away. *You can't expect to be powerful in everything. The moment I met you I could see that your bonding talent is extremely strong and even though my own elemental magic is gone, I could see that yours is every bit as strong as your mother's.*

I suppose you're right, Justan said, but Deathclaw knew that if anything, the conversation had just made him feel worse. The man had so much raw power, but could control so little of it. Deathclaw couldn't imagine how he would handle such a burden. His control was all he had.

Now, I'm sorry, but I really need to speak with Deathclaw, Beth said and the raptoid felt her attention shifted to him. *Listen, dear, I know you have another goal you are pursuing, but it is vitally important that you are with us until this siege is over.*

Why am I needed? Deathclaw asked. *The giant can speak to his bonding wizard at the Mage School when you need. Your man can scout.*

True as that may be, we need you. I can't explain it better than to just say that I know it, she insisted. *Sometimes I know the way things may happen. Sometimes it's with a vision, but with you, it's just a certainty. You may be fine out there alone, but if you're not with us, we will die.*

How can you know such things to be true? Deathclaw said.

It's spirit magic, Justan said. *It can do mysterious things.*

Perhaps, Beth said. *I'm not sure how this gift fits into the four spirit magic types, but I know it works.*

Deathclaw sulked. He should leave them to worry about their own survival. They could fend for themselves. Hunting Talon was the important thing. Ending her pain was his purpose. It wasn't his responsibility to keep the others alive.

But it is, Justan said and Deathclaw realized he had been thinking too loud. He had grown too careless around the human. Justan sensed his irritation. *I have narrowed my voice to you alone. Beth shouldn't be able to hear what I have to say.*

Explain, then, Deathclaw replied.

Their lives are in your hands now, Justan said. *This became your responsibility the moment you learned the results of leaving them. If Hilt and Beth and Charz die because you refused to stay with them, their deaths will be your fault.*

I do not accept that thinking, Deathclaw said. *Talon is my responsibility. As long as she lives, she will continue to kill without purpose. Will those deaths not also be my fault?*

I agree that ending Talon is an important mission, but she will have to be dealt with later. Right now watching over Hilt and Beth and Charz is your responsibility, Justan said. *Think of them as an extension of our pack. You couldn't willingly leave any of us to die knowing your presence could save us. Could you?*

Deathclaw growled. *I dislike being forced.*

Justan gave a mental shrug. *So do I. But that is an unfortunate part of life when you try to do the right thing.*

Deathclaw chafed under his logic. This human concept of right and wrong that Justan believed in seemed to stray often from the law of the pack, but in this case they agreed. One did not leave one's pack members to die. Not unless the situation was hopeless. Begrudgingly, he increased the volume of his thoughts and said, *I have thought on it, Beth. I will come to you.*

Oh, good! Thank you, dear, she said. *I will tell the others.*

Wait, Beth, Justan sent. *I have some information I think you should know.*

Oh?

The prophet spoke to some of us today and told us the identity of the mother of the moonrats.

Her interest was piqued. *Please. Tell me.*

While Deathclaw acted as the bridge between their minds, Justan told Beth the story of Mellinda and Stardeon. Though he found it interesting, the telling of the tale took longer than Deathclaw liked. The temporary bond with Beth was too weak to shove complete memories through, so it had to be retold directly.

As time passed, Deathclaw had to reel in more and more of his senses to focus on the connection. This left him feeling insecure in his hiding place, but eventually he became so enveloped in the story that he let his worries slide.

John did not see Stardeon again after the day he left with Samson, Justan said, reaching the end of the tale. *He left him without any bonding magic and with only his rings to power his magic. More than that John would not say, but we do know that the rings somehow ended up in the Dark Prophet's hands.* Justan said.

I would venture that Mellinda had something to do with that, Beth said, her thoughts a dark glower.

That would make sense to me, Justan agreed.

Somewhere at the edge of his senses Deathclaw heard something. It was faint, but haunting. He ignored it at first, but the sound repeated until it pierced Deathclaw's concentration. It echoed through his mind, a mournful chittering moan.

Moonrats! Justan and Beth said at the same time.

Deathclaw opened his eyes to find the forest floor flooding with pairs of glowing orbs of dim light. Most of the orbs were yellow in color, but scattered among them were pairs glowing a sickly green. As they moved, the moans rose in response to each other. It was a chorus; a chorus of mourning and hate and hunger, three emotions Deathclaw was intimately familiar with.

He hissed inwardly and dropped his connection with Beth. He had been foolish and overconfident and allowed himself to focus too much on their communication. He had covered his tracks well, but these creatures would smell him out soon enough. He prepared his mind for battle,

Justan sensed that he was about to cut off their communication. *Wait! Let me show you what I know about fighting moonrats.* The human slid his memories of fighting the creatures into Deathclaw's mind. It took only a few seconds, but that slight delay gave the moonrats the chance to catch his scent.

Hisses and screeches echoed out from the surrounding forest. Dozens of the creatures gathered at the base of the tree, while others made their way through the interlocking tree branches towards him. The information Justan had passed through the bond was useful though. Deathclaw now knew that individual moonrats were weak and that their eyes were their weakest point. Those glowing orbs were the source of the witch's power over the creature and easy to see in the dark.

The moonrats climbed from below and crawled through the branches with their many claws. Deathclaw kept completely still until the first one drew near, then his tail barb burst one of its yellow eyes and pierced its brain. The creature convulsed and fell into the milling mass below. As Justan's memories had predicted, the rest of the creatures tore into the body the moment it struck the ground.

Deathclaw willed time to slow down around him. He slid down the tree, knocking loose several climbing moonrats and sending them crashing into the others. Six feet before reaching the ground, he leapt away from the trunk and fell among them. He lashed out with claws and tail in calculating fashion, tearing every glowing eye within reach.

Once he had cleared a space around him, he drew his sword. The night was dark and deep and he knew that Star was at its full strength. Star caused a burning pain when it struck in daylight, but at night it turned flesh to cinders.

He slashed at the moonrats around him, using the shifting swordwork forms that Justan had taught him. Wherever the blade struck, searing flame erupted from the wounds. The air was pierced with chittering squeals of pain and terror as moonrats ran with pelts ablaze.

Deathclaw screeched in response to their pain and lay about him with his blade more fiercely than before. The night was soon ablaze with burning moonrats, their wounds bright with glowing coals. The putrid smell of their burning fur and cooking flesh, made his stomach turn, but he kept on with his attack until he saw that his efforts were having little effect. Dozens of moonrats lay dead or dying around him and dozens more fed on their bodies, but there seemed to be no end to the orbs streaking in from the forest's heart. It was time to move.

This was unlike any fight he had faced before. Though in some ways it reminded him of battles with packs of dragon spawn, this time he had no pack around to help him. Deathclaw fought alone and not for food. This was for survival.

He darted forward, dancing through the clusters of creatures, slicing any that came too close with his tail or sword. Their movements seemed slow and predictable to his focused awareness. Each animal that fell distracted several others, yet it wasn't enough. They swarmed after him with numbers unceasing. On he ran, leaving death and confusion in his wake only to find more in his path.

The night breeze changed direction and Deathclaw caught another scent. Screeches of hunger joined the voices of the moonrats.

Trolls.

But these trolls smelled different than the large trolls he had encountered earlier in the day. Those had reeked of the wizard Vriil's power and though their scent had an acrid tang to it, that tang had been muted. The smell of these new creatures was dangerous in a way different from those other trolls. They gave off fumes that stung his nostrils with a sharp intensity and caused his eyes to water. He then realized these trolls were flammable.

They soon came into view, lit by the glow of the moonrats around them, tall gangly creatures that dripped slime as they ran towards him. Their charge was fierce and mindless and every bit as hungry as the moonrats'. In their furor, several of them tripped over the moonrats beneath them. But that only slowed them down momentarily. They scrambled to their feet and kept coming.

Deathclaw didn't slow to face them. He knew that would be folly. But the moment one drew close, he lashed out with Star. The reaction was much more intense than with the moonrats. The troll was instantly engulfed in flame. It screeched and crashed to the ground, lighting every moonrat it touched.

The intensity of the reaction knocked Deathclaw off balance and he nearly fell in surprise. His focused awareness vanished and the battle around him sped up. He lashed about wildly with his sword, forgetting Justan's teachings. Another troll rose in front of him with claws outstretched and toothy maw gaping open. Star pierced its chest and the troll erupted so quickly that Deathclaw was struck with flaming spatter.

The troll slime clung to his skin as it burned, searing through his scales, but he couldn't afford to take the time to beat out the flames. He ignored the pain and kept running. Pain was temporary. His flesh would heal soon enough if he survived.

The next troll approached and as he raised his sword again, he noticed that Star's blade had begun to glow red. He lashed out at the screeching beast and the troll erupted as the others had before, but this time, the force of the blast was directed outward in a fan-like pattern away from Deathclaw, lighting several moonrats and another troll on fire.

This minor distraction gave Deathclaw time to refocus. The world slowed down for him once more. He continued forward, grateful that the sword's handle at least was cool in his hand. Each strike he landed with Star caused a more intense reaction than the one before, but he didn't have time to stop and think about the reasons why.

Fire blazed through the forest all around him in a long trail leading back to the place where the battle had begun. The winter's leaves, dried out by the spring breezes, were burning. Yet the moonrat mother drove the attackers on. Often they were aflame before they reached him. He lashed out, combusting one enemy after another and soon his sword blade shone white hot.

Star's transformation was a mystery. He had only used the blade at the time of its full power once before. But on the night he had battled Talon, the blade hadn't reacted like this. If it had, he would have killed her back then. There was no time to dwell on it now.

Each time Star's white-hot blade touched an enemy, they were thrown from him as they burst into flaming pieces. He took advantage of its power, clearing the path before him and turning his attackers into burning missiles that should have sent his enemies into disarray.

Still, the press of creatures grew thicker. They surged forward, many of them nearly dead from the heat before they reached him. The witch had driven even the fear of burning from their minds. His pace slowed and every step forward was hard won. Deathclaw knew that his survival was unlikely. They were going to overcome him with sheer numbers alone.

The power of the sword blasted them back; immolated them. The night air filled with the screech of dying trolls, the horrible noise punctuated by the sound of moonrat eyes bursting as they boiled from within, each one popping with a sound like an infant cry.

Deathclaw was not immune to the blaze either. Though the sword directed its power away from him, his scales smoked from the intensity of the fires around him. He found himself thinking of his demise with calm detachment. The feeling was puzzling. As a raptoid he had faced death with an intense instinctual fear. He should have been frantic in his attempts to get away, but he was able to fight on in full control and awareness. What had changed?

A brief quiet suddenly fell over the creatures. Something had shifted. Deathclaw didn't know what it was, but the air itself felt somehow different. The moonrats and trolls froze, even the ones on fire. This paralysis lasted only a few seconds, but when it ended everything changed. The trolls and moonrats tore into each other. Only the closest few came at Deathclaw and he dispatched them quickly with explosive thrusts of his white-hot blade.

A thudding sound pulsed through the night air next and Deathclaw saw the bodies of moonrats flung through the air from the darkened forest before him. A guttural laugh rang out and the bulky form of Charz came into view. He had a slimy troll gripped in both hands. The crystal pendant around the giant's neck swung as he raised the screeching beast over his head. It clawed at him with wicked talons, but they barely scratched his stony skin. He threw it into a burning patch of forest leaves where it immediately went up in flames.

An arrow cut through the night air, carrying the sound of a hissing snake and struck a nearby moonrat right in its glowing green eye. The rat fell over to be swarmed by its brethren and Sir Hilt ran into the fray, his twin blades dancing through the beasts, cutting them into neat pieces.

"Come, Deathclaw!" Beth's voice said from the darkness and he could just make her out, standing between two thick trees. Her bow was held slack in one hand, her other hand clutching a low hanging branch to keep herself from falling over. "I have cut off her presence from this place for now, but she's pressing me hard. We must get out of here before she . . . ugh, breaks through!"

Deathclaw ran to her, arriving just in time to cleave a troll that had been running towards her from behind. Its flaming pieces lit the forest beyond, setting fire to multiple troll trails that ran into the distance.

"Watch your surroundings!" he warned.

Beth gave him a weak grin. "I sensed it was there. And I knew you would get here first." She glanced at Star gleaming in his hand. "Nice sword."

"Charz!" Hilt shouted from behind them. Deathclaw turned to see him lop a moonrat's head off. "Grab Beth and let's go!"

"Fine," Charz sighed and booted a moonrat aside on his way. He lifted Beth's weary form in his arms and gave Deathclaw a shake of his head. "Nice job lighting the forest on fire, lizard. Now the witch has no doubt where we are."

Deathclaw hissed back at him. This wasn't his fault. He hadn't wanted to rejoin them in the first place. The giant stomped into the forest and Deathclaw turned to see if Sir Hilt needed his assistance.

The named warrior danced through the confused enemy, striking with fierce precision, making slashing cuts far deeper than the blades of his swords should have allowed. The trolls and moonrats feasted on each other, but any that looked coherent enough to chase after Charz and Beth were sliced in two.

Whenever Hilt came upon a small fire, he whipped a sword in its direction and a gust of air fanned the flames.

He glanced at Deathclaw. "Run with them! Charz can't fight while he's carrying her!"

Deathclaw nodded and darted after the giant. Once again, a human was telling him what to do. He knew that this fact should have bothered him more than it did, but perhaps he had gotten used to being a pack member instead of a pack leader. He narrowed his eyes at the thought.

He caught up to the giant quickly and ran beside him, Star's blade held out far from his body. The blade still glowed white, though perhaps not as bright as it had been, and he didn't know what to do with it. He was afraid that it would burn right through its sheath if he put it away.

He reached up with his free hand and grasped the tiny wood whistle hanging around his neck. *Beth . . . are you ill, woman?*

Just tired, came her mental reply. *I've been using spirit magic almost nonstop since we assaulted the army this morning and I'm concerned that the mother of the moonrats is starting to figure me out.* She grunted as Charz jumped over a downed tree. *And this big oaf does not make a comfortable carriage.*

He is hard, Deathclaw said, knowing that the human woman's soft body would be bruised by the giant's movements.

It's not just that. It's his soul. The poor dear is trying to change, but he has been such an awful thing for so long, he has a lot of regrets. Being this close to him just gives me a headache.

Changing . . . is not easy, Deathclaw said knowing the long path he was still on.

Don't compare yourself to him, she sent. *You were never evil. Just ignorant.*

Deathclaw frowned as much as his scaly face would allow. How did she think she knew him so well after just a short few moments listening to his heart?

It's part of my magic. It's what a listener does, she replied to his unspoken thoughts.

Charz gave them both a wary glare. "Is she talking about me?"

"Oh don't worry, you big boulder," she grumped. "Try

not to jostle me so much and I'll stop griping."

"Where are we going?" Deathclaw asked aloud.

"Out of this forest," the giant replied.

We are retreating into the foothills of the mountains east of here, Beth sent. *The further we are from the center of Mellinda's activity, the easier it will be for me to keep us undetected.*

But what does that matter? Deathclaw asked. *The giant's tracks will lead them right to us anyway.*

No. Wizard Locksher gave us a solution to that problem before entering the portal, she explained. *Look for yourself.*

Deathclaw slowed down a bit and watched the trail that Charz left behind. There was barely a discernable trace of the giant's heavy foot falls. With effort, he caused his sight to shift into mage sight as Justan had taught him and Deathclaw saw that the giant's boots radiated an earthy blackness.

"His boots have a spell on them," Beth said with a yawn. "Every footprint fills back in as soon as he steps out of it. It's the rest of us that need to be careful."

Deathclaw sent her a mental nod of understanding and altered his gait for stealth. *What will we do once we have reached these mountains?*

We scout, she said. *The Mage School needs to know everything we can tell them about the forces besieging them.*

Deathclaw ran alongside the giant, feeling unsettled. He looked at his sword and noticed that the blade's glow had faded to its familiar dull shine. He slid it into its sheath over his shoulder. He felt a twinge of pain in his hand when he let go of the pommel and flexed his fingers. He hadn't realized how tightly he had been holding onto it.

He looked at his hand and to his surprise, glowing in the center of his palm was a tiny rune in the shape of a star.

Chapter Seven

The witch! The witch had to die!

Across Dremaldria every moonrat let out a moan, echoing Mellinda's rage. This had been a costly day. A disaster! Ewzad had decided to play it off as a victory, but he had been far too lighthearted since finding out the queen was pregnant with twins.

A third! Fully a third of her children had been destroyed when the academy exploded. Several of her servants called out to her at once, asking if they could aid her, but she just growled at them in reply. All their input was giving her a headache. Ewzad thought her affection for the moonrats was sentimentality on her part but it wasn't. A small portion of her capacity for thought was stored in each living moonrat. She used their little brains to power her thought processes.

The day's losses had already weakened her ability to think when Ewzad's precious demon had set fire to her forest and killed over a hundred more of them. All in one day.

Mellinda hurt. Her very being hurt, but she could not let that slow her. Her own plans were still in motion. She just had to focus. Her children were multiplying faster than ever in their new breeding grounds. She would be able to replace the dead ones soon enough. Then all she had to do was wait for the new trait to emerge. One day soon a moonrat would be born with eyes of a new color. These new eyes would be more powerful than the orange. She could use them to transfer her mind to a new host and then be free to roam the lands again.

That would be her new beginning and it would come soon, she could feel it. The Dark Prophet had foretold her rebirth after all. But she needed to focus on the situation at hand. The academy was gone, but the Mage School remained. She had been ordered to assist Ewzad Vriil in his siege of the school, but Mellinda's larger priority was ridding herself of certain enemies.

Some of them she had already marked for death, like the bonding wizard, Sir Edge, who had killed so many of her children, and the girl from Malaroo, the daughter of Xedrion bin Leeths. That girl had come quite close to learning her true name and even worse, the name given her by the Dark Bowl.

Other enemies needed to die because they were too dangerous; like Tamboor, the soulless man whom she had learned had been named earlier that day; or Master Latva, the head of the Mage School, who knew far too much about her. But all of those enemies were secondary to the witch.

Mellinda hadn't understood at first how the human army had blocked her communications with her children in the area around the academy. She had been so distraught and frustrated and, most terrifying, blind during that attack. Then that night as her children were doing battle with Ewzad's pet, it had happened again. Mellinda had felt out the presence and attacked and for a moment, a brief moment, she had broken through the barrier. In that moment, Mellinda had grasped a name. *Beth.*

Names were powerful things, but only if one had the information needed to make them useful. In her walking days, Mellinda remembered Beth being a fairly common name but that was hundreds of years ago. Now perhaps things were different.

She reached out to her servants within the school, but the ones she could reach had not heard of this Beth. Where had she come from? The prophet had forbidden the teaching of spirit magic long ago and yet this witch was skilled. And powerful. As powerful as any witch that had existed during Mellinda's walking days. How had this woman become so good without being known?

Mellinda was also aware of her current limited reach. Perhaps this Beth wasn't from Dremaldria. Where had the academy found her then? Malaroo, perhaps? Surely the people of her old homeland hadn't completely forsaken spirit magic like Dremaldria. But then again, her people seemed to keep to themselves in Malaroo. She had learned that much while searching the girl Jhonate's memories.

Mellinda reached out to Arcon. As she surged into his mind, the mage was busy overseeing the transfer of more beasts into Ewzad's dungeons. He was directing those dirty dwarves as to where Ewzad wanted his new beasts placed.

"*Arcon, dear?*" she cooed.

The mage froze mid-gesture. *Yes, Mistress?*

"*I wonder, have you heard of a woman by the name of Beth?*"

Several, Mistress, he replied and she could tell that he was surprised at her kind temperament. *There are two by that name here on Queen Elise's staff as a matter of fact . . . Are you all right mistress?*

Was she all right? He had evidently been monitoring her moods. Mellinda scowled. Her struggle with the witch had caused her to lower too many of her barriers. How many of her servants had heard her pain and fear? They could misunderstand that as weakness. Unacceptable!

In a fit of anger, she wrenched at Arcon's pain centers, causing the mage to crumple to his knees. A blood vessel burst in his eye again and his heart pounded.

Will you kill me now, Mistress? He asked, his thoughts calm.

His response verged on insolence, but Mellinda reminded herself to be careful. She had come close to causing this one permanent damage on multiple occasions, and though he had deserved the punishment, Arcon was too valuable to throw away on a whim. He had a key seed inside of him after all.

She tried to make up for it by caressing his pleasure centers. "*Please, my love, tell me more. Who are these Beths you speak of?*"

Arcon responded by burying his emotions and relaying the things he could remember in a factual manner. Mellinda noticed him doing this quite often. It was a mental trick. He was hiding his resentments and rebellious thoughts somewhere deep within his mind. Sometimes she felt him retreat to this place when he thought she wasn't paying attention and she knew he plotted in there. She would root this place out someday if she felt the need, but for now Mellinda put up with it. That little bit of freedom helped him cling to his sanity and she needed him

95

capable.

He told her of different women named Beth he had met through the years, yet none of them were of any consequence. The mage's words rang true. He knew nothing of use. The girls he knew were just girls. She stroked the pleasure centers of his mind once again as a reward and let him be as she searched further among her servants. Mellinda grew more and more frustrated as each servant proved worthless. She went through them all, cutting off their communication as soon as she was sure they knew nothing. Finally there was one left. She let out a mental sigh. He was the one she hated visiting with the most.

Ewzad Vriil was in his laboratory, already playing with his new toys. Mellinda monitored his thoughts for a moment, knowing he was too focused to be aware of her presence. These six raptoids were fine specimens. The dwarves had managed to bring them all the way from the Whitebridge Desert virtually unharmed.

Ewzad had already transformed them into basic humanoid shapes as he had done with Deathclaw and Talon. He had learned much since his first encounter with raptoids and this time not one of them had died. They were paralyzed and strapped down on tables as a precaution and now he was deciding how to further modify them. As she observed, he was walking between them, giggling over the possibilities.

This was the one side of Ewzad Vriil that Mellinda identified with; the joy his creations brought him. Unfortunately, he often became so preoccupied with these toys that he forgot to look at the big picture. As it was, the lands were in chaos but he was not prepared to strike.

"And why are you so disapproving, Mellinda? Hmm?" he asked out of hand.

How did he-?

"Know you were there?" he finished. "My-my! I am not so foolish as you think me to be, no. You are not the only one able to ponder multiple things at once."

She refocused and hid her thoughts from him.

He gave her an exaggerated roll of his eyes. "Well? Tell me then, silent one. Are you not so wounded as you appeared earlier? Hmm?"

"*It is difficult, I admit,*" she said. "*As for why I am here, there was another incident.*"

"Oh? So soon?" Ewzad clicked his tongue as he reached out with wavery fingers, making small modifications to the raptoid before him. This one was female from the way he had accentuated her form. "My-my, what is it now?"

"*Your runaway dragon, Deathclaw,*" she said. "*He appeared in the outskirts of the forest tonight. He did battle with my children.*"

He was quite delighted, "Oh! And from your tone, dear Mellinda, I take it you were not able to destroy him?"

"*No, Master,*" she said with distaste. How she hated calling him that. "*He had a strange sword with him. He set fire to the forest in his bid to escape.*"

"Ha! Indeed! Yes-yes, how wonderful!" He reached out towards the female raptoid and stroked his fingers downwards causing flaps of flesh to grow over her mouth. The flaps began to take on the form of lips. "And just how many of your sweet children did he kill in this . . . escape bid?"

"*Too many,*" she replied, the words tasting sour in her mind. She could feel the smile on his face and wished she could make him reach up and tear it off.

"Ah, too bad. You do realize though, dear Mellinda, that if you had destroyed him, I would be quite upset with you. Quite upset indeed, don't you think?"

"*I was prepared to face your wrath if he had died, Master.*" she said sweetly. "*But my intention was merely to wound him enough to subdue him.*"

"Oh? And you were going to bring him to me, dear Mellinda?" he asked, busily fluffing out and darkening clusters of scales above the raptoid's eyes, giving them the appearance of eyebrows.

"*But of course,*" she lied. The trolls would have dragged him to her and she would have placed a sweet present deep within his breast. His bonding wizard would have had quite a surprise waiting the next time he tried to contact the raptoid. It was still her plan. If she had the chance to capture him again. "*Alas, he had help getting away.*"

"My-my, his new master was there with him, was he?"

97

Ewzad said and the smile died on his lips momentarily. He hadn't liked learning that Deathclaw had bonded with Sir Edge. Now Ewzad wanted that man dead as badly as she did.

"No, it was someone else. A witch helped him escape and a powerful one at that. It was the same witch that disrupted my thoughts during the battle for the academy. I should have recognized it before," Mellinda admitted.

"Indeed. A witch you say?" He paused for a moment and she could sense him communicating with the past Envakfeers. For some reason she didn't quite understand, she could never quite make out the words they said to him and, unlike when he spoke to her, he kept his conversations with them silent. When he had finished, Ewzad's smile returned, but there was no mirth behind it. "This must have been a powerful witch to overpower you, sweet Mellinda. Don't you think?"

"Very," she agreed. *"Yet this time I was able to break through just long enough to ascertain the witch's name. It is Beth."*

"Hmm . . . Beth, you say? Beth . . ." The wizard's eyes widened, then narrowed with uncertainty. He kept his feelings silent. "No. Means nothing to me. Still, you should hunt this witch down, don't you think? Yes-yes, she must be destroyed and soon so she does not harm our plans further."

"Of course, Master," The fool! Like she didn't know this already. She wondered at his brief uncertainty. Did he know something? Was he holding back some important bit of information?

"And what of my sweet Talon? Have you heard from her?" Ewzad had already returned his attention to the raptoids strapped to the tables in front of him. One of the males began to twitch and he froze it again, this time with a more intense spell.

"I have not found her as of yet," Mellinda said. *"I can only hope she turns up as she did the last time."*

"Oh, she will," he mumbled, running his writhing hands over the raptoid that had moved. He was growing excited. This one had potential. Not as great as Deathclaw perhaps, but it was a good sign that it had resisted the spell. A good sign indeed.

"Just remember your promise," she said. *"This time don't overlook her failure so easily. If she returns, you must plant one*

of my special gifts inside her."

"Oh must I? I mustn't do anything you demand of me, foul creature. No!" he snapped. Then he reduced hic voice to a purr. "But in this case I agree. When sweet Talon arrives, I will place your gift within her."

"Truly, master?" Mellinda grew excited at the thought. *"One of my special-?"*

"Yes-yes, fine. An orange eye if you want. I need her to command this group and I will not let her be tempted to run away with them. No, no indeed."

Mellinda was surprised. Evidently Ewzad knew Talon far better than she gave him credit for. Mellinda had been sure that if Talon was given this new pack, she would run off with them, leaving Ewzad dragonless. It was quite an amusing thought, actually. She chuckled, thinking of Ewzad pacing back and forth filled with anxiety knowing that he had lost his most favorite creations.

"Still," he said, bending over the raptoid that had twitched past his spell. He caressed its torso, causing its musculature to grow even bigger. Its skin ripped in several places, causing small scales to scatter across the table and onto the floor. He clicked his tongue and healed it just as quickly as he had caused it. "If I give her over to you and you betray me, I will be forced to reach through this eye and destroy you completely. The Dark Voice has given me the power to do so. You remember that, don't you? Hmm?"

"I understand, Master," Mellinda growled. She knew he spoke the truth. The last time they had nearly attacked each other, the Dark Prophet had told her so. The statement had infuriated her, but his voice had refused to answer when she had asked him why he would want his future wife submissive to a servant so weak.

"Hamford, you fool!" he shouted into the corridor behind him. "Bring me that red viper like I asked you! Yes-yes, and quickly! And don't cower in the corner this time, Hmm? These toys of mine won't hurt you unless I let them!"

As the wizard continued to berate his guard, Mellinda became more and more aware of a constant cry from one of her servants. She glowered. Several of them had tried to contact her again since she had cut her last communication off, but this one had been non-stop. She sent part of her mind surging through her connection with it, intending to deliver a swift punishment.

But when she finally paid attention to the words the gorc was babbling through his pain, she paused. Could it be true? She scoured his mind and soon found that he was indeed telling the truth.

Mellinda laughed in delight. This was the best news she had heard in a very long time.

*   *   *

The orange-eyed moonrat halted its gorging at the mother's command and left the corpse of its dead yellow-eyed brother to its other kin. It left the breeding grounds where it had been hard at work for most of its short life and traveled alone through the forest. It had never been alone before, but there was no room for fear in its tiny mind. Its thoughts were overwhelmed by the intense prodding of the mother.

It traveled throughout the night, reaching the edge of the forest before the light of dawn, then crept up the steep slope of the mountainside. The daylight pained it and the moonrat kept to the shadows as long as it could, then hid underneath a large rock for the heat of the day.

The mountainside was a foreign place without the cover of trees and filled with the whistling of wind along its unprotected slopes. The moonrat's nose sensed danger as well. There were creatures living in this place that smelled of hunger. The mother could keep most of those at bay easily, but there were also scents the mother warned it to stay clear of, wicked creatures with long legs and pointed sticks.

When the shadows grew long, the moonrat ventured out from its hiding place, ignoring the pain of the fading light. It headed further up the slopes, to a place where the earth shifted under its feet. It passed bubbling mud and hot pools and hissing spouts of foul smelling water. The moonrat avoided the areas the mother told it to and kept on.

The night deepened. Then before the sun rose again, it came to a place that stank of the tall slimy trolls. It had become familiar with these beasts of late, as the mother had brought so many of them into their forest. Many of them came running, screeching with hunger, only to be halted by the mother's gaze. The trolls then followed along behind the moonrat. More and more came and trailed meekly in its wake until it led a procession of over a dozen.

Other creatures fell under the mother's spell as they climbed. Snakes and spiders and rodents that had learned to live hidden from the trolls' hungry grasping claws crawled out from their little holes and joined the procession.

Soon one last slope reared ahead and the moonrat knew it was near the end of its journey. It climbed slippery, slime encrusted rocks until it reached the top. There it sensed the yawning mouth of a cave. The smell within was acrid and tinted with the sharp tang of smoke as if an intense fire had once filled the area.

Slime was pooled in the entrance and even more covered the floor of the cave. The moonrat was forced to trudge deeper and deeper until it was barely able to keep its nose above the surface. It moaned as the slime stung its eyes. As if in answer, a deep booming roar shook the ground around it.

The procession nearly crumbled and fled in fear, but the mother held firm. The tall trolls picked up the moonrat and the other creatures that wouldn't survive the swim and carried them through a tunnel in the rear of the cave. The troll carrying the moonrat had to crouch in the low ceiling of the tunnel as it waded through slime that was nearly knee deep.

The tunnel opened into a wide cavern with a ceiling that arched high overhead. The air was moist and hot and the moonrat could hear the bubbling of a heated pool of water somewhere near the center of the cavern. The air here smelled of smoke and slime and sickness.

An enormous shape shifted in the rear of the cavern and let loose the booming roar that the moonrat had heard before. The moonrat could not grasp its shape. It seemed to be made up of hundreds of waving limbs all connected to a central mass.

The big thing surged towards them and the mother called out to it. It roared back at her. The thing was hungry. As it came closer, the moonrat knew that it was also sick. It was emaciated

101

and would soon die of starvation. The mother sent calming emotions at it and the thing settled back, quivering; barely restrained.

The troll carrying the moonrat stepped aside and the other trolls walked past it into the chamber. A vertical split opened up in the side of the thing's central body revealing a gaping maw filled with rows of dagger-like teeth. One by one, the creatures in the procession walked to the big thing and stepped into the gaping maw, allowing themselves to be swallowed whole.

Finally, the other creatures were all gone. The last remaining troll held the moonrat out towards the big thing and waited as the mother communed with it again. This went on for some time and finally an agreement was struck. There was one last part to the deal. The mother told the troll carrying the moonrat to step forward.

"*Thank you, my sweet precious one,*" she said. "*You are special.*"

The moonrat didn't know or care why it had been singled out; why it was special. It didn't understand or fear the concept of death. It allowed itself to be carried into the gaping maw that opened up in the side of the sickly giant, secure in the knowledge that it was following the mother's wishes.

The moment the creature's mouth snapped shut around the moonrat, it felt sharp pain as its eyes popped loose. The orange orbs sprouted tiny clawed legs which latched on to the inner flesh of the beast. The moonrat chittered and moaned as the love of the mother withdrew from it completely and it felt what it was like to be truly alone for the first time in its short life. Then it slid further within the creature and was surrounded by burning liquid.

Pained and unable to breathe, the moonrat lashed out with its seven sets of claws and bit at the flesh surrounding it. Its struggling was cut short, as internal sets of jaws and teeth sprouted from the flesh around it, then crunched and sliced the moonrat to bits.

Somewhere, far back in the center of the darkest part of the forest, the mother was pleased. Very pleased.

Chapter Eight

"*Ho-ho, Willy, you bid wrong again!*" said the imp with a chuckle and he slammed his card down on the table. It was a high trump and took the hand. The dwarf sitting across the table from the imp raised a fist and laughed in triumph. "*We win, 513 to 383!*"

The dark clouds that made up the walls and ceiling of the room churned as if heavy with rain and lightning streaked through them, but the air was hot and dry. The clouds weren't rain clouds, but clouds full of smoke. Air and fire were the imp's magic talents, after all.

The kobald sitting in the chair across from Willum shook its head and put its rocky face in its hands, sobbing. This was the first time he had seen a kobald up close. It was similar in height to the dwarf, but wider chested and covered in stone-like scales. It was also overacting.

"This isn't a fair game, Imp," Willum grumped folding his arms and leaning back in his chair. He nodded his head at the kobald. "You can't partner me with him."

"*And why not?*" The imp asked with bushy black eyebrows raised over its red eyes. Ever since the battle at the academy, it had stopped bothering to hide itself. Perhaps it should have. The imp was portly and short with pasty white skin and had a pointed beak of a nose sitting over a mouthful of even white teeth. Its pointed ears and balding head of wispy black hair didn't help its appearance much either. Willum had found the overall effect a bit disturbing at first, but only because he had been expecting for it to look a lot more menacing.

It gestured with white hands tipped with black pointed

nails. "*We are playing the game of Unity, Willy. You must have a partner, and,*" it chuckled. "*If you and I were on the same team, these two would be at each other's throats. Dwarves and kobalds are mortal enemies, you know.*" The two other players looked at one another and growled in agreement.

Willum rolled his eyes, "You know I know that. But they aren't real, Imp. Only you and I are really here. Unity is not a fair game. No matter who you 'partner' me with, you are controlling them and therefore, your wins don't count."

"*Bah!*" it said in indignation. "*You accuse me of cheating? Willy, you wound me. I cannot cheat! Why that would be against the rules.*" The two other players pounded the table and nodded in agreement.

"How can you possibly control either of them, without knowing their hand?" Willum asked.

"*Ho-ho! I simply ignore the part of my brain that is monitoring him,*" the imp said, placing a hand on the kobald's shoulder. "*And believe me, the part of my mind that controls Bofus here is equally as smart as the part controlling Garson across from me.*" The dwarf nodded.

"I don't see how that's possible," Willum said with a frown.

"*Willy, Willy, Willy,*" it said, shaking its head. "*Willy-yum-yum, don't you understand that my mental capacities are far above those of humans. If not, what kind of match would I be for gnomes?*"

Then it dawned on Willum. "Oh, I understand now. You can't cheat if we are playing for points, but since we aren't using the ledger, you can do whatever you want."

"*Ha! Nonsense!*" It reached down and pulled the white ledger out of the smoke below and slammed it on the table, scattering cards everywhere. "*But I insist we go back to using the ledger! Without the ledger, games have no purpose. What good are games without wagers?*"

"Games are played for fun. I like games when I'm playing with friends." Willum said, then stood out of his chair and leaned forward, placing his hands on the table. "But listen clearly, if you are not willing to play like a friend, then we won't play at all, do you understand?"

104

"*Willy . . .*" it said with a warning glare, standing from its chair as well. It stood a good foot shorter than him, but still managed to look menacing. "*You took on a contract. You are bound by the rules.*"

"I am bound by the rules only if I agree to play," Willum said, meeting it glare for glare. "We discussed this before. I will not be bullied or tortured. I will play with you for fun only."

The imp growled and fell back in its chair, sulking. "*How is that fun? Games without consequences are boring.*"

"Fine. I don't mind having a friendly wager from time to time." Its ears perked up, and Willum added. "But understand me, I will not be making any wagers that leave me endangered on the battlefield because of some tick mark on that ledger of yours. If you start refusing to make attacks, I'll just have to use other weapons."

The imp frowned. "*Why do you insist on such silliness, Willy?*"

"Friends don't put each other in danger, Imp," he said. "I treat you like a friend, letting you converse with me throughout the day, playing with you when I have the time. I expect the same from you in return."

"*Oh-ho! This friends speech again,*" it said. "*If you mean it, calling me friend, then why-oh-why haven't you given me a name yet?*"

"That? Well . . ." Willum floundered for a moment. He didn't know, really. It seemed like such a simple thing, coming up with a name for the creature. In fact, he felt a little guilty just calling it 'Imp'. But whenever he tried, nothing would come to mind. It was almost like something was blocking him from doing so.

"*See! See, Willy? Friends? Ha!*" It glowered at him and its skin flushed starting from its eyes and spreading across its body, turning from white to red. "*I am just an imp to you. Ho! Just an axe! A weapon to be used!*"

"Come on," Willum said. "You know that's not the truth. Why don't you just tell me what you want to be called? Or better yet, tell me what your name is. You used to be called something, didn't you?"

"*I told you it doesn't work that way. You must give me the name.*" Its skin was completely red now and its eyes burned a flaming yellow. It reached towards Willum and he felt his stomach lurch. "*It must come from you. Just do it. NAME ME!*"

Suddenly the imp grimaced and clutched at its head. It sank back into its chair and its skin began to fade quickly from red back to white.

"Excuse me," said a voice from behind Willum. "I heard there were games to be played here?"

Willum turned to see a man wearing a white robe emerge from out of the churning clouds that made up the rear wall of the room. He was of average height and had short dark hair streaked here and there with white. He walked around the table and stood behind the kobald's chair.

"Do you mind if I sit here?" the man asked, his eyes glancing at the imp.

The imp didn't answer, simply staring at him wide-eyed, but the kobald shook his head vigorously, refusing to move.

"Thank you," the man said. He reached out with one hand and grabbed the kobald by the neck. He then yanked it up out of the chair as if it weighed nothing. Then while it struggled, he bent over and shoved it bodily down through the smoky floor at his feet. The kobald disposed of, he sat in the chair and leaned forward casually. His eyes met Willum's and there was a sudden electricity. "Willum, I need to speak with you."

"Who are-?" Willum asked. The man frowned and it was as if there was a crack somewhere in the back of Willum's mind. He became aware of a tremendous pressure he hadn't known was there before. He looked at the man again. "You're . . . Tolivar. But how are you here?"

"I'm sorry. I felt it was time to interrupt," the man said, then his eyes flashed.

The pressure in Willum's mind broke into a torrent of images and emotions that flooded over him. He remembered. He remembered everything. "No . . . oh no. Father . . ."

"*Willy!*" said the imp, concern and alarm spreading across its face. It snarled at the man. "*Why did you do that? Willum, I-!*"

"Shut up, Imp!" Willum spat and shoved the imp's dream world aside.

His eyes fluttered open. Willum sat up and cried out as he flung the axe. It spun and its keen edge penetrated the stone wall, where it stuck with a loud ping.

Willum was sitting in a soft bed in a medium-sized room with stone walls and a wood ceiling. Glowing orbs lit the area from sconces on either side and Willum saw that the room was made to fit two, with matching desks and dressers on either side. Sitting on the bed across from him, his back resting against the wall, was the man that had invaded the imp's world.

"That's a sharp blade," Tolivar said. He sat with one leg sticking straight out in front of him, the other drawn up close, one forearm resting on his upraised knee. He wasn't wearing a white robe like in the dream, but a clean linen shirt and breeches. The ornate hilt of a sword rose over one shoulder. "I'm sorry to have to wake you like that."

Willum had never met the man in person before, and yet he knew him more intimately than he had ever wanted to know anyone. Tolivar, formerly known as Tamboor the Fearless, was the man that had been chosen to replace his father.

"No. Not that," Tolivar said. *Never that.*

Willum blinked, still a bit disoriented. The moments after Coal had died were hazy in his mind. He had been giving his father's message to Sir Edge and then . . . at first there had just been pain and blackness. Then he had felt his father's arms around him. Around all of them; Bettie and Samson were there too. Somehow Coal had held them all.

Coal hadn't or maybe couldn't say anything at that moment, but Willum had then understood the true permanence of the bond. When the wizard dies, he pulls the spirits of his bonded into the next world with him. But Coal stayed close to his body and held them there with him, refusing to move on, his presence the only thing keeping them tethered to this world.

He remembered crying out to Coal, begging him to return to his body, begging him to stay. He knew that his father heard him, but Coal hadn't responded. He just held to Willum's spirit tighter and Willum knew that Coal wasn't going to be able to hold on for long.

Just as it seemed that Coal was about to fade away, there had been a bright light and though Willum couldn't make anything out within the light, Coal had. Their father had released them and stood before the light conversing with someone or something within. Then Coal had turned back to them and Willum had heard his father's voice for the last time.

Willum had felt the strangest sensation afterwards. It was an odd disconnect, as if his very soul had been removed from reality for a brief moment. Then when the sensation faded, Coal was gone. In his place, in the place where Coal had been since Willum was four, was a stranger. The spirit of the stranger was tattered and covered in great wounds.

The stranger had let out a piercing scream. There was a rushing sensation and their minds were joined. The stranger's memories were forced through his mind and at the same time, Willum knew that this man was living his.

"You can stop there," Tolivar said from the bed across from his, but Willum couldn't stop.

He shivered as the stranger's memories flooded his mind anew. They went by in a rush. He was Tamboor, son of Jarod, the young man eager to prove himself. Then he became the talented academy student making his name; then the confident warrior; the seasoned veteran leading the berserker guild; the legend fighting alongside Faldon the Fierce after the berserker guild was dissolved; then the academy retiree making a home in the mountains with his wife and children. Willum began to sweat. He tried to push away the part he knew was coming next. The terrifying event marched inevitably towards him.

He befriended the ogre, Fist. His children, his beautiful children, Cedric and Lina played around him as he worked the fields with his wife. Then came the outcry, the invasion of goblinoid troops, the frantic run towards his farm, only to find it was already surrounded. Then the wizard appeared-!

"*Stop!*" Tolivar commanded, both aloud and in Willum's mind. Thankfully, the memories ended as quickly as if Tolivar had slapped them away. The man was leaning forward, his face pained, his arm outstretched. Willum could see the naming rune emblazoned on the palm of his left hand. "I'm sorry. I hope you never have to relive that again. I . . . wish you hadn't seen it the first time."

"How did you survive that?" Willum asked, a tear rolling

down his cheek. "The pain . . ."

Tolivar's hand shook and he dropped it into his lap. He stared at the rune as he spoke, his brow furrowed. "I didn't survive it. John disagrees, but I tell you that the core of me died that day. That part went to hell and burned and screamed every second of every day over the last year. What was left inside this body . . ."

"Vengeance," Willum finished. He had experienced that part too. He had felt Tamboor's anguish and tenuous grip on reality. Over that year, the only time he had felt close to alive was when he was killing goblinoids.

"Perhaps. There was little else in my mind. I don't know how I held on, but John appeared there at the end. He stopped me from plunging Meredith into the Bowl of Souls and making my final mistake. He pulled me from the brink," Tamboor's eyes moved up to meet Willum's. "Then he used you all to tie those parts of me back together." He closed his runed hand into a fist. "I still don't know if it will take."

At the mention of the others, Willum perked up. "Are they okay? Where are they?"

"They're fine. Samson is at the stables with the other rogue horse, talking with . . ." He grimaced, his eyes closed. "With Captain Demetrius and someone else, I'm not sure who, about the feed conditions. As for Bettie, she is down at the forge arguing with her boyfriend again."

"So I'm the last one to wake?" Willum said. "How long was I asleep?"

"Four days," Tolivar said. "The rest of us were up in two." He took something out of his bulging shirt pocket and tossed it to Willum. It was a bread roll, slightly crushed, and heavier than it looked. "The wizards said that you wouldn't be hungry when you woke, but I brought it anyway."

The wizards were right. He didn't feel hungry. But as he raised the roll to his lips, Willum's mouth watered at the yeasty scent. He bit into it to find that the center was filled with a soft spiced goat cheese. He devoured it quickly.

Tolivar gave a slight smile. "There's more in the dining hall. They seem to keep a ready stock on hand for people to grab between meals."

Willum swallowed the last bite and his eyes moved to the axe still stuck in the wall. "Where am I right now?"

"In the Mage School dormitories. All of their regular students were moved inside the Rune Tower to free up beds after we came through the portal." His eyes followed Willum's to the axe. "Bettie and Samson were worried at how long it was taking you to wake up, but the prophet told us you might need more time than the rest of us."

"I had no idea how long I was in there," Willum said. "That conniving little monster tricked me. Somehow he suppressed the memories of father's death to keep me around. How could he do that?"

"I'm not sure exactly, but that creature has a powerful amount of spirit magic. It wasn't easy for me to break through," Tolivar replied.

Willum frowned. And he had thought they'd come to an understanding. He would have to deal with the imp later. He glanced back at his new bonding wizard. "And how did you do that? Break through, I mean."

"I'm not quite sure how to explain it, actually," Tolivar said with a slight shrug. "I looked through the bond, like Alfred has been teaching me, and in the place where your mind was supposed to be there was a block of some kind. From there I pretty much acted on instinct. I just pushed my way through."

"I'm glad you did," Willum said.

There was a bit of awkward silence then. Willum wasn't sure what to say to Tolivar. The man was his bonding wizard now, but even though he knew more about Tolivar's life than he ever knew about Coal's, they had just barely met. Neither of them knew how this new relationship was supposed to work. Tolivar wasn't going to replace Willum's father and Willum wasn't going to replace Tolivar's lost children. So where did that leave them?

"We'll figure this out sooner or later," Tolivar said.

"Yeah," Willum said encouragingly.

Tolivar slid off the bed and stood. "I'll leave for now. The other academy students are probably out at the wall if you want to join them." He walked towards the door, but stopped by the axe. "You might want to take this down. If you leave it there, people are going to stare."

"Right," Willum said.

Tolivar grabbed the handle and wrenched the blade from the wall, then looked at it for a moment. "Always did think Tad's axe was mean looking. Didn't know why he was so shy with it, though." He smiled. "I used to tease him, 'A man should never be afraid of his own weapon, Tad'. He never seemed to laugh." He held the axe out to Willum, handle first.

Willum blinked in surprise. "So you're just going to hand it to me after all that happened? You're not going to lecture me about it?"

"You're a grown man, Willum. Besides, we both know you have more experience with this spirit communication thing than I do."

Willum took the axe from him carefully and was surprised when the imp didn't speak up as soon as his hand touched it.

Tolivar grasped the door handle, but paused before opening it. "I should tell you one thing, though. You were reaching a dangerous moment when I walked into the imp's room. He had a mass of spirit magic poised over you."

"I knew something strange was happening," Willum said, his eyes moving over the red painted runes on the axe's blade. "He keeps trying to get me to give him a name. You know, it seems like such a small thing, but I've been hesitating. I'm not sure why it feels like a big deal, but it does."

"I don't know much about imps," Tolivar said. "But I'd suggest doing some research before you do what it wants. At least you're here. The Mage School is probably the best place to find out. Let me know if it gets too out of hand."

Willum nodded and Tolivar left. The moment the man shut the door behind him, the imp spoke up. "*Willy! Listen, Willy, that man, he-!*"

Willum dropped the axe on the bed and slipped out of the covers. He couldn't talk to the imp. Not now. Tolivar was right. He needed to find out what the possible repercussions of giving it a name were. But who to ask?

At that point, he realized that he was standing there completely naked. Why couldn't they have at least dressed him in his small clothes? He walked over to the dresser on unsteady feet and began opening the drawers. To his relief, his clothes were inside, cleaned and neatly folded. His scythes and sheathes had been laid in the bottom drawer all jumbled together as if whomever had put them in there didn't know what to do with them.

As he dressed, Willum realized that everything he owned fit in that one dresser. He didn't see his pack anywhere, so it must have been left somewhere on the battlefield. Everything he had left behind at the academy was gone for sure. The only things that remained were the few items he'd left behind at Coal's Keep. The thought of home brought a lump in his throat.

He sat down on the edge of the bed. Poor Becca. She was sitting at home waiting for them. There was no way she could know that Coal was gone. Oh how he wished he could be with her right then.

His thoughts were interrupted by a knock at the door. "Who is it?"

"Willum? Tam-, I mean, Tolivar told me you were awake. I was starting to wonder if you were alright."

Willum recognized the voice. "Come in"

Sir Edge opened the door with a ready smile on his face. Much like Faldon the Fierce, he was an imposing figure of a man; tall, wide shouldered, and thickly muscled. He wore a dark cotton shirt and leather breeches and was fully armed, with a gray wooden bow slung across his shoulder, a bristling quiver, and the hilts of two strange looking swords jutting up from his back. He stuck out his hand, and as Willum shook it, he felt the leathery thickness of the naming rune on the back of his hand.

"What brings you to see me?" Willum asked.

"Well, first of all, I wanted to thank you for watching over my mother while the academy was under siege," Edge said.

"I'm not actually sure that she needed much watching," Willum replied. "She pretty much watched over me."

Sir Edge chuckled at that. "Yeah, I know she seems that way, but she appreciated your help. She told me so."

"Oh," Willum said. He smiled a bit. He had grown fond of Darlan. "I'm glad I was of some help, then."

"So, um . . . " Edge scratched the back of his head.

"Would you like to sit?" Willum asked, pointing to the bed Tolivar had been sitting in earlier.

"Thanks," Edge said and sat down. "So, have you talked with Bettie or Samson since you woke up?"

"I haven't had the chance." Willum said. "I don't think Tolivar's learned how to keep the bond open yet."

"You should ask him. I can't believe Bettie and Samson haven't already done it," Edge said, then winced. "Uh, sorry. It's not really my business the way you do things."

"No, you're fine," Willum said. "We still have a lot to work out with Tolivar."

"Yeah, I guess you would." Edge said, and Willum wondered why he was really there. Finally the man leaned forward. "Well, here's the thing. I'm actually here to ask you a favor."

Willum blinked. What could Sir Edge possibly want from him? "Well, I suppose. Anything I can do to help. But why me?"

"Because you've done this before. You see, I've been given a mission to watch out for the witch's spies here at the school," Edge explained. "And I'd like for you to help."

Chapter Nine

"Willy! Willum, come now, you misunderstand what I did," the imp protested.

Willum shoved the axe into the half sheath at his waist. *We'll discuss this later.* He shuddered and followed Sir Edge into the hallway outside his room. "So how is the witch getting spies into the school? People come here as children."

"I'm not sure how it happens, but it was likely the same way it happened at the academy," said Sir Edge. "She had spies among the students when I was here at the school, but no one knew it at the time." He paused at the outer door. "Now be careful when speaking about this. Valtrek thinks the witch is aware that we know she has spies here. She could have someone listening at any time."

Willum nodded. "It was that way at the academy too."

"Yeah, but here the spies will be using magic." Edge opened the door into the bright sunlight. He paused and looked back at Willum. "Have you been to the Mage School before?"

"No, Father left the school before he found me."

"It might be a bit of a shock." He stepped out and Willum followed him through the door.

The grass outside the door was a verdant green and perfectly trimmed and the air smelled clean and sweetened by flowers. Willum stepped onto one of the stone pathways that crisscrossed the grass, leading to rows of finely constructed buildings. In the distance, he saw stable and a fenced-in pasture where horses grazed. Behind that rose a towering wall, higher even than the academy walls, that looked as if it was carved out of a single sheet of rock.

"Father showed me his memories, but it's so much bigger

than I thought," he said, awed.

"Then look behind you," Sir Edge said, a smile on his face.

Willum turned and stared. "By the gods!"

The Rune Tower was enormous, stretching into the heavens as far as he could see. Willum craned his neck and took several steps backward, trying to take it all in. Coal had talked about the Rune Tower often, but nothing his father had said or shown him had prepared Willum for this.

"I know. I was in awe the first time I saw it too," Edge said. "All the staring upward gave me a sore neck. Come on. We have some time before we go to the meeting. I'll show you around a bit."

Willum kept pace with Edge as he walked down the pathway towards the center of the school where a clock tower rose up. It had several large faces and was tall enough that Willum was sure he could make out the time clearly from anywhere on the grounds.

"About this meeting," Willum said. "Who is going to be there?" Sir Edge had been quite sketchy with the details.

"Just the people that need to be. Not much else was said to me," Edge replied.

He led Willum down a pathway that led towards the clock tower. The pathways were crowded with refugees bustling here and there, heading in and out of buildings, while out-of-place-looking academy students and trainees walked about staring at everything.

"It all seems so calm," Willum said. "I can't even hear the army surrounding us."

"Ewzad Vriil and the witch are handling this differently than the siege of the academy," Edge explained. "If they had the wizards as tightly surrounded as they had the academy, their army would be bombarded by magical attack day and night. Instead, they have settled on a soft siege. Ewzad Vriil's army has blocked the road to Sampo and the mother . . . No, we should call her by her real name. Mellinda has the forest areas and all other escape routes covered by moonrats, trolls, and whatever other monsters she can control."

"So we're not in immediate danger of attack, but we're

too outnumbered to leave," Willum said.

"Exactly. It's a perfect strategy for him. While all of his enemies sit here in one spot, waiting, he's able to build his strength and wait for a favorable time to attack. In the meantime, he has full control of Dremaldria."

Willum frowned. The beauty of his surroundings had suddenly lost their appeal. "How are we set up for supplies?"

Edge shrugged. "The wizards say we're fine. They produce enough food out of their own gardens and forests to supply the regular faculty and students year round. As for our additional numbers, all ten thousand of us, they say we could still hold out for years. They don't understand it yet, but with the addition of honstule plants to the gardens, even longer, maybe indefinitely."

"You brought honstule here?" Willum asked in surprise.

"My elf friend Qyxal made a thorough study of the plant while we were at Master Coal's keep. We gave a bag of the seeds to the elves and they are all quite excited about it. They began planting them in the gardens and Mage School forest the day we arrived here."

"There are elves here at the school?" Willum asked in surprise. Not thinking, he let his hand rest on the axe handle.

"Elves too? There's already dwarves around and don't think I didn't notice the gnome! I'm surrounded by enemies! What's next? Dragons? Willy, listen. Let's get out of here! We could-!"

"You alright?" Edge asked, noticing Willum jerk his hand back.

"I'm fine. Really," he replied, swallowing. How was he going to help Sir Edge with the search if he couldn't trust the imp?

"Alright then. Yes, the Silvertree elves were given asylum here at the school after Mellinda's children overran their homeland in the Tinny Woods," Edge explained. "They've been staying in the Mage School forest on the far side of the Rune Tower from here."

They walked into the center square and paused a moment to allow Willum to stare at the elaborate fountains surrounding the base of the clock tower. Multicolored arcs of water rose and fell in displays even more beautiful than the fountains Willum remembered seeing as a small boy around the Dremald Palace.

The square was packed with people but unlike at the academy where there was an undercurrent of fear, here there was laughter. The children ran around freely, some playing in the fountains. "So where are all the students and warriors?"

"They are still working out the details," Sir Edge said, "But all of the Mage School students and faculty have been moved inside the Rune Tower. The dormitories and class buildings to the east of the square have been taken over by the Reneul and Sampo refugees." He gestured to the far side of the square. "The dwarves have the class buildings on the west side."

Sir Edge led Willum down the center road away from the Rune Tower. Once they passed the rows of class buildings, Willum saw that the open stretches of manicured grass leading up to the main gates were covered with tents.

"Captain Demetrius' cavalry has the west lawn. The academy and their retirees have the east lawn and guards quarters." Edge shook his head as he took it in. "I still can't get used to it. When I was here before, I thought the Mage School was overly extravagant. Too much open space for so few people. Now it actually feels crowded."

"Crowded? I don't think you've seen crowded. This is positively roomy," Willum said, then realized he may have come off sounding somewhat rude. "Uh, no offense. I was just thinking about how cramped it was inside the academy."

"None taken. I see what you mean," Edge said. "Now we should go and wait for the others."

They turned around and headed back towards the Rune Tower and Willum asked, "Where are we going?"

"I told the others I'd meet them at the library before the meeting."

"Others?"

"Yes. Fist and Jhonate will be attending as well. I'd bring Gwyrtha if I could get her in there, but I'll just have to keep her informed through the bond."

"Oh. Good." Willum was relieved. The more people involved the better. He had no idea how he was supposed to help search out spies in a place this big and unfamiliar. "What about

Bettie and Samson? Or Tolivar?"

"You can let them know whatever you see fit. Tolivar is quite busy with his training or I would have asked him before. Also . . ." He gave Willum a hesitant glance. "How is he doing anyway? Fist says he seems better and he's walking around and talking almost as if there is nothing wrong, but everyone is uneasy around him. I think they're wondering if he might crack again."

Willum hesitated. What was okay to say? "Well he's still recovering, but I really don't think there's anything for people to worry about. Even when he was-, well . . . even back then he wasn't a danger to the people around him." That wasn't exactly true, but close enough.

"That's good to hear," Edge said.

They walked around the clock tower and approached the wide bridge that led to the main doors of the Rune Tower. As they stepped onto the bridge, Willum ran to the edge and looked down into the swift moving waters of the moat below. It was just as his father had described it. He could even see the dark forms of the perloi swimming sleepily deep within.

Sir Edge didn't wait, so Willum had to jog to catch up as he entered the tower. They walked down an elaborately decorated hallway and Edge stopped in front of some ornate double doors.

"The first time I walked through these doors a friend told me that all the knowledge in the world is kept in here," Edge said and as they walked inside Willum figured he could be right.

Once again, Coal's descriptions hadn't done reality justice. The library was huge, open, and several stories tall with ladders and stairways to the different levels sprouting everywhere while a domed ceiling arched far overhead, painted with fantastic murals. The bottom floor was covered with chairs and tables for people to study at. The place was packed with students from both the Mage School and academy who were reading.

Sir Edge grabbed his shoulder and pointed towards the center of the floor. "Here, I want to introduce you to one of my favorite people. He's the head librarian here." Sir Edge gestured and Willum's eyes settled on the large circular desk at the center of the library's ground floor.

It was like the nerve center of the library, where every book was taken to be checked out or returned. Several students wearing sashes designating them as library assistants manned the desk while others carried books in and out of the library proper.

Sorting through piles of books was a tall, thin gnome with droopy ears and a long pointed nose. He was wearing a pair of spectacles perched precariously on the end of his nose, along with another set resting on his forehead. The students milling around checking out and returning books seemed to avoid speaking with him. Instead they waited in line to speak with the library's student workers.

Sir Edge whispered as they approached, "Now here's the thing you should know about Vincent. He's so full of knowledge, but he gets easily sidetracked. The best thing to do is to redirect him if he starts wandering too far afield. It can be a pain at first, but you'll get the hang of it. Just watch me."

Sir Edge cleared his throat and approached the tall gnome. "Vincent, may I speak with you a moment?"

"A moment?" Vincent's head popped up and the spectacles on the end of his nose clattered onto the table in front of him. "What a small amount of time to speak in. What could you hope to learn in-? Why Sir Edge, so good to see you again so soon. When you left last night I feared I might not see you for another year. I jotted down a note about it. Let's see . . ." He bent down to shuffle through some notebooks under the desk and as he did so, the set of glasses on his head fell to join the other pair on his desk.

"Vincent, I'm staying for a while," Edge said. "At least as long as we're under siege."

The gnome chuckled. "Under siege indeed. The Mage School hasn't been under siege in over two hundred years. That was the War of the Dark Prophet. There is a whole section on it. Floor two, north end, aisles c-f." His eyes widened. "Sir Edge, are you wearing swords in my library? Now that is against regulations. I've told you that before."

"Vincent, we spoke about that yesterday," Edge said calmly. "Those regulations have been waived ever since the academy refugees arrived. You'll find it in the most recent

119

edition of the rulebook, section five, chapter two, paragraph one."

"Ah yes," Vincent gave the end of his nose a tug. "It's all a bit silly if you ask me, changing rules and traditions just to avoid inconveniencing a few warriors. Rupert Rolph said it best in his soliloquy on the rules of Alberri's capitol. It's a fascinating read if you care to look into it. Floor five, aisle-."

"Vincent, I would like you to meet my friend, Willum, son of Master Coal." Edge said, dragging Willum forward.

"Willum son of Master Coal? Where have I heard that?" The gnome said frowning. "Now where are my glasses?" He patted the top of his head and gave his nose another tug.

"There are two pair on the desk in front of you, sir," Willum offered.

"Ah, so there is," the gnome said and put both sets on the top of his head. "Thank you, Mister . . ?"

"Willum, son of Coal," Willum said and turned around but Sir Edge was no longer standing there. The named warrior was sitting at a table a ways across the floor, a thick book already propped in front of him.

"Ah yes, Coal. Would that be young Master Coal, named at The Bowl of Souls some thirty years ago?" Vincent asked.

"Yes. You knew him?"

"Of course. He studied here late many a night. Sometimes with that goblin friend of his. Now when you see him again, be sure to tell Coal he never did bring back that book on demons he borrowed. 'Count Reynard's Illustrated Book of Demon Anatomy'. It's a rare one, missing from its shelf on floor three, aisle seven, half way down on the second shelf."

"I-I'm sorry, Sir," Willum said feeling both sad and touched that the gnome remembered his adopted father. "He died a few days ago."

"Dead? Master-, ah yes, I heard about that. So tragic. What a loss. Master Coal was a great one. Always kept quiet and returned his books on time. Except for that one book, 'Count Reynard's-'."

"Tell me, Vincent," Willum interrupted, placing one hand on the pommel of his axe. "What can you tell me about imps?"

"*What are you doing, Willy?*" the imp asked. "*Ho-ho,*

that's not funny."

"Imps? What a fascinating subject!" Vincent said, giving his nose an excited tug. "You know, I wrote a treatise on the enmity between imps and gnomes back in my younger days. Why I must have been, oh, two hunded or two-hundred-two or something. I published it just before William the Raft published his account of his journey to the imp town of Pull. He was so perturbed. You can find his book on floor-."

"I'm glad you are an expert, Sir, because I happen to have an imp with me here at the school," Willum said.

"Don't tell the gnome that!" the imp cried.

"Truly?" Vincent asked, eyebrows raised. He gave the end of his nose a sharp tug. "How very fascinating! I haven't encountered an imp in decades." He frowned and mumbled, "When was it? Surely it was before Councillor Muldrew wrote his autobiography. That was . . . forty six years ago? Or was it after he put out the second edition? Yes, that's it. After he added the chapter about how he researched his treatise on the constantly sinking old capital city of Malaroo. Fascinating subject really. Floor five, aisle eight, second shelf, between-."

"Yes, well this imp I know is always wanting to play games," Willum said. "Have you ever played games with an imp?"

"Good gracious. Games with an imp? I learned my lesson years ago," laughed the gnome. Then his lips turned to a slight frown and he cocked his head. "My father always said, 'never play ledger games with an imp'. You can read his advice in, 'The Life Lessons of Head Librarian Reginald of Alberri', chapter twelve, page 477, paragraph three."

"Yes, well I have convinced the imp to play games without using the ledger," Willum said.

"Stop it now, Willy. I am not amused," it snapped. *"You will ruin my reputation."*

What reputation? No one knows you exist, Willum said.

"Without the ledger?" Vincent reached up and slowly pulled one of the pairs of glasses down to settle firmly on the bridge of his nose. "Now that is interesting. And you say the imp is here? At the Mage School?"

"Okay-okay, Willy. No more funny time, no. This gnome

is focusing," the imp was sounding panicked.

"Yes," Willum said. "It's here. And it keeps asking me to give it a name."

"Oh does it, now?" Vincent said and Willum could see that his whole demeanor had changed. He was no longer fidgeting and his eyes were completely focused on him. "Come, young Willum, follow me."

Willum looked back at Sir Edge, but the warrior was absorbed in his book. He wanted to ask him how much time he had, but the gnome was already heading towards one of the staircases leading up to the upper floors. Willum sighed and followed.

"*Ho-ho, you've done it now,*" the imp said. "*And you claimed we were friends.*"

After the way you tricked me and blocked off my mind, I'm not so sure about that anymore, Imp, Willum responded and let go of the handle as he followed Vincent up the stairs. They climbed all the way up to the fifth floor and past it.

"Wait, six floors?" Willum said in confusion. "My father always said there were five."

The gnome paused. "Ah yes, well we had to add a floor after the prophet lifted his ban on spirit magic. So many books were brought out of storage, you see."

The logistics of adding a floor to an enormous library at the base of an enormous tower were lost on Willum, but he shrugged and followed the gnome as he continued up past the sixth floor up to the bottom lip of the dome ceiling. The stairs ended at a plain doorway marked simply, 'Head Librarian'.

Vincent opened the door and as he stepped inside, a light flickered on within. "Come. Come on in."

Willum stepped in, unsure at what he would find. It was a large room with a long bed in the corner and a wide oak desk pushed up against one wall. The walls were painted a light green color and the floors were of highly polished wood. It was extremely tidy and uncluttered, almost as if its only use was a light dusting from time to time.

"Huh," Willum said.

The gnome sat at the desk and pulled out a thin drawer. "What was that?"

"I guess I expected more books, Sir," he replied, looking at the one small bookcase beside the gnome's bed. There were only maybe a dozen books on it.

"Call me Vincent, please," the gnome replied. "This room is just my private quarters, after all. If I brought the library's books in here, I'd forget them. Likely, I'd just harass some of the students looking for them and that wouldn't do at all."

Willum watched the gnome pull open a drawer and take out a thick book bound in green leather. This Vincent was acting completely different than he had been earlier. The gnome reached into his suit coat and withdrew a slightly bent quill.

"So, Willum, son of Master Coal, you have an imp here at the school with you." He turned and faced Willum with quill and book in hand. He jotted down a couple notes. "So how did that come to be?"

"I, um, inherited the imp from a friend," he said cautiously.

"You inherited it? How odd." He jotted down some more notes and Willum noticed that he never dipped the quill in ink. He shifted to mage sight and saw that the quill was dancing with colors. As was the book itself. And the glasses the gnome was wearing. "Is this imp a fighter or a player?"

Willum's brow furrowed. "What do you mean, sir?"

"Well, imps are much like gnomes in some ways. There are some whose goal in life is to trick or outsmart their enemies. There are others who only want to fight, to maim, to destroy."

He placed his hand on the handle. *Which are you?*

"*Ho-ho! No-no, Willy. I'm not telling you that! Not when you're blabbing to the enemy!*"

"He's a player then," Willum said.

"*Stop!*"

"Ah, a tricky devil. That's good," said the gnome as he jotted down another note. "And where are you keeping this imp?"

Willum hesitated. Sir Edge had vouched for Vincent, but Willum had just met him. *Imp, are there any moonrat eyes in this room?*

It snorted. "*Don't be ridiculous. She wouldn't try.*"

Everyone knows gnomes are immune to bewitching . . . ugh, why am I helping you?"

"I have it with me, sir," he said and pulled the axe from the sheath. He made sure to hold it by the head, so he wouldn't seem threatening. "It is bound inside my axe."

The gnome nodded thoughtfully, a smile curling the pencil thin mustache on his lip. "An imp bound to a weapon? That is quite fascinating." He made a few more notes, then scooted his chair back. "Would you mind placing it on my desk please?"

"You don't seem surprised," Willum said, hesitating.

"Oh, I'm definitely surprised. Imps are rare nowadays."

"But you didn't blink when I said it was in my axe."

Vincent laughed. "Well an imp spirit bound to a weapon makes a lot more sense than any other way you could bring an imp inside the school without causing an uproar."

Willum found himself smiling back. "I suppose you're right. It's just that it's so rare for people to know about spirit magic at all, much less binding magic."

"Don't fall for it, Willy. No-no, gnomes are tricky. He's trying to charm you."

I don't think so. Do you sense anything that would infer bad intent from him?

"HE'S A GNOME."

"Young Willum, the prophet's memorandum on teaching spirit magic has until recently been honored at every mage school in the known lands. The gnome capital, however, has never been under such restrictions," he said. "You see, since imps use spirit magic, all gnomes are taught about it as children."

"Of course they are. They're our e-!"

Willum made up his mind. He placed the axe on the desk.

"Hmm," Vincent leaned over the desk and peered at it. His fingers hovered back and forth over the metal, but he was careful not to touch it. Willum saw the wispy glow of spirit magic surrounding the gnome's fingers. "Hoo, that is interesting indeed!"

Vincent giggled and ran over to the small bookcase beside his bed. He pulled out one of the books and ran back, smiling all the way.

"Did you learn something?" Willum asked.

"I believe so!" said the gnome. He flipped through the pages. "What do you know about the relationship between the species that have blood magic and the opposing demon races?"

"Just that they're enemies."

"Oh? And why is that so?" asked the gnome.

"Uh . . . I don't know exactly. Just that the demons were created for that purpose," Willum replied.

"True, true. Now the identity of who created the demons is a fact lost to time. The prophet himself is perhaps the only one who knows. What we do know is that they were created as a counterbalance to those of us with blood magic. Can you imagine why the creators of the demons felt that was necessary?"

"I remember asking my father that question once. He didn't know the answer, but suggested that their creators likely made them because they were afraid that blood magic was too powerful," Willum said.

"Good! Yes, the elves with their overflowing life, the dwarves with their toughness, the dragons with their adaptability and regeneration, and we gnomes with our mental capacity. All of us have an advantage that the other species do not."

"Long life?" Willum suggested.

"Good, yes, long life. But it's more than that. You see, the elemental and spirit magic that humans and some of the other races have is rare. Only a select few have it. But in our races, blood magic is omnipresent. Every gnome has the gift of intelligence, just as every dwarf has the gift of toughness. If one of the blood magic races grew large enough, they could quite easily conquer and subjectify the other races."

"I never thought of that," Willum said.

"That's my theory anyway. I believe that the creators of the demon races hoped that whenever one race with blood magic became too numerous, the demons would rise up to take them down." Vincent raised a finger. "However, this hasn't been the case. The enmity between our races has been fierce and there have been clashes and large battles, especially in the past, but whenever one of our races gained too much power, it wasn't a demon that took us down. It was a calamity, be it a weather phenomenon, or invasion of orcs or humans. When it comes down to it, the demons have never truly been needed to fulfill their purpose."

Willum's eyes widened. He was impressed with this gnome. "I find this all quite fascinating, Vincent, but what does that have to do with the imp in my axe?"

"Ah, well, the population of demon species has somehow always been linked to the need for a race with blood magic to be opposed. My people in particular, despite our numbers, have never truly been a threat. Our focus is both our greatest strength and weakness. Very few of us have ever felt it necessary to try to subject others. Most of us are scholars, and those of us that study the art of battle are inevitably too busy protecting the rest of us to bother going on the offensive."

"Therefore, imps are rare," Willum concluded.

"Precisely," Vincent said with a nod.

He already knew that, though. "And my axe?"

"What I have been getting at, young Willum, is that with imps so rare and with spirit binding of intelligent beings so difficult to accomplish, it is very likely that there would be record of the creation of such an axe," Vincent said with a smirk.

"And you found it in that book?" he asked.

"I believe so, yes," he said. "I noticed right away that the runing style of the blade was not human or dwarven. This blade is of impish make. It is of the style of the imp warriors thousands of years ago. The runing, however, is of kobald make, and the iron in the runes has been infused with the blood magic of all four races."

Willum swallowed. "That sounds bad."

"Oh yes. This blade was built with quite an evil purpose. It is designed specifically to kill those with blood magic," Vincent smiled wringing his hands in excitement. "There were four such blades made; each one bound with a spirit of a different race of demon. They were created by a coalition of dark wizards and given to four warlords that desired to conquer the known lands."

"And to top it off, mine is the one with the spirit of an imp bound to it," Willum said, feeling sick. "The most vicious of the demon races."

"Not at all," Vincent said. "The demon races mirror their

counterparts. Bandhams are the most vicious of the demon races. The imps, on the other hand, are the most intelligent and most talented in the use of magic."

He lifted the book and turned it so that Willum could see the illustration. It showed four weapons; a sword, a bow, a spear, and an axe, each one quite wicked looking. "Your axe, as you can see, is not exactly as pictured but I believe that's just because the artist hadn't seen it in person. Inaccuracy is one of the most common foibles of scholarly work."

"Right," Willum said, feeling sick to his stomach. He couldn't imagine this having gone any worse.

"However, the translation of the runes is quite accurate." He pointed to the red runes on the axe. They were currently glowing a dull red, which meant that the imp was either angry or showing off. "If you read around the runes of power that grant the axe its sharpness and resiliency, there is an inscription. It reads, 'With my mind, I hew thee'."

"Great," Willum replied, rubbing his face with his hands.

"You seem disappointed," Vincent said, his brow wrinkled in confusion. "I have just told you that you own an extremely powerful magic weapon. This axe alone could make you a legend."

"What this is, is a disaster. What you've told me is that I own an ancient weapon of evil, forged by evil men, holding the spirit of an evil imp. That's the kind of power I don't need, thank you."

"That isn't what I said," Vincent replied. Then he frowned and cocked his head. "Well, perhaps it is what I implied, come to think of it, but it most likely isn't the truth. I never said the imp was evil."

"And how is that?" Willum asked.

"The demon races are made up of individuals, just like any other. They may have general tendencies towards viciousness, but that could very well be cultural. As individuals, they could potentially be every bit as good as any human or gnome. If raised correctly, that is."

"I understand that, but this imp was picked for the axe by evil wizards."

"Ah, but the dark wizards made a mistake when binding

this imp to the axe. You confirmed that to me earlier. The wizards picked a player and not a fighter. You see, the book states that when the axe was finished and delivered to the warlord, he spent weeks communing with it. During this time, his campaign crumbled. He complained that the axe refused to obey him and he hunted down the dark wizards that had made it one by one, killing them with the very weapon they created. He disappeared soon thereafter and the axe isn't mentioned again."

"That does sound like something the imp would orchestrate," Willum said with a sigh. "So what am I supposed to take from that tale?"

"Hmm. I'll tell you what, why don't you tell me how you came to own the axe? That could help me explain," Vincent said, lifting his green bound book and snatching up his quill.

"I . . . should probably get back to Sir Edge," Willum said, looking back towards the door.

"He knows where I reside if he needs you," the gnome said. "Please tell me your tale. It is a rare thing for me to learn something new about my field of expertise."

Willum scratched his head, but did as the gnome requested, telling him a condensed version of what had happened with the axe. The gnome asked very few questions, but took fastidious notes and giggled at odd times. When Willum ended his tale with the way the imp had blocked his memories, the gnome pursed his thin lips, deep in thought.

"Well! I would say that your own experiences should have given you the answers to your questions," Vincent said finally.

"I don't follow you."

"Well, for one your imp had multiple opportunities to betray you and it didn't. It could have cast you aside at any time," he said.

"He says it's because I amuse him," Willum said.

"Perhaps," Vincent said. "But if his intentions were evil, why would he ask you to name him?"

"I don't know. It felt important when he said it, though. What does it mean anyway, naming him?" Willum asked. "He asked Tad to name him too."

"Ah, well that is one of the rules of this particular type of binding magic. Any creature bound to an item in this manner is forced to follow the wishes of whatever creature picks it up. However, if the bearer of the object communes with the spirit bound to the item, he can claim it as his. This is done by giving the spirit a new name. If the spirit accepts this name, it becomes bound directly to the new wielder and is useless to anyone else."

Willum frowned. What was the imp hoping to gain? "What exactly does that entail? If I was bound to the axe, I mean."

"It means that a link would be created between you and the imp. Think of it as a lesser form of the bond you have with your bonding wizard. The connection would allow you to stay in contact with it when you weren't touching it, for instance. Also, no one else would be able to wield the axe." Vincent explained.

There was a knock at the door and Vincent stood so fast, he swayed on his feet. The gnome blinked and his brow furrowed with brief confusion. He looked at his bed as if startled to be sitting in his room. "Wh-who is it?"

"It is me," said a deep rumbling voice.

"Ah, well come in then," The gnome replied.

The door opened and was immediately filled by the crouching form of a musclebound ogre. Willum recognized his face immediately from Tolivar's memories. It was Sir Edge's bonded, Fist. Only he was dressed much differently that he had been in Tolivar's thoughts. Instead of wearing furs and skins, his muscles were bulging under a button down shirt and leather breeches. Somehow he even had an enormous pair of work boots covering his feet.

"Hello, Mister Vincent," said the ogre.

"Good gods, an ogre at my door!" the gnome said in surprise.

"I'm Fist, Mister Vincent. Justan introduced us the other day."

"He's bonded to Sir Edge," Willum said, giving the gnome an odd look. The focus had gone out of the gnome's eyes and his glasses had slid back to the end of his nose.

"Oh, yes. Of course. Sir Edge's ogre. Fist. Yes, forgive me. Come on in. Just don't track mud on my floor."

Fist looked down and lifted his boots, smiling when he

saw that they were quite clean. "Willum, Justan said you might be up here."

"Right. I'll be right with you, Fist." Willum said and turned back to Vincent. "Well, thank you so much for your help."

The gnome smiled and nodded and the second pair of glasses on the top of his head clattered down to join the other one perched on his nose. "Of course. Any time, young Willum. You are welcome in my library. All I ask is that you return the books you borrow on time."

Willum glanced at the book containing the story of the axe. "Would you mind if I borrowed that book, Vincent?"

The gnome swallowed and picked up the book, clutching it in his hands. "It is . . . part of my personal collection. But you can visit again and read it if you would like. I would like to hear more about what happens with your axe."

"Of course," Willum said. He looked to Fist. "Did they start the meeting already?"

"Yes, but they have just been arguing so far. Justan thinks we won't miss anything if we hurry down."

"Okay. Thanks again, Vincent." Willum picked the axe up off of the gnome's desk and slid it into the sheath at his side. Oddly, it had nothing to say.

Chapter Ten

Fist shut the gnome's door and let out a small sigh of relief. It had been much too clean in there. Most of the rooms in the Mage School were too clean and the wizards tended to stare at him as though afraid dirt might fall off of him at any moment. He glanced at Willum to see that the human looked almost just as relieved to leave the gnome's room. He flashed Willum a smile and got a hesitant nod in return.

"Please tell Sir Edge that I apologize," Willum said. "I didn't know how long my conversation with Vincent was going to take."

"Okay," Fist said and sent, *I found him in Vincent's room. He says he's sorry for not being there.*

It's not a problem. Just get down here as soon as you can, Justan replied, then added a few more choice words.

"He is not mad at you," Fist told Willum. "But he wants us to hurry. Wizard Valtrek insists that they wait for us, but the other wizard council members won't shut the hell up in the meantime . . ." He scratched his head. "Maybe I wasn't supposed to relay that last part."

"I am glad to meet you, Fist," Willum said with a laugh. "Both my father and Tolivar had fond memories of you."

"I am happy to meet you, too," Fist said with sincerity. "Miss Becca asked me to tell you that she misses you very much."

"She did?" Willum said, his smile fading.

"Yes, she was very nice to me. She made me a pillow."

"I miss her too." Willum said. "I'm worried about her. I don't know how she'll cope when she learns that father's gone."

Fist found it hard to keep smiling. He had wondered the

same thing. But it seemed like he should be encouraging, so he told Willum what Justan had told him when he had asked that same question. "She will survive. She has Benjo and you to watch over her."

"I hope you're right. I don't really know what's going to happen when this siege is over. I'm bonded to Tolivar now. I'm not sure where he'll want to go."

"He is a good man," Fist said, hoping he was being comforting. "He will do the right thing for you."

"I hope you're right," Willum said.

They started down the stairway, Fist having to step carefully on the narrow steps to keep from slipping. Nothing in this place was big enough for him. It had been true at Coal's Keep too, but the adjustments he had needed to make were minor in comparison. Here there were stairs everywhere and all the chairs had narrow seats with confining armrests. Even the doorways were narrow. He often had to hunch over and edge in sideways to get in.

He looked down into the library below as they descended. From the topmost steps, the people milling about looked tiny, but at the same time the library somehow looked even bigger from up there than it did from below. Fist had been in the library multiple times over the last four days and he was still in awe of how many books there were. Humans had so much information. Why hadn't the Thunder People ever tried to learn like humans?

He felt the pouch at his side move and knew Squirrel was trying to push the flap open. Fist paused on the library's fourth floor.

"No, Squirrel. Stay," he whispered.

Out, Squirrel insisted and pushed the flap again.

Fist held it shut. Squirrel had been learning more and more words lately. Fist was proud of him. Still, *We are in the library. I'm not supposed to have you in here with me.*

Not eat, Squirrel said, intimating that he didn't intend to eat any of the books. He didn't like the taste anyway.

"Your, uh, Squirrel wants out?" Willum asked.

"Shh!" Fist hushed putting a finger to his thick lips. He looked around to make sure no one heard and explained in a gravelly whisper, "He likes it in here. The smell of the books is very . . . appealing to him. But on the first day here, he chewed up an old book to make a nest up high and the wizards found out. He was banned from the library."

"Oh," Willum replied.

Squirrel didn't like his explanation and tried to push open the flap again, *Look!*

"I don't believe you, Squirrel," There was no way Squirrel would just get out and look around. *You would get into trouble again.*

Squirrel stopped pushing and sulked. Fist continued down the stairs, knowing that he would hear about it again. In fact, he'd probably wake up with an ear full of seeds in the morning. Why did Squirrel have to be so unreasonable? Justan never had it this bad with his bonded.

"I'm sorry that you had to come up here looking for me," Willum said, interrupting his thoughts.

"Oh. That's okay. Justan had a pretty good idea where you were. Besides, the meeting started off with wizards questioning why I was there, so I didn't mind coming to get you," Fist said as they reached the bottom floor.

Justan had warned him that it would be hard to get humans to accept him and he had expected to face some people that hated him for being an ogre, but that hadn't been a problem here. Everyone at the Mage School was perfectly polite. What he hadn't been prepared for was the way they seemed to discount anything he did or said. Some looked at him like he was just an intellectual oddity, while others treated him as if he were Justan's pet or something.

They reached the library's main doors and Fist turned down a long hallway. After a short distance, he turned and led Willum down a wide hall with marble floors.

"You really know your way around here," Willum said, impressed.

"Justan has shown me the way. He says I need to know my way around to be a student here. It is too easy to get lost," Fist said.

"You're becoming a student? Here at the Mage School?" Willum asked, eyebrows raised.

"I became a cadet yesterday!" Fist said with enthusiasm.

"Master Latva had me sign the big book and everything."

"Father mentioned that you had bonding magic, but he didn't say anything about you having elemental magic," Willum said. "He-. Where are we going?"

Fist had stopped in front of a plain doorway. "We are going down." He led Willum down some rough stone stairs. "I do have some magic, but we don't know how much yet. Professor Locksher is going to test me after the meeting."

"Good, um, why are we meeting here?" Willum asked when they reached the bottom of the rough hewn stairs.

Fist opened an old door. "Wizard Valtrek's office is down here."

Fist took him down an overly dusty corridor that at that moment was covered in multiple foot prints. He lifted his hand to knock at another plain door, but Justan answered it first and whispered, "Come on in and . . . just both of you do your best to look like you're good at hunting spies."

They entered to the stares of the assembled group. Valtrek had told Justan and Vannya to add an accomplice or two; someone they knew they could trust. Vannya had brought only Locksher, but Justan had brought in Fist, Jhonate, and Willum. He would have brought his mother too if she hadn't been so busy with her job as provisional mayor of Reneul.

At any rate, Fist knew that Justan hadn't expected the Mage School High Council to attend the meeting. The wizards had been difficult to deal with, complaining about every choice Valtrek had made. They didn't like Justan being chosen because he was too well known at the school; they disapproved of Vannya bringing in Locksher because they felt he was too obvious a choice for rooting out spies; they thought Fist would stand out too much as an eight foot tall ogre, though they grudgingly admitted his usefulness when it was learned he could use spirit sight. Now it seemed they were disputing the choice of Jhonate.

"I for one wonder why her presence is necessary at all, Valtrek," said Wizard Auger, the council historian, ignoring Fist's and Willum's presence. "We already have a warrior involved, a fact that makes her redundant. She knows nothing of the school. She would stick out like a sore thumb among the students, and she has no way of sensing moonrat eyes."

"That is incorrect, Professor Auger," Justan said and Auger's eyebrows rose in surprise at being contradicted. Fist could tell that Justan was losing his patience. "Jhonate knows how to use mage sight and when I told her how I use the bond to help me use spirit sight, she discovered something." He paused and turned to her. "Why don't you show them?"

She was scowling at the wizards. "I am disinclined to prove myself after such a rude greeting. I should refuse, but since Edge has asked me . . . Very well."

Jhonate lifted her gray quarterstaff in front of her and caused the end to widen and flatten. A round hole formed in the center of the wood. She lifted it to her eye and as she looked through it, Fist switched to spirit sight and saw the white haze of spirit magic stretched across the opening like a wispy bubble.

"Right now I can see Edge's connections to his bonded as well as the haze surrounding that man's axe," she said, pointing to Willum.

Locksher grinned. "I see. She has peered through her bond with her Jharro staff as a means of seeing into the spiritual spectrum. Ingenious, Jhonate!"

She grunted. "I can also see the bond Master Latva has with his dagger." She then turned and focused on Wizard Auger. "It seems to me that you council members are the only ones in this room without the ability to use spirit magic."

Auger's mouth dropped open and he stammered at being spoken to in that manner twice in one meeting.

Wizard Munsey, the council fire wizard cleared his throat and gestured at Willum. "What of Master Coal's son? How do you expect him to help in your search, Valtrek?"

Everyone turned their eyes on Willum. He shuffled his feet, looking completely unsure of how to respond. Justan gave him an encouraging nod and Fist nudged him.

"Uh, well, like the others, I can use spirit sight. My father taught me how to do it with the bond."

"He was the one who found the spy on the Academy Council," Justan added.

"Well, that was my axe, actually," Willum said.

"Truly?" Locksher said, an eyebrow raised.

"Very interesting. And how did your weapon do that?" Munsey asked.

Willum mouth hung open for a moment before he responded. "It, uh. It was Tad the Cunning's axe actually. Um, he left it to me upon his death. It has the ability to sense several things and one thing it has learned is how to smell out the witch's magic. I can see the witch's eyes with spirit sight, but my axe can sense the effects of her magic being used nearby."

"Truly?" Valtrek asked. "Could it tell if someone has been in contact with the witch but didn't have a moonrat eye with them?"

"I don't know, but-," he paused, his hand resting on the axe's handle, and blinked in surprise. "Actually it thinks it can."

"The axe talks to you?" Locksher asked, his other brow raising.

"Yes, it has a-."

"Can you prove this, young man?" Auger interrupted and his dubious gaze was echoed by several of the other council members.

Willum blinked and looked around the room. "Well, I could tell you what I see here, but the daughter of Xedrion already pointed out the other sources of spirit magic in the room."

"I don't see why he should have to prove anything," Justan said. "I was told to involve only those I knew for sure I could trust. He meets that criteria."

"Young man," Auger started. "I am quite tired of your rude interrup-!"

"I agree with Sir Edge," Valtrek said, cutting the wizard off and Auger's cheeks went red. "All this complaining is just wasting time. Each of these young people is more than qualified to help."

"Very well," Master Latva said raising a hand. He fixed Valtrek with a stern glare. "We shall not dispute that these people are qualified for the task. The question I have is why you have seen fit to invite all of them to this meeting."

"The things I brought you here to discuss could very well be helpful to them when searching out the witch Mellinda's spies," Valtrek explained.

"But is it necessary that they know everything?" Wizard Randolf asked, having remained silent up to this point. "I understand the hope that this . . ." He glanced at Justan, his lips twisting. "*Sir Edge* can keep his ogre under control, but what of these two?" He gestured at Jhonate and Willum. "They are academy students, whatever their qualifications. Can we trust them not to go running off to their superiors as soon as this meeting is over?"

Fist could hear the creak of Jhonate's hands tightening on her staff. He expected her to shout at the old men and put them in their place, but despite the glower in her eyes, her lips remained pressed together.

She's too proper for that, Fist, Justan sent. *She was raised to respect those in authority. But I agree. If Randolf weren't a council member she would have clouted him with her staff already.* From his tone, Fist could tell that he wanted to do it himself.

Would you like me to hit him? Fist asked jokingly.

I'm tempted, Justan replied.

"If you remember, Randolf," said Valtrek. "I wanted to invite the Academy Council from the beginning."

"I agreed with him," said Master Latva.

"As did I," said Wizard Beehn, fixing Randolf with a glare.

"You three seem to be agreeing on most everything these days," Randolf mused. "But you were overruled by the rest of us. Even the prophet agreed that we should keep this information to ourselves."

"You do prattle on, Randolf," Valtrek said with a shake of his head. "I wasn't planning on speaking of that particular information until they had left." He turned to them. "Don't worry, the information he is speaking about won't affect you."

What don't they want to tell us? Fist asked.

I'm not sure, but if the prophet agreed that we shouldn't know, I'm not too worried about it, Justan said, but Fist knew it wasn't completely true.

"As for the rest of this meeting, I take full responsibility for them," Valtrek said. "They have proven themselves against our enemy's forces and each one of them has good reason to want this siege lifted as much as the rest of us."

"Once again, Randolf, I agree with Valtrek," Master Latva said. He looked at the rest of the council. "Do we have a consensus? Who here objects to Valtrek's decision?" Wizard Auger was the only one to raise his hand. Wizard Randolf simply folded his arms and gave Justan a disdainful look.

"Good!" said Valtrek. "Now we can finally begin. First things first, I have some information regarding the prophet. He left the school last night."

"W-without speaking to us first?" Auger said in surprise.

"When has he ever bothered to ask permission before?" Randolf said.

Fist was disappointed. He had been waiting to speak with Big John. He had so many things to say to him. So many questions to ask. But every time he tried, the prophet had been too busy.

"Did he say where he was going?" Justan asked.

"He did not," Valtrek said. "He came to my offices and asked if he could go down and speak with the prisoners alone. When he returned a short time later, he said only that he would return before the first attack on our walls."

"So he told you nothing," Vannya said.

"Actually he said a lot," Locksher said, one eyebrow raised. "This means that we have at least a short time before the enemy forces make an assault. This also tells us that his return is a sign that an attack is imminent."

"But there was no time frame given," Beehn said. "Not very helpful."

"Nevertheless the Academy Council should be informed," Justan said. "This could help them when preparing their defenses."

"I will broach the subject when the War Council meets later this evening," Latva said. "Did he say anything else? Anything at all?"

"No. I asked him what he thought of the prisoners and he just said that he would be leaving," Valtrek said.

"Yeah, well he wasn't exactly helping much anyway," said Randolf.

"How can you say that?" asked Wizard Munsey. "He

warned us of the attack on the academy."

"All I am saying is that he has a huge amount of knowledge, but he won't tell us everything we need to know," Randolf said.

"He is acting under constraints," Master Latva reminded him.

"So he says," Randolf replied, then sighed. "Go on Valtrek. Everyone knows my opinion on the matter."

"Indeed," said Valtrek.

Out! Fist felt Squirrel nudge the flap to his pouch again.

This isn't a good time, he replied.

Hide, Squirrel promised.

With a sigh Fist gave in. *Okay. Just stay out of sight. Don't make trouble.* He could understand not wanting to be cooped up in a pouch all the time. He made sure no one was looking and lifted the flap just wide enough that Squirrel could escape.

Good. Squirrel slid out and darted behind one of the many desks in the room. Fist returned his attention to what was being said.

Valtrek was speaking. "Perhaps more importantly, I have finally heard back from our contact inside Dremald for the first time since the academy was evacuated. Some of these things I plan on bringing up at the War Council meeting anyway, but I felt I should let those of you that won't be there know right away."

"Good!" Latva said. "So what do they know?"

"Well, bad news first, they are aware that the academy forces escaped here," Valtrek said. "That much we already assumed, but the detail that they know is quite astounding. They have troop counts and at the least a general idea as to how the wall is being manned. They also know the names of all our leaders."

"That is pretty bad," Justan said.

"However, they do not know any of the plans discussed in our meetings, so we know the War Council at this time at least is clean," Valtrek added.

"So we still have spies to deal with, but the things they know could be discovered by anyone that can freely walk the grounds," Locksher mused.

"We should keep an eye out for those in cleaning crews or kitchen workers," Jhonate mused.

"As well as any students spending a lot of time watching the warrior camps, especially if they are taking notes," Justan added.

"Can you give us some good news, Valtrek?" Randolf asked.

"Well, for one, the tactic of using the destruction of the academy as a weapon was a good one. The enemy army was decimated and the mother of the moonrats was gravely wounded. From what my source said, the destruction of moonrat eyes hurts her in some way."

"That is true," Jhonate confirmed. "I have felt her pain as I destroyed them."

"However," Valtrek said. "Ewzad Vriil seemed amused by the whole thing. He feels that she will soon be back to full strength and is satisfied with having all the forces that oppose him within our walls."

"But what of his army?" Willum asked. "We destroyed most of them."

"He viewed them as fodder anyway; pawns that could be easily replaced. Even the creatures that he created are of no consequence to him. He expected them to perish. Evidently they are unstable."

"Yes. They melt away," Fist said.

"He has already begun replacing his army of beasts," Valtrek added. "My source was concerned in particular about a pack of assassins Vriil plans on sending after us. He intends to target our leaders."

"We must let them know," Jhonate said.

"We will. We will," Valtrek said.

"Do we know how soon he plans to attack?" Willum asked.

"Not as of yet. My source says he seems to be in no particular hurry."

"This source is awfully well connected," Locksher mused. "Who is it?"

"That is one of the things I cannot say," Valtrek said

apologetically. "If one of the moonrat mother's spies found out, their life would be forfeit. My source is close to Ewzad Vriil. I can say no more than that."

Chapter Eleven

"Is there any other information that you can tell us?" Justan said. "Anything that could help us in our search?"

"Well, one thing I noted is that the moonrat mother has expressed no concern whatsoever about those of her spies that we have apprehended already, which means it is likely she has no idea they were captured," Valtrek said.

"Or she isn't worried because they know nothing that could help us fight her," Justan suggested.

"That is a very real possibility." Valtrek admitted. "Though I hope that's not the case."

"Who are these spies anyway?" Locksher asked.

Valtrek sighed, "The council members know this already, but I suppose that I should show the rest of you. Their identities may be of some use as you search out their comrades."

"By the gods! A rodent! On your shoulder!" Professor Auger exclaimed, his eyes wide as he pointed a shaking finger at Master Latva. Fist grimaced as everyone looked to see Squirrel perched on the master's shoulder.

Squirrel froze, staring back at them, one hand reaching out to accept a crust of bread from the old wizard's hand. Master Latva looked back at Auger in confusion. "Yes, what is it?"

"Do you realize how many plagues have been started by rodents? That thing could be riddled with disease! We must dispose of it immediately!"

"Nonsense," Latva said, reaching up to stroke Squirrel's head. "He is Cadet Fist's bonded and well cared for. He is perfectly clean." As if to prove a point, Squirrel pulled a nut from his cheek pouch and placed it in the master's mouth.

"Oh. Thank you," Latva said and chewed it calmly. "See?

Nothing to worry about."

Fist's face flushed with embarrassment. *Squirrel! I've told you not to share your cheek nuts with humans. They don't appreciate it as much as other squirrels!*

Squirrel ignored him and began chewing the crust the wizard had given it.

"But," Professor Auger said in anguish. "It's-it's . . ."

"Come on," Valtrek said "This way." The wizard headed towards a door in the back corner of his offices and as everyone else began to follow, the council historian continued to stand there with that exasperated look on his face.

He doesn't handle being interrupted well, does he? Fist sent to Justan.

Justan glanced back at Auger before motioning Fist through the door. *Definitely not. He used to issue punishments to students whose eyes wandered away from him in class. It happened constantly. His lectures were so monotonous, it was difficult to focus. Still, apart from Vincent, he likely has more knowledge than any other wizard in the school.*

Oh . . . Monotonous? Fist asked as he followed the others down a drab twisting stairway.

Sorry, uh, it means boring and repetitive, Justan said.

Like all these stairwells in the Rune Tower? Fist said after he nearly slipped on a particularly narrow step. He had to be careful, if he fell now, he might take half the High Council with him. At least the stairwell was tall enough than he didn't have to hunch over.

Right, Justan sent with a laugh. *Just take it as your new word of the day.*

"But my word today is caterwauling," Fist complained. It was the word that Justan's mother had used to describe Lenny and Bettie's arguing earlier that morning. He liked that word. It reminded him of a bunch of treecats roaring.

"So you can use monotonous tomorrow," Justan replied in a whisper.

"Maybe," Fist said. He supposed that it was a useful word after all. But what if he heard a better word between now and then? There were so many wonderful words used around the Mage School.

143

While he pondered this, Fist's left heel caught on the broken edge of a rock-hewn step. He stumbled forward, trying to catch himself. He was able to turn sideways and dodge between Willum and Wizard Munsey, but he was losing control. Finally he reached out with his long arms and slammed his hands into the walls on either side to stop his momentum. He strained his muscles and came to a halt, but not before his broad chest collided with the soft form of Mage Vannya and sent her sprawling.

With a yelp, she careened down the stairs. Jhonate turned and, seeing her coming, pulled Master Latva to the side, but Wizard Locksher wasn't so agile. His eyes widened in surprise, but Vannya plowed into him anyway, knocking him down the last two steps and landing on top of him at the base of the stairwell. Wizard Valtrek, who had had been opening the steel framed door at the base of the stairs with a long brass key, jumped and whirled around with a shout.

"Sorry!" Fist said with a grimace.

Locksher laid stiffly with his back against the stone floor, letting out a soft wheeze. Vannya, who was laying face down over him, pushed herself up until she was straddling his hips. "Professor Locksher, are you okay?" She moved her hands over his chest, feeling out with her magic, and finally he let out a gasp.

"I'm fine," Locksher said "Fine! Just had the wind knocked out of me. Could you, um . . . stand up now?"

"Oh." Her face colored and she climbed off of him. Fist arrived at the base of the stairs, grasped Locksher's arm, and pulled him to his feet.

"I'm really sorry, professor," he said with a grimace.

"You may want to see about getting those stairs fixed, Valtrek," Master Latva said, pointing to the chunk of missing stair.

"Yes, I see," said Valtrek. "Well, follow on."

Valtrek headed through the door and the others began filing through after him. Fist stayed behind for a moment to apologize to Locksher again, but the man wasn't paying attention. He was staring after Vannya wordlessly as she passed through the door.

Fist followed Justan through the door. *That was embarrassing.*

More for Professor Locksher than for you, I would think, Justan replied with amusement. *I thought your dance moves were terrific.*

That's not funny, Fist grumped. *Where are we going, anyway?*

I'm not sure, Justan said. *But this area looks even in worse repair than the corridors leading to Valtrek's office. If this wasn't the Mage School, I would think we were headed to a regular dungeon.*

At first glance it looked like a regular dungeon after all. Not as dark and cramped as Ewzad Vriil's had been, but the area was dimly lit and the air was unpleasantly humid. The floor and walls were carved from rough-hewn stone. But that was where the similarities ended. All the cells were empty and lacking bars or doors of any kind and, to Fist's mage sight, the walls were humming with elemental magic.

"Let me first show you our most recent capture," Valtrek said and he snapped his fingers. The ceiling above them shuddered and in the cell directly across from Fist, a steel-barred cage lowered down from above.

Sitting in the cell on a thin cot was a dark haired woman in a black robe with a blue hem. Her eyes were red-rimmed and her cheeks tear-stained. She glared at them balefully and shouted something, but there was no sound.

"Mage Lolly!" Justan said in surprise.

"Ah, you know her?" Valtrek asked.

"I sat with her in Professor Auger's class at the beginning of my second year. I didn't know her very well, but she seemed nice." *She had a knack for replying to Auger's questions in such a way that everyone in the class knew she was making fun of him, but he never seemed to notice,* he added to Fist.

"I cannot hear her," Jhonate said, standing next to Justan. Her hand was resting against his in a casual manor, but Justan was keenly aware of her touch.

"This area was designed to hold those with elemental magic," Valtrek explained. "It cancels out their power and at the same time muffles all light and noise outside the cell. To her, we

145

are all blurs right now."

"How did you know she was in league with the witch?" Jhonate asked.

Valtrek looked at Professor Locksher.

"Oh, Vannya was the one who identified her," Locksher said.

Vannya gave them a proud smile. "I noticed that Lolly was spending a lot of time standing near the doorways leading to my father's offices. She never went down the stairs, but she did peek inside the doors and she always had her hands inside the pockets of her robes when she did it.

"I decided to keep an eye on her and saw her going through some old maps in the library. So I procured Professor Locksher's help and we decided to follow her. She was very cautious but we saw her leave her room after hours and open an old passage."

"I knew where the passage led," Locksher said. "It was a back way to this very tunnel. So we took a faster route and were waiting for her when she came out on the other end."

"She had a moonrat eye in her pocket," Vannya said proudly. "A green one."

"But wouldn't the witch have seen you capture her spy?" Willum asked.

"She wasn't touching the eye when we grabbed her," Vannya said. "And we were very careful not to touch the eye ourselves."

"But wouldn't she still see with it?" said Wizard Munsey.

"Not with a green one," Jhonate said. "She can use the green eye to enter the mind of someone who is holding it, but she can't see out of it. Only the orange eyes have that power."

"And how do you know this?" Munsey asked.

"I have some of the witch's memories stored in here," she replied, touching one finger to her temple.

"Ah," Valtrek said, gazing at her with interest. "If it is possible, I would like to speak with you some time about this information."

"Of course," Jhonate said.

Valtrek snapped his fingers and Lolly's cell rose back into the ceiling. "The other two prisoners were discovered by

Beth when we had her listen to those of us that needed to know the secret of our plan to evacuate the academy."

He snapped his fingers again and the two cells to the right of Lolly's lowered from the ceiling. The man in the first cell was dressed in worker's clothes and curled up on his cot staring blankly forward, drool running out of the corner of his mouth.

"That's Jeffrey, the stableman," Justan said and Fist could tell that he was saddened by the revelation. "I'd been wondering why he wasn't with the horses."

"Yes, it's too bad," Valtrek said. "I always liked him. Still don't know how long he had the eye. It was in his pocket when we searched him. He hasn't spoken a coherent word since we took the eye from him."

The occupant of the second cell had everyone's attention by then. He stood with his right hand grasping one of the bars, his left hand clenched into a fist. He wore a silken black robe richly embroidered with golden runes. His face was twisted in anger and he tapped his foot impatiently.

"Master DeVargas!" Locksher said. "But why is he here? I thought he was out doing research when Ewzad Vriil attacked the academy."

"Beth pointed him out right away. The prophet had us search his apartments and we found a moonrat eye," Valtrek said. "We couldn't tell people what really happened to him. It would have been all over the school and the moonrat mother would have known something."

DeVargas was the earth wizard on the council and was the only member besides Master Latva that had been named. Fist didn't need to read Justan's emotions to know that a named wizard in league with Mellinda was a bad thing.

"As it is, the witch has to know something is going on," Latva said. "With a prize this good she would have noticed when he didn't check in and her other spies would have told her that he had left the school."

Fist noticed that Squirrel wasn't on the wizard's shoulder any longer. He was still in the room though. Fist looked around and saw him sniffing at the stableman's cell. He didn't like the smell of it.

"I want to speak to him," Master Latva said, looking at

the named wizard in the cell.

"Are you sure, Master?" Valtrek asked. "If I lower the barrier, he will be able to see all of us."

"I know," Latva said. "But that doesn't matter anymore. Lower it."

Valtrek nodded and the air around the cell shimmered briefly.

"Ah, there you are," said Master DeVargas, ignoring the rest of them and focusing on Master Latva. "Finally ready to release me from this cage, Latva? I hope you've told Valtrek that I am going to see him stricken from his post for doing this to me."

"You are not being released anytime soon, DeVargas," Latva said. "Not until you are willing to talk about your connection to the mother of the moonrats."

"You keep saying that, but I don't even know what you're talking about. I know nothing of moonrats except for the terrible sounds they make when we pass through their woods!" he insisted. "And you have no evidence otherwise so why do you insist on keeping me here?"

Squirrel stepped over to DeVargas' cage and sniffed. *Stinks.*

"The prophet's assistant felt you out," Valtrek said. "And then there is the matter of the moonrat eye in your possession."

"What? Are you moaning about that bauble again?" De Vargas snapped. "For the hundredth time, Valtrek, you corner-sniffing fool, I found it in the forest and sat it on my shelf. It was an item of curiosity, nothing more!"

"We found it in a polished mahogany box lined with velvet, locked away in a drawer beside your bed," Valtrek said evenly. "Who keeps the shriveled eye of a dead rodent as a keepsake?"

Justan and Vannya looked over to Locksher, who was scratching his head innocently.

"I sensed there was some magic in it, of course," DeVargas said. "But at no time did I communicate with anyone through it. That's a preposterous idea and you know it!"

Master Latva frowned. "What do you think, Willum, son of Coal? Do you sense Mellinda's presence on him?"

Willum narrowed his eyes and stared at the prisoner, but unless he had better spirit sight than Fist, he didn't see anything. "He's been away from the eye for a while, so I can't see anything, but maybe . . ." He swallowed and placed a hesitant hand on the handle of the axe. Willum's eye twitched and a frown formed on his lips.

This went on for a few moments and Wizard Randolf grumbled, "Come on, this is absurd."

"There's nothing to find," DeVargas said.

"Give him a moment," Valtrek replied.

Willum finally let out a sigh and removed his hand from the axe, "He's definitely been in contact with the witch. My axe says that there are still traces of her magic on him."

"Squirrel smells it too," Fist said. Squirrel pointed at DeVargas and nodded in agreement.

"Ridiculous!" DeVargas spat. "Squirrels? Please. And Coal's son or not, what ability does that young man have that would let him know such things?"

"It is true that we haven't been given proof of that yet," Auger said.

"The prophet came down here last night, DeVargas," said Master Latva. "I can only presume he was here to see you. Would you care to tell us what he said?"

DeVargas paled and clenched his left hand so hard it shook. "That was between John and I. Now you have no good reason to keep me here. I demand that you let me out!"

"DeVargas!" Justan stepped forward, his mind filled with direct purpose, "Show us your hand."

The wizard's face twisted into a snarl. "How dare you, apprentice? How dare you speak to me like that?"

"He's right," said Auger. "Despite what he is accused of, Master DeVargas was named at the Bowl of Souls. You must use his honorific. To do otherwise is to insult the bowl itself."

Fist could feel Justan's anger spike.

"You seem to forget that I was named too, Professor," Justan said, thrusting his left hand palm out, showing his wizard rune. Auger flinched. Justan turned his palm to the rest of the council. "Many of you have conveniently forgotten that."

Fist had noticed it as well. All of the professors in the

school had been avoiding calling Justan by name. Most of the mages too. Even if they spoke his name, it was 'Sir Edge', as if they could acknowledge that he had been named as a warrior, but not as a wizard.

"Believe me, we haven't forgotten," Randolf said.

"Professor Valtrek, where is his naming weapon?" Justan asked.

Valtrek's brow furrowed. "His dagger is kept over there in that warded box," he said pointing to a short black box in the corner of the room. "But I wouldn't touch it. His cell is shielded against magic use, but he might still be able to reach through his dagger."

"I don't think so," Justan said, walking over to the chest. He lifted the lid, his thoughts full of confidence.

"Be careful!" Fist said as Justan reached in.

Justan pulled out an ornate dagger, covered in multifaceted jewels. He gave a grim nod and held it out so that the rest could see. There was a great crack running down the length of the blade. The naming rune was split in two.

"He has no bond with this dagger," Justan said.

"Impossible," Wizard Munsey said.

Master Latva snatched the dagger out of Justan's hand and shook it at the caged wizard. "Show us your rune, DeVargas!"

DeVargas trembled, but raised his fist towards the bars. He slowly opened his left hand. His rune had a crack down the middle mirroring the crack in his dagger. Where the thickened skin of the rune had split blood seeped, clotted in a few places. "I . . . cut myself. It will heal."

"Will it, Professor Auger?" Justan asked.

"No," the historian answered, his jaw open as he stared at DeVargas in disbelief. "It won't. The rune is broken. That can only mean that his naming has been revoked. That is something that's only happened a handful of times since the beginning of the bowl's history."

"Like Stardeon," Fist said, feeling pity for the man. DeVargas had risen so far and somehow the witch had still been able to corrupt him.

"Yes," said Justan. "Like Stardeon, he has broken his

promise to the bowl."

It had been the last vision John had shown them the night they arrived at the school. While Samson had waited outside the broken laboratory, Stardeon had knelt on the floor weeping uncontrollably. John had reached out and placed a hand on his head. Stardeon had let out a wail of despair and the prophet's last sight of him had been the wizard staring at the broken rune on his hand.

Latva's sharp eyes weren't filled with pity. He hurled the broken dagger to the ground and stared right into the ex-master's face. "The bowl has made its decision. In the records of the Mage School, your name will be changed back to Wizard Nikoli. The council will reconvene to decide your fate once the extent of your crimes are known!"

"Latva," the wizard formerly known as DeVargas fell to his knees and pleaded. "Master Latva, wait. There is a misunderstanding. Bring the prophet back here. He'll change his mind. I-."

Valtrek waved his hand, putting up a sound barrier that cut the master wizard off mid-sentence. He then clicked his fingers and the prisoners' cells rose into the ceiling again.

Latva whirled to face Valtrek. "In two days I want you to bring him back down and interrogate him again. Maybe some time to think will have changed his mind. Hint to him that if he speaks, he might be able to avoid quelling after his trial."

"B-but we don't know that he's done anything worthy of quelling," Professor Auger said.

"No, but Nikoli knows," Valtrek said with a nod. "I'll do that, Master Latva."

"If I might make a suggestion," said Justan. "You may want to try bringing Stout Harley along with you. No one knows Mellinda's tactics better than him."

"But are we certain he can be trusted?" Latva asked.

Justan looked at Willum, who looked surprised at being singled out.

"Well, I-uh do believe that he has forsaken his relationship with the witch, sir. I'll go and check him out for you if you would like."

"Do it," Valtrek said. He looked around at the others. "I

think this ends our meeting. Be discreet about what you have heard here. There will come a time when the need for secrecy will end, but I would like the moonrat mother to remain unaware of our efforts for as long as possible."

Chapter Twelve

Squirrel cocked his head in confusion and proffered the nut again.

"No, Squirrel. No thank you. I'm fine," Justan said for the third time.

The animal shrugged and chewed the nut itself, not moving from its perch on Justan's shoulder. Justan sighed and leaned forward in the stiff chair, planting his elbows on his knees and resting his face in his hands. He didn't remember it taking so long when he had been tested.

The long hallway that ran down the center of the Magic Testing Center was dimly lit and cool. The chairs outside the other rooms were unoccupied save for the last room on the far side. An apprentice that Justan had never seen before sat there patiently taking notes. The hallway was mostly quiet except for the occasional muffled thud that could mean someone's magical experiment was going extremely well. Or extremely bad.

He wished he could be inside with Fist, but Locksher had been adamant. Justan wasn't allowed in the room because it was too dangerous. He wasn't allowed to observe through the bond either for fear that the presence of his magic within Fist would disrupt the test results. Justan listened to the bond carefully instead, trying hard not to push any of his thoughts through to Fist.

He sensed that Fist's emotions were full of excitement, but there was also fear. Justan couldn't blame him. Fist had been given several days to worry over whether or not his magic would even be strong enough to bother training. When Justan had been tested, the moment had been thrust upon him suddenly.

Fist's excitement rose. Justan glanced over to see Squirrel

sitting very still with his eyes closed, concentrating. Justan found it difficult to resist entering the bond himself. He knew what was happening. This would be the moment where Fist reached for that knot of power deep inside him and released a pure blast of elemental magic. He heard a strange whooshing sound in the bond and a surge of energy pushed through it, causing Justan's heart to race.

It was done. The testing was over. Justan tried to recall if he had felt any vibration; anything that would tell him how strong the blast had been.

Locksher says you can come in now, Fist sent. *He is painting a piece of paper with some stinky oil.*

Justan stood quickly and opened the door. The room was empty except for the two chairs Locksher and Fist sat in. The ogre was grinning from ear to ear despite how uncomfortable that narrow chair looked under his wide frame.

"So what did you find?" Justan asked. He looked around the room, remembering how the magic from his own testing had cracked the ceiling. The room seemed undamaged.

"We were just about to find out," Locksher said, laying the oiled sheet of paper on the ground. He held out a glowing orb and looked up at Fist. "Now this orb has absorbed as much of that blast as possible. It will project the pure elemental mix of your magic on the paper. Are you ready?"

Fist nodded excitedly and Locksher placed the glowing orb in the center of the paper. A mix of colors left the orb and bled across the page. After a few seconds, Locksher removed the orb and held up the sheet. It was smeared with a wide swath of black with blue and gold streaks running through it.

"It seems that your strength is earth magic," Locksher said. "Your secondary strength is either air or water. It is hard to tell. Their levels look to be about the same. Your talent in fire appears to be negligible."

"But how strong is my magic?" Fist asked. Justan found it hard to tell, looking at the page. When he had been tested, the entire sheet was blue and gold. The color on Fist's sheet didn't reach all the way to the edges.

"Your earth magic is above average, and your air and water slightly below average," Locksher said, then added, "For a

154

human that is. For an ogre, according to the research I've done, your talent level is very high."

"Congratulations, Fist!" Justan said, giving the ogre a tight hug.

Fist laughed and stood, lifting Justan off the ground. Then he released Justan and the ogre hugged a surprised Locksher as well. "So what does this make me? A mud wizard?"

Locksher coughed and patted the ogre clumsily on the back. "Perhaps. With a mix of water and earth you have the makings of a mud wizard. That means you could become a good healer. Or you could as easily become a lightning wizard with your mix of earth and air. It really depends on what areas of magic you decide to research. You could even become a mix of the two, though it is likely that you will find you have an affinity for one over the other. Only time will tell."

Locksher waved his hand over the sheet of paper, drying it instantly, then folded it in half. He pulled a cylindrical metal tube out of his robes and used it to write a short message on the back of the paper. He handed it to Fist.

"Take this to Wizardess Landra. She is in charge of assigning classes to new cadets. The faculty offices are in the Rune Tower, right across from the library."

"Yes! Okay! Thank you, Wizard Locksher!" Fist said. He looked to Justan. "What classes should I pick?"

"Just choose whatever interests you," Justan said. "And don't forget to call the wizards 'professor'. As a cadet, that is the proper term."

"Are you coming with me?" Fist asked.

"I can't. Not this time. I'm supposed to meet with Professor Beehn." *But if you have any questions about it, just ask me through the bond.*

"Okay," Fist said and headed out the door. "Come, Squirrel," he said and Squirrel darted out the door after him.

"I hope they don't give him a hard time about keeping Squirrel around," Justan said. "Maybe I should have a talk with Wizardess Landra about it later."

Locksher chuckled. "You sound like a parent sending their child off to their first day of school,"

"I kind of feel that way," Justan admitted. "When Fist

and I first bonded, he was like a child in many ways, with so much to learn. But he learns fast. People here underestimate his intelligence because of the earnest way he talks. He is going to surprise a lot of professors with how much he understands."

"I hope so. I was truly surprised with how much magic he had. I was expecting a blip. I barely made my shield strong enough for the blast," Locksher said. "I came close to loosing an eyebrow."

"Do you want to know the strangest thing about this?" Justan said. "Here we are, talking about what classes Fist should take and meanwhile, the entire Battle Academy is patrolling the walls of the Mage School waiting for a possible enemy attack. It's made it hard for me to be as excited for Fist as I should be."

"It is an odd juxtaposition," Locksher agreed. "But we have to go on with life, don't we? Otherwise we do what? Sit here sharpening swords for who knows how long? The students here couldn't handle an existence like that. "

"I know you're right," Justan said. "Still it feels strange."

"Are you heading over to Beehn's now?" Locksher said, changing the subject.

"I should. I told him I could come over right afterwards."

"Would you mind if I walked over with you?" The wizard asked.

"Of course." Justan said.

Locksher blinked in surprise. "Oh . . . Alright then. I'll see you later." He turned to leave the room.

"No, wait," Justan said before Locksher could leave. "I meant 'of course' as in 'of course you can come with me.'"

"Oh. Good," Locksher said. "You should be more clear about such things, Edge. It is best to avoid confusion when one can."

"I'll keep that in mind, Professor."

"What is it that you and Beehn are doing anyway?" Locksher asked. "I noticed that you've been spending quite a lot of time there since we arrived."

"He . . . thinks that he can unleash my offensive magic," Justan said. "I had decided that it was just the way my magic worked-."

"Which is a perfectly reasonable theory," Locksher said.

"Everyone's magic is different and though I haven't yet been able prove it, I am sure it has something to do with variations in one's bloodlines. Why, I once knew a mage that could only heal broken bones. All other injuries were beyond him. In the end, he became a specialist and would assist other wizards when a particularly difficult case came in. I believe he lives in Alberri now. Great rock climbing there. And many tall buildings. Lots of ways for people to fall."

"Yes, well, Professor Beehn feels that my inability to use my magic offensively comes from a block similar to the one he had before the golem attacked," Justan said. "He has me meditating and focusing on my spine. He's convinced that's where his block was." Justan's face fell. "He has me focus for hours while he plays soothing music on a flute. I don't think there's anything to find."

Locksher shrugged. "It couldn't hurt I suppose, though I would think that sort of block would reside in the mind. If it is indeed a block, but I have been surprised before. Please let me know if there's any progress, would you?"

"Yeah. Sure," Justan said.

"Shall we go, then?" Locksher asked. They left the room and headed down the corridor of the Testing Center together.

"You said you had something you wanted to discuss." Justan said. "Is it about the Scralag? At one point you had suggested trying to unleash it and talk to it."

"Oh, no," Locksher said, with a nervous shake of his head. "Not now, during the siege. Can you imagine if it were to get loose and go on a rampage? Not a good idea. No, I wanted to speak to you regarding the prophet."

"The prophet?"

"Yes, it's been bothering me ever since the meeting. You know, when we learned that he had left."

"I did think it was strange that he left us while we were still under siege," Justan said.

"It's not that. The prophet is busy," the wizard replied. "I would expect him to come and go as he needed."

"Okay." Justan said, though he didn't necessarily agree. "But what could the prophet have to do that would be more important than helping the only people left that could stand up against the Dark Prophet's servants?'"

"I can't say as I know. I've never understood his methods or reasoning and he almost never explains himself." Locksher replied as they exited the building. They turned and headed down a side path. "You know, that's one of the things that has always bothered me about him. That and the fact that his powers don't make any sense according to the types of magic we know . . . and the fact that no matter how little sense it makes at the time, he somehow always ends up making the right decision."

Justan nodded in understanding. "I can see how that would frustrate you. But what can I say? He's the prophet. He's like a force of nature. You can't control what he does. You just have to deal with what he says when he comes."

"Yes! That's what I'm dealing with right now," Locksher said emphatically. "I keep wondering what I'm supposed to learn from his visit. I have been analyzing everything he said since we came through that portal and a few things have become evident to me. Especially about the meeting the day we returned."

Justan slowed his steps. "You mean when he told us about Stardeon and Mellinda?"

"Yes, exactly. Now one thing I know about the prophet is that he is amazingly efficient with his time. He does nothing without a specific purpose in mind," Locksher said, both eyebrows raised as he spoke. "Think about the people he invited to that meeting."

"Yes?" Justan asked.

"He didn't invite any of the leadership. Well, except for Master Latva I suppose. Instead, he brought all the bonding wizards and their bonded. He explained why he had all of you there. Called you his 'champions'."

"I think when he said 'champions' he was speaking of everyone in the hall that day, you included." Justan said.

"Perhaps. That is unclear. But at the least, he explained the reasons why he invited everyone there except for two of us. Myself and Jhonate," Locksher replied.

"But you asked him about that," Justan reminded him. "He said something like he 'felt impressed to bring you' or something."

"Actually Jhonate was the one who asked him," Locksher

said. "She said that some of us weren't bonded and he gave the reasons that he had invited Lenui and Zambon there. But when it came to Jhonate and I, what he said was, 'this tale will affect the two of you most directly'."

"That's right. I remember that now," Justan said. "But I left before he finished the story. I guess I assumed he had explained while I was gone. Fist didn't mention anything about it when he filled me in on the details, but-."

"That's likely because the prophet didn't explain," Locksher replied. "It bothered me, so I tracked him down later that night. When I asked him why he had felt that I needed to be there, he told me it was because I was Stardeon's heir."

Justan stopped as they neared Wizard Beehn's door. "Stardeon's heir? What does that mean?"

Locksher grimaced and looked around to make sure no one was in hearing distance. "I . . . it's somewhat of an uncomfortable secret, so I would ask you not to mention it to anyone, but suffice it to say, that Stardeon is one of my ancestors. I didn't believe it at first, but he said that my family line came from the child Stardeon had with his first wife. The thing that finally convinced me was a hereditary trait that Stardeon and I both share. You see, like myself, Stardeon didn't have a primary elemental talent. He was equally powerful in all four elements."

"You're as powerful as Stardeon?" Justan asked in surprise. He had no idea Locksher was that strong.

"No-no. I'm not as powerful as Stardeon. Dear me, he had the kind of power that comes along once in a millennia. No, I'm just above average at best. Our commonality is that we were both born with equal levels of strength in all four elements. There is only one family line with that particular trait and I happen to be the last surviving member." Locksher frowned. "That I know of anyway."

"So why is that such a secret?" Justan asked.

"Most of my ancestors were of, lets say, an unsavory nature," the wizard said uncomfortably. "It's not something I'm proud of. In fact, in order to get into the Mage School, I had to change my name."

"You have a family name then? You're a noble?" Justan

asked.

"No. My family had their rank rescinded over a century ago," Locksher said.

"You're a Blatche?" Justan exclaimed. In Dremaldria's history, only two noble houses had been stripped of rank and only one had been stripped because of their magic. The Blatche's had produced some of the most evil wizards in the country's history.

Locksher placed a hand over Justan's mouth and looked around to make sure no one had heard. "I told you it's a secret. A secret! Do you know what that word means?"

"Sorry," Justan said, though he was still shocked. "What does it mean that you are Stardeon's heir then? Does the prophet expect you to do something?"

"I don't know!" Locksher said. "I'm still trying to figure that out. It's been driving me crazy."

"So . . . Why are you telling me about this?" Justan asked. "I mean, it's fascinating information for sure, and I'm flattered that you would want to share it with me, but why?"

"It's because of your betrothed," the wizard explained and this time Justan was the one looking around to see that no one heard. "The prophet never explained why it was important that Jhonate be there. I was hoping that you might have an idea."

"Well," Justan thought about it. "Jhonate is from Malaroo. Mellinda was from Malaroo."

"Yes but it has to be more than that. Remember the vision of Mellinda the prophet gave us? Jhonate has the same eyes. The same nose. The same hair."

Justan frowned. "So you think she might be descended from Mellinda, like you are from Stardeon? But the prophet didn't mention Mellinda having any children."

Locksher nodded. "True, but the prophet never finished Mellinda's tale. He said he would tell us the rest at a later date. We know what happened up to the point she left Stardeon to learn from the Dark Prophet, but there is a large gap of time between that point and the point where she was imprisoned under the tree."

"I see," Justan said thoughtfully. He wondered how Jhonate would feel about this. "What do you want me to do with this information?"

"I tried to speak with her about it, but Jhonate refused to listen. She said that this was a matter between the prophet and herself."

"Ah." Justan nodded, then looked Locksher directly in the eyes. "You realize that she'll say the same thing to me."

"But perhaps you can get her to think about it. Like I said before, the prophet does nothing without reason and if he has a specific role in mind for Jhonate, she should be prepared."

"Well, I appreciate your concern and I promise to bring it up to her," Justan said. "But if I know Jhonate, she's already been thinking about it."

"Of course I have thought about it!" Jhonate snapped. "The idea that I might be descended from that witch is a terrible stain on my family!"

It was just after dark and the two of them had hidden themselves in one of the guard outposts that were spaced here and there along the base wall. It was sparsely furnished; basically just a tiny room with a field stove and a cot in case a guard wanted to nap between patrols. Before the siege they were rarely used. Now there were so many guards on the walls, they had been lucky to find one unoccupied.

"I told him you would say that," Justan said and the glower on her face made him want to kiss her again. It was strange. At one time, he had feared that glower. Now he was fond of it. "Locksher was just saying that you should be prepared in case the prophet has plans for you."

"I am quite sure he does," Jhonate said. "I only hope his plans include me destroying that creature! At the very least, I intend to be there when it happens, whether I am descended from her or not."

"I understand how you feel." Justan felt the same way about Ewzad Vriil. But moments alone with Jhonate had been so rare, he didn't want to spend them talking about their enemies. He pulled her in for a kiss instead. He was relieved when she didn't resist. She wrapped her arms tightly around him instead. He breathed in her familiar scent. It was earthy and clean. He found it intoxicating. Justan didn't want the kiss to end. He never did, but she broke it off and put a warning finger to his lips.

"We must not become too ardent, Justan," Jhonate said breathlessly. She swallowed, bringing herself under control. "If we lose control of ourselves even once, my father will consider our betrothal nullified."

"But-."

"And he will most likely kill you."

Justan blinked. She brought up her father's temper often. It was as if she were reminding herself. "Jhonate, I respect your people's traditions, but it is going to be a very long time until we'll be able to get your father's permission to marry."

She gave him a questioning look. "That is no excuse for impropriety."

"Impropriety?" That was the kind of word used only by high nobility. Then again, Justan supposed she was high nobility. Or at least it's what he had gathered. "I'm not suggesting we do anything improper. The thought hadn't crossed my mind," Justan said. It was only a minor lie. To do so would be to disrespect her, and he would never do that, but his dreams weren't always so honorable.

"It had not?" she said, raising an eyebrow. She laid a hand on his chest and he could feel the heat of her hand around his icy scar. "It has crossed mine."

Justan's heart beat harder. "W-well-."

"It is perfectly natural to have such thoughts about one's love, Justan," she clarified. Her cheeks reddened and she removed her hand. "However, to act on those feelings would be to destroy any chances that we could be together."

"I-I wouldn't want that to happen," Justan said. "What I was suggesting was . . . What if we married here?" Her eyes widened and he added, "I'm not saying right now, but after this siege is over."

"No," she said firmly. "My father would not acknowledge a marriage done outside our tradition. Besides, it would shame him in front of the other families. I have done so enough as it is."

"Who is your father, Jhonate?" Justan asked. "I know you don't usually speak of it, but I should know. Is he the king of your people?"

"We do not have kings." Jhonate said. She thought on it a moment and sighed. "Very few people know this. Only your father and the other members of the Academy Council are aware and I asked them not to speak of it. I . . . did not tell you, Justan, because I did not want you to think differently of me."

"It couldn't possibly change my feelings," Justan said, placing his arm around her. He kissed her cheek. "I would love you if you were poor or rich, if you had the most detestable family in the world, or if you had none at all."

"Why?" she said, looking into his eyes. "Why do you love me? When I trained you, I was . . . stern. Then we didn't see each other for so long. Why?"

"You changed my life. That year we spent together, sure I hated you in the beginning, but that turned to respect. Then at some point, I decided that you were my closest friend. You pushed me in the ways I needed. Why that turned into how I feel now, I don't know. I didn't understand how I felt until after we were apart."

"I knew how I felt earlier," she replied.

"But why? I was an ungainly idiot back then," Justan said.

"Do not disrespect yourself!" She punched him in the shoulder so hard his fingers tingled. "That could not be farther from the truth. You were ungainly perhaps, but never an idiot. You were too smart. You relied on your brains too much. It was when you started to trust me that I first began to feel for you. The day you rescued me from that . . . that bardatchi, I was so humiliated that I had to be saved by my own pupil." Her eyes softened. "You saw my weakness, but you did not hold it over me. You helped me hold onto my dignity. That is when I knew I loved you."

Justan was astonished. "I wish I had known how you felt then. I might have-."

"You might have done what? Would you have stayed in Reneul? Given up your chances at entering the academy? Forsaken learning your magical talent? For me?" She shook her head. "I would never have allowed it."

"Yes, I know you're right. And I probably would have chosen to go anyway. But all the same, it would have been nice to know."

"I could not have told you. I was . . . relieved when you left." She laid her head on his shoulder. "I pushed any feelings for you out of my mind so that I could concentrate on my studies. For a while I thought I had succeeded, but I was fooling myself. Your father could tell. Locksher could tell. Even Mage Vannya could tell."

Justan didn't know what to say. All those nights where he had lain awake thinking of her and she had been thinking of him as well. Suddenly waiting for her father's blessing didn't seem so bad after all. The thought prompted him to say something he'd been avoiding.

"You know, I think it might be a bad idea for us to keep hiding away like this," Justan said.

She lifted her head from his shoulder and looked at him. "Why do you say this?"

"Sir Hilt gave us permission to court. We have no need to hide our feelings for each other. Your father will hear sooner or later."

"I would not be able to do as we are doing now if people could see us," she said.

"You kissed me in the middle of the battlefield," he reminded.

"That was different," she replied.

"But people have already noticed we are together. We're hiding away to be alone, but what do you think the guards think we're doing in here?" Justan asked. Jhonate's face colored and he knew he had just ruined future possibilities of alone time between them.

"If-if they even suggested such a thing, I . . ." Her eyes grew cold. "I would not allow such talk."

"I know. You would strike them and the rumors would increase," Justan said. "They all expect it has happened by now."

"We have been betrothed for less than a week," Jhonate said, aghast.

"Among my people, two people in love aren't so chaste as with your people. Especially during war," he said.

"War is no excuse." Jhonate stood and held out her hand. "Come, we cannot stay in here."

164

He took her hand and stood. "Then let's stop hiding altogether."

"Very well," She laid a hand on the doorknob, then turned and kissed him so hard he wondered if his lips would bleed. She pulled back. "Thank you for telling me, Justan."

They stepped out of the guard shack and climbed the narrow stair beside it that lead to the top of the wall. The path along the top was wide enough that five people could walk side by side without brushing the waist-high walls. A few academy students paced by and nodded respectfully as Justan and Jhonate walked to the outer edge.

The moon was full and the air cool. Justan looked out over the expanse of cleared land and the forest beyond. It all looked so peaceful.

"You asked about my father," Jhonate said. She rested against the edge and looked at him. He could see the green of her eyes even in the moonlight. "But I suppose you should really know about me.

"I am Jhonate bin Leeths of the Roo-Tan. My family was with those that were brought to the Jharro grove by the prophet after our homeland was destroyed by the Troll Queen. My ancestors signed the contract with Yntri Yni and the Elf Council that made us owners of the land surrounding and protectors of the grove itself. My family has ruled over the Roo-tan for over fifty years, my father for the last thirty."

"So you are like a princess," Justan said.

"I am no princess," she snorted. "My father has seven wives and twenty five children. In our people, the leader is not chosen by lineage, but by vote of the people. I am one of the least of my siblings and I have no desire to rule."

"You have seven mothers and twenty four siblings?" Justan said in surprise. He couldn't imagine the dynamics of a life like that.

"My mother is Jhandra bin Tayl, my father's sixth wife. She is a witch and very unpopular among my father's other wives. I have many brothers and sisters that are stronger and more well respected than me."

Jhonate was giving Justan so much information that he was having difficulty deciding what to focus on. Her mother was

165

a witch? "Then why is your father so particular about what you do?"

"My father is very fond of my mother and he . . . dotes on me. He has called me his favorite many times in the past. Sometimes in front of the others."

"He is a warrior?"

"Xedrion bin Leeths is as powerful a warrior as any in the Battle Academy. He spars with Sir Hilt regularly and often beats him," Jhonate said.

"What will I need to do for him to allow our marriage?" Justan asked.

"It will not be easy," she said. "Your naming will help. Your Jharro bow will help. I will do what I can as well. But it may come down to battle."

Justan laughed.

"I do not see the humor in this," she said.

"Everything comes down to battle," Justan said, looking out at the calm night. "I'll do whatever is necessary, Jhonate. I promise you."

"As will I," she said, linking her arm in his.

"I wish we could go now," Justan said. "But who knows how long this siege will last."

"I do not like being trapped," Jhonate agreed. "And with no one to battle."

"I wouldn't say that," said a gruff voice behind them.

They whirled to face the voice, Justan with a hand on the hilt of his sword, Jhonate with her staff at the ready. Sir Lance stood there, his arms folded. His white hair was pulled back and his grizzled face grinned at them. Neither one of them had heard him approach even though he was wearing scale armor.

"You ain't the only ones achin' for a fight," Lance said.

"Were you listening to us?" Jhonate asked with a glare.

"I only heard that last part," the named warrior replied. "Thought you two might be interested in some action."

"What kind of action?" Justan asked.

"The kind of action that gets us closer to gettin' out of here. See, I'm planning a sortie," the old warrior's smile was wolf-like in the moonlight. "Care to join me?"

Chapter Thirteen

Beth watched the orc camp from the darkness just beyond the treeline. She maintained her web of bewitching magic at a low and steady hum, just strong enough to nullify Mellinda's eyes in the area, but not strong enough to alert the witch of their presence. It was a delicate task, but Beth had done it so often over the last month that it had become second nature to her. The difficult part was what came next.

She closed her eyes and sent feelers of bonding magic out through the camp, identifying every living creature in the area. She could not read the detailed thoughts of creatures at this distance, but she could tell their temperaments and moods. There were eight orcs in the camp. Two were sleeping on straw mats, while four of them sat around a campfire, alternating between arguing and laughing loudly. She had hoped that more of them would be sleeping at this time of night.

The final two orcs were on watch. They were relatively efficient at it, showing that they were veterans at least. Hilt had told her of orc watch techniques. The two orcs were stationed at opposite ends of the camp. They paced clockwise around the perimeter of the camp at a measured pace and watched the woods beyond, keeping the fire to their backs so that their night vision wouldn't be compromised.

Hilt was right about another thing. These orcs were very alert, their swords in hand as they paced. This likely meant that Mellinda was keeping them on their toes. The witch knew there were enemies somewhere in the area.

Beth reached further with her magic, beyond the edges of the camp and felt the position of her companions. Hilt was hiding behind a bush just a short dash from the sleeping orcs, while

Charz, wearing his stealthy boots, was crouched behind a large tree just outside the reach of the revealing firelight. Deathclaw was in a tree whose branches arched over the camp and one of the guards was pacing towards his position.

Beth took a deep breath and opened her eyes. The moment she did so, her awareness of the others faded. She couldn't maintain all her powers and use her other senses at the same time, something she was working hard at improving. She drew an arrow from her quiver and tightened her hold on the viper skin grip as she pulled it back to her ear. She sighted the orc guard pacing closest to her.

Ready, Viper? she asked the bow. The spirit inside the bow hissed with anticipation. Viper loved to strike.

Ready, Deathclaw? The other orc guard was nearly under his tree.

His reply was quiet, the way it usually was when he wasn't holding the Jharro whistle in his hand. *Ready.*

I will wait for your attack, she replied.

She felt the raptoid tense up as the orc walked under his tree. Deathclaw dropped from the branch high above, his tail pointing straight downward, stiffened like a spear. His tail barb popped through the top of the orc's skull, killing it before the rest of his body landed on top of it, slamming it to the ground.

Beth fired on the other orc guard. A portion of the viper's spirit rode the arrow with eagerness, extending itself outward like fangs on the tip of the arrowhead. The arrow pierced the guard's throat and the viper struck its nervous system. The orc stiffened and fell, unable even to gurgle before it died.

Good, Viper, Beth said as the viper's spirit returned to the bow. She drew another arrow even though she already knew she wouldn't need it.

As the two guards dropped, Hilt darted from concealment, his dual swords drawn. He ran past the sleeping orcs and swiped both swords behind him. Thin blades of air flew from the swords tips and slashed through the orcs and into the ground beyond, neatly lopping off their heads.

Charz, who had a more difficult time seeing the precise moment to move, chose that moment to run from his concealment. By the time he arrived at the fire, Deathclaw had already torn one of the orcs' throats out and Hilt had run two of the others through.

The last orc barely had time enough to scream before Charz grabbed it by the head. The rock giant lifted the orc high over his head, then grabbed its legs with his other hand and slammed it down over his knee, breaking legs, back, ribs, and neck simultaneously.

He grunted in disgust and smashed it to the ground. "Don't even know why I'm here sometimes. You guys kill 'em all before I get there."

Hilt let the two orcs slide off the ends of his swords. "You got one this time, Charz. Besides, if things had gone wrong, you would have had plenty to do."

The giant snorted. "Right. We all know that the two of you could've handled a group twice this size all by yourselves."

"True," Deathclaw said in agreement, his arms folded, standing with one foot resting on the corpse of the last orc he'd killed.

"And we know you could've handled them all by yourself," Beth said, joining them from her concealment. "But this group was the size it was. Like I told you before, you'll have the chance to fight all you want. I have foreseen it. Before our task is done, we'll see more than enough battle. You'll be lucky to escape alive."

"So you've promised," the giant grumped. He kicked the smashed orc into the fire.

"Good thinking, Charz," Hilt said with a grin. "Let's drag the others to the fire too, but lets just shove their heads in; leave their bodies hanging out. That should give the others something to wonder about when they find them."

Part of their mission was to disrupt the enemy forces as much as possible. That had been the easy part so far. The four of them had hit two supply wagons and four orc camps similar to this one already. Unfortunately, their major mission hadn't been as successful. Their scouting efforts had met with little success. They had yet to find a major encampment.

Evidently Hilt had been thinking along the same lines. "I think we need to travel further east into the foothills," he said, dragging one orc to the fire. He stomped its head into the coals.

169

"We've seen about all there is to see in this area. All the orcs we've found seem to be heading in that direction anyway."

"I agree," Deathclaw said. The raptoid had been quiet since joining them. He did what they asked him to do, keeping watch and reporting anything Sir Edge needed them to know, but he mostly kept to himself.

"Whatever," Charz grumped. The giant stomped over and picked up the bodies of the two orcs that had been sleeping, then kicked their heads in the direction of the fire.

Beth knew she was going to have to speak with both Deathclaw and Charz sooner or later, but she had been putting it off. Keeping up her field of magic was a constant drain and whatever their issues were, she knew it was going to take a lot of emotional effort to resolve them.

Beth smiled as she watched her husband retrieve the body of the orc guard she'd killed. She loved him more every day. To think it had only been two years since they'd met. It seemed like she had known him forever. But perhaps that was because she had seen so much of his future.

Hilt was the stabilizing force in their group. He took charge when needed and joked around to keep Charz from getting too despondent, while giving Deathclaw space when he needed it. He was a natural leader, doing all of this instinctually, something she would have never been able to do without her spirit magic to guide her.

While the men worked, she spread her web of bewitching out farther, just so she would know if the smoke or the nasty smell that accompanied it drew any other enemies towards their position. That done, she walked to the pile of supplies the orcs had brought with them. Her spirit sight picked out the silvery glow of the orcs' moonrat eye right away. It was nestled in one of the packs, likely the leader's. She moved aside some filthy clothing and pulled it out. It was a green one and fairly fresh, only partially shriveled.

It was strange. Each eye they found seemed to be fresher than the one before. Beth considered the idea that Mellinda was running low on moonrats, but that didn't necessarily strike true. Her power seemed as strong as ever. Another thought came to her.

She walked to the fire. "I had a thought," she said as she tossed the eye in.

"Oh?" Hilt said with a teasing smile.

She gave him a playful glower. "The eyes we find are getting newer and newer. The Mage School's source mentioned a moonrat breeding ground. What if it's somewhere nearby?"

"Hmm," Hilt said. "Then perhaps east is the wrong way for us to go. These orcs have been heading east. But if these eyes are new, they've been getting them to the west. The moonrat breeding grounds could be that way."

"That could be true," she agreed. "And it would make sense, since that would take us deeper into the forest." She looked to Deathclaw and Charz. "What do you two think?"

"Ask Edge," Deathclaw offered.

"Yeah, and I could talk to Alfred later, see what he thinks," Charz said.

"Then let's head back to camp," Hilt said.

They rummaged through the orcs supplies, taking anything useable and tossing whatever they didn't want into the fire, then headed into the forest. Deathclaw darted ahead of them, but Charz stayed with Beth. Hilt followed at a slower pace behind them, making sure they didn't leave a useable trail for their eventual pursuers to follow.

"How are you and Alfred doing?" Beth asked the giant as they walked.

"You always say that like we were married," Charz said with a shake of his head.

"You are bonded," she replied. "It isn't that different."

"Oh isn't it?" Charz chuckled. "I ain't seen him in eighty years and even before that we weren't snuggling at night."

"You know what I mean," she said. Alfred had kept the giant chained to a cave until just a few short months ago. But he had let Charz loose, which meant something.

"We exchange information. That's it. He still doesn't like me much."

"What happened the last time you saw him?" she asked.

"It was twenty years after they left me at that cave." The giant frowned uncomfortably. "He came to tell me how Master Oslo died."

171

"Oslo?"

"He was the wizard that first bonded me. The bond was shifted to Alfred when he died," Charz explained. He looked pained as he spoke. "Alfred blames me for what happened to Oslo. He's right, too. It was my fault."

"Would you mind telling me how that happened?" she asked.

"I . . . don't like sayin' that kind of thing aloud," he said.

"Then carry me," she said. "I can listen as we walk." Charz picked her up in his arms and Beth settled her head on his granite chest. It wasn't a comfortable spot. "Try not to jostle me if you can avoid it."

"Why are you so curious, anyway?" Charz asked. "You don't even like me that much."

She smacked his chest with her hand hoping it was hard enough that he could feel it. She knew she bruised her palm. "That's not true." *Not exactly anyway. It just ticks me off that it took you so long to figure out what an evil bastard you were.*

"I knew," he said, then added mentally, *I always knew. I just ignored it because fighting was so much fun. You sure you want to know me better?*

Yes, she replied. *I think I need to.*

The giant sighed and, with reluctance, pushed the memories through to her. The truth wasn't what she'd expected. By the time they arrived at their camp, her tears were streaming down his chest.

"I'm sorry," he said as he gently set her on her feet.

"No, Charz," she said, patting his arm. "I'm the one who should be sorry. I didn't know."

He raised a rocky eyebrow. "That helped? You sure you don't want to order me to leave?"

She patted his chest. "Shut up and get the fire going."

They moved their camp every few days to make sure they didn't get too predictable and so far it had worked. Their current camp was under an overhanging rock next to a small stream. Hilt had a powder that made a fire smokeless when sprinkled over the wood, so all they had to worry about was the light. Beth's magic told them if anyone was coming close.

Deathclaw had arrived quite a while before them. The

raptoid had been busy. There were three squirrels and a raccoon lying next to the fire pit, already gutted and stripped of fur.

Thank you, she sent, looking up at the tall tree she knew he was perched in and received a mental grunt in response.

"What? We're supposed to survive on that?" Charz complained, then swore as another dead raccoon fell from the tree above, bouncing off the back of his head. Deathclaw had only just started gutting this one and its entrails decorated the giant's shoulder.

"Thank him next time," Beth said. "He would have handed it to you."

Charz grumbled, but he got the fire going.

By the time Hilt arrived, the sky was brightening. The sun would rise over the eastern mountains soon. The warrior had a badger tossed over one shoulder and was happy to see Beth seasoning the rest of their meal. With Mellinda's troops in the area, there was no big game to be found and their options were limited.

"It's good not to be the only hunter around," he said. "Though I must say, I sure am tired of rodent. Almost as tired as I am of these," he said, pulling a thin black snake out of his jacket pocket. "Deathclaw, I've got your favorite."

The raptoid made very little sound as he slid down the tree and approached. From the smear of the blood on his jaw, he had already eaten, but he readily snatched the snake out of the air when Hilt tossed it.

"Thank you," Deathclaw said and bit off its head.

Beth cooked their meal and smiled contentedly as they ate. She leaned her head on Hilt's shoulder. They didn't have it so bad, really. Conditions weren't the best, and they were under constant threat, but she knew deep down that as long as they stayed together, the four of them would survive.

These feelings or impressions had started when she had first met Hilt, but they had increased in frequency over the last year, ever since she communed with Yntri's Jharro tree. Sometimes the feelings came with a specific vision, sometimes not. The prophet had called them, 'the Creator's blessing'. She wasn't sure what that meant, but she had learned to trust them anyway.

173

By the time the sunlight touched their camp, they had bedded down for the day. Charz fell asleep right away while Deathclaw kept watch from the tree above them. The raptoid didn't tend to sleep for long hours at a time, instead taking several small naps during the day when he wasn't needed.

Beth snuggled up next to Hilt under his pink elven blanket. It was thin, but somehow on cool nights it kept them warm and on warm nights it kept them cool. She found it difficult to sleep, though. Charz's memories continued to run through her head. She tried for a while, but finally nudged her husband.

"Hmm?" he said.

"I need to talk to you." she whispered.

"Can it wait?" he asked with a grumble.

"Would I bother you if it wasn't important?"

"Yes," he responded. "But fine." He yawned and turned over to face her. "What is it, Beth?"

"Shh, don't wake Charz," she said. "I can tell you with bonding magic if you want."

"You know I don't like that," Hilt replied. "Just talk quietly."

He didn't like the feeling of someone else's voice in his head. Beth found this particular dislike quite annoying. Mental communication was so much easier. "Fine. It's about Charz."

"That's what I assumed when you told me you didn't want him to hear," Hilt replied.

She scowled at him, "I finally got him to speak about his past today."

"You do tend to pry."

"Just shut up and listen," she said. "I've . . . been wrong about him. At least somewhat. He's not a regular rock giant. Did you know that?"

"I assumed. I've fought rock giants before and though many of them were bigger, none of them had skin that hard, or healed that fast," Hilt said.

"Charz wasn't always like this," she said. "He was taken as a child and sold to wizards in Khalpany. They made him like this. They raised him to fight in the arena.

"These wizards used their magic to make his skin harder

174

and make his reactions faster. Then they put these gemstones inside his body that made him heal very fast," she said. "They would send him into the arena for champions to challenge and as long as his head was attached, he would heal afterwards. There was no way he could escape. They had his gemstones linked to that crystal pendant that he wears. They kept it in a strongbox and if he strayed too far from the crystal, he collapsed."

"That's a sad existence," Hilt said. He glanced over at the sleeping giant. "It could drive someone mad."

"That's just it. He had seen others go crazy and become little more than rabid animals. All of them ended up dying sooner or later. Charz chose to enjoy the battle instead. He saw each fight as a challenge."

"How long was he in there?" Hilt asked.

"Nearly a hundred years. He was the reigning champion. No one could beat him. He was popular for a while, but eventually the people tired of him. They wanted him to lose. The owners even stacked the events against Charz, hoping that a gladiator would finally be able to beat him, but Charz never lost." Beth said. "Eventually they started letting popular gladiators fight their way through the competition without facing him.

"Then one day, a named wizard called Master Oslo visited Khalpany. He watched Charz fight a horrific battle and they bonded. Oslo was outraged by the way Charz had been treated. With Alfred's help, he stole the crystal and let Charz free. But he didn't understand what Charz really was. It wasn't long before Charz thirsted for a challenge. He went on a rampage, stirring up the countryside against them. When Oslo finally sealed Charz up in that cave, it was because he had no other choice."

"I see," Hilt said. He kissed her lips gently and stroked her hair. "He's changed, Beth. Don't worry that he is going to lose control again. You'd know if that was going to happen."

"It's not that," Beth said. "I know he's sincere. I felt it when I listened to him the first time. He had a true change of heart. The problem is me. Ever since I first listened to Charz and felt the weight of his hundreds of years of bloody fighting on his shoulders . . ." She sighed. "Even though I knew he'd changed, I

175

couldn't forgive him for what he'd done. I put up with him being around because I knew it was necessary, but I haven't been kind to him."

"I hadn't noticed," Hilt said with just enough sarcasm that Beth had to resist the urge to knee him in the stomach.

"What I realized today," she said with clenched teeth. "Is that it's not my place to judge him. He has enough doubters, himself and his bonding wizard included. We need to support him and just maybe we should look for ways to make him feel like a more needed part of our group."

"I agree. You know, Beth," Hilt said, stroking her jawline. "I fell in love with you because of your courage and determination and, quite frankly, because you gave me no other choice." He chuckled. "But I stay in love with you because you always try so earnestly to make the right decision. And because you always let me sleep."

"Alright, go to sleep then," she said and turned over, putting her back to him.

"And?" He reached around her and pulled her close against his chest. She could feel his heartbeat against her back.

"And I love you, too," she said.

"Good. I am asleep now," he said and that was true just minutes later.

Did you hear what we said? Beth asked Deathclaw through the Jharro wood, knowing that he had. His hearing was that good. Even from way up in the tree, he would have heard.

That you two love each other? the raptoid asked. *It is to be expected among you humans, I suppose.*

No. What I said about Charz, she clarified.

Yes.

When he didn't elaborate, she added, *And doesn't it strike you how similar his story is with-.*

We were both changed by wizards and bonded to a human, yes, Deathclaw interrupted, sounding somewhat offended by the comparison. *But that is all we have in common.*

I wasn't comparing him to you, Beth said. *I was comparing him to your sister.*

Deathclaw was silent in thought for a few moments. *How?*

He was once broken, just like she is, Beth sent.

He was never like she is, Deathclaw said.

Beth frowned. *Charz eventually changed, is the point I am trying to make*.

Deathclaw snorted. *I cannot wait a hundred years for her to change*.

But-.

Have you foreseen this? Deathclaw demanded. *Have you had a vision of a change in her?*

No, she admitted.

Then as with Charz you must learn that it is not your place to judge her, the raptoid said. *I am her broodmate. I am her Deathclaw. I have judged Talon*.

Beth blinked, surprised at being reprimanded. *I am sorry. You are right. It wasn't my place to say*.

Sleep, Beth, Deathclaw said.

Her mind churned in embarrassment, but she couldn't think of anything to say. Sleep was difficult for Beth to find. Deathclaw's reprimand sat sourly in her stomach and it was some time before she drifted off.

When Hilt woke her it was well past noon. The sun was at its Zenith and the heat of the day was on them. Beth hated sleeping during the day. She always woke with a headache, feeling like her brain had been stuffed with cotton.

"Beth," Hilt said, shaking her gently.

"Oh, what is it, damn you!" she snapped.

"We need to get moving," Hilt replied. He handed her a tin cup filled with water. "Charz has spoken with Alfred and it seems that their spy among Ewzad Vriil's people has some new information."

"What is it?" she asked sitting up. She drank and found that the water was cool and had been flavored with waking herbs. Hilt knew her so well. Her mind had begun to clear by the time she finished it.

"Their informant says that the mother of the moonrats has established a troll farm somewhere to the east of us. She told Ewzad Vriil that she expects to have a sizeable army by summer's end. It's probably where the orcs we've been running into were headed. The council is worried that she may be making more of those modified trolls there."

"Then I guess our decision has been made for us," Beth said. She stood and began folding the gauzy blanket.

"Yes. We head east. But the question I have is even if we do find this farm, what do we do then? Regular trolls we could set on fire, but if she has a large number of modified trolls, we won't be able to handle them."

"We need pepper," Beth said.

"I ate the rest of the peppered beef," Charz said.

"No we need a lot of pepper," she said.

"I know there used to be some farms to the northeast," Hilt said. "I don't know if there's anything left of them now, but they could have some."

"No," Beth said as a flash of intuition hit her. "I know where we could find a whole barrel."

"Where?" Deathclaw asked.

"Pinewood," Beth said.

"That's almost a week's travel to the north, through moonrat-infested land. That's the opposite direction from where we want to go," Hilt said.

"I know, but I have a feeling."

Hilt gave her a wary look. "Are you sure you want to go there, love? It would be a dangerous trip and we have no idea what we'll find when we get there."

"I understand that," Beth dreaded it herself. She had lived in Pinewood for a decade and left many friends behind. No one she had spoken to knew what happened to the town, but most of the refugees in the dwarf caverns assumed it had been wiped out. "But Pinewood is where we need to go."

Chapter Fourteen

Talon crouched on the roof of what had once been the mayor's house, wondering just how many of the humans had gotten away alive.

Pinewood had once been a proud town full of hardy forest folk. They were situated perfectly at the edge of the Tinny Woods right next to the main road from Sampo to the academy. Fear of the growing moonrat menace led them to wall the town, but that hadn't prepared them for Mellinda's purge. When the academy was surrounded and the protective wards covering the forest roads had been broken, Pinewood was one of the first casualties. Moonrats had swarmed over the walls, taking them by surprise.

Talon had spent some time searching for survivors when she first arrived. The gates had been flung open at some point and human tracks led away in all directions. But most of the tracks she had followed disappeared suddenly or led only to inedible remains.

Talon grinned at the thought of all the humans running and screaming. She felt a twinge in her jaw and reached up to caress the spot where the ogre had struck her. No trace of the injury remained, but she felt it still. Sometimes she dreamed of that blow. She had never been struck so hard, not even by that rock giant. She wanted to face that ogre again. She would let it strike her again, just to feel the power of it, feel her bones break and her muscles burst. But then she would kill it. Then she would taste its blood, mingled with her own.

She was hungry. Trolls and moonrats had taken anything edible in the town weeks ago. Talon had found a few homes or shops with glass jars full of vegetables or preserves that the moonrats hadn't known what to do with. She had broken them open and ate them, but even though she enjoyed the way the glass cut her mouth and throat, these meals were meager and unsatisfying.

This town had sustained her for the time since the great battle, but there was little left to eat anymore. Most wildlife around Pinewood had been hunted clean long before she arrived. This was likely why the moonrats and trolls had left. Otherwise, it wouldn't have become Talon's refuge. Here, she was able to stay unmolested by the moonrat mother until she decided what to do.

Talon knew that she had failed Ewwie's orders. She had only killed one of the wizards. Her brother's wizard still lived. If she returned to Ewwie now, he would put another moonrat eye in her and the moonrat mother would make her numb again; make her obey again. Talon couldn't bear the thought of that.

She had spent the last few days tearing up the floorboards of houses. She had discovered that humans liked to hide things there. Unfortunately not much of it was food. Talon had found trinkets, weapons, armor, and strange potions that tasted intriguingly bitter, but did nothing to assuage her hunger.

The house she stood on was the only place she had yet to search. She wasn't sure why she had stayed away thus far. It should have been her first target. It was bigger than the others and it even smelled of food, but still she had stayed away. Even now as she sat on the pinnacle of the roof, she felt a strong compulsion to go elsewhere. The feeling confused her. She listened to it; rolled the feeling over in her mind.

Why should she leave? She did not know. Talon pushed the feeling away and slid down the wooden shingles. She hung by one hand for a moment then dropped twenty feet to the muddy road below. Again, she felt the compulsion to turn around and leave, perhaps check some of the other houses again.

She went around to the back of the house instead. There was a rear door. She really didn't want to open it, but she lifted the latch anyway. She pushed on the door. It wouldn't move. She put her eye to the crack between the door and the jam. The door was barred from the inside. There was a small window in the door, but surely the glass was too strong to break. Talon's fist burst through the glass and she reached down for the bar. The bar was going to be too heavy for her to lift, though. She lifted it anyway, and pulled the door open. The smell that wafted out caused her mouth to water. There was meat inside, and something else. Something living.

It was time to leave. Her hunger left. She was sleepy. She was too sad to go inside. Talon ignored all the feelings and crept inside, ready to kill whatever lived there.

She was in some sort of small hallway. Muddy boots lined the floor and coats were hung on hooks that protruded from the walls. She rounded the corner into a room with long counters and various metal instruments, but she didn't stay to investigate it further. She heard a yelp from the room beyond and heard the thudding of footsteps.

Talon was buffeted by thoughts and emotions. The sound was nothing. It was a mouse, no, a dragon. Ignore it. It would be best to leave.

She chased after the sounds and entered a room with a long wooden table surrounded by many polished chairs. At the head of the table, a chair was pulled back. A plate was set there, with a half eaten jar of red lumps of sweet smelling vegetables. Talon heard a creak and darted forward through another doorway, focusing her senses and ignoring her emotions.

In the next room, cowering in the corner, was the living creature she had sensed. Its eyes were wide and black, its teeth sharp. It held a long kitchen knife.

"Stay back!" it said, it's voice shaking.

Talon's instincts told her to run and never look back. This was the most terrifying creature she had ever encountered. Talon's eyes, however, told her that this was merely a gorc. A female. It had mottled leathery greenish skin and for some reason was wearing some kind of fancy human dress, the material red and shiny with lace at the edges.

Talon stalked forward, her teeth bared.

It squealed and dropped the knife and all the conflicting emotions left Talon's mind. "I'm sorry! P-please tell the mistress I'm sorry!"

"Misstress?" Talon hissed and leaned forward, sniffing at the gorc. It smelled like flowers and human things and stale gorc sweat.

"Yes! Please! Tell the mistress I weren't hidin'. I was just . . . scoutin' this place."

"I do not sserve your misstress," Talon said and licked the gorc's neck. The acrid taste of human perfume filled her mouth. She whispered in its ear, "I sserve only Ewwie."

"D-don't know no Ewwie, lizard lady," the gorc female replied with a shudder.

Talon flexed her fingers, feeling the urge to tear its throat out and play in its innards. "He iss the barldag'ss messenger."

"Oh him," the gorc said in relief. "I never heard him in my head. Just heard the mistress."

Talon stepped closer, tracing a claw lightly down its face. "You hearss her?"

"I-I don't hears her no more," it whimpered. "I don't gots her eye no more. Lost it. Please don't tell her!"

"I hatess your misstress," Talon hissed, drawing back her arm. She would make the thing scream for hours before silencing it.

The gorc looked relieved. "Me too! I hates her nasty rat guts. I do! Threw her eye down the poop hole! I-I'll serve yer Ewwie, though. I'll do whatever Ewwie wants!"

"You hatess her?" Talon asked, lowering her arm slowly.

"She makes me do things I don't want to. Eat things I don't want to. A-and hurts me if I don't do what she wants. Makes me use my witchy-witch magics all the time."

"Witchy?" Talon cocked her head.

"I'cn make things do what I wants sometimes. With my brains," it said, pointing to its head. "Hurts if I gots to use it too much. Makin' you stay gone was real hurty."

"You made me sstay away?" That bombardment of feelings had been caused by this loathsome creature? It must have powerful magic.

"Didn't work too good though, 'cause you's here," it said and smiled shakily. "I-I'm Durza. What's the name you was given?"

"Talon, gorc," she said.

"Th-that's a good one. Better than Durza fer sure 'nuff." It edged towards another doorway. "You hungry, Talon?"

182

Talon licked her lips. "You look like food."

Durza laughed nervously. "I wouldn't taste no good! I got lots better foods here. L-let me shows you."

Talon let it back away. If it tried to escape, she would enjoy chasing it down.

The gorc edged around a small table and backed through the doorway Talon had chased her through earlier. "This way, Talon. The foods is this way."

Talon followed it, hoping the gorc had set some sort of trap. But it simply led her past the area with the large table and back into the clean room with all the countertops. Durza opened a door and went down some creaking steps into a basement area. The scent of food was strongest in here. Drool escaped Talon's lips and dripped off her chin as she descended the steps. The steps opened up into a room long and wide with earthen walls, lit by glowing orbs.

"The peoples in this place keeped lots and lots of foods here," Durza said, showing Talon shelves upon shelves laden with glass jars similar to the ones Talon had found in other houses. The entire town's food surplus must have been stored in this place. The gorc walked to the back and opened another door to a room that was cold. Talon could sense the magic within. Great sides of beef hung from hooks in the ceiling, mixed with whole pigs and chickens and ducks.

"Meat!" Talon said gleefully and pulled a pig down from one of the hooks. She dragged it out of the cold room, but was disappointed to find that it was frozen solid.

"It'll thaw," Durza said. "Try this."

The gorc grabbed a jar off the shelf and pried at its metal lid with some sort of instrument. There was a pop and the lid came off. A pleasant meaty aroma wafted out.

Talon pulled the jar from the gorc's hands, irritated that this gorc had known how to open the bottles when she had not. She reached in. The meat she pulled out was red, but looked cooked. The humans had somehow formed it into tubes. She tore into a piece to find that it was extremely salty, unpleasantly so, which piqued her interest. After she swallowed, a heat built up in her mouth and continued down her throat. She reached in her mouth with her fingers expecting to find flames, but there was

183

nothing there."

"I likess thiss," she decided and shoved more into her mouth, enjoying the way her tongue burned and tingled.

"Them's sausenges," the gorc declared. "They gots lots of bottles of 'em here. They also gots soft-soft beds and even a hole you'cn poop in. Right down here, in the corner."

"Poop?" Talon asked.

"In the hole in the corner. It goes way down deep. It barely even stinks none."

Talon narrowed her eyes at the gorc. She could pump its body full of poison and stuff it in the cold room to eat later. After it screamed for a long time, of course.

"Y-you'cn say here with me if yous like," Durza offered, blinking worriedly. "Just don't hurt me'n I'll use my witchy-witch magic to keep otherns out."

"Sstay with you?" Talon cocked her head. Could it be useful enough to keep it alive?

"Sure!" It said with a cautious smile. "We'cn play games and stuff and eat the humans food until the mistress is killed by them wizards. Then we'cn both go wherever we wants to."

Talon blinked. Was it possible that the moonrat mother could be killed? She had seen the power of the wizards that the mistress and Ewwie faced. They had destroyed the academy place and melted the bodies of a dozen of Ewwie's pets outside the cave. If they could kill the moonrat mother, she could return to Ewwie. He would forgive her she was sure. He might hurt her for a while first, but that would be fun and then he would forgive her.

Yes, that would be good. This creature would be an entertainment in the meantime. It could keep the moonrat mother from discovering her and if she tired of it, she could kill it and eat it.

"I will letss you live," she decided, giving Durza what she thought was a charming smile. *For now.*

Chapter Fifteen

"You wouldn't . . . make any changes to them, my dear. Would you?" Elise asked and Ewzad could see the fear in her eyes.

As her belly had grown, Elise had become more and more confident in her abilities and her handling of the citizenry. The babies inside her were the only things she feared for. He ceased the magical energies and willed his fingers to stop their writhing. He gave her swollen belly one last caress, enjoying the way her belly button pressed out against the shiny fabric of her wedding dress.

"No-no, my dear. Of course not. Never. The thought hadn't crossed my mind," he cooed as he rose to his feet. But of course it had. At the very least he had been tempted to make slight alterations to make sure they grew strong. But the other Envakfeers told him that babies in the womb were already quite unstable. Any slight change could have a disastrous result. "My talents are not for children, no."

Fortunately, both children seemed quite strong enough without his help. The Vriil bloodline was known to produce sickly young, but the Muldroomons were strong. The dark voice had known what he was doing when he picked the two of them to raise the heir.

The only thing Ewzad could do was surround them both with elemental and spirit magic energies in hopes that their tiny forms might somehow absorb it. One of the Envakfeers claimed that their son had grown to become a powerful wizard with such treatment. The others thought he was a fool, declaring that such talents came from lineage only.

"I was merely checking on them, yes?" he said. "They are

strong. Oh so strong, dearest Elise."

She gave him a nod and held out her arm. "Are you ready?"

She looked so beautiful, standing in her satin dress of purest white, studded with pearls and sparkling jewels, her shining crown on her brow. The royal seamstress had refused to alter it for Elise's condition at first, offended by the idea of modifying the traditional royal wedding dress. But after Elise had strangled the woman, her replacement had done a marvelous job.

"Oh yes," Ewzad purred. He took her arm in his and nodded to Hamford and Arcon. They signaled the royal guards and Elise and Ewzad walked towards the throne room.

They could hear the trumpets' fanfare echo down the proud hallways of the palace. Ewzad giggled in anticipation. He had been looking toward this moment since childhood. He had been ten years old when he fell in love with Elise.

He remembered the day well. His father had left him in Dremald at the palace to spend some time "getting to know the royalty". In reality, Ewzad knew he had been left behind so that his father could spend more time focused on his sister, Jolie. She had reached marriageable age and they were tired of Ewzad getting in the way while they attended ridiculous balls and tedious social engagements. Father didn't care for him. He had regretted marrying Ewzad's mother after his first wife had died. Ewzad's mother had told him so, and even though Jolie was kind to him, he knew her kindness was a facade.

So he had sat alone while the other noble children had chortled and flitted about brainlessly. The days were filled with tedium. But then Elise had come to sit with him. She had been his same age and unlike the other children of the nobility, she didn't look down upon him just because he was a Vriil. She laughed while he mocked the others. It was her laugh more than her beauty that had won his heart that day.

Ewzad looked at his queen as they approached the great doors of the throne room and smiled. He was so excited he had to force his legs to keep their shape. It wouldn't be very kingly if he fell and slithered across the floor to his wedding, now would it? No, this was to be his greatest day; his finest hour. All his plans had been set for this moment. Ewzad Vrill, King of Dremaldria, and Elise, the queen at his side.

They walked into the throne room to thunderous applause. The enormous light orbs near the ceiling had been increased to twice their usual brightness and great marble pillars had been decorated with shimmering streamers as per tradition, half of them plastered with Muldroomon's red and white sigil, the others with House Vriil's gold and black. The royal guard's armor had even been painted to match.

The entire event had been put together in a week's time. It had been difficult to arrange everything on such short notice. Usually there were months of feasting and revelry in preparation for a royal wedding. But circumstances had precluded tradition. Elise's pregnancy had become public knowledge, and as word spread, she began to worry that if the twins were born out of wedlock, they would be considered illegitimate and non-heirs to the throne.

In addition, word of the academy's destruction had spread throughout the city. The truth of the situation with the Mage School had been leaking out, something Ewzad was sure was being perpetrated by Mage School spies. The peasants, who had already been unruly, were now rebellious. Several of Ewzad's men had been attacked, some of them killed. Elise was convinced that many of the nobles were stirring them up. The leadership of the Dremald garrison had fractured as well. The slow stream of desertion had turned into a flood.

Ewzad had dismissed her concerns in the beginning. He had wanted to wait for the Mage School's destruction before announcing their marriage. But then a plan had formed in his mind. If all went well, the populace would be subdued, the nobles taken under heel, and Ewzad would be free to leave Dremald and attack the Mage School at his leisure.

They approached the steps to the throne where the Minister of Religion was waiting for them. Ewzad glanced at the crowd. The ranks of the assembled nobles and dignitaries were thinner than Ewzad would have liked, but Elise had filled the gaps with merchants and supporters. Ewzad noted with amusement that many of those assembled wore gemstones glued to the back of their fingers. It was an affectation spreading

187

among those who had chosen his side. Some had even begun having gemstones surgically embedded in their flesh with metal studs, all in an attempt to look more like him.

The Minister of Religion stood in full regalia, a jeweled scepter in one hand, while in the other he held a cushion with a crown nestled on top. His position was a long held and sacred tradition in Dremaldria. As their country did not have an official religion, his robes were decorated with a plethora of symbols representing all of the gods worshipped by Dremaldria's various peoples.

Elise and Ewzad stood before him and bowed their heads as he began the ceremony. It was long and boring, full of intonations and symbolic gestures. Ewzad more than once considered forcing the man to get to the end. But Elise had foreseen his impatience and made him promise beforehand that he would put up with the tedium.

Somehow he made it through to the end, though part of him wanted to kill the man. The minister had Ewzad and Elise raise their hands clasped together and his scepter spit out a ring of light that settled around them. Then he lifted the king's crown from its velvet cushion and settled it on Ewzad's brow.

It was done. They were wed. Ewzad was king.

The assembled group applauded once more. Music played and Ewzad danced the traditional Dremaldrian wedding waltz with his new bride. Then Elise raised her hands and called for silence.

Ewzad amplified her voice so that when Elise spoke, all the assembled heard her speak with queenly authority, "Let us walk out to the people! Let us show them their new King!"

Elise and Ewzad exited through the main palace doors, the nobles streaming out behind them. The royal guard had been prepared in advance and lined the road, creating a clear path towards the gates to the inner city. The guards had been busy on the other side of the gates as well. A large area of the central square had been cleared and a platform raised.

The inner city was home to the noble and wealthy, but anything said or done here would make its way out to the peasants in the rest of Dremald by the end of the day. The citizenry surrounding the square had mixed reactions on seeing

Ewzad and Elise walk from the palace gates. There were cheers for Elise, but almost as many jeers for Ewzad and there were many others who merely stood in silence unnerved by the appearance of four figures, bound and hooded, being held at the base of the platform.

Once Elise and Ewzad had climbed the stairs to the top of the platform, Elise raised Ewzad's hand into the air and shouted, "My people! My beloved people of Dremaldria, I introduce you to my husband, your king! King Ewzad Vriil!"

Ewzad amplified and extended the reach of her voice so that even those outside the inner city walls could hear. Then he cleared his throat and spoke.

"People of Dremaldria! Yes-yes, my people! I come to you this day newly crowned and wed to your sweet-sweet queen, to bring you news. To tell you the truth, yes!" Ewzad grinned with excitement, barely able to keep his body under control. "I have grave-grave news to tell you this day!

"Yes, as many of you have heard, the Battle Academy has fallen! But there is more. They defeated the greater part of the army surrounding them! Yes-yes, those brave souls fought well. But they were betrayed! Yes, their very walls were destroyed! Not a trace of that proud Dremaldrian institution remains! Who betrayed them, you may ask? Yes-yes, I can tell you! They were betrayed by magic!"

There was a rumbling in the crowd at this. Ewzad's men had been sewing rumors for weeks that the wizards were responsible for the academy's destruction. Now it was time to grow those seeds.

"Yes! They were betrayed by wizards!" he shouted. "I know, I know it is hard to believe that our own protectors, our own Mage School would do this. I wouldn't have believed it myself, no-no I wouldn't, if not for new evidence! My men have uncovered new truths about poor King Andre's death. The men who snuck into our great palace and murdered my dear friend were not just from one foreign kingdom as we had thought, but from many! Yes-yes, what's more, they had magic help!

"Magic got them in past our people undetected. Yes, magic got them past our great-great guards! For years, long unknown to the people here, the wizards of the Mage School have been trying to take command of Dremald! Yes, our beloved King Andre and sweet Queen Elise, they did not want to trouble you with this disturbing fact, no, but the High Council has been petitioning to have one of their number serve as the ruler's advisor for years!"

That much was true and no great secret. The Mage School representatives brought it up every time they came to court.

"When the Mage School could not gain power through the correct methods, they contacted other countries. Other kings! Yes, our neighbors in Razbeck, our friends in Alberri, even our cousins in Khalpany, they all conspired with the Mage School to kill King Andre that night and would have slain dear Queen Elise too if I hadn't stopped them!"

The crowd roared, a few of them in agreement, but most of them in protest. The Mage School was trusted by the majority of Dremaldrians, whether their methods were liked or not. But Ewzad was ready to bring the proof that would convince them.

Ewzad caressed Elise's cheek. "Our sweet queen had her suspicions. Yes, so she sent to the academy for aid right away. The wizards knew the academy would help us, yes-yes they did! And so the High Council unleashed a horde of monsters to surround our dear friends. But the warriors would not let themselves be stopped, no-no they wouldn't. They gathered their strength and fought the beasts back and when the warriors had the battle won, the wizards panicked. The Mage School knew they could not let them escape. So they ignited the spells that strengthened the academy's walls, incinerating them all!

"And all along, they kept us here, paralyzed with fear! Unable to help, yes!" He stepped forward, ignoring the building outrage in the crowd, and pointed to the men bound at the base of the platform. "The queen and I only wish now that we had known, so that our proud garrison could have come to their aid. But the wizards had help. Yes-yes, many of our own people, yes, true sons and daughters of Dremald spread malicious rumors, trying to keep us from the truth!"

He gestured and the royal guards pulled the hoods from the bound men. They were the heads of the highest noble houses. The men stood in filthy finery, gagged and bruised. The crowd rumbled in confusion.

"Yes! Terrible, isn't it?" Ewzad shouted. "Yes-yes it is! Those foul wizards enlisted many of our own proud nobles, yes! They worked against us!"

Elise looked at him questioningly. Some of these men were her strongest opposition among the nobles. They were the ones working up the rabble, but Ewzad hadn't told her about this part of his plan. It was his surprise to her.

The crowd began to cry out, many of them demanding to hear from the men.

"You wish to hear from them? I will allow them to speak in their defense, yes! But before I do, let me tell you, yes, that this conspiracy is more foul than you know. These men conspired to murder Queen Elise this very morning. They had her cornered with magic at the ready when my men captured them!"

He let the cries among the crowd build. The royal guards had to struggle to keep some of the other nobles back. Ewzad reached out with his magic and caressed the seeds of power he had placed within the bound men the night before. The seeds had ripened, matching the bodies they inhabited. He tightened his fist and the four men lurched in unison.

He turned to Hamford and Arcon and whispered. "Guard Elise, you fools!" The two men shuffled to stand at either side of her, but Ewzad erected a protective shield around her anyway before turning back to gaze at the bound men.

"Cut their gags free!" Ewzad commanded the guards below. "Yes-yes, let them speak in their defense. See if their foul words can convince us!"

The moment the gags fell away, the seeds of power sprouted. Before the noblemen could speak, their bodies began to swell. The ropes binding them burst free.

Nudro, the leader of House Pross sprouted great horns from his head. His tongue swelled and grew from his open mouth sprouting suckers and undulating like a reaching tentacle. Tombas, the leader of House Stots sprouted buzzing wings and his face hardened as if carved of stone.

"No-no-no! They're after the queen!" Ewzad shouted. "Protect the queen!"

The mutated noblemen, confused and horrified by their sudden transformations, flailed about and let out horrible cries. The crowd screamed and backed away. Many ran. The royal guard, trained by academy graduates and made of sterner stuff, did not break ranks. They drew their swords and advanced on the mutated men.

Stensil, the leader of House Roma, now a four legged hairy beast whose head was that of a falcon with red eyes and flames pouring from its mouth, leapt to the top of the platform, Ewzad in his sights.

Ewzad smiled and pulled a jeweled sabre from the belt at his waist. He had been hoping this would happen. Let the people see what a hero he was. He pointed the sword at the beast and shouted. "For Queen Elise and Dremaldria!"

Stensil leapt at him, opening a beak filled with flames. Ewzad wasn't a swordsman, but he had been trained in the basics as a young boy as all noblemen were. He paralyzed the beast with one writhing hand, then spun and swung the sword down. As the sword touched its forehead, Ewzad sliced with his magic. Elise yelped as the former head of House Roma fell into two pieces and his body began smoking.

"The wizards!" he shouted. "Yes, the wizards are behind this!"

He surveyed the scene below. The guards had managed to kill the leader of House Tensow, who had become a slug-like creature. But Tombas of Stots was hovering above them with his buzzing wings. His upper body was carved from living stone and his lower half had become a swollen black abdomen with spider's legs,

"Bowmen!" Ewzad cried. "Kill it! Kill it! Shoot it! Don't let it reach the queen!"

Tombas tried to escape, but his heavy body was barely held aloft by his wings and the best he could manage was to bob through the air slowly hovering over the screaming masses of spectators. Arrows arched towards him, some missing completely and striking innocents below, others bouncing off the stone-like skin of his upper body. His lower half was not as well protected though, and the arrows easily pierced it.

He let out a keening, buzzing cry and struggled to rise

higher in the air, but the next volley of arrows found their mark and he plummeted to the ground. His swollen body burst upon contact with the street below.

Ewzad turned his attention to his final victim. Nudro of Pross screeched up at him from the street below, the bodies of royal guards strewn about him. The beady eyes on his horned head were filled with rage. His body had become a twisted mix of spikes and armored plates.

"For Queen Elise and Dremaldria!" Ewzad cried once again and he leapt off the platform towards the beast. His leap was propelled by magic and the blade of his sword shone as if forged in the sun. He arced through the air, surrounding the beast with a cloud of steam and when Ewzad struck him, he ignited the noble from within.

When Ewzad emerged from the cloud of steam, he carried the melted remains of Nudro Pross' head. Many of the crowd that remained cried out in praise at Ewzad's heroism. Others cried out in horror, but Ewzad was confident that the tale of his greatness would spread.

He climbed back to the top of the platform where Elise stood with a hand to her mouth, her face pale. He then turned and hurled Nudro's head to the street below. "This will not stand, no! No it won't!" His voice carried throughout the city Dremald and into the countryside around. "There will be retaliation, yes! AS LONG AS I PROTECT THE QUEEN, THE WIZARDS WILL NOT RULE DREMALDRIA!!"

As his voice faded into the air, he took Elise's arm and headed back towards the palace, Hamford and Arcon at his side, the ranks of royal guards clustered protectively around them.

"Y-you were magnificent, my husband." Elise whispered and Ewzad could feel her trembling. "But why didn't you tell me your plans? We could have used others. Wh-why I nearly had Nudro Pross convinced to join our side and House Roma had always backed me."

"Yes-yes, I know. I know, dearest, but doesn't that make it even better?" Ewzad said with a giggle. "The nobles know who our backers are, don't they? Will this not make my story all the more believable? My performance that much more real? Why would we strike our own supporters, hmm? Unless the wizard

193

conspiracy is real and pervasive, don't you think?"

"I see," Elise blinked in surprise, and looked at him with a mix of respect, admiration, and horror. "This no longer becomes about houses vying for power in Dremald."

"Yes! You see, don't you? This is Dremaldria versus the Mage School!" He giggled.

"Very good, Master," Mellinda said from inside his mind. *"Even I sometimes forget you aren't the foppish fool you seem. Your speech was even half convincing. I imagine the peasants will make it sound much grander when they spread the word of it."*

Ewzad's smile faded. "What is it, witch? Yes, why must you disturb me now at the day of my crowning?"

"The warriors are planning something," she said. *"I believe they plan to strike out against us somehow. They have been arguing with the wizards for weeks about it, but I think they have finally come to a resolution."*

"Well, what is it?" he spat. "What do they plan?"

"It is hard to say," she said reluctantly. *"My sources inside the walls of the school have been thinned."*

"Thinned? And how has that happened, Mellinda?"

The witch simmered over him saying her name aloud. *"The eyes belonging to my highest ranking spies have been destroyed. I believe my spies have been captured. I know where at least some of them are being held."*

Ewzad scowled. "Is your information useless now, then?"

"Far from it, master," she said. *"I have learned some very important things. First, whatever the warriors have planned, it will happen tomorrow. I have fortified my forest, but your men must be prepared."*

"Very well. Tell them then, yes?" he said.

"Secondly, it seems that the Mage School has a spy of their own. They have been made aware of certain things; things only one closest to you would have known. For instance, not only do they know that your wife is pregnant, but one of my sources overheard that they also know she will have twins."

"How could they know this?" Ewzad snapped, coming to a stop in front of the palace doors. He had kept that information quiet. Certainly no one could know, but perhaps Hamford and

Arcon.

"What is it?" Elise asked, but Ewzad ignored her.

"You may not remember spilling this secret, but you do have loose lips, master," Mellinda chided. *"You have mentioned this fact several times within the palace walls. 'how are my babies, love?', 'Come, let me feel the twinnly twins, Elise.'"* She snorted, *"There are servants everywhere here and they love to gossip amongst themselves. If the Mage School has even one spy in the palace, they could know many things."*

"Then you send Arcon around with one of your eyes," he said through clenched teeth. "Test every maid, servant, and guard in the palace until you find them!"

"Of course," she purred. *"I live to serve you, Master."*

Arcon stumbled suddenly and he gave a bow. "I-I will get on it right away, my king," the mage said and hurried away.

"My feet are tired, dear husband." Elise said, tugging his arm, her face concerned, as it usually was when she was listening to his side of an argument with the witch. She gestured through the open doors towards the end of the throne room where he saw that a second throne matching the queen's had been added to the dais. "Can we sit?"

"Of course, my queen," Ewzad said, his grin returning. Yes, he couldn't let Mellinda's trifling words muddy his day of triumph, now, could he? They entered the throne room and climbed the steps to the dais together.

As they sat next to each other on their plush thrones, Ewzad laughed. He kissed Elise's hand. Now they ruled as husband and wife. Soon they would usher in the return of the Dark Prophet. And then they would conquer the rest of the lands; Ewzad and Elise Vriil, together.

"And now?" Mellinda said. *"What would you have me do about the Mage School?"*

"I think it is time we sent the wizards a message, don't you? Yes-yes, my new creations need to stretch their legs," he said with a wicked grin. "Send me five of your orange eyes, dear Mellinda. Without sweet Talon here, you will need to guide them for me."

"With pleasure . . . my king," Mellinda said.

"Has sweet Clara found Talon's trail yet?" he asked.

"*She is close.*"

"When she does, have her tell Talon that I need her back right away. Yes-yes, right away," he said.

"*And when Talon returns, what shall you do?*" Mellinda asked.

"As I promised, don't you think? Yes, I shall place an eye in her as well. We mustn't have her running free again."

"*As you command,*" Mellinda said and Ewzad could tell she was very pleased. Yes, very pleased indeed.

Chapter Sixteen

I envy you your battle, Deathclaw said.

Oh? Justan asked from his soft bed, feeling guilty knowing that Deathclaw was resting in the branches of a tree. He reminded himself that the raptoid liked sleeping in trees. *And why?*

We are three days from Pinewood. The moonrats and trolls are thick here, but Hilt will not let us fight. We must travel slowly to avoid them, Deathclaw grumbled. *At least we travel during the day now instead of at night.*

Please listen to him, Justan sent. *Hilt knows tactics as well as anyone.*

It is sound strategy, Deathclaw replied. *But it is tedious. All this hiding and sneaking, just to obtain some flavoring.*

Pepper is poison to trolls, Deathclaw.

I know this, the raptoid replied. *And yet I would rather be with you, scouting ahead.*

I would rather have you here as well, Justan said and smiled. There seemed to be true affection in the raptoid's thoughts. Deathclaw had changed so much in the last five months since they had bonded.

A raptoid is always loyal to its pack, Deathclaw said. He had fallen back into the practice of monitoring Justan's inner thoughts again lately. *Affection is a human emotion that has nothing to do with it.*

Oh, come on, I know you miss Fist, and riding with Gwyrtha, Justan said. *Don't worry, they miss you too. Gwyrtha mentions it at least once a day.*

I . . . Deathclaw paused, unsure how to respond to Justan's teasing.

Don't worry, I'll tell them you miss them, Justan said.

I will speak to you again tomorrow, Deathclaw replied with irritation and his thoughts faded from the bond.

Justan chuckled and sat up. There was no use trying to go back to sleep. It would be daybreak soon. He dressed and strapped on his swords. He was staying with his parents in one of the visitor houses near the front gate. His mother had commandeered it when she first arrived. It was small, with just two bedrooms and a small sitting room with a table and chairs. Darlan had grumbled a few times about its lack of a stove, but the wizards always fed their guests lavishly and likely figured one wasn't necessary.

Justan would have preferred boarding elsewhere. He hadn't been comfortable staying separately from his bonded and especially in a house with his parents. It seemed a step backwards. But Fist was staying with the other Mage School students in the Rune Tower and Gwyrtha was in the stables. Besides, once Darlan made up her mind, there was no changing it.

He slung Ma'am over his shoulder and headed into the sitting room. There were a few apples in a bowl on the small table and as Justan sat down to munch on one, the door to his parent's room opened.

"Morning, son. I'm surprised I didn't have to wake you," Faldon said.

Justan shook his head. "Not when we have a fight ahead of us."

Faldon was dressed for battle, wearing his short sleeved chainmail shirt under a scalemail vest and iron bracers, while the long pommel of his sword, The Monarch, rose from behind his right shoulder. Darlan followed him into the room, wearing rich robes of red and black that Justan had never seen before.

She saw him staring. "These are my war wizard's robes."

"She was wearing those the first time I saw her," Faldon said. He sat in the chair across from Justan and smacked Darlan's rump. "Still just as stunning now as she was then."

Justan smiled. This was the kind of morning banter he remembered as a child when his father was home. "I think you look great, mother."

She did, too. Living at the Mage School seemed to be good for her. Her face was fair and vibrant, her hair shining. If Justan didn't know better, he would think she was ten years younger.

"Why thank you, dear," Darlan said and kissed his cheek. "See, this is why I wanted you to stay with us. Why, I couldn't possibly kiss your cheek with your friends around, now could I?"

"Definitely not." He took a bite from the apple and savored the sweet and complex flavor. That was one benefit from his bond with Deathclaw. Everything tasted so much better. "These apples are almost as good as the apples in the elf homeland. You can almost feel the energy entering your body."

"The Mage School gardens are made of soil from elven homelands, dear," Darlan reminded. "Why else do you think the wizards here live so long?"

"Right." Qyxal had told him that once. Justan wondered if the food was what made his mother look so youthful. If so, his father hadn't had nearly the same benefit.

"Don't eat just that apple, son," Faldon said as he grabbed one for himself. He bit into it. "We have a major battle ahead of us and you'll need all the energy you can get."

"I'll head down to the dining hall, then," Justan said and stood from the seat. "I'll see you in an hour or so."

Justan headed out to find Jhonate. He jogged past the line of tents and tethered horses that belonged to Captain Demetrius' cavalry. She was staying in the guard barracks with the other female warriors, but if he knew her, she would already be up and exercising in the training area.

Justan! Several horses reared as Gwyrtha bounded past them, sliding to a stop at Justan's feet. *Ride!*

Justan scratched behind her horse-like ears. "I'm just going over to see Jhonate," he said, Gesturing to the training area less than a hundred yards away.

But we must ride, Justan.

"I know we haven't had the chance to ride much since we've been here." There were no open spaces to ride in. In truth, they hadn't been able to spend much time together at all. Gwyrtha was finding their stay at the Mage School boring. She spent most of her time with the elves in the Mage School Forest.

"Hey, but we ride today. The big battle, remember?"

We ride and we fight, she agreed happily.

"Right. Why don't you go find Fist and bring him to the dining hall for me?" Justan said, knowing that Fist was already awake. From the direction of the bond, Justan could tell that the ogre was just leaving the Rune Tower. Fist was likely heading for the dining hall anyway, but it would at least give Gwyrtha something to do.

Fist! Come to the food place! Gwyrtha sent.

Okay, Fist replied.

He is coming, she told Justan.

"Good . . . Thank you, Gwyrtha," Justan said and sighed. So much for alone time with Jhonate, "Alright, come with me."

The guards' training area was out behind the barracks and against the wall. The other academy students were just getting up, most of them going about their business tiredly, but as he had expected, Jhonate was in the training yard working with her Jharro staff. Her personal warm up was a dazzling mix of staff work, spear work, and sword work, her staff changing forms as she moved. Despite the hour, she already had a handful of wide-eyed student observers.

Justan and Gwyrtha waited for her to finish and come their way. A short time later, she jogged over to them, a sheen of sweat on her brow. "Good morning, Justan," she said quietly when she knew no one was close enough to hear.

"Good morning," he said and kissed her. It was a short kiss. She had begun to allow a certain amount of affection to be seen in public, but she still kept tight reigns on what was allowed.

Gwyrtha nudged her. *Morning! Ride, Jhonate?*

"She wants to know-." Justan began.

"No, Gwyrtha," Jhonate said. "I do not wish to ride this morning. We are preparing for battle."

I am waiting, Fist said. The ogre had arrived at the dining hall already and was standing in line.

Just a minute, Justan sent. He looked at Jhonate. "Fist is at the dining hall already. Have you eaten?"

"I have not." Jhonate said. "Tell him I need three eggs and some hot porridge."

We'll be there in a minute, Fist. Can you get our food for us? Justan asked.

The ogre let out a frustrated sigh. *Again? They already look at me like I eat too much. When I tell them some of it's for you, they think I'm lying.*

Please? Justan asked.

Fine, the ogre grumped.

Justan told him what they wanted and walked with Jhonate towards the dining hall. Gwyrtha pranced along behind them as they discussed the morning's plans.

"Did your father tell you what the council decided?" Jhonate asked. "I know only that we are still attacking today."

The whole assault had nearly been derailed the night before when an emergency meeting was called. Valtrek's source had told the wizards that Ewzad Vriil had, in essence, declared war on the Mage School after his wedding and coronation. In addition, the source told Valtrek that Mellinda knew about their planned foray from the Mage School. The witch didn't seem to know any details, but she was alerting Ewzad's men to expect something.

"The meeting didn't end until late. Mother said that the arguing was split fairly down the middle. But yeah, it's happening. They decided not to reveal the details of the plan until after we leave in case her spies might overhear them. They don't want to allow Mellinda time to plan for what's coming."

She raised an eyebrow. "Then we are supposed to plan the assault as we go?"

"Sir Lance left with Hugh the Shadow and Oz the Dagger right after the meeting. They're going to find out what kind of last minute preparations Ewzad's men are making. They're supposed to meet us on the road with a plan," Justan said.

"Well, it is less than ideal, but . . . I am glad that we are making some kind of move," she said.

Justan nodded in agreement. The constant waiting had been hard on everyone.

It had taken a month to convince the wizards to move in the first place. Sir Lance's plan for a sortie had met with a lot of resistance. The War Council was worried that the remaining spies within the school would leak word of it and their troops would be heading into a trap. Ewzad and Mellinda could simply be waiting for them to send out half their forces and then attack the school while they were gone.

Sir Lance was adamant that they take control of the war and he was able to convince the leadership of the academy to join his side. If they could break through the barricade crossing the road to Sampo and scatter Ewzad's men, they could gather up additional forces in Sampo and march on to Dremald. Captain Demetrius agreed, assuring them that the Dremald Garrison would switch sides as soon as they showed up.

It was the announced wedding of Ewzad Vriil to Queen Elise that finally convinced the wizards. They couldn't continue to wait while Ewzad did as he wished with the rest of the kingdom. A series of scouting parties had been sent to Sampo to assess the situation. The news was mixed. Ewzad's troops around Sampo now numbered close to ten thousand. The good news so far was that they were still only lightly armored and no monsters had been seen with them. The council set the day of the sortie. They would attack the day after Ewzad's wedding, while his men were still celebrating.

Gwyrtha waited outside the dining hall while Justan and Jhonate went in. Fist was at a table waiting for them, several plates of food piled around him. He was sitting next to Zambon and Willum, both of whom were almost finished eating.

"How did it go, Fist?" Justan asked as they took a seat. He passed Jhonate her plate and grabbed a plate of eggs and porridge for himself. "Did the kitchen workers give you any problems?"

"They were suspicious," Fist said with a frown. He glared over at one of the workers who was eyeing the ogre with a slight scowl. "Especially Chef Richard. He didn't want to give me the extra eggs. He says I eat too many!"

"I don't see how he can say that," Zambon said, glancing at the eight hard boiled eggs on the ogre's plate.

"I know," Fist said with a wide-eyed nod. "But I told him that the extra eggs were for Jhonate and he didn't dare say no."

Jhonate glanced at the chef and gave him a nod of dismissal. The man hurriedly turned his attention back to the food line. She looked at Fist's plate with disapproval. "You must eat more than meat, Fist. Protein alone is not enough. Your body needs grains of some kind for proper fuel."

"Oh," the ogre said. He looked at her plate and his face fell. "I don't like porridge."

"Have some bread then," Justan said and tossed him a roll from a platter on the center of the table. He turned his attention to Zambon. "Hey, I didn't get the chance to talk to you last night. I'm sorry about Elise."

Zambon smiled and shook his head. "I knew there was no chance for us the day I left her at Castle Vriil and went with my father. I realized then that she wasn't anything like the girl I had thought her to be."

"You had a thing for the princess?" Willum asked in surprise.

"She's queen now, I guess," Zambon said, then shrugged. "I was stationed at the palace for awhile and . . . anyway it's a long story."

"He kissed her," Fist said, elbowing Zambon.

"A few times, but like I said, nothing came of it, okay?" Zambon said.

Willum grimaced. "You kissed the woman Ewzad Vriil got pregnant?"

"I didn't know that would happen at the time!" Zambon retorted.

"Consorting with a client? Such behavior rarely comes to anything good," Jhonate remarked absently as she ate.

"Such behavior?" Zambon said. He and Willum looked at each other, then stared back at her. They knew how she and Justan had met each other.

Before either one could say anything, Justan changed the subject, "Are you two joining us today?"

"Yeah. I'm in Lyramoor's company," Willum said. "Sabre Vlad had to stay behind so Lyramoor asked me to come along."

"I'll be joining him," Zambon said, shoving a piece of bacon in his mouth. "I'd be in Riveren's company, but they have to stay and man the walls. You know, since he's Captain of the Guard and all."

Justan nodded in understanding. "What about your

father? Is he coming?"

"No," Zambon said. He chewed slowly. "Father isn't . . . ready to return to battle yet."

"Are his wounds not healed?" Jhonate asked in surprise.

"Physically he's fine," Zambon said. He shrugged. "It's Alfred's suggestion."

"Alfred is concerned that a pitched battle might cause Tolivar to fall back into his rage," Willum explained. He glanced at Zambon. "Tolivar doesn't disagree."

The guard shrugged again.

"What do you think?" Justan asked Willum.

"He still feels . . . unstable sometimes. I think it's a smart move," Willum replied.

"The Howlers don't like it though," Zambon pointed out. "Old Calvin the Red was talking to him about it the other day. Their argument got pretty heated. I think the Howlers feel abandoned by him."

"Why does Calvin the Red not lead them then?" Jhonate asked between bites of porridge. "Was he not the guildmaster before Tolivar?"

"That's what father told him to do," Zambon said, wiping up the last bit of egg yolk from his plate with a crust of bread. "The old man spat on his shoes and stormed out." The guard shoved the bread in his mouth, then pushed back his plate and stood. "I need to go get ready."

"Will you be wearing your father's sword into battle?" Jhonate asked, eyeing the pommel of Meredith sticking up from Zambon's back.

"She's my sword now," the guard replied. He reached up and touched the pommel. "I've renamed her."

"What do you call her?" Justan asked. He hadn't gotten around to naming his own swords yet, something that Lenny liked to give him grief for.

"Efflina," Zambon said.

Fist grasped the guard's shoulder. "That's a good name."

"I'll see you later," Zambon said and headed around the tables to the door.

"I should go too," Willum said.

"We should all go," Jhonate agreed and stood. She

carried her plate and the one that Zambon had left behind to the sinks.

"You ready, Fist?" Justan asked.

The ogre stood, popping the last egg in his mouth. "It will be good to fight again." He had enjoyed his classes so far, but even Fist was getting stir crazy.

"Let's go, then," Justan replied.

Ride now? Gwyrtha asked hopefully from just outside the building.

Yes. Justan said. *We ride.*

Chapter Seventeen

"Yes, sirs?" Justan asked, sliding from Gwyrtha's saddle to stand next to his father. He nodded to his mother and the other leaders. "You needed me?"

They had made it half way down the road to Sampo without any resistance before their scouts had stopped them. Now their entire force, six thousand strong including the wizards accompanying them, was at a standstill.

They were measured out into twelve divisions, each commanded by an academy graduate and each one accompanied by a team of five wizards or mages. As they marched, the leaders had clustered together at the front with the cavalry discussing plans.

Now that they were stopped, the men rested while the wizards maintained a series of wards in a wide area around their forces in case the enemy had placed watchers along the road. So far there hadn't been any surprises. Evidently Mellinda hadn't bothered to bring any forces this close to the school. Still they stayed diligent, watching the area just to make sure.

"Edge, we have a problem," said Hugh the Shadow, his ever-confident grin unwavering. "Vriil's troops have erected barricades reaching from the ravine to the west, across the road, and all the way to the river's edge. They are clustered in companies of thirty, nothing we can't handle really, except that we have no way of knowing how many of them can turn into monsters."

"We understand that you can," said Oz the Dagger.

"Yes, sir," Justan said. "I can make out which ones have been changed by Ewzad. It looks like a bright concentration of spirit magic focused in their stomachs. Anyone with spirit sight can pick them out, sir."

"Who else do we have that can do that?" Darlan asked.

"Anyone that is bonded. Fist, Gwyrtha, and Willum can," Justan said. "Jhonate too, and as far as I know, that's it. The others who have the ability remained behind."

"Only five of us," Captain Demetrius said with a frown. "And four of them in the same division. That will make it hard to avoid surprises."

"Then split us up," Justan said. "As long as one of us accompanies each division that's leading the charge, we could direct you to the problem areas in the enemy ranks. You could put Gwyrtha with the Cavalry and Fist with the Howlers."

Faldon nodded, "That is a sound strategy. Jhonate could stay with my group and Edge could direct the archers-,"

"Sir," Justan said. "If I may make a request, can I be part of an infantry group?" He had been giving it a lot of thought lately. He didn't want to be remembered only as a bowman. He had always wanted to earn his name as a swordsman. He was always relying on his bow in battle. It was his most powerful weapon, after all. But he needed to get to know his swords better and there was only so much he could learn while training. "My swords need some exercise."

Faldon gave him a questioning look at first, but finally nodded in understanding. "I suppose."

"But-," Darlan began, her brow creased in concern.

"Willum, son of Coal could direct the archers," Mad Jon said.

"Edge can fight with my group," said Sir Lance, his gruff voice sounding amused. "His swords will get plenty of exercise with us."

Faldon nodded, avoiding his wife's glare. "We have a consensus then. Let's go."

They split off to their different groups, Justan dispersing instructions to Fist and Gwyrtha through the bond. Jhonate gave him a disappointed glance. She had hoped to fight at his side. But Justan was sure this was the right tactical choice.

"Glad you're with me, Edge," said Sir Lance as they joined his troops. They were two hundred men strong, half of them academy retirees and the other half recent graduates. "We have the best job in the sortie."

"And what is that, Sir Lance?"

"We're leading the charge," the grizzled warrior said with a yellowed smile. "See, usually the cavalry'd do it, but Vriil's men have been busy puttin' up spiked barricades. Our job's to charge in and clear a space for the cavalry."

Justan nodded. "So when you say 'the best job', what you mean is 'the most dangerous'."

"You got it," Lance said, slapping Justan on the back.

"We'll have archers and wizards providing cover fire then?" Justan said.

"Exactly! They'll be tryin' to steal our fun!" Lance laughed and Justan realized he had never seen the man this jovial. It was kind of unnerving. The warrior turned to his men and raised his arms. "Right, boys?"

The men shouted in agreement, raising their weapons. Justan wondered if they knew what they were cheering about.

The signal was given and they started their march. Sir Lance jogged around within the group as they went, talking to the men, sometimes laughing loudly. The men grinned when he was around.

Justan was impressed. He hadn't known Sir Lance was such a natural leader. He listened close to what Lance was saying to the men and realized it wasn't much different from the things he had said to Justan. Lance bragged how dangerous their job was and, it seemed crazy, but the men lapped it up. Perhaps they did know what they were cheering about after all.

Justan waited for Lance to make his way back to him and asked the man, "Why are you so happy? When you were leading the Sampo refugees, you were always in a foul mood?"

"Was I?" Lance asked. He chuckled. "I suppose I was. The thing is, Edge, there's a difference between leading a group of warriors into battle and trying to protect thousands of families that can't fight. It's a whole different level of responsibility." He sighed. "I never wanted that. But this!" He waved his arm at the marching men. "This is what I'm made to do. Put me with a group of fightin' men and together we can raze mountains. As for today? In my time, I've led men against giants, trolls, basilisks. Hell, even a merfolk invasion. Ewzad Vriil's men?

Pissants!"

"Pissants, sir?" Justan said, unfamiliar with the term.

"Pissants! Right boys?" The men shouted in agreement and Lance laughed. "Tell me, Edge, what's the easiest way to get an ant off your boot?"

"You could flick it off, I suppose," Justan replied.

"Sure, if you want to bother bending over," Lance said with a smile and ran on down the line, sharing Justan's ignorance with the other men.

They marched on for another hour before a halt was called. Then Captain Demetrius rode over to them. "The blockade is just ahead. They've picked a good site, too. The enemy will see you coming a hundred yards before you can hit them," the captain said.

Lance laughed. "Good. We've got 'em where we want 'em!"

"We'll be right behind you. As soon as you get the barricades clear, we'll charge on through," Demetrius said. He glanced at Justan, nodded, and rode back to his men.

Ready to fight? Gwyrtha asked excitedly from her place at the front of the cavalry.

We are, Justan replied and included Fist in his next thought. *You two don't worry about me. In this battle you help the people you're with. They'll need you to guide them to the men with Ewzad's power in them.*

I can smell it already, Gwyrtha said in disgust. Justan breathed, focusing on the smells around him, but all he could smell was the cavalry's horses and the sweat of the men around him. He coughed and grimaced. His enhanced senses weren't always a blessing.

We know what to do, Justan, Fist said, then added in irritation. *These men, the Howlers? Fighting with them reminds me of fighting with ogres.*

Justan smiled. *That's why I recommended you.*

Thanks, Fist replied.

Lance unsheathed his enormous sword, raised it into the air, and the men began to jog to the front of the line. The men were eager. Sir Lance's enthusiasm had spread. Justan found his heart pumping with excitement as well.

He smiled. Finally he was doing more than walking around the Mage School. The entire month he'd been searching for moonrat eyes and he was the only one that had been unsuccessful. Vannya and Locksher found two spies, both of them young students. Willum had found two among the food workers by himself. Even Fist and Gwyrtha had found someone, the most crucial catch actually; a wizardess named Sprauna, who taught Fist's earth magic class.

Justan had looked into suspects, of course. He had been sure Pympol was a spy, considering how close the ex-mage had been to Arcon and his part in the creation of the plant golem. But he'd followed the mage, had Gwyrtha smell him out, and he'd come up clean. No, looking for spies had not been the kind of action Justan needed. This was what he needed; the chance to make a direct impact on Ewzad's forces.

The infantry jogged up an incline and, as they crested the top, their goal came into view. The road had been clogged by barricades, heavy logs supporting sharpened stakes angled upwards to pierce the chests of charging horses. Behind the barricades stood ranks of scruffy men, looking much like those Justan had faced when helping Lenny free his people. The difference was these men were alert and ready for battle. Their archers already had arrows notched.

Sir Lance signaled for a charge and the men began to run. Justan switched to spirit sight. His excitement turned to concern. He had expected a few of Ewzad's changed men scattered through the ranks, but the entire line glowed with the wispy white of spirit magic.

"Sir Lance!" Justan called. "It's all of them! All of them have Ewzad's power inside!"

"That's good to know," Lance said but he didn't slow. He swung his sword above his head and a cloud of arrows arched over their heads from the troop of archers somewhere behind them. "Run at 'em, men!"

The academy archers were far superior to the scruffy men in both training and skill. Their arrows struck before Ewzad's forces even fired. Many of Ewzad's men fell. Others started to change, their forms swelling and distending.

Then the wizards got involved. Lightning struck among

the enemy ranks, knocking dozens down at a time, followed by fireballs that exploded in their midst, sending bodies flying. Smoke rose from the barricades, partially obscuring large bulking shapes that rose from among the fallen men.

Justan's chest was pounding. He drew his swords and was relieved when the calm of his left sword took over, clearing his mind. His right sword buzzed with energy, eager to release the emotions it had been storing since Justan arrived at the school.

The world slowed around him and Justan saw everything clearly. A barricade loomed in front of him and Justan didn't slow his charge. He swung his right sword and the moment his blade touched wood, he released the power stored within. The barricade exploded outwards, pelting the mutating men beyond in a shower of pointed stakes and splinters.

Justan ran among the enemy, knowing he was now leading the charge.

A large green-skinned monster was his first target. Its torso was bulging and misshapen, its arms hanging low to the ground with fists like knotted roots. Its body had been punctured in multiple places by shards of wood.

Justan stabbed deep into its leg with his left sword, absorbing its pain and confusion. Then he spun and sliced into its hip with his right sword and released its pain back at it in an explosion that tore it nearly in half.

He turned and, out of the corner of his eye, saw Sir Lance shear the arm off a wolf-like beast. The rest of the men were pouring through the breach in the barricade Justan had created. Many of them set to work clearing more barricades to the side.

A tall spindly beast with a trunk-like torso and insectile limbs swung a spiked arm at him. Justan arched his back and let the arm pass mere inches above his face, then sliced his left sword into the joint at its knee. Its emotions flooded into the sword and Justan had a brief moment of understanding. These men of Ewzad's were frightened by the changes inside them. This one hadn't known what the wizard's power would do to him.

Justan's blade sheared through the joint and the beast fell. Justan left it there for the others to deal with and sought out

211

another. A beast with the body of a lizard and head that seemed to be a mass of teeth with eyes darted out of the smoke towards him. This one moved fast.

Justan focused and time slowed even further for him. The beast wasn't so fast anymore. He thrust his left sword forward towards its eye and let the beast run right into his blade. He had another flash of insight. This one had known what Ewzad's power inside it could do. It had transformed once before and embraced the feeling that came when its body changed. These thoughts flickered through Justan's mind for mere fractions of a second before the tip of his sword passed through its eye socket and into the brain beyond.

Justan spun and pulled the sword out of its head as he watched the oncoming charge of a truly enormous monster. It was three times Justan's height and shaped like a centaur. It had four trunk-like legs and a lower body covered in thick gray folds of skin, its upper body was that of a giant with a lumpy half-melted head.

It reached down for him. Justan dodged its grasping fingers and swung his right sword into the beast's front leg. The resulting blast blew off its foot and the monster reared back, its ragged stump spewing blood. Justan ran under it and thrust his left sword into its underbelly. He absorbed its pain and rage as he ran forward, slicing along, letting its insides fall to the ground behind him.

Justan fell into a rhythm, absorbing emotion with his left sword and expelling it with his right. The mutated monsters could not move fast enough to hurt him and their grotesque nature held no fear for him. He understood them now.

He moved faster as his confidence built, his senses enhanced to their utmost. He could see every detail of the enemy around him, hear the sounds of the battle, and pick out where each sound came from. He could feel the weight of his swords change as they passed through different types of flesh. He realized that he wasn't tired. He didn't even need to draw energy from Gwyrtha.

His eyes shifted. Lines of white energy mixed with blue and gold had sprung out in every direction, connecting him to each monster. This was very much like the armed combat test in the academy arena nearly two years ago. He didn't understand how he was doing it, but he was pulling energy from the crowd around him.

His sword's names came to him then. It should have been obvious a long time ago. Their names were in their natures. His left sword was Peace, his right sword Rage, and when he held them, Justan was a whirling mix of both. The enemy fell around him like they were nothing, some glassy eyed and confused, others blown to pieces. He was might and magic, calm and action; he was Edge and he was unbeatable.

Justan! came Gwyrtha's frightened voice.

Justan! shouted Fist.

A centipede-like monster with human arms instead of legs rose before Justan. Rage blew off its head and Justan ran along its back as it melted. *What?*

You're out there alone, Fist said. Justan got the sense that the ogre was in a pitched fight of his own and that his berserker unit was losing.

Justan glanced back over his shoulder in their direction. He could see nothing but the hulking forms of other monsters. Somehow he had lost track of the others. Where was the rest of his unit?

I'm coming back, Justan sent. He dodged a monster's spear-like appendage and ran back the way he had come, following the trail of melting bodies. *Gwyrtha stay with the cavalry. Don't come for me!*

Mutated beasts were in his way, their backs turned to him as they pushed to reach the front lines. Justan cut them down from behind, slicing out hamstrings and blowing legs off entirely. They crumpled around him, howling in pain. Justan sucked that pain away with Peace and silenced them with Rage.

The monsters edged away in confusion at being attacked from behind and Justan finally broke through. The situation was more dire than he had expected. The academy's troops had been pushed back. Monsters had surged forward and a pitched battle was being fought in front of the barricades.

How had it happened? The situation had seemed well in hand. He looked up and saw lightning strikes and fireballs exploding in the air high above them. The wizard's spells were being deflected somehow. Justan shifted to mage sight and saw the problem. Somehow the enemy had erected a bubble-like shield to repulse the spells. He looked down the line of battle and saw nothing that could be causing it.

Fist, there is a shield deflecting the spells! he sent.

Justan swung Rage and blasted a slimy beast that seemed to be leaking some sort of acid from holes all over its body. Parts of it spattered the other creatures beyond it, causing them to howl in pain and stagger backwards. The men surged forward.

I see it, the ogre replied and Justan could tell that the berserkers were locked in a losing battle of their own. *The wizards know it's there. It blocks arrows too.*

Justan cursed under his breath and ran back to join his unit. The men had been routed. They must have lost half their force. Bodies lay everywhere and only a small number were holding the beasts back.

"Rally to me!" Justan said as he cut a tall stork-like beast's legs out from under it and it crashed to the ground, tripping up a scaled monstrosity with a single eye instead of a head. Justan splattered the eye with Rage.

"Rally to me!" he said again, and the men responded, stumbling in his direction, many of them dragging wounded comrades. He could see right away that they were in no shape to continue. "Fall back! Take the wounded to the wizards!"

"But the order hasn't been given?" one man complained.

"I'm giving it now. Once the wounded are out of the way, you can come back and fight!"

"Yes, sir," the man said.

Gwyrtha, where's the cavalry? he asked.

Fighting, she replied. He sensed that she was covered in small wounds and her mouth was full of the blood of Ewzad's mutated men. *Lots dead.*

Justan turned to see that three warriors from his unit had refused his orders and were standing near him, swords in hand. They were all recent academy graduates, young and unafraid. He recognized one of them as Kathy the Plate, the assistant to Stout Harley. Her plate armor was distinctive, glowing blue to his Mage Sight.

"They have enough men to carry the wounded back

without us. We can still fight," she said. Justan didn't bother to argue. They were defense guild. They were tough.

"Where is Sir Lance?" he asked her.

"He went in after you," Kathy said.

Justan shook his head. "The old man better not die on my account. I'm going after him," He ran back towards the gap in the barricade where he had last seen Sir Lance. "You should remain behind."

"We're with you!" Kathy replied and charged after him.

Mutated monsters stood in the gap, keeping the army from busting through. There seemed to be a momentary lapse in the fighting at this area. Infantrymen stood several paces back from the barricade breathing heavily, while the monsters stayed behind the protective bubble barrier, safe from spells and arrows.

Justan shoved past the men and rushed the beasts. He slashed about him with his swords, catching them off guard. He slew four of them before they fought back.

Kathy was right behind him. Her axe seemed unnaturally sharp, its blade gleaming a dull black, and she wielded it like a hammer, smashing and slashing her enemy at the same time.

Justan soon saw Sir Lance's trail, a line of smoking monsters, each one smote cleanly in pieces, leading off in a different direction than his own. He followed the trail with his three companions in tow, felling any hideous creatures in their way.

Finally, the grizzled old warrior came into view. "Sir Lance!" Justan cried.

Lance fought proudly, surrounded by wary monsters, his white hair matted with blood as he swung his huge sword with one hand. Smoking hulks littered the ground around him, the other beasts slipping in the remains of their brethren as they attempted to reach him.

Lance turned to face him and Justan saw that his face was very pale. The named warrior's left arm was gone, ripped off at the shoulder.

"What're you doin' here?" Lance shouted, his lip curling in anger. "Retreat, you idiots!"

They're calling retreat, Fist said. *Come!*

Come back! Gwyrtha said, and Justan knew she was

coming after him.

"Come with us!" Justan said.

"Missing an arm?" Lance cocked his head at Justan. "Why, boy? I'm dead." As if in confirmation, a huge hairy giant swung a heavy fist, crumpling the named warrior to the ground.

"What do we do?" Kathy asked.

"Do as he said," Justan replied. "Retreat! Re-!"

Justan felt a strange pain in his chest. He looked down and saw the fletching of an arrow sticking out from the center of his chest. Standing between the monsters was a single archer fumbling for another arrow.

In disbelief Justan said, both aloud and through the bond, "*I've been hit.*"

Justan! Gwyrtha and Fist cried out at once.

Justan shivered. He felt the hands of two of his companions grasp his shoulders and pull him away. The monsters crowded in and Kathy the Plate ran forward, fighting them off with wide swipes of her axe.

One grabbed for her with arms made of stone, but it was no match for her axe and she left it with stubs. Another one, a squat beast, thick but no taller than a man, shot spikes at her from a cannon of a mouth. The spikes struck hard, staggering her, but bounced away unable to penetrate her armor.

"Wait," Justan said numbly. He felt cold and his vision was going blue, no, blue and gold. His breath frosted in the air. "Wait!" he shouted.

He looked down at his chest and saw that the shaft of the arrow had been encased by a shard of ice. It was then he knew that the arrow had pierced the center of the frost rune. He reached through the bond. The blockage between him and the Scralag was gone. Icy cold poured through the bond. He could feel the Scralag's pain and anguish. Icy power built within his body.

"Let go of me!" He shouted at the men dragging him. Peace had stopped draining his emotions and his panic spun out of control. The icy power within him built until a torrent of frost, like frozen fog, spewed from his wounded chest. The men let go and backed away. "Kathy, run! Get out of here!

He pointed Peace at one of the beasts assaulting her. A

great lance of ice shot from the tip of the sword and skewered the beast. Kathy turned and looked at him in surprise. Instinctively, he fired another lance of ice over her head, piercing another beast that had drawn too close.

"Go!" he shouted. "Don't let the magic touch you!"

The frost spewing from his chest became a white torrent of ice, like a living river. The magic flowed across the ground and every beast that touched it froze in place. Justan stumbled backwards and swiped with Rage, shooting a similar torrent of white ice from the blade. A wall of ice sprang up from the ground where the magic landed, freezing beasts mid-stride.

We're here, Justan! came Fist's voice.

"No! No, stay back. It's too dangerous! *The Scralag is coming!*"

More of Ewzad's mutated men charged around the barrier of ice towards him. Justan slashed with his swords, sending waves of ice crashing into them. The creatures froze and burst to pieces.

Justan felt one of Fist's strong hands grab him by the sword sheathes on his back. He was lifted off the ground and they began to move away from the beasts, but Justan sent blasts of frost towards them anyway, sending towers of ice springing from the ground behind him.

Absently he wondered why Fist was holding him so high off the ground. Why was he moving so fast? White ice poured from his chest as they moved, freezing a swath of the road, causing men to dodge or be frozen themselves. Justan knew he was losing control.

Where was the Scralag? Was it still coming, or was it dead? Was this his magic unleashed like Professor Been had been hoping?

He was placing men in danger, but there was nothing he could do. Random blasts of ice shot from his blades, springing up into high crystalline walls wherever they struck the ground. Men screamed. He tried to drop his swords, but he couldn't move his hands.

Fist, he sent. His vision was beginning to fade, the blue and gold giving way to blackness. *Fist, put me down. I'm hurting people. I might . . . hurt you.*

No, Fist said.

I'm sorry . . . blackness consumed his vision. *I'm sorry* . . . then he felt nothing; no cold, no sensation of movement. Maybe Peace was working now. Maybe he had simply frozen over. Maybe . . . maybe the arrow had killed him.

Faintly he thought he heard voices. They could have been Fist and Gwyrtha or maybe even Deathclaw, but they were too quiet. Then the voices faded altogether.

I'm sorry . . .

Chapter Eighteen

Talon prowled through an endless field of soft purple flowers that gave off a pleasant scent. Boring flowers. The sky was blue and clear spotted with small puffy white clouds. It was a boring sky.

She hungered, but there was no prey. Just insects; fat worms which popped satisfyingly in her mouth but had no flavor; plump bees that tried to sting her but could not pierce her scales with their little stingers; and butterflies. The air was full of pretty pink and yellow butterflies that had a dusty texture and taste. Boring butterflies.

It was a boring place altogether. A hateful place.

Talon tore apart the flowers. She ate the grubs, squished the bees. But it was idle fun and unsatisfying. The sun still sparkled cheerfully and the petals of the flowers were still pretty even if they were shredded and scattered about. The butterflies ignored her, flitting from place to place even though the flowers were destroyed.

Talon took out her irritation on the butterflies next. They were a bit more erratic in their flight than the bees, zig-zagging and bobbing in seemingly random patterns. It was challenging in the beginning until she got the hang of it. But then she engaged in pure butterfly slaughter. Knocking them out of the sky, catching them and tearing off their wings.

Then the fun of butterfly killing began to fade. They had no voices to scream with. They died so easily. Looking around her, Talon realized that very few butterflies were left. Soon they would be gone. One of them floated towards her and landed on her finger. She reached with her other hand to crush it, but stopped.

The grubs were gone, the bees. There were no other animals, nothing but the sky and miles of broken plants. If the butterflies that were left died, she would be alone. She released the butterfly and followed it. The small number of butterflies flew together lazily in the fading sun and Talon walked behind them, not wanting them to fade out of sight.

Then one of the butterflies fell, clumsily fluttering out of the sky. Talon found it and picked it up. It was dead. Another one fell, silently dying, and another. Talon grew worried. Their numbers were decreasing. She hadn't done anything. Why were they dying?

More butterflies fell dead from the sky until there were only a handful left. Talon finally realized why. The butterflies drank from the flowers and the flowers were all gone. She had destroyed them. Talon scooped up armfuls of flower petals and rushed after the remaining butterflies, urging them to eat. But the butterflies continued to bob about, ignoring her, dropping one by one.

The sky darkened as the cheery sun sank until there was only a red haze on the horizon and soon only one was left. Talon gently plucked the last butterfly from the air and held it close, trying to get it to eat the shredded remains of flowers. The tiny thing's wings beat slower and slower and then as the light faded from the sky, it stopped moving.

Talon was alone. No stars shone in the sky. There were no sounds but the soft rustle of a breeze. Then the wind stopped. Talon shivered.

"Talon!" said a raspy voice. "Talon!"

Talon opened her eyes. She was laying on luxuriant softness. She was on the broken remains of the mayor's bed. She'd been sleeping on the feather mattress. She had destroyed the rest of the room, peeling bright paper from the walls, breaking the furniture to pieces. But the mattress, it had felt too good to destroy.

"Talon? Mistress Talon?" Durza said.

Talon hissed and lashed out with her tail, missing the gorc's face by inches. Durza took a few hesitant steps back. She was wearing a different dress today, this one blue with short sleeves. And she had a wig on her head, with long curly dark hair.

Talon hissed at the gorc again. Was that dream Durza's doing? "You did thiss? Givess me thiss dream?"

"Dream? N-no, I-I I'm sorry. I waked you up, Mistress Talon. You was sleepin' a long time," the gorc babbled.

Talon scowled. Why had it been so hard for her to wake from that awful dream? The slightest sound or movement should have done it. Her instincts were honed. The moonrat mother was surely looking for her. Why had she continued to sleep?

Maybe it was the stupid feather mattress. She tore at it and tufts of downy feathers spilled out. "No!" she said, instantly regretting it.

"I-I can fix it Mistress Talon," Durza held out a jar of those spicy sausages Talon liked. "I brought you some foods to eat."

In the two weeks Talon had been there, she had eaten most of the sausages. There were only a few left. Talon had nearly killed the gorc the day before when she had found out Durza had been hiding some of the jars away. Durza was trying to save them so they wouldn't be all gone, or so she said.

The gorc was a nuisance. Talking all the time, complaining when Talon broke things and then cleaning up after her. Talon ordered her not to clean up the broken things. She liked broken things. But Durza would wait until Talon left the room and clean it anyway. Then there was her habit of calling Talon 'Mistress'. Talon hated that.

"Why did you wakess me?" Talon asked.

"Th-there's sonethin' outside wants to come in," Durza said hesitantly. "I-I been usin' my witchy-witch magic to make it stay away, but it keeps sniffing 'round."

"Doess it?" Talon asked. She darted to the window and peered into the street below. "I seess nothing."

"It's on the other side of the house," Durza said. "By the kitchen place."

"What iss it?"

"I don't knows. It feels like . . . like you, Mistress Talon," Durza said.

"Like me?" Talon smiled. Could it be Deathclaw? Had he found her?

"Yes, its brain feels like you. It wonders why it don't want to come inside this place."

Talon's smile faltered. If it was Deathclaw, he could be a nuisance. If he found his way inside the house, Talon would have to fight him again. That would be fun but she could no longer stay in the house. The house was her hiding place. Without it, the moonrat mother would find her.

"I go," Talon said. She would lead Deathclaw away. Lead him far into the forest. "I will be gone for some dayss. Then I will come back."

"Really? You must go?" The gorc looked heartbroken. "Don't leave me, Mistress Talon."

"I am not Misstress!" she hissed.

"Can't you just kills it and come right back?" Durza pleaded.

"No," she said. Not this time she couldn't. Deathclaw was not to die. "I will comes back. Wait here."

Talon crept down the stairs and peered out the window by the front door. She thought she saw movement in the street. She moved through the sitting room and the dining room into the kitchen and looked out the narrow crack between the door and jam.

Durza crept up behind her. At least she was good at being quiet. The gorc leaned towards Talon and whispered. "It's in the house crossed the street. It smells somethin' there, I think."

Talon knew what Deathclaw smelled. It was her. She had been careless and let herself bleed on the floor in that house when she had cut herself out of boredom one day.

She raised the bar on the door and slipped outside, nodding in satisfaction when she heard Durza bar the door behind her. That wouldn't keep Deathclaw out, but it could help if anything else came while Talon was gone.

Talon crept along the street in the opposite direction of the house Deathclaw was in, releasing the pheromones that would mask her scent. She couldn't let him find her too close to the house. He might come back if he thought she would return there. She paused at the city gates and turned off the pheromones. She urinated to be sure he would smell her, then chirped. It was a teasing command, one they used as small ones in the desert sands. It meant follow me. She heard a crash from within the walls and knew he had heard her.

Talon darted into the forest, staying west of the road, away from the places thickest with moonrats. It was mid-day and unlikely they would be hunting, but it never hurt to be cautious. She left her tracks visible, knowing it might make him suspicious, but also knowing he would follow anyway. After an hour of running, she paused and waited to see if he had.

She listened intently for the slightest rustle of leaves. If he was as eager to chase her as he usually was, he wouldn't bother to stay silent just yet. Five minutes passed by and there was nothing. Was it possible he had lost her trail? Surely he wasn't that inept.

A moonrat moan echoed through the forest. Talon turned and sniffed the air. The sound had come from the south of her. Another moan echoed out, this one to the west. Those were hunting calls. Moonrats didn't hunt during the day.

She heard the rustle of leaves a moment later. Finally he was coming. She climbed the nearest tree. It was tall, with thick branches. A good place to hide in. She would pounce on him when he arrived.

She waited and another moonrat moaned, joined by several more. These were also to the south, but closer now. She must make this fight with her brother quick. She would defeat him, then run to the east towards the road, then double back with her pheromones active, leading him to think she was hiding in the moonrat mother's lair. These moonrats would make things even better. They would give him a merry fight, giving her more time to sneak away.

Finally his steps approached her tree. Talon tensed up in anticipation. More moonrats called out. To the east and west, but this did not matter. Deathclaw was here, except . . . The creature that walked under her tree was not her brother.

For a moment she had no idea what it was. It was female, with a shape similar to hers and a long tail with a barbed tip. But it had a full head of hair like a human. Long flowing red hair. Then she understood. This was a raptoid. A new raptoid. Ewwie had been busy.

It looked up at her and Talon saw that it had lips just like she did as well. But its skin was not the same grayish green. This creature's skin was a bluish green unlike any raptoid Talon had ever seen.

"Talon," it said. "You are Talon?"

She dropped from the branch and landed on the ground before the thing. She peered up at it with a questioning chirp. "Yess. And what are you, thing?"

"I am Clara," it said. "I am a raptoid. King Ewzad sent me to get you. You must come home."

"Ewwie ssent you?" Talon's laugh was a throaty hiss. "No. The moonrat mother ssendss you."

Clara cocked her head. "The Mistress follows King Ewzad."

"Sshe doess not," Talon spat. "You know this, Clara thing. Sshe hatess Ewwie. Sshe betrayss Ewwie."

"She did not send me," Clara said, Ewwie had given her thick eyebrows and she raised them earnestly as she spoke. "King Ewzad misses you. King Ewzad loves you. He says come home."

Talon stood to her full height. She noted with satisfaction that she was slightly taller than this new raptoid. "You lie. The moonrat mother ssendss you."

"Why do you say this?" Clara asked, and by the way the color of her face deepened, Talon knew she was angry.

"Your eyess," Talon said.

It blinked at her with eyes an azure blue. "They are gnomes eyes. King Ewzad gave them to me."

"Not those eyess," Talon pointed a long finger at the orange eye embedded in the center of Clara's forehead. "That one."

"The Mistress guides me. Tells me King Ewzad's words," Clara said with an angry hiss.

Talon slid up to her and reached out to cup Clara's jaw. "Sshe hurtss you, yess?" She traced Clara's lips with one taloned finger. "But not like Ewwie. Her hurtss make you obey. Her hurtss are not fun."

Clara slapped her hand away. "You will come with me. King Ewzad wants you home. He has work for you."

"I will not have one of her eyess in me," Talon said

stepping closer, moving her body sensuously in the way that Ewwie had shown her, the way that would unnerve her prey.

Clara leaned forward and whispered into Talon's ear, her voice sounding like the moonrat mother's. *"You will have no choice. You will be mine, Talon."*

Moonrat moans echoed again, this time from every direction. Talon stepped back and hissed. She crouched in attack posture, tail curved, claws extended. Moonrats streamed in from the forest all around her. Their green eyes gleamed even in the dappled sunlight. Talon could feel the weight of the moonrat mother's mind upon her.

She heard the female voice in her mind and Clara's lips mouthed every word. *"You will come to me, Talon. Your precious Ewwie has given you to me. I will reign you in and if you are obedient, I will place you in charge of these new raptoids."*

"No. You will not," Talon hissed.

"Then you will be punished."

Talon felt it then, the sensation she dreaded more than anything else. A numbness crept in on her, starting from her fingertips and toes and creeping up her body.

"No!" Talon screamed. She clawed out the eyes of the moonrat closest to her.

"Stop now," the female voice commanded. Clara took a threatening step forward and the numbness continued to spread.

"No!" Talon stabbed another moonrat with her tail, piercing its heart.

"Stop it!"

Talon threw herself at the moonrats, killing another, then another.

"Stop!" Clara collided with her, taking Talon to the ground, her long claws piercing Talon's flesh. Clara rolled to the top, pinning Talon's legs with her knees and grasped Talon's wrists in her claws. *"You will ob*ey."

Talon barely felt the pain. The numbness spread further. Her vision weakened. She would not let this happen! She whipped her tail about and pierced Clara's lower back near the base of her spine with her hollowed barb. She pumped Ewwie's poison in to the raptoid's body. "Die."

Clara hissed and trembled, then rolled off of Talon and stood on her feet. The raptoid's breathing was labored. "King . . . Ewzad thought you might do this. He has made me . . . strong against the death . . . whisper poison."

"That much poisonss?" Talon asked. Ewwie had made her poison gland very large. Even if the strength of the poison was somewhat diluted, the amount she had used was the equivalent of a hundred death whisper stings.

"I . . . am . . . strong!" Clara insisted.

Talon leapt at her, claws extended. But Clara was fast. The raptoid moved aside before Talon could reach her. Clara lashed out, her claws scoring deep gashes in Talon's side.

This was a pain Talon felt and she gurgled in pleasure at it. "Thank you, Ugly Clara."

"You . . . thank me?" The raptoid was still breathing heavy. She frowned and cocked her head. "Ugly?"

"Your ugly hairs," Talon taunted. She began circling Clara, struggling to fight off the encroaching numbness. "Your ugly colors. Your ugly orange eye! You are ugly as the moonrat mother!"

Clara screeched in rage. She darted forward, quicker than Talon had anticipated. Clara dove for the ground and rolled, whipping her tail forward. Her tail barb slashed diagonally across Talon's chest, scoring down to the bone.

"You . . . are the ugly one!" Clara hissed. "Bald! Gray!"

Talon gurgled a laugh. The wound hurt. She focused on the pain. Her vision cleared. She began circling Clara again, ignoring the spurts of blood that poured down her belly.

The moonrats smelled the blood. Despite the mother of the moonrat's tight reign on them, some of them began feeding on their dead. One came too close to Talon's legs and she stabbed out with her tail, piercing its green eye and into its brain.

"Talon is beauty. Clara is ugly!" Talon said, readying herself for another attack. Clara hissed but did not charge this time. The raptoid's legs were shaking. Talon blinked, thinking of another taunt she could say. Then an idea came to her. Something Ewwie had said. Something the moonrat mother did not like. Talon smiled. "Mellinda." Clara tensed up. "Mellinda is ugly!"

Clara screeched and charged again. She dove forward in her rolling attack again, but this time Talon was ready for her speed. Talon caught Clara's tail in her left hand and when the raptoid tried to roll to her feet, Talon slashed out with her right hand. Her claws raked Clara's face, tearing her lips and splitting the orange eye on her forehead.

Clara screeched and thrashed on the ground, clutching her head. Talon's numbness faded and she shuddered, enjoying the return of sensation to her limbs. The moonrats growled and began to back away.

"Mistress! I can't hear you!" Clara hissed.

Talon frowned at her. Was this raptoid broken too? "You are free from your misstress, Ugly Clara. You will kill these moonratss with me?"

Clara stopped her writhing and climbed to all fours. She glared at Talon with her wounded face and hissed, her tail swaying back and forth. "You will come back. The Mistress wants it! King Ewzad wants it!"

"No! I lovess Ewwie, but I hatess your misstress!" Talon declared.

Clara sprang at her. Talon let her come. She grasped Clara's reaching hands and fell backwards, bringing her knees up to her chest. Clara came down on top of her, biting into Talon's neck.

Talon kicked out, digging the claws on her feet deep into Clara's abdomen, tearing through scales and muscle. Talon shoved her to the side, enjoying the way the raptoid's teeth tore her throat. Clara tried to stand, but the poison had weakened her and her insides were pushing through the tears in her belly. She clutched at her stomach, trying to hold them in.

"Would you comess with me, Ugly Clara?" Talon rasped, her torn throat making it hard to speak. "We will come to Ewwie when the moonrat mother is dead."

Clara glared. "No."

Talon thrust out with her tail, piercing up through the soft underside of Clara's jaw and the roof of her mouth. Talon squeezed her remaining poison into the raptoid's brain. Clara went still.

Talon turned to the moonrats, who had watched the

exchange without comment. She could feel her wounds closing already, and enjoyed the itching sensation of her flesh knitting together.

"*I will have you,*" the female voice said.

Talon licked her lips. She could not return to Durza. The moonrat mother would find her there now and both of them would be captured. There was only one thing left for her to do.

"I will killss you, Ugly Mellinda," she promised with a gurgling giggle. "Then I will returnss to Ewwie."

"*Come then, foolish thing,*" Mellinda replied. The moonrats turned and slunk deeper into the forest.

Talon smiled. Then she set about removing Clara's head just to be sure she stayed dead.

Chapter Nineteen

Hilt put his arm around his wife's shoulders. "I'm sorry."

Beth stood at the gate of Pinewood. She looked inside the walls, one hand raised to her mouth, her brow furrowed. "I-I knew what I would find, dear. It's just strange. I expected more . . . destruction."

Deathclaw looked inside the gates and saw what she meant. The glass in most of the buildings was broken. There was clothing and odd garbage in the streets, but the town was more or less intact. It just felt empty. Suddenly a scent wafted to him.

Deathclaw's heart raced. He ran to the edge of the open gates and crouched down, sniffing the metal hinge at the bottom. "Talon was here!"

"Here?" Charz turned around as if expecting to find her on his back.

"Do you smell her?" Hilt asked, though his attention was still focused on his wife.

"She . . ." Deathclaw tried to think of a word he could pronounce. Not peed. "Watered here."

"She drank something?" Charz asked. "You can smell that?"

"She . . ." Deathclaw mimed squatting and gestured.

"Ohh," Charz said.

Now Deathclaw was glad he had stayed. He had nearly left his companions several times since Justan's thoughts had suddenly disappeared from the bond three days prior. The only reason he knew Justan wasn't dead was the dull certainty remaining that he was somewhere to the south and west where the Mage School was. Charz had communicated with Alfred and found out that Justan was injured, but alive. Beth's assurances that Justan was in the care of the best healers in the known lands had been of little comfort.

Deathclaw looked around for sign of Talon's trail. The urine was over a day old. Why hadn't Talon bothered to hide her scent? Did she know he was here? Did she want him to find it?

"Is there anyone alive in there?" Charz asked. "Can you tell with your magic?"

Beth shook her head. "I can't feel any . . . any . . . wait!" Her eyes widened. "Get your swords ready."

Hilt drew his weapons and took one step in front of her. Deathclaw drew Star. He could feel an odd pain when the star emblem on her grip touched the star-shaped scar still embedded in his palm.

"Is it Talon?" Deathclaw asked.

"I don't think so," Beth said. "But I felt a hostile resistance to my magic just now. I reached out to hide us from Mellinda's eyes and I contacted another magic that was trying to do the same thing."

"Are you saying there's another witch? Here?" Hilt asked.

"That's how it feels," Beth said. "When our magics touched, it recoiled, then it sent threatening images at me."

"Ain't scared of witches," Charz said as he walked through the gates. "Where should I go?"

"I'm feeling that out," Beth said. She had her eyes closed and one hand was held out, reaching towards the town. "I think . . ." She blinked her eyes open. "I think it's coming from the center of town."

They stepped cautiously through the gates and down the main road. The streets were criss-crossed with the footprints of humans and moonrats pressed deep into the dry dirt. It had been muddy the night Pinewood was attacked and whatever rain had fallen since then hadn't fallen hard enough to destroy the signs of the battle. From the way the various moonrats and occasional troll tracks were overlaid on top of the human tracks, Deathclaw knew that the monsters had roamed around the place for a while after the humans left.

"It's strange that Mellinda has abandoned this place," Hilt said, examining the same tracks. "You would think that a town this size could be of use to someone building an army. The buildings are already here. It's defendable. It would be perfect for a supply outpost, or prisoner camp, or troll farm."

"Or trap," Charz said, bending over to pick something up off the street. It was a child's dress. It had been blue once before being muddied and trampled. "Enemy could charge in at any moment."

"No," said Beth. She stopped in front of a large two story house, her hand on her chin as she stared up at it. "There are no enemies for at least half a mile in any direction."

"Huh," said the giant. He stood there with the filthy blue dress in his hand, looking around for a place to put it down. For some reason he didn't seem willing to toss it back in the mud. "So not a trap."

"Not unless the trap is in here," she said gesturing to the building in front of her. "This is the mayor's house. It's also the meeting hall and the town storage. Does it feel strange to you?"

Deathclaw glanced at the building. It looked in remarkably good repair compared to the others. There were a few broken windows on the upper story, yet the doors and windows on the lower level were undamaged and curtains drawn so that he couldn't see inside. He cocked his head. "It's nothing."

"Yeah, forget that place," said Charz.

Hilt was staring at the front door, one hand resting on a sword hilt. "I really don't care about this place, Beth."

"And yet, that's where the pepper is," she said.

Deathclaw shook his head. Why was she staring at something so unimportant? They should be worrying that Talon was here. That was just a house.

"There could be pepper in one of these other places," Charz said. He stooped and walked inside one of the other buildings and Deathclaw could hear him moving things around.

Beth looked at her husband. "If you don't care about this place, Hilt, then why are you staring at it?"

"Because I should care," he said, frowning. "Whatever's inside there must be very powerful."

"Exactly," Beth said. "This is where the bewitching magic is coming from." She waved her hand over them. "Do you understand now?"

Deathclaw's indifference faded. He crept up to the front door and crouched. The front porch was completely clean of debris and he could see tiny gouges in the wood that could have been left by Talon's claws. He pressed his nasal slits against the door jamb where a tiny draft of air leaked out. He hissed as he processed the scent from inside. "Talon was here!"

He reached for the door handle but it would not open. He rammed his shoulder against the front doors, but they would not budge.

"Wait, Deathclaw!" Beth said.

Deathclaw moved to the side and launched himself at one of the front widows. He collided against it face first and bounced back, his neck wrenched and bruised by the impact.

"Those are strong windows," Beth said. "I helped install them. We should go around back."

"What's going on?" Charz asked, poking his head out of the door of the house across the street.

Deathclaw rotated his head and felt his neck bones pop. The window had cracked. He launched himself again, this time shoulder first, and the window shattered inward.

Deathclaw landed on all fours, glass imbedded in his skin in several places. But the pain was easy to ignore. The scent of Talon filled his nose. She had been here for some time. And there was something else. Another scent.

As he left the front room and headed upstairs, Deathclaw could hear Sir Hilt knocking the remaining shards of glass from the window frame. The scent was issuing from up there; something acrid and sweet, covering something more unpleasant.

He tore open one of the doors at the top of the stairs. Talon's smell was strongest here. The room had been thrashed, ripped apart, and on a rumpled mattress in the center of the room, curled up in a quivering ball, was the source of the other scent in the house.

It looked like most gorcs, with a bulging nose and warty face. But this one was whimpering and sobbing and wearing a yellow lace dress and a blond wig. He rushed over and grabbed the creature by its arms.

"Where is Talon?" It didn't respond. He shook it, his claws piercing the dress' sleeves and the skin underneath.

232

"Where is she?"

"Mistress Talon is gone!" it cried. "She left me all 'lone. Durza is all 'lone!"

"Don't kill it!" came Beth's voice from the room below. "Bring her down here. I must speak with her!"

"Can't fit through this window!" Charz yelled from outside. "Will someone open the door?"

Deathclaw dragged the gorc from the room and down the stairs, losing its wig along the way.

"My hair!" it cried.

Deathclaw threw it at Beth's feet. "It's a gorc."

"I can see that," Beth said. She crouched beside the creature and laid a hand on its shoulder. "What a pretty dress you're wearing. What is your name, dear?"

"My hair!" It wailed, clawed hands covering the thin scraps of hair that clung to its mottled green scalp. "My pretty hair!"

Beth looked up at the stairway. "Deathclaw, would you please retrieve her hair?" Deathclaw hissed, but he went back and threw the wig down to her. Beth caught it and handed it to the gorc. "There you are, dear. It really is pretty hair."

It pulled the wig on crookedly, the strands of hair sticking out sideways, and nodded, "I likes this one. It is nice and yellow."

"It goes well with your dress," Beth said in agreement. She looked at Hilt. "Hold her arms."

The gorc didn't resist as Hilt came up behind her and lifted her to her feet. He gripped her wrists behind her back and warned, "Careful, Beth. She could scratch you pretty good with the claws on her feet."

"Not wearing those shoes," Beth replied as she stood, gesturing to the shiny white boots that bulged from the gorc's oversized feet. She prodded the creature and turned its head back and forth, then placed her head against its chest. The gorc's eyes widened. After a few moments Beth withdrew her head.

"You can let her go, Hilt. She's not going to try to hurt me." Beth sighed and scratched her head. "Mellinda sent her in after Pinewood was attacked to try and find out if there were still any survivors hiding out here. Evidently some of the people were unaccounted for. When she saw the stores here in the mayor's house, she got rid of the moonrat eye she had been given and drove the others out."

"Threw it down the poop hole!" the gorc said proudly.

"Poop hole?" Beth asked, then shook her head. "At any rate, Talon found her here a while ago. They have been hiding from Mellinda together."

"You got big witchy-witch magic, lady," the creature said.

"As do you," Beth said. She smiled at the gorc. "My name is Beth and this here is my husband Hilt. The giant sticking his head in the window is Charz. We aren't here to hurt you."

"I'm Durza," the gorc said with a cautious smile. Then she pointed an accusatory finger at Deathclaw. "He hurt me!"

"That's Deathclaw. He's Talon's brother," Beth replied. "He's worried about her."

Durza scowled. "He hates her! Mistress Talon loveses him but he hates her. He wants to kill her!" Deathclaw hissed and she recoiled. "He'd kill me too!"

"Deathclaw, dear," Beth said. "Apologize to this young lady."

"What?" he said.

"Young lady?" Charz laughed, banging his fist on the windowsill outside. Hilt settled for a bemused smile.

"Yes, young lady," Beth said, fixing the three of them with a stern glare. "Durza is a proper young lady and must be treated as such. Do you understand me? Apologize."

Deathclaw swallowed. What was Beth going on about? He folded his arms, "Sorry."

Beth looked back at Durza. "See? He won't hurt you again. Please tell me, where has Talon gone?"

She pointed at Deathclaw, "One of him was sneakin' 'round outside and sh-she went out to lead him off. B-but she didn't come back. All night long I waited but she didn't come. Even last night, she didn't. Now I'm all 'lone!" the gorc sobbed.

"I was not here," Deathclaw hissed. What had Talon gone to do? Had she known he was coming?

"It was like you," the gorc insisted. "Felt like you."

"Another raptoid?" Hilt asked and Durza shrugged in

response.

"She doesn't know," Beth said. "But to her spirit magic, the other creature Talon led away felt a lot like Deathclaw."

"Hey, you guys gonna leave me out here all day?" Charz complained.

Beth walked over and unlocked the heavy front doors. "You can come in, but you're not going to fit down in the food cellar."

"Cellar?" Charz asked as he lumbered in. The ceiling was high enough here that he was able to stand without hunching over.

"Let's not forget why we came here," Beth said. She headed towards the door at the side of the room. "Come on."

Deathclaw followed her and Hilt through the rooms beyond. What was this thing that 'felt like' him and Talon? Could the wizard have made more? He needed to tell Justan, but he could tell that nothing had changed in the bond.

Beth entered a room filled with counters and human dining implements. Durza scurried up to her. "Are you here to take my foods?"

"No, Durza," Beth said. "At least not much of it. We're here for something specific."

Deathclaw followed them down a narrow and steep stairway with earthen walls. He did not like the feel of this place at all. It was too tight. He pushed down a surge of panic. Surely Beth would not be leading them down this way if it was unstable.

He was so uncomfortable that he did not smell the food until he reached the bottom. Here the floor and ceiling were wooden, though the walls were still made of hard packed earth. The cellar was large and filled with shelves upon shelves of glass bottles.

"You have gone through a lot of the stores," Beth said.

"Mistress Talon eats too much," Durza conceded. "But I hides some of it from her."

Hilt stopped at some barrels lining the walls. "Beans, turnips, potatoes . . . no pepper here, but maybe we could take some of this with us? Make a stew?"

"It's not here. Further back," Beth said she went to the rear of the cellar to the far right corner and stopped. "What the . .

. oh."

"You want to use the poop hole?" Durza asked.

They were standing in front of a circular hole. Deathclaw could see that it had been cut at the front of a hinged door in the floor. He could see edges of a wooden ladder when he peered in. The door could be lifted by grabbing the edge of the hole, though it did not look pleasant to do so now.

"That's not a poop hole," Beth said with a grimace. "That's the trap door to the wine cellar."

"Did you say wine cellar?" yelled Charz hopefully from the kitchen above.

"It's also where we stored the spices," Beth sighed.

Chapter Twenty

Talon crept through black sludge and rotted vegetation. Rain poured down all around her, leaving deep puddles and sucking mud. She was getting close. There were very few living things this deep into the dark forest. Just vicious biting insects, snakes, and half dead trees. And moonrats of course, but they didn't bother her as long as she stayed hidden at night. Her pheromones hid her from their sensitive noses.

The bugs didn't bother Talon much either. She enjoyed the feel of their stings and they were the only thing she could safely eat in this place, flavorless as they were. The driving rain that had begun the day before had been welcome as well. The moonrats didn't prowl about as much in the rain and for some reason these bugs made her quite thirsty.

She opened her mouth as wide as she could and turned her face towards the sky, letting the water trickle down her throat. Talon swallowed and smiled. This would be the day. She was sure of it. This was the day she would find Mellinda and kill her.

She had been conducting a steady search of the Dark Forest, starting with a search around its perimeter, then circling inward just in case the moonrat mother wasn't in the exact center. Yet that seemed to be where Mellinda was, for the trees were getting more rotten and most of them were leafless. Several times she passed tall mounds of stinging ants and slid by small clouds of greenish flies.

It was nearing dark before she found her. The rain stopped and the moonrats had come out of hiding. Luckily they were mostly blind and Talon kept her movements slow, avoiding them as much as she could. Soon there were so many of them that Talon was forced to lay against the trunk of a tree as still as possible and wait.

She was grateful for Ewwie's gift. Her pheromones were powerful enough that a couple times moonrats crawled up her back without noticing she wasn't part of the tree. Her biggest struggle was resisting the urge to kill them. She promised herself that she would kill them all as soon as Mellinda was gone.

A short time later Talon saw her.

The moonrat mother rose up from the base of an enormous rotted tree not far from the place where Talon hid. Her skin was purest black and glistened in the dying sunlight in such a way that Talon could only make out the outlines of her voluptuous shape. Cascades of black hair fell about her shoulders. Mellinda lounged in the exposed roots of the tree and idly caressed the heads of a few orange-eyed moonrats that stood near her.

Talon's heart pounded. She was close. As soon as the moment was right, she would strike. She watched the moonrat mother for a while. Mellinda merely lay there, occasionally stretching or crooking her finger for another moonrat to come to her. It was as if she was practicing luring men, much in the way Ewwie had taught her. Then Talon realized that the moonrats all around mimicked the moonrat mother's movements. They turned their heads when she did, lounged when she did.

Her moment finally came just as the sun sank beyond the horizon and only the dimmest shade of red from the fading sunset lit the forest. The moonrat mother looked away from Talon, turning on her stomach and facing in the opposite direction. The moonrats turned and looked with her.

Talon darted towards the rotten tree and jumped, landing on Mellinda's back. Simultaneously she pierced the moonrat mother's body with her tail, pumping poison into her, and reached around to tear her throat out.

Mellinda laughed. Her body grew and she was no longer facing away from Talon, but embracing her. *"I'm so glad you finally came."*

"Die," Talon said, stabbing the witch with her tail over and over, squeezing out every ounce of poison she could.

"I'm afraid not, sweet Talon," Mellinda said. Her dark

238

body grew larger and larger until she was twice Talon's size. *"You cannot kill me. I am immortal."*

"Nothing livess forever," Talon hissed.

"I do," Mellinda said. Black strands of muck gripped Talon's arms, legs, and tail, immobilizing her.

"My poisonss will kill you." Talon could smell it already. The moonrat mother was rotting from the inside. "You diess already."

Mellinda chuckled and her black face smiled, showing a gleaming set of white teeth. *"Can your poison kill this?"*

Mellinda's black skin peeled back from her face, exposing the flesh within. Under her skin was a legion of tiny insects, flies and ants, all clinging to rotten leaves and small animal bones. The white teeth Mellinda had shown Talon were, in fact, small white beetles.

"My true body lies deep under this tree, you see." The insects moved along with the dead matter in a parody of living tissues, working a jaw, a tangled mass of worms mimicking a tongue. Her hair was made up of a tangle of fine roots. *"The body you are seeing, the body I show my rare visitors, is made of the living things and organic rot around me. I command it all. It obeys my will."*

"How do you do thiss?" Talon asked. She didn't quite comprehend what she had seen. "Why sshow me?"

"I do this because I cannot be contained," Mellinda said and the black sludge that made up her skin flowed back over her hideous insides, giving her the illusion of life again. *"I tell you, because it amuses me."* She grew larger and hunched over Talon's form, peering at her with oily black eyes. *"Because you are mine now."*

"No," Talon hissed. She strained, trying to thrash, trying to dislodge herself. This had been a foolish attempt. She needed to get away. She would have to run. She could run away forever to get away from this thing. Her body barely moved.

"You would abandon your poor Ewwie?" Mellinda asked in mock surprise. She chuckled again. *"Oh you would, wouldn't you? Your love for him is a hollow thing, an affection built out of a need to survive. You had to love him or hate him. Hating him would have been useless, since he controlled you. But your love*

239

amused him. It earned you freedoms."

"No. I lovess Ewwie," Talon gurgled.

"*Then why do you disobey him? Why do you run away?*" she asked.

"I runss . . . from you."

"*Ah, well that isn't possible anymore.*" Mellinda reached towards the forest and the sea of glowing moonrat eyes and crooked a finger. The moonrats moved aside, to let another come forward. This moonrat was larger and more muscular than the others. Its teeth were longer and sharper, its claws more vicious. And its eyes glowed blue.

The blue-eyed moonrat came to Mellinda obediently but proud, not cowering like so many of the others did. She reached towards it and her hand shrunk as she did so until it was just the right size to stroke its head and rub its flank.

"*This, Talon, is my masterpiece. I've spent centuries building for this moment. You see, this wonderful little child of mine will bring my freedom.*" She scratched under the moonrat's chin and her voice sounded regretful as she said, "*I am so sorry my sweet.*"

Mellinda grasped one of its bulbous eyes and twisted. The moonrat squealed as she plucked the eye free. She brought the eye up so that Talon could see it. In the back of the eye, where a nerve should have been, was a tiny grasping claw.

"*The orange eyes are powerful conductors for my power. One orange eye can contain a vast amount of thought, perhaps an entire human's mind and memories. But they are too weak to contain me. This,*" she held the blue eye close so that its grasping claw clutched at Talon's face. Talon flinched away. "*This one beautiful little eye can hold my entire being. All my centuries of knowledge and power.*" She reached out with one black finger and touched Talon's chest. "*Don't worry, I won't numb this for you. I know you'll enjoy it.*"

"Ewwie! Helpss me!" Talon hissed as Mellinda ran her nail across her chest. Talon's skin parted under the moonrat mother's finger as well as the flesh and bone of her ribcage. She could feel the tearing and see her own lung inflating and deflating in her chest, but the wound did not bleed.

"*Now, Talon.*" Mellinda shoved her hand deep into

Talon's chest, pushing the blue eye past her lungs and heart until it nestled at the back of her spine. Talon could feel it moving around inside her as Mellinda slipped her fingers back out of the wound. *"I don't want you to think that you are my first choice for a host. Your appearance has much to be desired. But you will make a fine backup in case Ewzad loses this war and nothing better steps forward. After all, I could make further modifications to your body as needed later on. I do love the way you raptoids adapt."*

"No," Talon sobbed, despite the exquisite pain. "Ewwieeeee!"

"There is a chance you will never see him again. You definitely won't if he loses, though you can help with that I think. Nevertheless, you are mine now, Talon," The black face smiled, showing her white teeth again. *"You may even be me someday. So if I might make a suggestion, choose to love me now. Love me more than you love him because I control you far more than your Ewwie ever did."*

She ran her black finger across Talon's chest again and the wound closed. Talon shuddered. The healing hurt far more than the wounding. She would have enjoyed it, were her mind not screaming in terror.

"Now." She released the bands holding Talon and set her down. Mellinda's huge form shrunk back down until they stood at the same height. She caressed Talon's face and this time she didn't move her lips as her voice spoke in Talon's mind, clearer than ever before. *"You have much work to do."*

"Yess, misstress," Talon said.

Chapter Twenty One

Justan was cold. He always had been. At least his only tangible memories were of being cold. There were times he could vaguely remember warm days, family and friends, but every time he tried to grab hold of such memories they faded away like wisps of a dream.

His life consisted of one long trudge down frosty corridors with walls of milky ice. His only clothing was a short sleeved linen shirt and a worn pair of leather pants. He had no shoes and his bare feet were mostly numb as he walked across floors made of damp black stone. He wondered from time to time if this dampness was because the walls were melting, but they didn't seem to be. When he touched the walls, they were covered with a film of frost.

There was no ceiling in this place, just a dark and cloudy sky. It looked like snow should fall at any moment, but none ever did. He had thought about climbing the walls to get a better perspective of where he was, but the tops were too high for him to reach and there were no hand or footholds in the ice.

Every time there was a junction in the icy corridors, Justan took a right. He remembered reading that strategy somewhere. If one were to ever find themselves stuck in a maze, take only right turns.

When he thought on it further, there was something ridiculous about that memory. How could he have read anything? There had been no life before this maze. Justan stopped walking. But there must have been. Something must have happened before he was in the maze. Otherwise, where did his clothes come from? For that matter, where did he come from? He knew that for a human being to be born, they had to have parents. Why didn't he remember parents? Had he struck his head and lost his memory?

Justan looked up at the sky and tried to piece things together. What did he know? How had he learned it? What did his knowledge tell him about himself? The more he questioned what was going on, the more he knew, and the more he knew, the more confused he became. How had he gotten in this situation?

He struggled to keep his thoughts together. Every revelation seemed a bit slippery. His name was Justan. He knew that much. He knew how to read, therefore there must be a place with books in it, which meant there was someone writing books to be read. He knew he existed, therefore he had a beginning. If he had parents then they must also have had parents, so there was a history to his world.

Somewhere off in the distance Justan heard a faint voice, but he ignored it. He was sure that if he let his attention wander, he would forget everything he had learned. So what else did he know? He knew he was cold and that he hadn't always been cold. There was warmth somewhere in his past which meant there was likely a way he could be warm again. Too bad there was nothing to burn. Wait, he knew something about creating warmth. A fire! Yes, there was something called a fire, but you had to have materials to create it.

A voice sounded off again, closer this time. Justan didn't dare listen. This was good. He was getting somewhere. He could create a fire and a fire would make him warm. He would need wood and wood came from trees! Yes, trees were plants that grew very tall and had branches and . . . and . . . why was this important? He wasn't sure, but it was something about fire. Yes, fire came from wood. But there wasn't any wood.

Justan frowned. What did that matter? The voice called out again, this time close.

"Sir Edge!"

Justan stomped his foot in irritation. He was going to lose everything at this rate. "What?"

"Sir Edge? Do you hear me?"

It was an annoying voice, somewhat high pitched and with a musical quality, but . . . wait. A voice? "H-hello?"

"Ho-ho! I believe you did!" The voice laughed.

Where was the sound coming from? "Where are you?" Justan asked. "Who are you?"

"I'm a friend I suppose. Yes, in this situation, I am most definitely a friend," the voice said. "Ha! What a ridiculous situation."

"You're my friend?" Justan smiled. He had a friend. "Where are you?"

"I'm right here. On the other side of this ice wall," the voice said. Justan heard some scratching. "If you rub off the frost, you might be able to see me. Yes, it's not completely translucent, but you might."

Justan turned around. Which wall was it behind? He looked up and saw a faint glow emanating from behind the wall on his right. He rubbed away the frost with the side of his hand and indeed there was someone on the other side. The image was distorted and blurry, but there was someone there. It held something glowing.

Justan laughed in relief. "Do you have fire?"

"Why, yes. Yes I do," the person said.

"Could you maybe . . . melt through this wall?" he asked.

"Ho, yes. Yes, of course I could, but only if you want me to," the person said.

"I do!" he said. The image behind the ice shifted and the glow grew brighter.

"Okay, well do you believe I can melt the wall? Wanting me to and believing I can are two different things, you know," it said.

"What do you mean? Fire can melt ice." Justan said, his hope fading a bit. The fire on the other side flickered. "Is your flame too small to help?"

"Of course not!" The person sounded indignant. "Why I have the power to melt this place down to the ground. But only if you believe it. You are in control here, after all."

"I am?"

"So do you believe me?" the person asked. "Do you believe that I, your friend and rescuer, can melt down this wall between us?"

"Yes!" Justan had no reason to doubt his friend.

The person chuckled. "Then stand back. I wouldn't want

you to get burnt."

Justan took a shuffling step backwards and watched in awe as the glow behind the ice burned brighter. Steam rose into the air and a trickle of water ran past his feet. The water was warm. The image behind the ice wall was obscured by steam, but the light grew stronger. It was coming through.

Justan smiled, "You're doing it!"

"I am," the person agreed.

The water spreading around Justan's feet was warmer now. He reached down and felt it with his hands. He splashed it on his clothing. Oh, to feel warmth again!

A hole appeared in the center of the wall and flames poured out. Justan stumbled backwards in surprise, the brightness leaving trails in his vision. The hole melted wider and the flame died down. A head poked through the hole.

It wasn't the kind of head Justan had expected. The person was balding and had pasty white skin and pointed ears. A pair of spectacles sat on its pointed nose. "Ho-ho, there you are," it said and stepped through the hole.

"Y-you are naked," Justan said in surprise. The person was short and portly and had a long forked tail.

The person looked down and its bushy eyes rose. "Why yes I am. Ho-ho, how unfortunate! Would you prefer I was dressed?"

"W-well, yes. That would be preferred," Justan said.

It cocked its head. "Do you mind turning around? I prefer not to dress in front of people."

"Sorry, of course," Justan said. He turned his back, then frowned. "Wait, why does that matter? You're already n-." He turned back around and the person was dressed in a full set of fancy finery, a white fluffy blouse under a long velvet vest and a pair of green velvet trousers. But its feet were bare. It had long white toes with black pointed nails on the end. "That was fast."

"Ho, well I am a fast dresser," it said and smiled, showing a set of even white teeth.

"What . . . are you?" Justan asked,

"Y-you've forgotten? You've forgotten me, your close friend?" It clutched its chest in mock pain. "You wound me!"

"I'm sorry," Justan said, his brow furrowed. Was it

teasing him?

"Ho-ho, you're fine," it said dismissively. "I'm an imp, of course. What else have you forgotten?"

"I-I don't know," Justan said. How well had he known this imp? "I don't remember much. Um . . . I remember that my name is Justan."

"Ah, Justan. Yes, I've always thought it such a pretty name." It gave him a deep bow and peered up at him, its grin growing wider. "And might I say, I have always thought you were a most beautiful young lady."

"L-lady?" Justan looked down and realized it was true. There was a large, but firm bosom under his shirt and his hips were nicely rounded. "W-why thank you, imp."

It chuckled. "Well, Miss Justan, I would say our next course of action is figuring out how to get you out of here. Your friends and family are missing you so very much, you know."

Justan reached up and touched the long brown hair that fell about his shoulders. Why hadn't he noticed it before? "I have family and friends waiting?"

"They are all very worried. Especially your Auntie Fist. She is beside herself really. And your father, Darldon the Fierce hasn't left your bedside. He brings flowers every day. Lilies. Your favorite," it said and linked its arm with his.

Justan blinked. Much of what he said sounded familiar. Those names . . . images swirled about those names in his mind. They were blurry, but that was more than he had remembered in a long time. "Can we just go out the way you came in?"

"Hmm, that seems a bit too easy, but let's see, shall we?" the imp said.

He led Justan through the hole in the wall. There was another wall beyond and the corridor stretched for quite a ways in either direction before Justan saw a bend.

"I thought so," the imp said. "I am sorry, sweetheart, but you will have to think our way out. What have you tried so far?"

"I've been making right turns," Justan said.

"Ho-ho, that's a good strategy for a simple maze, but a good maze has a series of gypsy turns just to stop that kind of solution," the imp said.

"Gypsy turns?" Justan asked.

"Ha! Yes, a place in the maze that is its own self-contained riddle. If you keep taking rights or lefts, you'll loop back on yourself," the imp rubbed its hands together. "This is delicious. Ho, a good riddle of a maze."

"You seem happy," Justan said.

"Oh, I love games, pretty one." It let go of his arm and rubbed its chin. "Hmm, what strategy to use . . ."

This imp was so strange. Justan folded his arms under his breasts, ignoring how strange it felt to have the weight of them resting on his arms. Why didn't the imp seem more familiar to him? "What was your name, imp? I'm sorry, I don't remember."

"Oh that. Well our mutual friend Willamena hasn't given me one yet, I'm afraid. She's still 'thinking it over'."

"You don't have a name?" Justan asked in surprise.

"Not currently," it said and adjusted the spectacles on its nose. "Now we could leave a trail behind us so that we will know if we have doubled back on ourselves." It reached into its vest and pulled out a bulging bag. "I have plenty of glow stones."

"How do you not have a name?" Justan asked. "Didn't you ever have one?"

It sighed. "A long time ago, but that doesn't matter, that name's no good anymore. Willum needs to give me a new one if our connection's going to work." It paused, its mouth open, and looked up at him. "Willum's my pet name for Willamena, you know. Now, let me think. We need a strategy to get out of here."

"Why don't you use your fire to melt our way out?" Justan asked.

It scowled. "That would be cheating."

"Why?" Justan said. "Are there rules?"

"Why of course there are . . . well that depends, I suppose." It peered at him. "Are you the type of girl who sets rules, Justan?"

Justan scratched his head. "I don't know."

"Hmm. Well, you did seem to think that taking right turns was a rule, but that didn't work for you. I suppose that it's possible there are no real rules in this place. We could leave a trail of stones behind us, but if the walls shifted around or simply continued on forever, that would get us nowhere." It stomped its foot. "Drat! I was so hoping for a good game!"

"I really don't care if there are rules to this place," Justan said. "I'm tired of this maze. Please, just burn it all down like you said you could."

It blinked at him and a smile started across its face. "Ho-ho, well there is some fun in that too."

It reached out and an orb of fire appeared between its two clawed hands. "Now this fire can be as big as you want it to be, you know."

Justan didn't understand why his wishes had anything to do with it, but the imp seemed to know what it was saying. "Then I want it big and I want it to melt right through these walls like they were nothing."

The imp giggled. "Ho, then let's do that!"

It stretched out its arms and the fireball grew larger and larger until it was as tall as the imp itself. Then the imp shoved the ball towards the wall across from where they were standing. As Justan had desired, it rolled forward and melted through the ice like it were paper thin. The ball kept rolling, melting through another wall, then another, and they followed through the holes it made.

The ball rolled on at a steady pace, burning through wall after wall until it had burned through ten, then twenty. The imp looked at Justan and said, "Darling, I want you to know that there are only five walls left before we are through this maze. Only five. Do you understand me?"

"Good," Justan said as the fireball rolled through another one. "Are you sure? How do you know? You didn't know that a few minutes ago."

"Imps just know these things, my dear," it explained. "Do you believe me? It's the truth."

"You haven't led me astray yet," Justan said. And it was true. Everything seemed to be the way the imp had said so far.

The fireball burned through four more walls and then, just as the imp had promised, it rolled into open space. Justan ran through the last wall in excitement. The ground beyond was made of the same moist black rock as before, but there were no more walls. Instead, there were trees; a grove of trees made entirely of ice. And lying on the ground in the center of the grove was a strange creature.

"Let's go another way," the imp said, its eyes fixed on the creature. "We can go around the trees. Maybe the exit is on the other side."

"It kind of looks like you," Justan remarked. The creature was long and thin, probably twice the height of the imp, but it had similar sickly white skin and its long arms were tipped with black talons just like the imp's were. Its head was turned away from them.

"I do NOT look like that," the imp said. "Oh ho, believe me, we have nothing in common."

The creature slowly turned its head to face them and Justan saw that the imp was right. The creature had a skeletal and noseless head and its open jaw was filled with razor sharp teeth. It hissed, a steamy cloud of frost leaving its mouth. As it shifted, Justan saw a large hole in the center of its chest. A glowing wisp of golden magic escaped from the hole.

Justan took a step back. It seemed familiar. Why did it seem so familiar?

"The fireball," the imp said. "It isn't stopping."

The large fireball was still rolling forward and Justan watched it melt right through a large tree of ice. The upper half of the tree crashed to the ground, shattering as the ball kept rolling.

"Stop it," Justan said.

"I'm trying!" the imp said, waving his arms frantically, but the ball kept rolling. It cut down another tree. "You need to believe it's going to stop."

"What does my belief have to do with it?" Justan said, his eyes widening in panic. "It's going to hit the Scralag!"

The moment those words escaped his mouth, Justan stumbled. A flood of memories poured into his mind. He saw the day in the strategy test when Benjo had shoved him down the rocky hill. He saw the Scralag tracing a symbol on his chest. He remembered Master Coal telling him that the Scralag was inside of him. He saw it pull itself free from his chest and freeze the bandham.

He turned to the imp. "You lied to me."

"Wh-what do you mean?" it asked, its eyes still watching the ball roll towards the injured ice elemental.

Justan grabbed its shoulder. "Who are you?"

"I-I told you. I'm-."

"Your Willum's imp, aren't you?" Justan accused.

"You should be focusing on that fire," the imp said as the fireball melted through another tree. It was coming close. The Scralag lifted a weak arm towards it.

"How did you get here? What are you doing in this place?" Justan demanded.

The imp watched the fireball's inexorable roll with a grimace. "You've been unconscious a long time. Everyone's worried. The wizards can't wake you. Your bonded can't reach you. Wizard Locksher had this idea that since I inhabit a world within the axe, I might be able to enter the world you had entered."

"So I'm in the Scralag's place," Justan surmised. "I'm inside the ice rune."

"Yes! Or what's left of it," the imp said. "Will you stop that damned ball! If that creature is destroyed, we might cease to exist along with it!"

"The fireball is nothing," Justan said.

The fireball touched the Scralag's outstretched claws and froze solid. The Scralag shoved the ball away and struggled to sit up, more golden magic seeping from its injury. The ball of ice rolled into a tree, shattering on impact.

"How did you get here?" Justan demanded.

"It was everyone," the imp said. Somehow it didn't look relieved that the Scralag was alive. It watched with alarm as the Scralag stood. "They formed a circle. Fist held your hand and that Malaroo girl's and she and Willum grabbed your rogue horse. Then Tolivar and Willum grasped my axe and Tolivar grabbed your other hand. Ho, it was all really quite touching.

"Then Tolivar did something and shoved me into this place and the only way I knew how to find you was the line of spirit magic leading to you." It swallowed. "That thing is coming this way, you know."

"I see," Justan said, and he could. He could see them all now in his mind. His friends were all there waiting for him. The silvery cord that connected him to this place was dim, but he saw that too. It stretched off into the clouds high above.

"Can you, um, call your monster off?" the imp asked.

Justan heard the creak of a door. He turned and saw a small cabin at the edge of the grove. He was pretty sure it hadn't been there before. It was made of ice logs, as if it were built out of the trees in the grove.

The door to the shack stood open and a bearded man wearing a blue and gold robe leaned out, gesturing to him. A warm glow poured out from behind the man and the interior of the shack looked inviting.

Justan walked towards the shack, somehow sure that he needed to speak with the man. The imp shuffled along beside him. The man in the shack gestured insistently, his expression urgent. The Scralag came towards them on its long legs and stretched out an arm. A frozen rope of ice shot from its palm. The imp yelped as the rope wrapped around its waist.

"Call it off!" the imp growled and the skin of its face flushed a deep red. It grabbed the rope in one clawed fist and a stream of fire crawled up the rope towards the Scralag's hands. "I don't know that I can fight it in this place!"

Justan reached the door and the robed man withdrew inside. Justan looked back at the imp. Its skin had turned entirely red now and the rich clothing it had worn was gone, replaced by a fiery armor adorned with golden spikes. The flames had climbed to the Scralag's hand and steam burst from its palm. The Scralag smiled.

"Sir Edge!" the imp yelled. Its voice had grown deeper, more throaty. "I was sent here to help you!"

"You're tough, imp. And it's weakened. You can help me best by holding it off for awhile." Justan narrowed his eyes. "And by the way, convincing me that I was a woman? Not funny!"

He walked inside the cabin and shut the door behind him.

Chapter Twenty Two

The cabin was a small but tidy place. It contained a single room with a bed, a small table, and two chairs that stood next to a warm fireplace. The robed man eased into one of the chairs and gestured for Justan to take the other. As Justan sat, he realized that his body had returned to its true form. He now wore his common traveling clothes and trail-worn boots.

The man sitting across from him looked to be middle aged, with thick brown hair streaked with gray and an odd beard that stretched across his chin but did not cover his lips. He held a steaming tea cup in his hands and he was smiling at Justan fondly. Justan's spirit sight showed a silvery cord of magic connecting his chest to the man.

"I'm Sir Edge," Justan said. It sounded strange to use his new name, but it was the proper way.

The man chuckled and when he spoke his voice sounded somehow familiar, "I'm sorry. Please forgive me but it has been so long since I've spoken with anyone that I'm still gathering my thoughts. You see, it is hard to keep hold of one's self in this place."

"I've noticed. Are you the wizard that turned into the Scralag?" Justan asked.

"I suppose I am." The man blinked thoughtfully. "Yes. Now that I think about it, that is what you have been calling the elemental, so that makes complete sense. Thank you for reminding me."

"So . . ." Justan ran a hand through his hair. "Wow, I have so many questions for you, I don't know where to start."

"Our time together is likely limited. I can feel the elemental gaining in strength as we speak. I may not be able to hold my thoughts together for long, so why not begin with the most important questions," the man said. He took a long sip of his tea.

Justan's mind whirred. What was most important? "What happened back on the battlefield? Why am I here?"

The man swallowed his tea and nodded. "Ah, well that is the most immediate concern I suppose. The elemental's connection tying this place to your body was torn when you were wounded. The elemental had to turn all its focus on keeping you alive. That arrow had pierced right through your heart, you know. When that happened, your own magic raged out of control. It was quite impressive, by the way."

"That magic, the ice pouring from my chest, shooting from my swords, you're saying that was mine?" Justan was so stunned by the possibility that the fact he'd been shot through the heart didn't faze him.

"Oh, yes, you are very powerful, but you should know that by now," the man said.

"I . . . that's what the wizards told me, but I haven't been able to do anything with it. I can't make so much as a single snowball with my magic. I can only act defensively."

The man pursed his lips. "That is likely my fault. Well, the elemental's fault. Well, our fault, I suppose. It takes most of your magic for me to maintain this place."

"This?" Justan grew angry at the thought of his power being wasted to create the endless maze and the grove of icy trees. "You used my magic to make this place?"

The man winced. "Well, we had no choice. When you bonded with us, we were trapped there in the hills. We were tied to my old bones, you see. We couldn't leave the place without simply ceasing to exist. But the event of the bonding brought me a rare moment of clarity. I made the rune on your chest and created a realm where we could stay."

Justan grit his teeth. "I didn't ask you to come with me."

"If we hadn't come with you, the bond would have been for nothing," the man explained. "We had no choice and once we were with you it was difficult to stay there. We had to siphon your magic in order to make this place stable. The elemental's power is hard to contain."

253

"Why not use the Scralag's power to maintain this place then? And if my power is so reduced, why am I able to use it for things like shield spells?"

The man took another slow sip of his steaming tea and closed his eyes, savoring the moment before he swallowed. "Sorry, it's just that I so rarely have the presence of mind to make tea. As for your questions, both of them have a similar answer. Our power has a specific purpose. We are saving it for when it is needed. Until then, we do our best to protect you when you need us. You are a warrior. You don't need your elemental magic to fight."

"What right do you have to decide how I use my magic?" Justan demanded. "We are bonded. You should have told me that you needed it. If you had just spoken with me, we could have worked something out."

"My dear boy, that is a well reasoned argument and you are absolutely correct. That is what we should have done. However, intelligence is an infrequent visitor to our mind. Believe me, I haven't thought this clearly in over a century. We were unable to communicate to you in any way you would have understood. Our normal state is so cold and vicious, I felt it best to wall up the bond for your protection."

Justan digested what the man had said for a moment. While he did so, the man lifted his cup to sip from it again, but the liquid was gone. He looked into the cup sadly.

"It looks like our time is running out a bit quicker than I intended. The elemental has almost recovered and your imp friend is fading. We can only speak for a few more minutes."

"Then why didn't you speak to me sooner?" Justan asked. "Why put me in that maze for so long?"

"We didn't put you in there," the man said. "We were busy keeping you alive and then, keeping ourselves alive. I didn't even know you were stuck in here until your imp friend arrived," the man frowned and set the empty cup aside. "Why were you in there so long anyway? It is a fairly simple maze I made to keep the elemental preoccupied. Just a few left turns and you're out."

Justan covered his face with his hands. "Alright. Alright. So what do I need to know?" There was just so much. "Okay,

254

what is your name?"

"I don't remember," the man said. He laughed. "Oh, that's terrible. I can't even recall my own name."

"Well, you were obviously a powerful frost wizard. That's a rare talent, right?"

"Runs in the family," the man said, then shrugged. "I'm sorry that's all I can give you."

"Um . . . what about your purpose? You told me that you were holding your magic for a purpose, right?"

"Of course. I wouldn't be here otherwise. I would have passed on to the next life like most people, but instead I hung around and turned into this thing. But I can't remember what my purpose was. I just . . ." The man's eyes widened and he pounded a fist into his hand. "Ah! The book! The book I gave you has everything you need to know. I can't believe I almost forgot about it." He lifted his hand in front of his face and frowned. The man's nails had darkened to black. "This explains it. Our time is just about up, I'm afraid."

"But the book is unreadable!" Justan said. "We've tried everything."

"No, you have all you need. There is a nasty little spell on it, I agree, but you have the key. I was worried when you gave the book to that wizard, but he brought it back to you."

"No, we don't have the key. Locksher found your spectacles with the hole in them, but whatever goes in the hole is missing. He looked all over and couldn't find it!" Justan said.

The man's eyes were glazing over, the pupils turning red. "I don't . . . no, you have it. You've always had it. I left it for you. You have all you need . . . all you need." He shook his head and blinked. His eyes were all red now. He stumbled over and opened the door. "You must go. Go to your friend. I am afraid we have damaged him. He is . . ."

Justan grasped the man's shoulders and shook him. "Hey! Don't join with the Scralag yet. Listen to me! I'm bonded to you. You have to listen!"

"The elemental is me," the man said hollowly.

"No. Look!" Justan pointed to the cord of spirit magic flowing from his chest to the man's. "See the bond? The elemental has been outside this cabin the whole time, but this

255

bond has always been here. I am connected to you, not your magic that's turned into that thing."

The man frowned and blinked some more. The redness faded from his eyes. "I-I."

"Listen!" Justan said. "I've been thinking about our bond, wondering why it happened in the first place. What was the mutual need? What did we gain from each other?" Justan grasped the sides of the man's face, willing him to stay coherent. "I believe that I needed my bond with you to increase the strength of my magic. Now you needed me to get free of those hills, but I think there's more. I think what you've gotten from me is the ability to think again. You don't seem to remember anything from the day before we bonded, but you seem to be aware of everything I went through since then."

The man swallowed and gave a brief nod. His eyes were normal now, but frost had begun to crust over his hair. "That is possible."

"Then focus! When I am gone, you need to gain ground with the Scralag. Take control. I can't have your unmanageable power inside me like a bear trap waiting to spring at any second. I will need to speak with you again. You must gain control!"

The man nodded again and pulled Justan's hands from his head. His black fingernails had become claws. "I will try. You are quite a remarkable boy, you know. Your grandfather would be so proud. Now go. Help your friend!"

Justan looked back and saw the imp lying on the ground. It was naked and its skin was a pasty white again. He ran two steps towards the imp before he realized what the man had said. "My grandfather?" He looked back but the man was gone. The cabin stood empty and standing in front of it was the Scralag, the hole in its chest was closed and looked as if it had been stitched together with golden thread.

He ran to the imp and knelt beside it. Its chest rose and fell slowly, but there was a hole in its belly. Wisps of gold were leaking out.

"Are you okay, imp?" Justan asked. He put his hands out over the wound and focused, but his magic wouldn't do anything. He could sense the wound but couldn't interact with it.

The imp coughed and scowled at him. "You jerk! You

selfish son of a wizardess! I come to help you. Me! Helping a human and you leave me to die!"

"You may have come to help. But you lied to me," Justan said. "Aren't you supposed to always tell the truth?"

"This is your place, not mine. Only your rules apply." It laughed, then winced in pain. "Ho-ho, it was funny when you thought you were a girl, though. Ha-what a good girl you made, too. Nice proportions! At least I had one good joke before I died."

"You make it hard to regret leaving you to fight without me," Justan said. Still, the imp was right. It had come to help and it was Willum's axe. He couldn't let it die. "What did the Scralag do to you?"

"Ho, the stupid thing tore the air magic right out of me! Used it to seal its own wound. Now I'm the one in trouble." It clutched at the hole in its belly. "My air magic helps bind me to the axe. Without it, I'll die. I'll pass on to wherever imps go. I don't know where that is. Maybe it's nowhere. Then the axe will just be an axe."

"If you had enough air magic, could you repair yourself?" Justan asked.

The imp snorted. "Maybe, but it would take a lot. I could repair it on my own if Willum went out and killed enough things, but ha! There's no time."

"Can you take my magic? I'm strong in air," Justan suggested.

It shook its head weakly. "No. Yours is all tied up in this place. You couldn't give it to me without tearing this place apart."

"Then we need to get you out of here," Justan said.

"Yeah? How?"

"Just hold on while I do it." Justan reached into the bond and found the strand of spirit magic connecting him to this place. He pushed his mind through it until he found the barrier that blocked the Scralag from the rest of the bond. He picked the barrier apart strand by strand, until he could push through.

He sensed his bonded again. Fist and Gwyrtha were close by, Deathclaw far away. They called out to him, but he couldn't speak with them yet. He sensed Tolivar holding his hand, maintaining the imp's connection. He reached out to Tolivar and pulled the man through.

Tolivar appeared next to them in the Scralag's world. He looked down at the wounded imp, then back at Justan. "Are you okay, Sir Edge?"

"Ho-ho, ignore the imp. Of course he's okay!" the imp said weakly. "Now listen, Tambaloor, Tolivan, whatever your name is now, tell Willum I did what he wanted. Now it's his fault I'm dying. He owes me. He owes me a . . ." the imps voice faded and his head lolled to the side.

"Take him back please," Justan said.

Tolivar nodded and reached down to grasp the imp's arm. They disappeared.

Justan took one last look at the Scralag. It blinked its beady red eyes and reached an arm out towards him. Justan heard a single word.

Go.

Justan eyes opened to the view of tight clusters of icicles hanging from a stone ceiling.

"Justan!" Fist exclaimed.

He sat up. He was in a bed in a large stone room. His friends and mother were gathered around him, all of them wearing heavy winter coats. Icicles hung everywhere and the walls and floor were covered in a thick coat of frost.

Jhonate hurled herself across the bed and threw her arms around him. Her scent filled his nose and he felt a little dizzy as his mother joined her, clutching him too. Everyone began talking at once, both aloud and through the bond, asking him questions.

"*Stop!*" he exclaimed. The room went quiet. He kissed his mother's cheek and Jhonate's lips, then carefully began prying their arms off of him. "I'll speak with you in a moment. Willum!"

Willum was holding the axe, his brow furrowed in concern. "What happened, Sir Edge? The imp isn't responding."

"Listen, the imp needs air magic or it will lose its bond with the axe. Is there an air wizard in here??

"No," Darlan said. "Locksher and Vannya left with Valtrek about an hour ago. I can call for them."

"No, we need air magic now and the imp can't use mine."

Justan swallowed. There was only one other solution. "Where is my bow? It's here in this room, I can feel it."

Jhonate lifted Ma'am from the side of the bed and handed it to him. "We brought everything you were bonded to. Alfred thought it might help."

Justan took Ma'am from her and was relieved to see that it was still strung with the dragon hair string. He unstrung it hurriedly. "Willum, take this bowstring. It's full of air magic. Tell the imp to take what it needs."

"Justan, that is a rare gift," Darlan warned.

"I know," Justan said.

Willum took the string hesitantly. "Are you sure? I don't know what it will do."

"Neither do I, but the imp helped me. I only hope its enough." He looked at Jhonate, hoping she wouldn't be offended that he had used her gift to him in this way. She looked at him with searching eyes, but she didn't seem angry.

"I-I'm not sure how to do this," Willum said. He wrapped the string around the shaft and pommel of the axe and closed his eyes.

Justan switched to mage sight and saw the bright golden glow of the string flare. Then with a small pop, the golden magic began to flow into the axe. The string's glow ebbed and faded. After a few moments it was gone all together. The string was no thicker than a regular hair and when Willum tried to unwind it, it broke.

Justan swallowed. The golden string had been in many ways his most powerful weapon. Now it was gone and the war wasn't finished. "Was it enough?"

"I think so," Willum said. "It's talking to me now. Actually it's demanding I go kill some things with it so that it can absorb more energy."

"There's nothing to fight right now," Fist said.

"Take it down to the kitchens," Tolivar said. "See if they need any help slaughtering chickens."

Willum laughed. "It doesn't think that was funny. Still, that might be all it's going to get."

"Alright. Now that's settled." Justan said. He folded his arms. "Where am I?"

Chapter Twenty Three

"You're in the Magic Testing Center, dear," Darlan said. She reached out and smoothed Justan' hair. "As you can see, your magic was too far out of control for you to stay anywhere else."

Justan ran his fingers up to the scar on his chest. The frost covered rune was still there. There was nothing more than a little extra scar tissue to show he'd been shot.

Justan, Gwyrtha laid her big shaggy head across his legs. *You were gone too long.*

"I know." *I missed you sweetie*, he assured her. He looked at the others. "How long was I unconscious?"

"A month!" Fist said. "Four whole weeks we been worried." He frowned. "I mean, 'we've been worried'."

"A month?" Justan couldn't believe it. A month of time spent walking in circles? The pure waste of it gave him shivers.

"Your mother has been taking care of you," Jhonate said. She gripped his hand and her green eyes were intense. "Few other wizards were able to come near you. The rest of us could only visit you if she or Wizard Locksher was here."

"Did I hurt anyone?" Justan worried.

"Not since we put you in here, no," Darlan said.

Justan swallowed. "And before that?"

Darlan and Jhonate exchanged glances.

"You must have wiped out twenty or thirty of Ewzad's monsters," Willum said enthusiastically. "I saw it. It was amazing! Huge towers of ice freezing them or falling on them. Your attack allowed us to get away."

"So we lost," Justan said. He had thought it was the most likely case, but had hoped otherwise.

"We were at a tactical disadvantage," Jhonate said. "There were far more of those creatures than we had expected and our archers and wizards were rendered ineffective because of those shields they erected."

"I saw them," Justan said. He hadn't seen any shields like it before. "I didn't know they had any wizards on their side."

"They didn't," Darlan said her lips pursed in irritation. "I would have seen them. Somehow they must have generated the shields in another way. Locksher has been looking into it, but as far as we can tell, they must have had a magical item of some kind that produced them."

"How bad were our losses?" he asked.

"Nearly a third," Tolivar said. He looked down at the floor as he added, "Over half of the Howlers."

"It's not your fault, Tolivar," Fist said sadly and Justan could tell they'd had this conversation before. "They wouldn't stop fighting."

"They would have if I had been there," Tolivar replied.

"Berserkers always take heavy losses," Willum said. "Tad the Cunning told us that was one of the reasons the academy disbanded them."

"Not while I was in charge!" Tolivar said and for a brief moment his eyes looked like the eyes of the Tamboor Justan had met in Ewzad Vriil's dungeons, full of pain and rage. But the moment passed. He placed his hand on Willum's shoulder. "Next time I will be fighting at their side. If I start to lose myself again, I will have you and Samson to bring me back." He smiled slightly. "Bettie might just cheer me on."

"Two thousand men dead." Justan shook his head slowly. That was more than had died during the rescue of the academy warriors. "How many of our men did I kill?"

The room grew quiet.

Jhonate gripped his hand. "Wizard Valtrek's spy says that Ewzad Vriil was very upset about his own losses. He considered it a major setback. The majority of his changed men were killed, including his commander. He has been replacing them as fast as he can, but the witch has filled the gaps in their lines with goblinoids in the meantime."

He let out a slow breath and looked into her green eyes.

"How many of our men did I kill?"

"It . . ." Jhonate's brow furrowed.

"None that we know of for sure, dear," Darlan said, patting his arm comfortingly. But Justan didn't look away from Jhonate's eyes. His mother would try to make him feel better, but Jhonate would tell him the truth.

"There are too many men unaccounted for," Jhonate said. "We cannot be sure. There has been some talking among the men. Your magic caused a lot of destruction and the journey back to the school was dangerous. There were . . . injuries."

"What happened?" Justan asked. He felt sick to his stomach.

Fist spoke up, gesturing excitedly. "You were spraying cold stuff out of your chest and shooting ice out of your swords! Men were running to get out of the way. Monsters were freezing and breaking to pieces! Then Gwyrtha brought me to you and I pulled you up with me and we ran."

It was cold and you were hurt, Gwyrtha complained. She pushed some frantic memories through the bond; memories full of ice and roars and screaming.

I'm sorry, sweetheart. Justan sent as he rubbed her head. He frowned. "Wait. Fist, did you say you pulled me up with you?"

I got big, Gwyrtha said.

"Yeah, she was big enough to carry me and you," Fist said, smiling. "And Mistress Darlan."

"You did that on your own?" Justan asked Gwyrtha. He hadn't known that was possible. Samson wasn't able to do that.

She nodded. *I remembered how to get big.*

"I had to ride with them to keep your magic under control," Darlan said. "The ice pouring from your chest slowed down while you were unconscious, but it still burst out from time to time"

"Some men were trapped by your magic," Jhonate said. "But the wizards with us were able to thaw them. There were a few frost related injuries-."

"I almost lost two fingers!" Fist said, holding up his right hand. Two of his fingers were missing their nails, but they looked to be growing back.

It was cold, Gwyrtha agreed. *My tail hurt.*

"However, as your mother said, there is no proof of fatalities," Jhonate assured him. "When you arrived back at the Mage School, your magic was still flaring out of control. You were taken here instead of the infirmary so that none of the other patients would be in danger. Your mother resigned as mayor so that she could care for you."

"Why did you go and tell him that?" Darlan said, shooting Jhonate a glare. She smiled at Justan. "That's not exactly how it went, dear. I was only provisional mayor. I didn't want the position anyway and there are other people just as qualified."

"They're still arguing about who should replace her," Tolivar said, his arms folded. "If you ask me, she is really the best person for the job."

"Nobody asked you, Tolivar!" Darlan snapped. "I never wanted to be mayor. I was only doing it for Tad."

"Are you sure? You've always liked being in charge, Darlan," Tolivar said. His mouth was twisted in amusement.

She scowled. "I like it when things get done properly. Sometimes it means that I need to kick a few butts to make sure things happen. That doesn't mean I enjoy it. I find it damned irritating when people can't do their job." Her hand flew to her mouth and she shot Justan an embarrassed glance.

"Right." Tolivar chuckled. "Well, speaking of jobs, Willum and I have wall duty tonight. We should get going." He nodded to Justan. "I'm glad it worked."

"Thank you for helping me," Justan said and looked to Willum. "Willum, thank you for helping. I'm sorry I came so close to killing your imp."

"You saved him," Willum said. "I'm sorry about your bowstring."

Justan shook his head. "Just tell him that if he ever breathes a word about the little joke he played on me, I'm sending the Scralag into his world."

Willum looked extremely curious, but he just said, "I'll tell him."

Once the two men had left, Justan looked to the others and sighed, "I'm sorry I've been so much trouble."

"Don't you worry about it," his mother said, leaning in to hug him. "You heard what I told Tolivar, this is what I wanted to do." She kissed his cheek and stood back. "Besides, I have been able to get back into doing things I actually enjoy."

"She's been teaching me magic!" Fist said with a wide grin.

"Really?" Justan asked, giving his mother a surprised look.

"We've been here in the testing center with you anyway," Darlan said. "I simply requested the room next door and took over Fist's schooling while you were . . . away. I figured he could use some training from a war wizard."

Justan liked the thought of the two of them spending time together. "How is he doing?"

"He learns quickly," she replied, smiling at Fist proudly. "He struggles somewhat with the more scholarly aspects of school here, but he has an instinctive grasp of the way magic works."

"I can make my mace lightning!" Fist said.

"I have taught him some basic war spells," Darlan said. "He can worry about theory and mathematics and runework after the siege is over."

"Wizardess Landra was okay with this?" Justan asked. Landra took her job as assigner of classes quite seriously. No student dared step on her toes and any wizard that tried to override her got the sharp edge of her tongue.

"She was resistant at first, but we came to an understanding," his mother said matter-of-factly. "I spoke to Valtrek and we convinced Master Latva and Beehn that Fist is a special case. Randolf and Auger were against it, but I was able to convince Munsey and they were overruled. We skipped this whole cadet nonsense and raised him to rank of apprentice. Then when I brought the decision to her, I told Landra she could burn for all I cared and since I was the one who taught her the job in the first case, there was nothing she could say about it."

Justan's jaw dropped. "You convinced the council to make Fist an apprentice? After a month as a cadet?"

"It wasn't easy to say the least," Darlan said. "I'd forgotten how much the council drags their feet. It took me two

264

whole days to convince them to make the right decision."

"You stood before The Bowl of Souls?" Justan asked Fist.

"That wasn't necessary," Darlan said before Fist could answer. "We're at war here. The advancement ceremony is nothing but a symbol of the Mage School's arrogance. It's not part of The Bowl of Soul's true purpose. They started doing it a hundred years ago to make it seem like advancing in rank was a bigger deal. I find it offensive to tell you the truth. The Bowl of Souls is for naming, not for prancing about in front of."

Justan was used to his mother's long winded opinions, but this one surprised him. If he hadn't gone through the advancement ceremony, he wouldn't have dipped his dagger into the bowl. Then again, perhaps that proved her point. The bowl's purpose was naming.

"So . . . you took Fist on as your personal apprentice?" he asked.

"She's a really good teacher," Fist said.

"You don't need to blow sunshine at me, Fist," Darlan said.

"Yes, Mistress," Fist said obediently.

"I believe that I am the best teacher for someone of Fist's talents," Darlan said. "The main skills he needs to know are healing and fighting. Those are the ways he can be of best use to you. And Squirrel, of course," she amended.

As if on command, Squirrel leapt from the headboard of the bed to Darlan's shoulder. Justan hadn't realized Squirrel had been there. Darlan noticed his surprise.

"Squirrel has been keeping an eye on you for me when Fist and I are next door," Darlan said and reached into her pocket to hand Squirrel a cracker. "Good boy. Now don't you get any crumbs on me, understand?" Squirrel nodded and began nibbling the cracker very carefully.

"But if you-," Justan began.

"Enough about what we have been up to," Jhonate said sternly. "Tell me what happened to you."

Justan noted everyone's expectant stares. "Well, I . . . It is a bit difficult to explain."

"We know that you were trapped in that rune of yours

with the Scralag," she said. "What were you doing all this time?"

"For most of the time, nothing," Justan said honestly. He told them what had happened, only leaving out the part where the imp had him convinced he was a woman. He ended with his words to the man inside the Scralag.

"Do you think it will work?" Darlan asked. "Do you think you'll be able to communicate with the elemental?"

"With the wizard inside it, yes. I plan to work on it at least," Justan said. "What I really need to do is find out what the key to the book is." An idea came to his mind. "Mother, the man said something to me at the end that seemed important. He said, 'Your grandfather would be proud of you.' Do you know what that could mean?"

Darlan's brow furrowed thoughtfully. "I suppose he could have been one of your grandfather's contemporaries. My father never mentioned having any wizard friends himself. He was a fighter." She gave a slight smile. "He was always worried that his lack of magic would pass down to his children. He was so glad when I had my awakening, he wasn't even angry that I burned the barn down."

Justan felt a surge of irritation, but he pushed it down. Since finding out his mother was a wizardess, it seemed like all her stories were new. She had hidden so much of her life from him. "Think of it this way, mother. Were there any powerful frost wizards around when grandfather was? Any strong enough to leave an elemental behind?"

She shrugged, "There were a few frost wizards around. None that powerful that I can remember, though. It was nothing like back in your great grandfather's day. Now he was a powerful frost wizard."

"Great grandfather?" Justan's eyes widened. "You just said he was a traveler. Why didn't you ever tell me he was a wizard?"

"I was in hiding. I didn't want anyone to know magic ran in our family. If you told someone your great grandfather was the great Frost Wizard Artemus, they could have figured out who I really was," she said.

"You should have told me," Justan said. He would have figured it out by now! "You should have told me all of it! I wasn't a stupid child. I wouldn't have told your secret!"

"I was well aware of how smart you were, dear," she said. They'd had this discussion several times since arriving at the Mage School and it was a sore subject. "Children can't keep secrets. Believe me, I have seen it enough times to know."

"I would have!" Justan grit his teeth. "I shouldn't have had to wait until I was twenty to find out that my mother was the War Wizard Sherl!"

His mother's face went red. "I'm sorry, Justan. I-I don't know what else I can say."

Justan threw back the blankets and swung his feet over the bed. Jhonate gasped and turned away. Justan paused, glad to see that he was wearing his small clothes.

"Thank you for taking care of me, mother. This is the first time I've awoken from an injury to discover I wasn't completely naked." He whistled as his feet touched the frosty ground.

"Where do you think you're going?" Darlan demanded.

"I need to go see Professor Locksher. Please tell me my clothes are in here somewhere."

"They are over here," Jhonate said. She kept her eyes averted as she handed them over. Justan pulled on his pants.

"I don't like this, son," Darlan said. "You have been through a lot of trauma. You should rest."

"I've rested for four weeks!" Justan replied. He pulled on his boots and stood as he tucked in his shirt. "This can't wait." He hoped she wouldn't call him out on that. It wasn't necessarily true, but he didn't want to wait.

"Yeah," Darlan said with a shake of her head. "You'll start feeling it any second."

She was right, too. Half way through strapping on his sword sheaths, he started breathing heavy.

"You have been lying prone in bed for a month," Darlan said. "My magic has helped keep your muscles from atrophying, but your body doesn't know that. You should rest."

"I can't," he said. "I've been waiting for this moment for two years. I need to see Locksher."

"Fine," she said. "We'll take you over there. If this has something to do with grandfather, I want to hear it. Locksher

267

said he was returning to his rooms."

Justan re-strung Ma'am with a regular string, sheathed his swords and they headed out the door.

They left the Magic Testing Center to a setting sun. The sky was ablaze with orange and red. Justan smiled at the hot evening breeze. He had slept right into the middle of summer.

Ride? Gwyrtha asked hopefully.

He didn't dare refuse her at this point. Besides, he really didn't want to. He was exhausted just from walking this far. *Okay, but don't go fast. It's not that far away.* He climbed onto her saddle and swayed a bit before leaning forward and grasping her mane.

"Are you okay, Justan?" Jhonate asked.

"I'll be fine," he said. "I'm not looking forward to climbing all those stairs to Locksher's rooms, though."

Take my energy, Gwyrtha urged.

Thank you, Justan said. He didn't know why he hadn't thought to ask sooner. He reached through the bond to Gwyrtha's powerful energy source and pulled. He sat up higher in the saddle. His fingers twitched. His vision swam. He had pulled in a little too much energy, but he felt so much better than he had before.

He breathed in deep and extended his senses. He closed his eyes and listened to the footsteps of those around him. Fist's were heavy and widely spaced. Jhonate and his mother had similar weights and both walked with firm and purposeful strides, but Justan could tell them apart by the lengths of their steps. Jhonate's legs were a bit longer.

A quiet voice echoed through the bond. *Justan, you are there*!

Justan focused in and the thoughts grew louder. Deathclaw was surprised he was there.

Justan smiled. *It is good to hear you.*

I had wondered if you would wake. Deathclaw actually sounded happy. *Beth told me you would, but I doubted her.*

She seems to be right most of the time, Justan said, remembering her telling Sir Lance that his time was nearly finished.

Then I must warn you, Deathclaw said. *Beth has a bad*

feeling. She is worried that something horrible is about to happen.

Tonight? Justan asked.

She is not sure, but soon.

To me? Justan asked.

That is unclear. Deathclaw said. *It could be to us. But she said we should warn those at the Mage School just in case. Charz spoke with Alfred this afternoon. He says the guards have been alerted. Her feeling is vague, but very strong.*

"Justan, are you alright?" Darlan said, interrupting his thoughts. "We're at the Rune Tower."

"He's talking to Deathclaw, Mistress Darlan," Fist said.

I have more to tell you, Deathclaw said, sensing his distraction.

Can it wait another hour or so? I have much to tell you as well, Justan sent.

Deathclaw hesitated. *Perhaps.*

Okay, if Beth feels anything else, let me know.

I will. Deathclaw said. *I . . . am pleased you are awake.*

Me too, Justan said.

"He says Beth's worried that something bad is going to happen soon, but she doesn't know when or to whom," Justan said. He slid from the saddle and was glad when his legs didn't buckle. Gwyrtha's energy had been exactly what he needed. "We should be on our guard."

"Your father told me earlier," Darlan said, her brow was furrowed in concern. "That's why he wasn't with us when you awoke."

"The guards are on alert," Jhonate said.

"Good," Justan said. But it didn't really make him feel better. Somehow the fact that everyone knew was of little comfort. He felt a sense of dread in his stomach.

They crossed the moat, but Justan stopped before they went in. He could feel the heat of Gwyrtha's breathing against his back. He turned and scratched behind her ears. "Gwyrtha, I'm sorry but you know you can't go in there with us. I need you to wait out here."

Gwyrtha snorted in irritation. *I can't go anywhere here.*

"I'm sorry, sweetie. I'll see you soon," he said "I'll tell

269

you what. I'll sleep in the stables with you one night this week, okay?"

Promise? she said dubiously.

Yes, he said.

Okay, she replied. She turned and walked back across the bridge, but made sure he knew she was unhappy about it.

He sighed and grasped Jhonate's hand as they went inside. Darlan led the way, Fist right behind her, and when they passed the library and came to the spiraling stairwell that led to Locksher's rooms, Justan paused and stared at them in anguish. This was going to be a long climb. He was going to need all the energy Gwyrtha had given him.

Darlan and Fist started up first. Justan placed his foot on the first step, but Jhonate grabbed his arm, stopping him. He gave her a questioning look, but though her eyes were intense, she said nothing. The moment Fist and Darlan climbed out of view, Jhonate grabbed his head and pulled him in for a deep kiss. Oh how he had missed her.

She turned his head so that she could whisper in his ear. "We need to be alone if I'm going to kiss you the way I need to kiss you." She kissed behind his ear and the side of his neck. "Never leave me like that again, Justan, you understand?"

"No necking down there, you two," Darlan called from somewhere above.

Jhonate pulled back, her face red. Justan looked back at her, his eyes wide. How had his mother known?

Jhonate cleared her throat and composed herself. She brushed past him and headed up the stairs. Justan's knees were weak, but he had no problem keeping up with her.

Chapter Twenty Four

When Justan reached the door to Locksher's rooms, his mother was standing outside it with one eyebrow raised. Jhonate, still blushing, gave her a cool look, but Justan's sensitive ears immediately picked up what his mother was raising an eyebrow about. A giggle echoed from Locksher's rooms. An intimate sounding giggle.

Justan knocked. "Professor Locksher, are you in there?"

"Is that you, Edge? Come in! Come in!" the wizard replied excitedly.

Justan opened the door and his nose caught the flowery scent of Vannya just before she ran into him. She wrapped her arms around him in a tight hug and Justan couldn't help but return it. She had been doing her best to avoid him for so long it felt very nice.

"I'm so glad you're okay!" she said. Her eyes moved from Justan to Jhonate and she took a step back. Vannya cleared her throat. "We've all been very worried."

Justan glanced back at Jhonate and was pleased to see that she didn't look angry. "It's good to be back, Vannya."

She smiled and ushered them in. They walked in to a room quite different from the one Justan had seen nearly two years before. Gone were the random stacks of books and jumbles of items. In their place were several rows of bookcases, each one holding neat rows of books. The assortment of hooks adorning the walls had been replaced by shelves. Each one was clearly labeled for the objects that sat on it.

Even Locksher's desk had undergone a transformation. Though still covered with papers, the stacks looked tidy, and all his experiments had been moved to two workbenches that had

271

been installed to either side of the desk. One was covered by odd jumbles of bottles filled with various liquids. The other held a wide platter that held some sort of opaque gelatinous mass.

"So very good to see you awake, Edge!" Locksher grabbed Justan's shoulder and shook his hand with enthusiasm. His neatly trimmed beard was split by a wide smile. "I see that the imp in Willum's axe was able to contact you?"

"Yes. I very nearly killed him, but we're both fine," Justan said.

"I'm surprised you made it up the stairs after a month of bed rest why . . . Oh yes, of course. Your rogue horse." He laughed. "You bonding wizards are quite fortunate."

Fist, who had never been in Locksher's apartments before was staring around in awe and bumped into one of the wizard's bookcases. The bookcase rocked and several rows of books spilled across the floor.

"Sorry!" the ogre said. He bent down and started to pick them up.

"Wait," Locksher said. "Just leave them there."

"It's okay, Fist," Vannya said. "We'll put them away later. Professor Locksher likes them in a specific order."

"Locksher, we're here to discuss the creature in Justan's chest," Darlan said. She refused to call him Edge. She said it's a mother's right to call her son by the name she gave him. It made others uncomfortable, but Justan preferred it that way. Faldon, on the other hand, avoided the situation altogether by just calling him son all the time.

Locksher's eyebrow rose. "Yes! Good. I'd been hoping he would learn something while he was in there!" He walked to his desk and pulled out a small notebook and a metal cylinder. "Now, Sir Edge, tell me what you've found out during the last month."

Justan told his tale, surprised to see that while Locksher took notes, Vannya was doing the same with her own notebook. The two of them exchanged interested glances several times while he spoke. When he brought up the name of his great grandfather, Locksher nodded excitedly.

"Aha! Wizard Artemus! Yes, I had him on my list." He flipped back in his notebook and showed Justan a row of hastily scribbled names. "I went back through the archives and looked up all the frost wizards in the Mage School's past that could have been strong enough to leave a frost elemental behind. Artemus was the most recent one and I highlighted it because his name started with the letter 'A'. Only two of the wizards on my list started with 'A'."

"Why the letter 'A'?" Darlan asked.

"Because of the cover of the Scralag's book," Vannya said. She opened one of the drawers in Locksher's desk and pulled out the weathered book. "The front cover is torn, but look. The title starts with 'Bo' on the first line and 'A' on the second."

"The Book of Artemus!" Locksher and Vannya said in unison.

"Well, maybe," Locksher amended. "It's an idea anyway. I never would have thought Artemus would be your grandfather though. It makes so much sense thinking back on it now that I know your family line. Strength in complementing elements must run in your family. Sherl being a magma wizard. You and Artemus being frost wizards. There would be a tight family connection to you for whatever part of Artemus was left inside the Scralag. The only reason I hadn't considered the possibility was because Artemus disappeared during the War of the Dark Prophet."

"But that was two hundred years ago," Justan said. He stared at his mother. "You told me great grandfather had disappeared, but . . . How old are you?"

Darlan's cheeks colored. "What a rude question. Never ask a woman her age, Justan."

"I know wizards can live longer than regular people, but grandfather was a warrior, not a wizard." Justan did some quick math in his head. "He had to at least be conceived before Artemus disappeared. Even if you weren't born until he was fifty, you would have to be at least-."

"Don't finish that sentence!" Darlan demanded.

"That's quite impressive, Sherl," Locksher said.

"You must have a lot of elven fruits in your diet to maintain such stunning good looks," said Vannya, nodding appreciatively.

"And to remain fertile enough to have a son twenty years

ago," Locksher added.

"I have half a mind to slaughter you all," Darlan growled.

"How does this work?" Jhonate asked.

"Good question," Justan said, folding his arms. "I've always heard that wizards used magic to extend their lives, but they never said anything about it in my classes. How does it work?"

"It's not something that is discussed openly," Locksher said, looking a little uncomfortable. "Working with magic does tend to slow aging. That's why races with blood magic are so long lived. Magic is working inside of them all the time. With humans, our use of magic isn't constant, so the benefit isn't as pronounced. Most wizards, if they die of old age, can live to be a hundred, maybe a hundred and ten. For us to live longer, it usually means we are around a lot of elven magic. For instance, the soil in the Mage School gardens is made from elven homeland, so the fruits and vegetables we eat here extend our lives. I am forty five, myself."

"And you don't look a day over thirty," Vannya said.

"Thank you," Locksher said. "Valtrek is in his eighties. The oldest wizard in the school is Master Latva and he's nearly two hundred. There had been some talk that he was eating a little too much elven food. But now that we know he's bonded to a gnome, it makes sense."

"The Roo-tan have long lives," Jhonate said. "The elders say it is because we commune with the Jharro trees. My father is seventy years of age, but he is still a warrior in his prime."

"How old are you?" Justan asked. "Not that it matters, but-."

"Twenty two," she said, her head cocked. "Am I too old for you, Edge?"

Justan swallowed. "Not at all."

"I'm nineteen!" Fist said proudly.

"Enough of this age talk," Darlan said with a scowl. "We are here about the Scralag."

"Khalpany olives!" Justan exclaimed. He pointed at Darlan. "A messenger used to bring you a box of Khalpany olives several times a year. You said an old friend sent them, but those were elven olives, weren't they?"

274

"I have some former clients that owe me," Darlan said.

"Those are a rare treat," Locksher said, impressed. "The Pruball Elves. Their olives are highly concentrated magic. On the edge of being illegal. What did you do to make them that grateful?"

"That is not information you need to know, Locksher," she glared and said slowly, "Or should I call you by your real name?" the wizard's eyes widened in alarm.

Justan's hand flew to his mouth. "Does father know how old you are?"

"Of course he knows!" She shouted. "He's a bit older than he looks too. Now that is enough of this discussion, young man, do you understand me?" Her eyes flared and this time actual flames blazed into existence in front of her eyes. Jhonate gave her an approving nod and Justan was sure Jhonate wished that she had that ability.

"Yes, let's get back to the subject at hand, shall we?" Locksher said. He swallowed and flipped through his notebook. "So Wizard Artemus, your great grandfather, whom everyone thought went missing, was somehow killed in the hills near the Battle Academy during the War of the Dark Prophet." He pursed his lips and picked up the book. "That tells us quite a bit, but we still can't read this without the key. Perhaps what you said to him will work, Edge. Maybe you can coax more information out of him at a later date."

"But we have the key," Justan said. "Artemus told me so. Do you have the spectacles?"

"I do," Locksher said, both his eyebrows raised.

He turned around and dug through a drawer, mumbling to himself. Finally Vannya tapped his shoulder and pointed to a different drawer. With a relieved smile, Locksher opened it and pulled out a pair of wire frame spectacles. The wire was made of some type of gold alloy and the lenses were square and not very thick. In the center of the right lens was a circular hole.

Justan took the glasses from him and looked at his mother. "When you told me who Artemus was, I finally understood. What was the one thing of great grandfather's that you held on to all these years?"

"His ring, but how . . ." She looked at the hole in the

glasses and her eyes widened in understanding.

Justan pulled the copper colored ring off his forefinger. He shifted to Mage Sight and looked at the intricate engravings. "To think I've been wearing it all this time! How could I not have noticed . . ." His spirits fell. He didn't see any elemental magic. He switched to spirit sight and there was nothing there either.

"May I see that?" Locksher said and Justan handed it over feeling numb. He had been so sure. Locksher squinted at the engravings. "Hmm. There is magic here, but it is very faint. Perhaps it's because these runes are incomplete."

Locksher held out his hands and Justan handed the glasses over. The wizard studied them for a moment, then shrugged and placed the ring into the hole in the right lens. It settled into place with a tiny click. A golden glow ignited around the lenses.

Locksher let out a hoot. "It's ingenious actually. The missing parts of the runes are actually carved into the glass of the lens! The sequence is incomplete until the ring is set into place!" He laughed, shaking his head, and handed the glasses back to Justan. "Artemus went through a lot of trouble to make sure no one read that book."

Justan's hands shook as he put the glasses on. His vision shimmered and everything went slightly out of focus. But when he brought the book in front of him he could see it clearly. In fact he could see it more than clearly. It was as if every detail stood out to his eyes.

He opened to the first page.

I Howell, son of Zack, start this journal because my mother made me. She says that good scholars need to keep journals for posterity. Who wants to be a scholar, though? Just because father is a great wizard doesn't mean I'm going to be one. Even if I am, I don't want to spend my time in a musty old library all day. I want to make fireballs or magma streams. I want to fry goblinoids like father . . .

Justan frowned and flipped through a few pages. The boy

complained about his chores, worried that he might never have an awakening, gushed about a cute girl. "This is a child's journal. It's written by a boy named Howell, son of Zack. It doesn't say Artemus anywhere."

"Wizard Zack was Artemus' father," Darlan explained. "He was a decent magma wizard, one of the first war wizards to die battling the Dark Prophet's forces. Perhaps Howell was Aretemus' name before he stood before the Bowl of Souls. May I see it?"

"Of course." Justan took off the glasses and handed the book to his mother, feeling a bit foolish. Of course Artemus would be a named wizard.

Darlan began to read. "Oh, Justan, I should have made you keep a journal." She read a bit further and smiled. "I have that pie recipe!"

Justan sighed and looked to Locksher. The wizard shrugged. They all stood there for a while, watching Darlan read, grinning and muttering to herself.

"Doesn't the ring thing get in the way while you read?" Fist asked.

"That is what I was wondering," Jhonate said.

"No," Justan said. "When you have them on you can't even see it."

"Ohh," the ogre replied and everyone nodded in understanding.

They waited a little longer before Locksher finally picked a book up off his desk and started to read. Vannya pulled a chair over for Darlan and the wizardess sat with barely a wave of acknowledgement.

"Anything interesting, mother?" Justan asked. She gave him a dismissive shake of her head and went back to reading, a smile of amusement stuck on her face. She chuckled to herself and turned another page.

Justan! Gwyrtha's thoughts interrupted Justan's irritation. She was standing in front of the bridge to the Rune Tower, her ears pricked and her hackles raised.

Yes, sweetheart?

Come quick. I smell Deathclaw's sister. She growled. *Talon is here somewhere! Many Talons!*

"We're under attack!" Justan announced, startling everyone but Fist, who had heard Gwyrtha's warning and already had his mace in his hand. Darlan even looked up from the book. *How many?*

I smell four, she sent. *There might be more.*

"What is it?" Jhonate said.

"Somehow Talon is somewhere on the Mage School property and she is not alone," Justan says. "Gwyrtha says there are at least four, maybe more and they're raptoids like her and Deathclaw."

"There are more of them?" Locksher said in shock.

"Somehow," Justan replied. He shuddered to think what Ewzad could do with even a small army of raptoid soldiers.

"Beth was right. This will be a bad night," Jhonate said. She twirled her staff and ran for the door. Fist followed close at her heels.

"Assassins," Darlan said. "Valtrek's spy warned us that assassins were coming. But no one thought they'd be able to get inside the walls."

"We'll go and alert the guard," Justan said. "Locksher and Vannya, tell the rest of the council. Talon could be after them. If anyone sees her, watch out for her tail!" He ran after Jhonate.

"I'd better warn Valtrek," Darlan declared, stowing the book and glasses in her robe and hurrying after him.

Justan ran down the hallway and started down the stairs, hoping to catch up with Jhonate, but she had flown down the stairs and Fist was in his way. The ogre was having difficulty descending quickly with his large feet. Finally he moved aside so Justan could get by.

Justan focused, putting his mind in a battle ready state as Deathclaw had taught him. His mind in complete awareness and control of his body, he ran smoothly, taking the stairs four at a time. He reached the bottom and ran past the library, dodging startled students, and pounded across the bridge. Jhonate was nowhere to be seen, but Gwyrtha was waiting, growling, her body in a half crouch.

Where is Jhonate? he asked, breathing heavily. He pulled more energy from her as he talked. His body needed to hold up!

278

She went that way, she replied and her mind showed him Jhonate heading towards the center square. *But I can smell one of the Talons this way.* Her mind showed him the buildings to the right of the Rune Tower. That was where the academy students were staying.

Take me there. Justan wanted to be with Jhonate, but the beast was more important. Gwyrtha ran. *Fist, stay with my mother.*

Fist halted in front of the library doors. He had taken a tumble at the bottom of the stairs and students were staring, some of them asking what was going on. *But-.*

If I was Mellinda, I'd want all the leaders dead. If they know Valtrek's in charge of spies, mother could be in great danger.

I . . . okay, Fist said reluctantly and ran in the direction Darlan had gone.

Gwyrtha sped off to the right, passing startled people as she followed the scent. She ran past the dining hall and the dormitories and to Justan's surprise stopped at the Hall of Elements. *One is in there.*

Justan slid down from her saddle and drew Peace. All anticipation and fear for everyone's safety left his mind and he focused on the task at hand. Why would an assassin enter the Hall of Elements? This wasn't a gaming night. His mage sight showed him that the building's magic was activated, but the sound wards were also on so he couldn't hear what was going on inside. He grasped the door with his right hand and pulled it open.

Inside the hall was a massacre. The enchanted tables were overturned in a jumble and cards were scattered everywhere. Red-robed wizards were sprawled across the room, torn and bloodied, very few of them moving.

As Justan stepped in, he saw a large figure, engulfed in flame, swipe down with one thick arm, tearing into a wizard's chest with fiery claws. The wizard stumbled back and Justan saw that it was Wizard Munsey. The High Council Fire Wizard had a pleading look in his eyes before he collapsed.

As Munsey fell, the flames around the attacker died down. Its skin was blackened and charred in most places, but

279

there was no mistaking what it was. The beast was a hulking raptoid, perhaps a half foot taller and twice as muscular as Deathclaw.

"See? Your burns meant nothing to me, wizard!" it said with a deep growling voice, and from the way it moved, it didn't seem to be pained.

It stomped on Munsey's still form and turned its head to look at Justan. Its eyes were yellow and slitted, its cheekbones broad, and its jaw thick and wide. An orange moonrat eye bulged unblinkingly from the center of its chest, looking only partially singed.

"You," it said. It pointed one steaming finger at him and smiled, the blackened scales on its lips splitting. "You are Sir Edge. You have been marked for death."

Chapter Twenty Five

"Just hide. We are under attack!" Fist told the students as he ran after Darlan. His grip on his mace increased his speed and he knocked a few startled classmates aside, but he didn't have time for apologies. Squirrel sat on his shoulder, shaking a tiny fist at the students too slow to get out of the way.

Fist's guts churned. He wanted to be with Justan. He had just gotten him back and with Talon around and possibly more like her, this was the worst time for them to be separated. *Keep him safe, Gwyrtha*!

We found one, she replied and the image of the burned and smiling raptoid flashed through his mind.

Fist stopped, his hand on the handle of the plain door leading down to Valtrek's offices. This was foolishness. There might not even be a raptoid down there. But he couldn't fault Justan's logic. Mistress Darlan was more powerful and capable than her son knew, but she had never fought anything like Talon or Deathclaw.

With a growl, Fist threw the door open. He was forced to put his mace away as he descended the stairs. He had enough difficulty navigating the stairs without having it speed up his movements. His back still throbbed from the fall he had taken at the bottom of Locksher's stairs on the way down. Squirrel was lucky he hadn't been crushed.

Half way down, he heard the door at the bottom slam. Mistress Darlan wasn't too far ahead. Squirrel sniffed the air and Fist felt a surge of fear coming from him. *Raptoid*!

There was one down there! He focused and reached the bottom as quickly as he could, not slipping once. When he opened the door, he saw the dust-covered hallway beyond had two sets of boot prints; one large, a man's, and the other Darlan's. Scattered between them, were another set of tracks. Claw marks.

Fist pulled his mace and rumbled down the low ceilinged corridor as fast as he could while hunched over. Valtrek's door was thrown open, light pouring from inside, and Fist could hear faint sounds of struggle. He surged through the doorway and saw papers scattered everywhere. Darlan was kneeling by a bloodied form, her arms held out over it. The sounds of struggle echoed from the doorway in the back of the offices.

Darlan glanced back at him quickly and turned her attention back to the body in front of her. Fist saw that it was Wizard Valtrek. His torn robes were more crimson than blue now and there were deep gashes across his face. Darlan closed her eyes and her brow furrowed as she poured elemental magic into him.

She licked her lips. "Fist, he's barely alive. I'm doing my best to save him, but whatever attacked him went through the door to the dungeons. There was screaming when I first arrived. Go! I'll be down as soon as I can."

"Squirrel, stay with Mistress Darlan!" he ordered. "Tell me if something happens."

Yes! Squirrel replied, leaping down to stand alertly by her side.

Fist spared one last glance for Valtrek and shoved aside a turned over desk so he could reach the open doorway. He heard grunting and hissing from down the stairs. He grimaced. These were the most treacherous stairs in the tower. He wished he had time to use earth magic to turn them to dirt so that he could go down them safely. Instead, he grimaced and half-ran, half-slid down them, considering himself lucky when he reached the bottom without falling.

"Slow down, you freakish beast!" Bellowed an angry voice from the doorway in front of him.

Fist barreled into the dungeon. The prisoner's cages had been lowered from the ceiling. All of them held the gory remains of Mellinda's spies, except for one.

Stout Harley stood in front of the last cage, facing off against a hissing raptoid with shield and hammer. Cowering in the back of the cage was the ex-wizard DeVargas, eyes wide with fear.

Stout Harley wore his full suit of platemail, missing only the helmet. The raptoid, a lithe and thin female, was dodging his hammer swings and striking out with clawed limbs that seemed to stretch out impossibly far in search of a gap in his armor. Only Harley's expert stance kept its attacks from making it through.

The defensive specialist shifted his arms and legs and used his wide shield to close any gap before her strikes could land. Despite his efforts, he hadn't gone unharmed. Blood poured down the side of his head from two long gashes that extended from the center of his forehead back into his hair.

His eyes never left the raptoid, but he noticed Fist's entrance. "Ogre!" he said, stepping to the side to keep the raptoid from darting around him. "Stay back. You're not ready for this one. It's fast and I think its claws are poison!"

Fist swallowed. Stout Harley knew his skill level pretty well. For the last month, he had been teaching Fist the use of shield and breastplate in battle. Unfortunately, Fist didn't have his shield or breastplate with him.

"No!" Fist said shaking his head. Stout Harley was hurt and if he was poisoned, he needed Fist's help. Besides, Harley didn't know everything that he could do. Fist sent black strands of earth magic plunging into the stone floor around him in preparation for a spell. He didn't have the sophisticated touch of many of the students, but the things Darlan had taught him didn't need it. "Hey! Talon's friend! Fight me instead!"

The raptoid leapt back to dodge one of Stout Harley's swings, and turned to face Fist. Its face was mostly razor-like teeth, its huge mouth taking up the majority of its head. Reptilian eyes sat near the top of its skull with two tiny nasal slits just above its teeth. Red bits of flesh were stuck in its teeth and bloody strands of saliva hung from its lower jaw. An orange moonrat eye was embedded at the base of its throat.

"Don't be a fool, ogre! You can't defend against this!" Stout Harley stepped forward and swung again, but the raptoid didn't even look at him as it dodged the attack, its body seeming to stretch to get out of the way.

"Go, both of you!" DeVargas yelled. He had stopped

cowering and stood. "It's here to kill me. The witch's been taunting me through that orange eye from the moment it came in here, so just either set me free and let me fight it or leave and let it kill me!"

"The witch's been talking to me too, Nikoli," Harley said. "She wants me dead just as bad as you."

"She wants us all to die," Fist said. He readied his mind and wove strands of air and earth up along his body and around his mace. He set the strands vibrating against each other, then pointed at the raptoid with his free hand and demanded, "Come at me!"

The raptoid slid forward, stopping just outside of the portion of the floor Fist had control of. It cocked its head and chirped. Fist worried. Did it know? Could it use mage sight?

"What is she saying to you?" Nikoli asked.

"Nothing," Fist said. He rolled his shoulders and kept his mace at the ready. "Are you too stupid to talk to me, Mellinda?"

At the sound of the witch's name, the raptoid screeched. It launched itself toward him and Stout Harley was right. It was very fast. It moved too quickly for him to enact the earth spell he had planned.

He brought his mace in a back swing, aiming for the center of the thing, but its body contorted out of the way. It ducked and kicked off the ground, reaching with stretching arms. As Fist knew would happen, its claws pierced his clothing and tore into the muscle of his chest.

Bright arcs of electricity flared from Fist's skin, running up its arms, sending its body into convulsions. He grabbed its throat with his free hand and squeezed as he commanded the stone under its body to surge upwards. The rock flowed soft as mud, encasing its jittering body, and stopping right under Fist's hand. He continued to pour the electricity into the thing, while squeezing its neck and willing the rock to harden.

Its neck yielded under his grip but there was no breakage of bone. The orange eye pressed against his palm and he distantly felt pressure as if something was trying to break into his mind but the bond was in the way. He squeezed harder until, finally, the orange eye burst.

He let go and stepped back, pulling the raptoid's claws

from his chest and cutting off the flow of magic. He staggered and grasped the bars of the cage next to him, breathing heavy and wincing at the pain of his wounds. Darlan had made him practice both of those spells but he had never tried enacting both of them at once. Using the mace and all that magic at the same time had taken a lot out of him.

The raptoid screeched wildly, its eyes bulging as it flailed the portion of its arms that protruded from the rock. The bones of its arms stretched, but it could only stretch so far. The rest of it was immobilized.

"Good work, ogre," Stout Harley said. His breathing was labored and he was leaning against his shield. "Didn't know you were that far along in your studies."

"Mistress Darlan is a good teacher," Fist replied.

"You're hurt, though," Harley replied. "We might both die from this poison."

Fist was starting to feel its effects. His skin was hot and his vision beginning to blur, but he wasn't too worried. "Mistress Darlan will heal us."

"Will you just kill the stupid thing!" Wizard Nikoli begged. The raptoid hadn't stopped screeching.

Fist looked down and saw the staring and unseeing eyes of Mage Lolly looking back up at him. He grit his teeth. "Yes, sir."

He pushed himself away from the cage and swung his weapon back. Electricity shot along the head of his mace as he brought the spiked end down on the raptoid's screeching face.

Heat buffeted Justan and the sound of crackling flames built around him as he stepped in to the fire section of the hall where the floor and ceiling were painted red. He edged to the right while Gwyrtha crept to the left through the gold painted air section, wind ruffling her mane.

Stay back, Justan warned her, keeping his eyes on the large raptoid in the center of the hall. It stood in the adjoining space of all four elemental sections on the broken and burnt remains of the great center table where the Elements Finals were usually played. One of its arms was in air, one in water, while its tail swayed back and forth in the rumbling earth section. It had

285

extended its grinning head towards Justan in the fire section, so far ignoring Gwyrtha. *Don't attack unless I have its full attention. We don't know what Ewzad has done to it yet.*

I am fast. I am hard. I am strong, Gwyrtha said and Justan sensed her body changing. *I am fast. I am hard. I am strong.* She repeated it like a spoken spell and Justan realized that while Fist had been learning from Darlan, she had spent the last month practicing taking control of her body's ability.

He pushed the train of thought from his mind, letting Peace take the interest away. He was proud of the growth of his bonded while he was gone, but he didn't have time to think about it now. His body was tired but he let Peace suck that away too.

The raptoid gurgled a laugh. "You think to surround me, Edge? You can try. But your pet horse is nothing. I am too strong. You can try to cut me with your swords, but I will heal."

As Justan watched, he saw that it was true. The blackened scales on its body were flaking away, exposing new undamaged scales underneath. This raptoid healed much faster than Deathclaw. It had taken on the spells of Munsey, the school's most powerful fire wizard and overcame them.

I am fast. I am hard. I am strong, Gwyrtha chanted.

Justan twirled his swords, feeling the power inside Rage build. It must have absorbed a lot of emotion from Justan while he was unconscious, because it was buzzing with it.

He focused in, the world slowing around him as he continued to edge around the room. His senses intensified and he ignored the bodies around him, stepping over them as he moved. He did not look at their faces. He could not. He might recognize one of them and that would be a distraction the raptoid could use.

"Are you coming, Edge?" it asked. "Or should I come at you?"

I am fast. I am hard. I am strong.

"Come," Justan replied. "Or wait until more of my friends arrive."

"You would have them die too?" it asked. "But they will all die soon enough."

"Is this you or Mellinda talking?" Justan continued to move. He placed one foot into the water section and felt its coolness encase his skin. The material of his pants lifted away

286

from his leg as if weightless.

Its eyes narrowed. "She doesn't like you using that name."

"Oh, but I should," Justan said. His hair lifted away from his scalp as his body was enveloped in the magic of the water section. He prepared his attack. "That's her true name. That's the name she had when she betrayed Stardeon with Gregory."

It cocked its head and when it spoke this time its voice was different. It was a bit higher, more female, and something about it buzzed at the edge of his mind as if trying to penetrate the bond. "Who told you this?"

Justan stopped his circling and stepped forward. "That was the name you had when your people rejected you. When you bonded with Dixie. Before you became the monster that was buried under a tree."

I am fast. I am hard. I am strong, Gwyrtha chanted and whatever she was doing was almost finished.

"I will enjoy your death," the raptoid said and it stepped fully into the water section. It moved towards Justan deliberately, not rushing, its arms ready, its clawed hands open, knocking aside any chair or table in its way.

Justan hopped up on a table in front of him and let it come, focusing in even tighter until its every stride was as slow as if the room truly was under water. It snatched up a chair and hurled it at him. The chair tumbled through the air end over end and Justan saw the raptoid run behind it. It jumped.

He ducked under the chair just as the raptoid jumped. It sailed at him, eyes wide with blood lust, claws outstretched. Justan dove under it, rolling as he hit the floor and felt the stinging lash of its tail across his back.

He rolled to his feet and spun, slashing with his swords, expecting the raptoid to be right on him. Instead he found another chair hurtling towards him. He knocked it to the side with Peace and saw the raptoid hurling the table he had been standing on just moments before.

Justan was forced to fall backwards to avoid it, bending his knees and letting the table pass just inches from his face. His back landed in a puddle of blood just as he saw the raptoid in the air above him, having jumped after flinging the table. Justan rolled to his left, slashing out with Peace as he spun to his feet.

The blade connected with the raptoid's outstretched hand and as Peace pierced its skin, an understanding flashed through Justan's mind. This raptoid was newly made and embraced its body. It was not broken inside like Talon had been. Ewzad had made it strong enough and durable enough that it feared nothing, but it was loyal to the moonrat mother. It also intended to eat his heart after it killed him.

The raptoid paused after the blade cut its hand, giving Justan time to scramble to his feet. He stood in the fire section again and the heat made the cut on his back twinge.

"This is the blade you struck Talon with?" It asked, holding its hand. The cut hadn't been too deep, slicing only skin and muscle. It didn't look frightened like Talon had been. Just contemplative. "She warned us about it. It has . . . an interesting bite. She warned us of your other sword too. I wonder how that feels?"

"I will be happy to show you," Justan replied. He forced his breathing under control, glad that Peace was sucking his fear away. "Where is Talon, anyway?"

"She is here. Killing your people." the raptoid said. It licked the wound. "No more talking."

I am fast. I am hard. I am strong. Gwyrtha was readying herself.

"What is your name?" Justan asked. He flipped Rage over so that the dull back side of the sword rested against his arm.

"Hungry," it said, licking its lips. "King Ewzad named me well."

"That's a terrible name," Justan said, hooking the tip of Peace's blade under the armrest of the chair beside him.

It came at him, not leaping this time, and Justan hurled the chair at it. Hungry spun, letting the chair collide with its shoulder, and whipped out with its tail. Justan brought his right arm up defensively and let the tail hit the edge of Rage's blade. The moment the edge pierced its scales, Justan unleashed half of Rage's stored power.

The force of the blast tore the raptoid's tail apart and sent it sprawling into a table in the earth section, scattering wood and blood across the black painted floor. Justan didn't wait for it to recover. He started towards it, ready to use the rest of Rage's power.

Gwyrtha got there first. Hungry barely had time to turn over before she was on him. Though Peace was still draining Justan's emotions, he couldn't help but pause for a moment, surprised by the changes.

Gwyrtha had not grown larger. Instead, her torso had shrunken in size, making her body more dense, her arms and legs a little longer. The scales on her body had enlarged and hardened, looking more like armored plates than scales and her claws had lengthened. Her mane stuck up from her back stiff and bristle-like and her head looked fiercer than before. Her teeth were longer and sharper and heavy scales protected her eyes and throat.

She wrapped her jaws around the raptoids head and they thrashed, slashing at each other with clawed arms and legs. Her claws tore through muscle and skin and scored bone while his bruised her belly and tore a few scales loose.

Gwyrtha's jaw tightened and a tooth pierced one of his eyes. Hungry thrust his taloned hands up under her ribcage, trying to tear her open, but even though his claws punctured through, he was unable to tear her toughened skin. She wrenched her head back and forth until finally there was series of loud cracks and the raptoid began to convulse.

"You can get off him now, sweetheart," Justan said, holding Rage at the ready. I can finish this."

I will! I am fast. She wrenched her head more wildly and the raptoid stopped moving. *I am hard.* She dug in her claws and pulled. *I am strong*! she said and strained until she tore its head free.

Gwyrtha spat its head to the side and Justan wrapped his arms around her bristling neck.

You were amazing! Are you okay, sweetie? he asked, checking on her injuries. Her belly was scratched and punctured in a few places, but the wounds were shallow.

I am strong, she said.

Yes you are, he agreed. He reached into the bond and healed her quickly.

Fist is hurt, she said.

He looked into Fist and found out she was right. The ogre had deep gashes in his chest and some kind of poison in his blood. Justan set to healing him, panicked that the poison was the same type that had killed Coal.

Justan, don't worry about me, Fist said. *Go and see if there are more of them.*

Not until I'm sure you're alright, Justan said. Fortunately the poison was much weaker and Justan was able to flush it from the ogre's system.

Now go. Mistress Darlan will finish once she has healed Wizard Valtrek.

Alright, fine, Justan said. He pulled back from the bond and looked down at the corpse of the raptoid in front of him. Its torso and belly were torn into ragged shreds, yet the orange moonrat eye was still staring from its chest.

"Goodnight, Mellinda," Justan said and stabbed it out.

Chapter Twenty Six

"Ho, come on, then. I risk my life to save your friend. Ho! Nearly die! And still you refuse to name me?" the imp complained.

Willum leaned on the wall's edge, looking into the calm night beyond and frowned. Ever since leaving Sir Edge's bedside, all the imp had done was whine about needing blood to recharge him or being named. *I'm still thinking of a good one.*

"A good one? Bah, I may not be able to read your thoughts yet, Willy, but I can tell when someone is making up a story. How good the name is doesn't matter!"

"It doesn't matter?" Willum scoffed. "Are you telling me you really don't care?"

"The name doesn't matter," the imp insisted.

"Oh? How about Barbara? Or Dorris? Or Jenifer? Suzy-?"

"You know what I mean," it said with a mental snort. *"A male name, but other than that, it doesn't matter . . . Just not something stupid, like Bimber or Plog or other Kobold names."*

"So it does matter," Willum said with a smile.

"Oh, you vex me Willy! Stalling the way you do. You've doubted me. You've wondered. You even took me in front of a blasted gnome! What more can I do to prove that it isn't a trick?"

It had a point. Despite the fact that the imp was an unrepentant trickster, it had proven that it wasn't evil. It had agreed to forgo its rules and behave itself for the most part. The gnome librarian had assured him that naming the imp meant only that he was claiming ownership of the axe. The downside was that their connection would be more akin to the bond. That was the thing he was most resistant to. The imp would be able to talk to him at all times, even when he wasn't touching the axe.

"Tell me the truth," Willum said. "Why is this so important to you?"

"You know," said a low monotone voice from behind Willum. "People will think you're crazy if you keep talking to your axe aloud."

The night was dark and moonless, but when Willum glanced back, he could see Swen's tall form silhouetted by the lights of the Mage School behind them. "Me? You talk to your bow."

The archer snorted. "And I talk to my arrows too. But I don't actually think they talk back."

Swen wasn't supposed to be on duty yet, but whenever he wasn't eating, sleeping, or making arrows, the wall was where he could be found. He preferred pacing the top of the wall to socializing with the other guards.

"*Hey Willy*" the imp said. "*Tell tall boy to move off. We're talking here!*"

Willum let go of the axe's handle. "People really don't believe that Tad's axe speaks to me?"

Swen shrugged. "I guess most do. And if anyone suggests otherwise, I make sure to set them straight. Still, they call you Willum Odd Blade."

"I thought that was because of my weapons." He was the only warrior in the school that dual wielded an axe and scythe. It was such a strange choice of weapon combination that some of the instructors had called him crazy for trying it.

"Could be," Swen said, shrugging again.

"Wait. Do you believe me?" Willum asked, noting the careful way the archer was phrasing his words. The big man hesitated. "Come on, Swen. Don't tell me that my best friend doubts me."

Swen moved over to stand beside him and bent to rest his elbows on the wall. He looked out into the night. "You truly consider me your best friend?"

Willum smiled and looked at the tall man's chiseled face. "Can't think of anyone else."

Swen shook his head. "What about Samson or Tolivar or

that named warrior you spent so much time with before he froze half the troops."

"Samson and Tolivar are more like family. And Sir Edge . . . I'd say he's a friend, but I really don't know him all that well," Willum said. "That freezing thing wasn't his fault, by the way."

"I heard that too," Swen said.

Willum pushed off the wall and faced him, "So do you believe me or what?"

"Alright. I guess you're my . . . best friend too," Swen said, looking away, obviously uncomfortable.

"No, I meant about the axe," Willum said with amusement at Swen's discomfort. "Do you believe it speaks with me?"

"You say it does. I can't doubt your word," the archer said with a shrug.

"Look, here," Willum pulled the axe from its half-sheath and held it out towards the man, handle first. "Let me prove it to you just to make you feel better when you have to defend me to the others."

"*What are you doing, Willy?*" the imp said. "*And what's all this talk? Aren't I your best friend?*"

Just tell him hello, imp.

"You don't have to prove anything." Swen said, looking at the axe dubiously. The imp was making the runes etched into the blade glow a fiery red.

"Just reach out and touch the handle, Swen," Willum said. "It'll speak to you."

"*No I won't. I'm not talking to your 'bestie best friend' unless you name me first.*"

Swen raised his hand hesitantly.

You had better speak to him if you wish to prove yourself to me, Willum said.

"*Oh ho! See this is where playing without the rules puts us into a conundrum, Willy boy. You think you can drag me along, making hints and half promises and I'll do whatever you say, hoping . . . hoping while you delay.*"

Swen touched the handle.

Just do it!

Swen drew back his hand with a gasp. He looked at Willum with wide eyes.

"What?" Willum asked. "What did it say to you?" *You didn't hurt him, did you, imp?*

"*I merely gave him a traditional impish greeting.*"

"It said . . ." Swen frowned. "'Hey wood face. Willy talks too much'." He reached up and touched his face. "Why wood face?"

Willum had to stifle a laugh. The imp must have overheard Tolivar tell him that Swen had a face that looked as if it were carved from wood. "It, uh, has a strange sense of humor."

"*Ho-ho! That was a good one. Right, Willy? I felt you hold back a giggle.*"

I don't giggle, Willum replied. *And just because I find it a bit funny, does not mean it was a nice thing to say to my friend.*

"*When did I say I was nice?*"

Willum put the axe away. "At least you know the truth."

Swen nodded slowly. Then he grew still for a moment. "Do you hear that?"

Willum turned and looked to the center of the school where the clock tower was lit up by the lights in the center square. It was faint, but he heard frantic voices. "What's going on?" He grabbed the axe handle again.

"*Something strange is happening, Willy,*" the imp said. "*Something smells . . . bad in the air now.*"

"Something like what?" Willum asked.

"Maybe we're about to find out," Swen said. They could see two figures running down the wall in their direction, giving instructions to every guard they passed by. One of them carried a torch and torches were only supposed to be used in case of an emergency at night. It dulled a guard's night vision and made them an easy target to archers below.

"*Ho-ho! It smells like the witch, Willy. An eye is nearby.*"

Willum pulled the axe from its sheath. *Is it coming from these two guards?*

"*I don't know. Somewhere close. Ho, be ready!*"

Willum reached through the bond and contacted Tolivar and the others. *Something's going on in the school. I can't tell what it is from the wall, but the imp senses a moonrat eye*

294

somewhere nearby.

There is a commotion near the center square, Samson replied from the stables. He jumped the pasture fence as he spoke, *I'm heading there now.*

I'm knee deep in the friggin' forge, said Bettie. *But Lenui and I will be there if you need help.*

I'm on my way to you, Tolivar replied. He was only a half mile down the wall to the north.

Willum elbowed Swen. "Something's coming. Be ready."

The big man didn't ask questions. He pulled an arrow from his quiver and notched it on his enormous bow.

Willum watched the guard's approach with a tight grip on the axe, but as they drew nearer, he let out a sigh of relief. The one carrying the torch was Sabre Vlad and the one with him was his assistant, Lyramoor. They ran to Willum's position and stopped, both of them with serious looks on their faces.

"Willum! Swen!" Sabre Vlad said. "We've gotten word that assassins have entered the school. We don't know how they got in, but it is our job to make sure they don't get out."

"How many are there?" Swen asked.

"*It's close! It's close, Willy!*" the axe said.

"The axe says there's something here now!" Willum shouted.

Swen and Lyramoor looked over the outside edge of the wall, while Willum and Sabre Vlad looked over the interior. Willum didn't see anything at first, but then he noticed that little marks on the stone beneath Sabre Vlad were actually the tips of claws. A shadow stirred beneath the warrior and before Willum could call out in warning, the creature shot up from the dark.

Sabre Vlad barely had time to pull his sword from its sheath, before it grabbed him and sank its teeth into his throat. The warrior let out a gurgle and the creature tore free with a spray of blood. Willum cried out, staggering backwards.

The torchlight showed Willum a nightmare. The creature's scaled skin was jet black and its face was reptilian with deep red slitted eyes. As it swung towards him, Willum saw that its torso was disturbingly female in shape and that an orange moonrat eye was embedded in the center of its chest almost as if it were a hanging pendant.

"*Name me, Willy,*" the imp pleaded. "*Quick! Do it now!*"

"Vlad!" cried Lyramoor and as Sabre Vlad fell back, clutching at his ruined throat, the elf darted forward, slashing at the creature with his dual falchions.

Swen grabbed Willum by the collar and dragged him back several paces. "You'll be in Lyramoor's way," the archer said and Willum saw it was true.

The torch lay on the ground where Vlad had dropped it and the fight its flickering light illuminated was something of beauty. Lyramoor was a consummate swordsman, perhaps the best dual wielder in the academy and despite his worry for Sabre Vlad, the elf's movements were poetry. He whipped about and danced, taking up the whole of the walkway as he fought.

I need a wizard here now! Willum called through the bond. *Samson, get one! Sabre Vlad is down*!

It's a mess here too, said the centaur and Willum caught a glimpse through the bond of students screaming in terror. *I'll try.*

Lyramoor's attack was flawless, but the creature was a blur. It dodged most of his attacks, but those it couldn't, it parried with a row of hardened and glistening scales on the sides of its forearms.

"Just give me an opening," Swen said quietly. Willum could hear the creak of his bow as the archer pulled an arrow back.

"*Name me,*" the imp said.

"Shut up about that!" Willum snapped. "Not you, Swen." *This isn't the time.*

"*It is!*" the imp insisted.

The creature went on the offensive, blocking Lyramoor's attacks and striking out with a long spiked barb on the end of its tail. The elf was hit once in the shoulder, staggering him back. He blocked two more strikes, but was hit once in the hip and once in the abdomen. He grunted and hobbled over to stand protectively over Sabre Vlad's struggling form.

"Me first," Lyramoor said and Willum knew that the fight was over.

The raptoid made two slashing feints with his claws, then turned and whipped out his tail. The barb caught the elf on the side of the head and Lyramoor tumbled over the edge. Willum watched with a sick feeling deep in his stomach as the elf fell to the inside of the wall, a drop of fifty feet.

A soft twang sounded as Swen released his arrow. At this range, nothing should have been able to dodge his shot, but the creature whipped its head around at just the right moment. The arrow, which had been aimed at the back of the creature's head, struck the side of its cheek instead, passing through its mouth and ripping out half of its upper jaw on the way out.

The thing stumbled back, but caught itself on the inside wall. Blood poured from its ruined mouth as it turned its red eyes on them. Swen stepped backwards, pulling another arrow from his quiver.

I'm coming, Tolivar said.

"Run, Willum!" Swen said.

"Just ready your arrow," Willum said, and stood with his feet planted, facing the thing. He pulled a scythe from its sheath at his lower back with his left hand, leaving the axe in his right.

"You're not ready for this, Willy. Just name me."

That won't help, he sent, angry that it wouldn't stop its nagging even at a time like this. *Just be ready with a force strike.*

The imp was right about one thing though. He wasn't ready. This creature was too fast and the axe's magic would be no good if he couldn't hit it. He'd been practicing hard, but switching from dual wielding scythes to fighting with a scythe and a waraxe had been a difficult transition for Willum. Even before making the change, this thing would have been too good for him and he'd only actually had a couple months of training with his new style.

"I'll try to help but I don't know if I have a force strike in me," the imp replied.

The creature leapt at him. The torch glow wasn't much to see by and its black scales didn't help, but Willum was able to block one claw with his scythe and strike its other forearm with his axe. The claws on the creature's feet struck his thighs, digging in deep, before the axe thrummed with power.

The sound of a deep bell echoed through the night and the creature was thrown away, tumbling end over end along the top of the wall. The impact tore its claws from Willum's thighs and all strength left his legs. He collapsed to the ground, crying out in pain.

"*Oh-ho, good hit! But Willy Yum, that blast was not as big as usual. My power is too drained. I'm no good to you now unless you name me.*"

The creature climbed to its feet and Willum saw what the axe meant. The hit hadn't been strong enough. Its arm was bleeding, but intact. It ran for him.

Swen fired. Somehow the beast dodged to the side and the arrow meant for its chest simply struck its arm. It staggered but kept coming.

How could naming you possibly help?

"*Trust me,*" the imp pleaded.

The creature darted forward blood pouring from its mouth and arm, its eyes crazed and focused on him. Willum knew it was too late.

Tolivar collided with the beast, shoulder first, driving it to the ground. He rolled over it and stood, swinging back with his sword as it sprung to its feet. His sword tip slashed along its back. The wound didn't seem to phase the beast and it came at Tolivar, this time both claws at the ready.

Tolivar's style wasn't anything like Lyramoor's and it wasn't like anyone else's Willum had ever seen. His technique was a mix of berserker and swordwielder guilds. He swung wildly, leaving openings too hard for the creature to resist, then somehow was able to come around and close them with an expert parry. If he ever did get hit, he knew how to move his body in such a way that the wound was very shallow, seldom more than a scratch.

"*Listen Willum,*" the imp said. "*If you name me, I'll be able to use more than just elemental magic in my attacks. My spirit magic is locked, see? I can't use mental attacks unless you unleash me!*"

Willum swallowed. He watched Tolivar battle with savagery and precision. The warrior was good, but even wounded, the creature's skill was even with his. He needed help.

Alright! Willum said. He shoved aside his doubts about the imp. Coming up with the name wasn't hard. He had picked out the name months before, not long after talking to Vincent about it. He just hadn't been ready. *I name you Theodore.*

"*Theodore?*" the imp chuckled. "*Oh, I like it. I like it, Willy. It's a very proper sounding name. A bit of a gnomish name perhaps, but good.*"

It was Tad's given name before he entered the academy, Willum replied. *He told me he changed it to Tad because he thought Theodore sounded like a scholar's name.*

"*I accept,*" the imp said. There was a strange click in Willum's mind and he had a flash of insight as he felt the imp's emotion's pour through him. It was happy, exhilarated. It tasted freedom from solitude and to Willum's surprise, what it felt towards him was something close to affection.

A sound echoed from the axe. This one was much different than the bell sound. It was more like a whooshing sound. Willum saw a wave of white energy rush from the axe's blade and strike the creature full-on.

The creature paused mid-attack, stunned. Tolivar struck out twice in quick succession. One swipe split its left hand in half, the other caught it in the chest just above the orange eye, cutting deep. He spun around and followed through with a kick that caught it in the midsection, knocking it towards the outside of the wall and sending it over the edge.

As it fell, Swen's bow twanged again and an arrow caught it in the abdomen, sending it spinning into the deep darkness below.

Willum let out a sigh of relief and fell to his side. *Thank you, imp.*

"*Ho-ho, it's Theodore now, remember? Don't forget my name already,*" the imp said. "*Your legs are cut up pretty good, Willy. It hit an artery. You'll bleed out if it's not tended to.*"

That's okay, Theodore, Willum said. *I think I'll be fine.* He was watching Tolivar crouched over Sabre Vlad. The fallen warrior wasn't moving.

Tolivar turned and came to him. His eyes gleamed sad in the flickering torchlight. "I'm sorry. Vlad's dead. Samson couldn't get a wizard to come with him, but he has two elf healers on his back and they're coming here now to check on Lyramoor."

Willum's eyes were droopy. "I'll sleep till they get here," he mumbled.

"*Don't sleep Willy*," Theodore cautioned.

"The axe is right," Tolivar said, surprised that he heard its voice. "Time to try this, I suppose. Stay awake for me."

Willum felt a strange feeling as if a door opened somewhere inside him and then he could feel Tolivar's energy inspecting the injury. He felt a warmth gather around the wound, then a jolt. It felt somewhat like when Coal had healed him in the past, but a lot more intense.

A moment later, Tolivar took a deep gasp and opened his eyes. Willum realized the man had been holding his breath.

"What did you do?" Willum asked. He felt wide awake now and the pain in his legs was gone.

"I don't have elemental magic," Tolivar said. "But Sadie's a healing sword. Alfred's been teaching me how to intensify her power with my spirit magic. He says it's only possible since she's my naming weapon."

"Sadie?" Willum asked.

"I hated the name Elise," Tolivar said. He sat on the ground next to Willum. The man was tired. Willum could feel it through the bond. Fighting the creature without going into a berserker state, along with healing Willum, had taken a lot out of him. "I didn't want a sword named after the stupid princess that broke Zambon's heart. Once Zambon changed the name of my old sword, I felt better about changing the name of his." He paused. "You know why I named my old sword Meredith?"

Willum shook his head. He was curious, but it seemed surreal that they were having this conversation mere feet from Sabre Vlad's body.

"*He's protecting you, Willy,*" the imp said, sounding impressed. "*He's keeping you distracted from what just happened. Oh-ho, your wizard's a true general.*"

"Meredith was the name of my first girlfriend," Tolivar said. "Oh, she was such a nag. She'd get angry at anything and she won every fight, it didn't matter what it was. Considering the sword's angry nature, her name seemed appropriate."

Samson called out through the bond, letting them know he'd arrived at the base of the wall. The elves he'd brought with him had found Lyramoor. To Willum's relief, he was still alive. His wounds were bad and he had multiple broken bones, but the elves thought Lyramoor would live. They had been quite surprised to find out he was a full blooded elf. He had hidden his secret from them all the time he'd been at the Mage School.

Are there more of those creatures out there? Tolivar asked.

We don't know, Samson replied. *The commotion seems to have died down, though.*

"So why did you call your sword Sadie?" Swen asked. He was standing next to them, another arrow cocked on his bow. His sharp eyes were looking out for any more danger, but it was obvious he had become interested in their conversation.

Tolivar lifted the blade in the torchlight and the white gem at its base sparkled, surrounded by fiery golden runes. "This sword's the opposite of Meredith. She's a proper lady. And she cares. She wants nothing more than to heal. So I named her after my own mother.

"Sadie was the best of women. She would heal a wounded bird. Even let spiders free if they got in the house." He climbed to his feet and Willum could see that Tolivar's wounds were closing up as he spoke. "Something else about my mother, she was fiercely protective of us. I once saw her beat a cork snake to death with a broom handle. That thing's head was bigger than mine. She broke my dad's nose once when he got too drunk and slapped my sister."

"That's a fine name, then," Swen said. Willum agreed.

Tolivar reached out his hand and pulled Willum to his feet. Willum's legs twinged slightly, but they felt whole.

You need to get down here, Bettie sent, interrupting their thoughts. *The leaders are gathering to assess the damage. This thing was bad.*

"I'm going down to meet Samson," Tolivar said. "We'll go outside the wall and check to make sure that creature is dead." He ran to the nearest set of stairs leading down to the ground below. *You head to the meeting for me. See what's happened.*

"Yes, sir," Willum said. "Will you man my post, Swen? I'll send some men back for Sabre Vlad."

The tall archer nodded and Willum ran.

Gwyrtha's new form was not made for riding. Her torso

was short and much narrower than before. It was a struggle to stay in the saddle. Justan was knocked about by every bump or jostle and was forced to grip her bristling wiry mane tightly.

They paused at the center square. People were milling about, some of them sobbing, and Justan saw several wizards tending to wounded on the ground. One of the raptoids had cut right through the center of these people, causing as much damage as it could on the way.

Several people screamed at Gwyrtha's appearance, but Justan was enough of a recognizable figure that no one tried to attack. He talked to one of the wizards and told him about wounded wizards in the Hall of Elements. Munsey was dead, but a few of them were still breathing when he left.

Jhonate, Gwyrtha said, sniffing the air. *She chased after this one.*

Go! Find her, Justan said, tightening his legs on her sides. Gwyrtha sped away, skirting the center square and heading for the main gates. They passed two fallen academy students along the way. One of them cried out, but Justan couldn't stop to help him. *Is it Talon?* Justan asked. *Is it Talon's scent you're chasing?*

No. Another, Gwyrtha said and Justan felt slightly better. Still, though Jhonate was as good a fighter as anyone with her staff, he doubted she'd faced anything like one of these raptoids.

Justan soon saw two figures struggling in the distance just off the lit section of the main road among the twisting walkways. Gwyrtha headed right for them. It was Jhonate. She had caught up to the creature.

The raptoid she was facing was male and tall, though not so big as the one Justan had faced. Its skin was dark green with diagonal stripes of gray. A long set of spikes ran down its back from its neck all the way to the end of its tail. The moonrat eye was set in the center of its forehead, surrounded by a row of protective spikes.

As Justan neared, he saw that Jhonate was more than holding her own. The raptoid's torso was covered in slashes and punctures and it was missing one long finger from its left hand. Jhonate seemed uninjured, though her shirt was torn and her leather breastplate damaged.

302

The raptoid hissed at her as it slashed, calling her all kinds of foul epithets, things even Lenny would never say. Justan's lips twisted into a snarl as he slid off Gwyrtha's saddle. He drew his swords, watching Jhonate fight as he edged around the beast.

If Jhonate noticed him, she gave no indication. She worked, spinning and slashing, her staff morphing into whatever shape she needed. It dove at her and she rolled to the side, slashing out with her staff. The sharpened edge caught the raptoid in the neck and as it turned to face her, bright gouts of blood sprayed from the wound.

It clutched at its neck with one hand and backed away a few steps, then spun around to run, but Gwyrtha was there, growling. It turned again, but Justan was ready for it. With a gurgle, it threw itself at Jhonate.

It screeched and when Jhonate slashed at it again, it caught her staff in its right hand. Jhonate morphed the staff again and spikes sprouted from the wood, bursting through its skin. It ignored the wound and pulled back on the staff, bringing Jhonate in close, then slashed down with its other hand.

Jhonate spun and its claws tore through her shirt, but glanced off the protective magic of her ring. Jhonate followed through with a high kick that caught it under the chin and staggered it back. She withdrew the spikes and pulled the staff from its ruined hand, then pivoted and thrust the now sharpened tip of the staff through its chest. With a twist, she made the tip of the staff sprout spikes again, this time through the heart and lungs of the raptoid.

It quivered and fell to its knees. "You will die," it gurgled. "The mistress will see to it."

She spat into the moonrat eye in its forehead. "Tell her I will see to her first."

Jhonate tore the staff free and severed its head with a two-handed chop.

Trevor H. Cooley

Chapter Twenty Seven

Faldon the Fierce slung the corpse of his raptoid next to the others. This one had black and green mottled skin and its body was covered in wounds, including one massive gaping gash that stretched from its right shoulder to its left hip. Darlan rushed over and hugged him, careless of the raptoid blood that covered his body.

"It attacked Hugh and I as we were exiting the infirmary," Faldon explained.

The Hall of Elements had been cleared of tables and the injured wizards taken to the infirmary along with the bodies of the dead. The Hall's magic had been shut down and the surviving leaders gathered to view the raptoids and decide what to do next. Reports were still coming in and they still hadn't heard from half of the High Council. Randolf was there, but Beehn, Latva and Auger were still unaccounted for.

"This thing was a nasty piece of work," Hugh the Shadow added as he tossed the raptoid's head down beside the body. "It took nearly everything I had before Faldon finally hewed it down." He began plucking the various thrown daggers and stars and blades that protruded from wounds in its body, tucking the retrieved weapons quickly into different places hidden within his assassin armor.

"Fascinating." Locksher's eyebrows were fully raised. The wizard was kneeling beside the bodies and examining them with tiny metal instruments. Every once in a while he would cut a tiny piece of a raptoid free and tuck it into a tiny pouch, then hand it to Vannya to put away. The mage looked both disgusted and intrigued at the same time. "This one's eyes seem to have been cut from a snow tiger. Somehow Vriil placed them inside this raptoid and adapted them seamlessly to its nerves."

"Still no sign of Talon," Justan said. They had killed four raptoids in all. The one Tolivar had kicked off the wall hadn't been there when he went to retrieve it.

"I don't know that she was here," said Valtrek, leaning on Fist for support. The wizard was still very weak from Darlan's healing, but had insisted on coming anyway. "There were supposed to be six assassins, but Ewzad Vriil knew nothing of Talon being here. According to my source, he still thinks she's missing."

"Gwyrtha smelled her. She's sure of it," Justan insisted. "Talon was here."

The door to the hall swung open and the room hushed as Alfred stepped inside. The tall, gaunt-faced gnome was grim faced as he walked towards them, the end of his polished cane making a loud click each time it struck the floor. His fine clothing had been torn, leaving half his shirt hanging in tattered rags, exposing sculpted and thickly corded muscle beneath. He didn't appear to be injured.

"Latva is gravely wounded," the gnome pronounced. There was fear in his eyes as he said it. "Wizard Auger and Wizard Beehn were able to get him stabilized before the healer arrived, but whatever poison the thing injected him with is vicious. They are still working on him." He threw the severed end of a raptoid tail onto the ground.

Gwyrtha growled at the scent of it.

"That's Talon's tail." Justan felt a surge of hope. "Were you able to kill her?"

"I cut its tail free just as it pierced Latva," Alfred said, then added bitterly, "I wasn't fast enough. We struggled and I stabbed the beast through the heart, but it managed to hurl itself from a window. I can only assume it survived the fall, because it's not there now."

"You stabbed it? Through the heart?" said Randolf with a snort. The air wizard's golden robes were pristine. He had been in the library teaching a late class when the attacks happened. "Since when did you carry a blade, gnome?"

Alfred thumbed the grip on his cane and pulled a long, thin blade from within the wood. A soft ringing split the air and the blade glittered in the light for a few quick moments before he slammed it back into the cane.

"Gnomish steel," Lenny's bushy red eyebrows were raised in wonder. "Ain't seen one of them in decades."

"Alfred was a gnome warrior before he was a bonding wizard," Valtrek explained.

"You're kidding me," said Hugh the Shadow, eyeing the gnome with admiration. Gnome warriors were rarely seen outside Alberri, but they were said to be the most dangerous of foes, a gnome that had eschewed scholarly pursuits at a young age to focus solely on fighting.

"And who gave you permission to give out such information, Wizard Valtrek?" Alfred gnome asked with a glare.

"What reason is there to hide it now?" Valtrek said with a roll of his eyes. "They know everything else about you and Latva and, since it seems that Talon survived, Mellinda does too."

"What are our known casualties?" Faldon asked.

"On the High Council, we lost Wizard Munsey," Valtrek said. "There were six other fire wizards with him, some of the most powerful in the school and only two of them survived. Wizardess Landra was one of the dead. We also know about a handful of mages and two cadets that were killed." He sighed. "Promising students all of them, and the numbers could rise." Justan noticed he didn't mention the slain prisoners.

"We lost Sabre Vlad," Willum said. He swallowed and his back stiffened. "It wouldn't have happened in a fair fight, but the thing just came out of the dark. Caught him by surprise."

The warriors in the room bowed their heads in respect.

"Don't forget Forgemaster Stanley," Bettie added. Her face was drawn and sad. She had gotten to know the academy armorer quite well since they arrived at the school. "He was in the center square when that striped one attacked."

"The loss of those two men alone would have been a heavy blow," Oz the Dagger said, rubbing his chin. "But beyond the loss of their skill, we have a bigger problem. Six creatures attacked us tonight. Only six! And they managed to get past our defenses and kill our leaders. How are the students and refugees supposed to feel safe now? What kind of panic will we be dealing with when a large force arrives?"

"We can't let them see it that way," Hugh said. "We need to show them that we survived. Let the people know we won."

"So we set the bodies of these things on display," Randolf said. "Let them see what we were up against."

"What? And give the students nightmares about those terrible things?" Darlan said in disgust. She shook her head. "No, you'll have them seeing raptoids around every corner." Randolf scowled at her tone, but she ignored him. "Show the creatures to the leadership and the wizards if you must. For the others, talk only of the heroes that defeated the beasts and the tragic loss of our great fallen. Make them angry. Make them proud so that when the enemy comes they will fight."

"And that's why they call her a war wizard," Faldon said with a smile.

"Why didn't these things melt?" Willum asked, looking at the raptoid remains. "All the rest of Ewzad Vriil's monsters turned into goo when they died."

Justan knew the answer but it couldn't be spoken aloud. If Ewzad Vriil ever learned the truth, he would find a way to make all of his creations stable. The damage he could do with that knowledge would be devastating.

"I'm not sure, Willum," Locksher said as he sawed at one of the spikes on the striped raptoid's back. "I'll do some tests when I get back to my rooms and let you know. Perhaps it's something unique with them being raptoids." Justan swallowed. He needed to have a conversation with the wizard later.

"I got a different question," Lenny said, his face pinched. His eyes were filled with something akin to guilt. "Where'd Vriil get six dag-blamed raptoids in the first place? Fer that matter, where's he gettin' all the blasted animals he's been makin' monsters with?"

"Dwarven smugglers," Valtrek said, eyeing Lenny's expression with interest.

"Dag-blast it!" Lenny said stomping his foot. "Someone should've told me sooner. Hell, I should've guessed it myself. Dag-blast it! Which ones are supplyin' him?"

"Dwarven smugglers?" Justan asked. He'd never heard of such a thing.

"Dark magic dealers mostly," Faldon said. "They're

responsible for most of the slave trading and elf contraband in the known lands. We have run-ins with them all the time when we're out on jobs."

"I'm, pretty sure he's dealing with a branch of the Corntown Smugglers, Lenui," Valtrek said. "They were masquerading as a dwarf menagerie and our spy described them as wearing handlebar mustaches."

"Garl-friggin' son of a dog!" Lenny swore. "Did he see their leader? What's his name?"

"According to my source, he didn't give a name," Valtrek said. "He just demanded they call him 'Ringmaster'. Other than that, the only other information I have is that he has black hair and had a larger mustache than the others."

"That dag-burned, hoop-skirtin', corn-jiggin', mother brother!" Lenny exclaimed.

"Do you know him?" Justan asked. He'd wondered about Lenny's past many times. Why had Gwyrtha hated him for so long? Why did he seemed worried about other dwarves who wore a mustache the way he did? But the dwarf never wanted to talk about it.

"Yes, durn it, he's my uncle," Lenny said with a scowl. "Name's Blayne."

"Can you tell us anything that could help us know what's coming next?" Valtrek asked. "What else might they bring him?"

"I can do you one better." Lenny said. "I can tell you what yer spy can say to call that coonhound off."

"You can get them to leave?" Valtrek said in surprise. "Break their contract with Ewzad Vriil?"

"I can tell you what to say to have 'em out of Dremaldria 'fore the sun hits their arses," Lenny promised. "No more raptoids. No more other monsters he can use, unless he's got another source."

"How could you know a thing like that?" Faldon asked, looking at Lenny with puzzled eyes. "I've battled with Corntown smugglers before. They won't leave a contract unfinished unless half of them are dead."

"Yeah, and even then they ain't 'posed to let up," Lenny agreed. "It's bad fer their reputation. My momma would kill 'em her dag-gum self."

"Your momma?" Bettie asked, her brow lined with confusion.

"My momma's their gall-durn leader," Lenny said with a sigh. He looked miserable just saying it. "Has been fer the last ninety years."

"Unbelievable," Hugh the Shadow laughed. "We have smuggler royalty right here! Bloody Maggie's son!"

Lenny's face was beet red. "Look, just tell yer spy to go to the main tent of the Menagerie. Tell 'em you got a 'price one message' fer the ringmaster. Remember now. Price one! Blayne'll be pissed when he comes, but just tell him exactly this. 'Lenui says there ain't no profit fer you here.' He'll demand to know why. You say 'Maggie's law'."

"Maggie's Law?" Valtrek said.

"That'll do it." He looked down at the floor. "You need me to repeat it?"

"I'll remember," the wizard promised.

"Good. I'll . . . be outside then," Lenny said and made his way out the door.

Justan stared after him, mouth open in wonder. Matron Guernfedt came into the hall a moment later with news on the casualty count. As the others talked, Bettie came over to Justan and pulled him aside. Despite the soot on her face, the muscular half-orc was looking prettier than usual. Justan's mother had told him that pregnant women had a glow about them. Maybe this was what she meant. If so, that was the only way Justan would have been able to tell. Her belly only showed the slightest bit of a bulge.

"Listen here," Bettie said, grabbing his earlobe. Her fingers were rough and callused and Justan winced as she pulled him close enough to whisper in his ear. Her whisper was as loud as most people's speaking voice. "You go and talk to Lenui. Find out what's bugging him. I've never seen him looking so sore."

"Why don't you talk to him yourself?" Justan asked, pulling out of her grasp.

She scowled and grabbed his ear again. "Ever since he learned he put a baby in me Lenui ain't been himself. Until he smartens up, I ain't lettin' him cry on my shoulder. Besides, he's got a soft spot for you. He'll talk to you."

Justan pulled free again, half expecting to leave half of his ear behind. "Fine. I'll go."

"Good! And make sure you set his brain on straight. Tell him he sure as hell better tell me about his momma. His future wife should know these things," Bettie said, punctuating her declaration with a firm nod.

Justan swallowed and walked to the door. Gwyrtha came right behind him. He was relieved to see that she had resumed her regular size and form. It was impressive how quickly she had done it.

Can I come too? Fist asked. He was still standing there propping Valtrek up.

I'm sorry, Fist. He looks like he still needs your help. The wizard was practically sagging in the ogre's arms. *Besides, you can let me know if any new news comes in.*

Could I at least get him a chair? Fist complained.

Justan chuckled. *I'm sure that would be fine*, he said and exited the room.

Lenny hadn't gotten far. Justan saw the dwarf walking towards the center square. Likely, he was going back to the forge to work out his frustrations. Justan hurried, hoping to grab him before the other dwarves pulled him aside. "Hey, Lenny!"

"Huh?" the dwarf said, looking over his shoulder. "Oh. Hey, son."

"What's going on?" Justan asked. "You got out of there quick."

"It's shame, Edge," Lenny said. "Dag-nab it, a past is a hard thing to hide from. You do somethin' stupid and it always comes back to bite you in the arse."

Justan frowned. "But it's your mother that's the smuggler, not you."

"But it weren't always-!" Lenny looked around, making sure no one had been close enough to listen, then grabbed Justan's arm and pulled him around the corner of the dining hall. It wasn't any more private. People were walking by, some of them nodding at them in recognition. "Well, I ain't talkin' 'bout this where folks'll hear."

"Okay, then," Justan said and led Lenny back past the Hall of Elements, bringing him to the edge of the Mage School forest. He stopped at the treeline. "Here we are, no one here to hear your shame."

"You ain't bein' funny," Lenny said with a frown.

"Come on. It can't be too bad. You're Lenny Firegobbler, Master Weaponsmith, The Hero of Lightning Gap!" Justan said.

"That's Thunder Gap," Lenny corrected. "But you don't get it. That ain't always been me."

Justan blinked. "So you were a smuggler too?"

Lenny shifted his feet. "Gah! Back in my younger days, yeah! Look, here's the thing. I'm from Corntown. If yer from Corntown, yer one of two things. Either a blacksmith or a gall-durn smuggler. Now the Firegobbler line is full of fine smithys. Grandpappy and daddy are both legends."

"And so are you," Justan said.

"Just listen, dag-gum it! Now I don't know why I'm feelin' like tellin' this story, but if you don't let me tell it proper, I probly won't."

"Got it." Justan reached up and mimed pinching his lips shut.

Me too, Gwyrtha promised.

Lenny gave them a suspicious glance, but nodded. "Right, then. So my daddy married twice. My stupid brother Chugk is from his second wife and so's my sister."

Justan's eyebrows rose at that, but he wisely kept his mouth shut.

"But I was born from his first love, Maggie. Now she was a Cragstalker and they was known trouble, most of 'em turned smuggler. Maggie's daddy was their leader at the time, but she promised him she'd left that life behind and my daddy let himself believe it. Grandpappy was pissed, but daddy married her anyways.

"I was born soon afterwards. Life was durn good fer a little dwarf. Daddy'd let me play 'round in the forge and momma'd tell me excitin' stories 'bout her daddy outrunnin' the law. Then one day, out of the blue, momma grabbed me'n took off. Now I was sixteen at the time and she was promisin' adventure. Daddy was keepin' me workin' in the forge and adventure sounded real good right then.

"So we left. Momma took me back with her to the

Cragstalkers. It was fun at first. They taught me how to ride horses. How to rustle critters. How to fight. But when I turned twenty, that's when they started takin' me on smugglin' runs. I saw some dark friggin' stuff then. The Cragstalkers did business with some nasty damned wizards, I tell you. I done seen things that'd turn yer liver green."

"My liver?" Justan asked, trying to picture how that was possible.

"But they kept me from the real bad stuff fer a couple more years. 'Till they thought I could handle it," Lenny said. His lip twisted in revulsion. "That's when they showed me my first elf blood slave. They called him Palky. Maggie's daddy'd stole him from his homeland when he was just a babe. They raised him stupid, so's he wouldn't be smart 'nough to run away. Then they'd cut on him or bleed him if a wizard paid 'nough for it. He was all scarred up'n wild."

He shuddered. "Now I didn't have nothin' to do with that part, but the point is, son, I was there. I was in the blasted thick of it. I didn't like it, but I didn't do nothin'. Least not then. Not till I saw them sell a rogue horse."

Gwyrtha growled.

Lenny walked over and rubbed her head. "I know darlin'. I know. I'm real damn sorry'n I understand if you hate me forever fer this. But I gotta tell the dag-gum truth to you right now." He looked into her eyes. "My grandpappy Cragstalker was the son of the dag-blamed dwarf who rustled yer kin."

"Your great grandfather captured the rogue horses?" Justan asked.

"He did," Lenny said and Gwyrtha growled again. "They was braggin' 'bout it. Called it the biggest Cragstalker score in history. Jedd Cragstalker was Stardeon's monster supplier back then. Helped him make the rogues. Now they didn't say Stardeon's name when they told me the story, but I figgered it out when Old John told us his story.

"They was content to act within their contract, but then the big quake hit the land. Stardeon run off, leavin' the rogues behind, so Jedd rounded 'em up and took 'em fer himself. Started sellin' 'em off to the highest dag-burned bidder. Them purse snatchers didn't care who they sold 'em to. Just whoever could pay. And they charged a king's fortune, too.

"Anyways, when I was with 'em they'd already done sold all the rogue horses 'cept fer two. They was real sweet too. I gotta ride 'em. Don't know what their real names was. The Cragstalkers just called 'em 'gold' and 'more gold'. One was part gorilla and one was part dog.

"I was there the day they sold the part-dog one. We took him to a place in Alberri. There was a real rich gnome there. A scholar. He paid fer it, took it, and slit its throat." Lenny's face twisted in anger and his eyes swelled with tears. "Right there in front of me, Edge. That friggin' gnome killed that sweet rogue like it was nothin'. Poor thing didn't even struggle. Just laid there lookin' confused. The gnome filled up a glass with its blood. Drank it, and cut some parts of it free. Then they left its corpse to rot."

Gwyrtha let out a keening moan and Lenny held her, telling her over and over that he was sorry. Her sorrow cut through the bond and Justan had to swallow back tears of his own.

Did you know him? Justan asked her.

Don't know, she said, but it didn't matter. *There were many with dog in them. Father liked dogs.*

"The night we got back, I went out to the pasture and rode the gorilla rogue. I took him to the edge and busted some of the dag-burned fence down, makin' it look like it was done from the outside. Then when I turned to set him free, I saw a man standin' there watchin' me. It was the dag-gum prophet. John asked me what I was doin'. I didn't want to say, but then he told me who he was. He called me by name. Don't know how he knew my name, but he asked me if a smuggler's life was what I wanted. I told him I didn't know. Then he took the rogue and left.

"I decided to leave the Cragstalkers, but I waited a week or two, just so's they wouldn't know it was me let the rogue go." Lenny gave a half grin. "Oh, them smugglers was dag-burned pissed. I was scairt, but I had a hard time keepin' from smilin' every time Grandpappy Cragstalker let out a curse. Then I went back to my daddy's house and asked him to take me back in. Told him I wanted to be a smithy like him."

Gwyrtha licked his face. Lenny grimaced and spat. "Hell, girl, if yer gonna eat me, just do it whole."

"She forgives you, Lenny," Justan said. He put a hand on his friend's shoulder. "You came out all right in the end, I think."

"Really, girl?" Lenny said. He turned her head so he could look in both of her eyes. She licked him again.

"Now you need to go back and tell Bettie this story," Justan said.

Lenny paused in his attempts to wipe the slobber from his face long enough to look at Justan like he was crazy. "You think I'm a dag-blasted idjit?"

"Bettie deserves to know all about the dwarf she's going to marry," Justan said firmly.

Lenny snorted. "Don't think that's gonna happen, son. Don't get me wrong, I ain't lettin my kid be raised without a daddy. But every time I bring up gettin' hitched, Bettie just looks like I asked her to eat a turd and throws somethin' at me."

Justan frowned. "That's strange. She told me she was going to marry you."

Lenny's eyes widened. "When'd she say that?"

"Just earlier tonight. When you left." Justan said. "She told me to come talk to you. Then she told me to convince you to talk to her about it because, she said, 'his future wife should know these things.'"

Lenny shook his head. "Well I'll be dag-gummed. What is that woman playin' at?"

"I don't know," Justan said. "But it sounds like you shouldn't give up."

"I wasn't gonna anyway," Lenny said with a scowl. He stormed back towards the Hall of Elements, muttering to himself.

Chapter Twenty Eight

The troll farm was tantalizingly close. Deathclaw could see at least two hundred of the slimy creatures, standing in clusters of ten to twenty. Each cluster swayed stupidly next to small wooden lean-tos where the moonrats hid, controlling them from the shade. The stench of these trolls was particularly strong. The fumes were so thick Deathclaw was developing a headache.

They're getting smarter, Beth said for the tenth time that afternoon, watching as an orc patrol passed beneath the tree they waited in. *She has them ready for us.*

Perhaps, Deathclaw replied, but he had to agree she was probably right.

When they found the first few farms, all Deathclaw had to do was light one troll trail and the entire place would go up in flames; hundreds of trolls and dozens of moonrats cooked at once. At first they had been able to make it look like a simple accident, perhaps started by an orc stupid enough to start a camp fire too close to the trolls. But Mellinda had started putting safeguards in place.

Hilt had been able to think ways around them so far, but this time the security was a lot more difficult to break through. The size and frequency of patrols had increased, making it harder for them to get close. In addition, there were goblins assigned to troll trail duty. Their job was to walk around the farm covering up troll trails with dirt to keep them from building up and becoming a hazard.

Beth and Deathclaw had only found their hiding spot after great difficulty and they'd been forced to sit there for hours as they waited for the right opportunity to strike. The orcs were getting too efficient in their duty.

Poor Charz, Beth said.

Deathclaw turned his head to look up at her perch two branches above him. She had done a great job camouflaging herself that morning, sewing leaves and twigs into her clothing. If he hadn't known she was there, he might not have noticed her. *Has he been wounded?*

No, but he's frustrated and I don't blame him.

Deathclaw shook his head and looked back down at the passing patrol. Charz and Hilt were out on the other side of the farm and had been waiting just as long as they had, ready to cause a commotion if Deathclaw and Beth needed it. Each one of them now carried a Jharro whistle so that Beth could coordinate attacks and movements, but to Deathclaw's mind, Beth spent too much of her time using the whistles to monitor everyone's emotions.

Charz is always frustrated, Deathclaw said.

Wouldn't you be? His naming wizard is distraught over Master Latva's coma, not knowing if he'll live. Charz doesn't feel like he fits in with the rest of us, and he rarely gets to do more than wait as a reserve when we do these raids.

Deathclaw sighed. He understood how Charz was feeling. He had spent an entire month cut off from Justan, after all. Yet he had still done what was needed without whining.

Perhaps we should have brought the gorc with us after all. Then he would have had something to play with. The giant and the gorc had gotten along quite well for the few days they had stayed in Pinewood. He hadn't been happy leaving her behind.

You're not being fair to him, Deathclaw, Beth chided. *And Durza's magic may well have been useful if we had taken her with us. I would have pushed Hilt to take her if I hadn't felt prompted to leave her there. For some reason, she needed to stay in Pinewood. Besides, she didn't want to leave with us anyway.*

Deathclaw had been relieved when Beth felt that particular 'prompting'. He had come to trust Beth's instincts about people, but that Durza creature would have been a difficult companion to have around. *Regardless, Charz has been tedious.*

And you haven't been? Beth asked with a mental snort.

What are you speaking of? Deathclaw asked.

You, with your constant worry over Talon. I'm always having to reign you in, to keep you from running off to either find her or try to rejoin Sir Edge at the Mage School.

I am not tedious, Deathclaw insisted. His reasons for wanting to return to Justan's side were legitimate. There had been multiple times where his presence near Justan could have averted disaster. He would have found more of the witch's spies. He could have killed the archer that struck Justan before it even cocked an arrow.

The news of the raptoid attack had been the hardest one for Deathclaw to ignore. If he had been there, he could have issued a proper warning. He could have stopped Talon. With Star in hand, he may even have been able to destroy them all by himself and the leaders that had been slain would still be alive.

And then there's your constant worrying over your sword, Beth added.

Star is . . . troubling to me, Deathclaw admitted. He glanced at his hand. The star-shaped scar at the base of his palm still hadn't faded. He had even bitten it off a few times, but once his tissue had healed, the scar had returned anyway. It was as if his body considered the mark a natural part of his skin now. *When I touch its hilt, I feel like it is watching me.*

This was a new development. Star had always been quiet before, but something had changed after his fight with the trolls and moonrats two months prior. It was as if the sword had come to life and since they started burning troll farms, the feeling had become more and more insistent.

Bound weapons do that, Beth said. *My viper bow is always watching me and every time I pick it up, it pleads with me to shoot something. I think the scar in your hand is the sword's way of saying it belongs to you now.*

Beth said that a spirit was bound to his sword. Deathclaw hadn't believed her at first, but when he looked at Star with spirit sight, he could make out a faint glow. He turned his gaze back out to the trolls. They were standing there brainlessly, waiting for their turn to be chopped up and turned into more trolls. He touched the handle of his sword. *I can feel it now. Star wants to cut the trolls. It wants to burn them.*

Hmm, Beth thought for a moment. *Perhaps the spirit in*

your sword has a specific purpose. Yntri Yni's people have bound items that have only one use. For instance, they have a spirit-bound gate that's purpose is to open only to people that achieve a certain rank.

You are saying that Star was made to fight trolls, Deathclaw surmised.

I don't know that for sure. It's just an idea. It's also possible the spirit inside the sword just doesn't like trolls or maybe it just likes how easily they catch on fire, she suggested.

Perhaps, Deathclaw replied. He leaned forward, narrowing his eyes. *Look there, at that first group of trolls.*

The pool of slime around their feet had flowed over to join with the slime pools of several other clusters. The goblins on duty with their shovels were not paying attention. They had gathered to the side and were playing some sort of game using small white rocks.

I see it, Beth said excitement pouring from her thoughts. *This could be our chance. Hilt sees it from his side too. Do you think you can get close enough to light it without being seen?*

Beth and Hilt were going out of their way to make sure that they weren't seen by anything that could alert Mellinda to who was causing her problems. On the way back from Pinewood, they had deliberately caused a commotion so that the moonrat mother would think they had traveled to the north. So far it seemed they were successful in keeping their identities secret, though all of them knew it would be unavoidable. Sooner or later she would know it was them. There couldn't be many groups attacking her army.

I can make it. Deathclaw watched the departing orc patrol. Their backs were turned to him and soon they would pass behind a group of trees. He could slide down and reach the slime pool before the goblins noticed.

Do it, then. Hurry, she said.

He backed down his branch and slid down the trunk of the tree, then picked up a small broken branch from the ground at the base of the tree. Glancing quickly to make sure no one saw him, Deathclaw snuck towards the area between the troll clusters where the slime had pooled.

As he moved, Deathclaw reached into a small pouch at

his waist and pulled out a narrow wooden tube with a leather cap. He removed the cap, revealing the fire-runed metal button on the end. Quickly, he rubbed it across the dry tree branch. Flames shot from the wood and Deathclaw tossed the branch on the slime pool.

He backed away, expecting a sudden flare as the slime ignited, but the fire didn't behave as expected. Flames crept along the slime trail slowly, and as they reached the first cluster of trolls, they flowed up their bodies deliberately as if the slime were only mildly flammable. The trolls should have run screaming before the moonrats could bring them under control, but these ones simply stood, swaying as if the flames didn't matter.

Deathclaw darted behind a nearby bush and watched the slow spread of fire with concern. *The fire is wrong.*

What is it? Beth said. *What's slowing it down?*

I don't know.

An orc guard saw the onward march of the flames and shouted. Cries rang out and the goblins stopped their game. With shocked yelps, they grasped shovels and buckets of dirt and ran towards the slime trails.

Deathclaw hissed as a goblin neared the critical junction, shovel in hand. It would reach it before the flames did. If the goblin stopped the fire's spread there, the rest of the trolls would go untouched and the orcs would search the area in full. Hilt and Deathclaw were stealthy enough to escape, but Beth and Charz were depending on the chaos of the fire to help them get away. Deathclaw readied himself to rush out and attack the goblin.

Wait. I'm trying something! Beth sent. It was obvious that whatever it was took a lot of concentration, because her voice was quite faint.

Suddenly a chorus of screeches echoed out. The cluster of trolls that had caught fire broke formation and ran. One of them jumped under the lean-to and attacked the moonrat, while others charged the goblins. The fire reached the junction and spread towards the other troll clusters. Soon the entire farm was ablaze and though the burn was slow, it was still effective.

As soon as they were sure that the frantic orcs would be unsuccessful in stopping the blaze, Beth called out, *I'm coming down. Hilt and Charz are heading to the meeting place.*

Deathclaw met her at the base of the tree and they ran into the woods together. Deathclaw took the lead, taking them down paths that would be harder for the orcs to track. *What did you do to make the trolls attack?*

It was difficult, but I was able to reach out and block that individual moonrat's power so that the trolls were released, she explained.

Deathclaw's brow furrowed in concern. *But wouldn't Mellinda know it was you?* All their precautions would be useless if their identity had just been given away.

I don't think so, Beth assured him. *I didn't cut the moonrat's presence off from Mellinda. I cut the moonrat's presence off from the trolls. I was careful. I don't think it would feel like a spirit magic attack. Hopefully she thinks the trolls went out of control because they caught fire.*

They should have done that anyway, Deathclaw reminded her. He led her up the center of a rocky bottomed creek. They were nearly there.

That's a good point, she admitted as they sloshed through the shallow water. *The only thing I can think of is that the moonrat watching them was particularly strong. That could have kept them from running.*

Hilt and Charz were waiting for them when they arrived. The meeting spot was a stand of trees marked by a large mossy rock that angled up from the forest floor. The named warrior was pacing back and forth, his hands on sword handles, while Charz was sitting on the rocky outcropping, idly crushing ants with one wide finger. Hilt grinned when he saw them while Charz just gave them a bored wave.

"That one got a bit strange, didn't it?" Hilt said with a chuckle. "I was worried you'd be seen up in that tree."

"Whoo hoo, you made it," the giant said, stifling a yawn. "Can we please find a way to fight next time?"

"We've talked this over," Hilt said. "As soon as we're seen, Mellinda will know it's us doing the attacks."

"I still don't understand why it's so important that we keep our identity secret," Charz grumbled. "I liked thumbing my nose at her. We were successful fighting that way before. Isn't the important thing that she can't track us down?"

Hilt sighed and said reluctantly, "He has a point, Beth. Mellinda has to at least suspect we're the ones setting fire to her farms. She did send a sizeable force looking for us last time."

"Look, I don't know the reason." Beth sighed, placing her hands on her hips. "I don't know why it matters. It's just a feeling. I can't explain it further."

The giant shrugged. "If it were anyone but you, Beth, I'd say that wasn't good enough, but," He chuckled and leaned back, putting his hands behind his head. "You're the witch here, not me."

Beth narrowed her eyes at him, her jaw working as she decided whether to be offended.

Hilt walked up and placed an arm around her shoulder. "Maybe we should return to camp. Is anyone pursuing us, dear?"

She pursed her lips and closed her eyes briefly. "There's a lot of milling about in the direction of the farm, but there's no one coming our way yet."

"Alright then, so let's talk about what just happened," Hilt said. "Does anyone have an idea why the troll slime burned so slowly?"

"Their . . . odor was strange. Stronger than usual." Deathclaw said. He'd been wondering about that. Why, if their smell was stronger, did their slime burn slower?

Hilt rubbed his chin. "Do you think they're somehow related to those modified trolls?" They'd only seen regular trolls since returning from Pinewood. After all that effort spent finding pepper, fire had been the only weapon they'd needed.

Beth frowned. "Their emotions didn't seem as complex as the modified trolls. But it can be hard to tell with moonrats controlling them."

"Maybe they're a mix," Charz said. "You know, a mix of regular troll and those changed ones. Think about it. The slow way those things burned would make 'em harder to stop on the battlefield."

Deathclaw nodded. He had been thinking the same thing.

"That's a possibility," Hilt said. "The question is, what's our next move? If the mother of the moonrats is somehow mixing modified trolls and regular ones somewhere nearby, we

321

need to destroy that farm."

Charz frowned. "Sounds like another long wait where I don't get to do anything."

"Not this . . ." Deathclaw wanted to say 'time'. Once again his lack of lips got in the way. "Not this one. Those trolls do not . . ." He wanted to say 'burn'! He hissed in irritation

"What he's saying, Charz," Beth said, stepping in to Deathclaw's rescue. "Is that if we come up against those modified trolls, we will definitely need you. The guards will be more numerous and simply setting fire to the place won't work on them."

"Do you have any idea where to look?" Charz asked, perking up.

"I . . ." Deathclaw clenched his fists. He wanted to say 'smelled'. "Scented these trolls. I can track . . . their scent to know where they-uh . . ." He wanted to say, 'Came from'. "Started."

"You mean originated?" Charz said with a slight grin. Deathclaw couldn't decide if the giant was mocking him or not.

"Good. That's a start. Why don't you do that, Deathclaw?" Hilt said, politely ignoring Deathclaw's difficulty speaking. Beth, however, gave him an understanding look that only made it worse. "We'll head back to camp and you can leave in the morning."

"I will go now," Deathclaw pronounced. He was itching to get alone for awhile. It would be good to go and track something without dealing with the others' feelings or sense of humor.

"Wait," Beth said. "Don't you want to eat first?" *You know it doesn't matter to us that you have difficulty saying certain words.*

Deathclaw bristled. Now she would be bothering him the whole time he was gone, trying to assuage his feelings as if he were some human. "I'll go now."

"Okay," Hilt said. "Let Beth know as soon as you've found something."

Deathclaw gave them a brief nod and started back towards the troll farm they had left burning. He'd see if he could catch further traces of that strong scent and track it to its source.

322

He brooded as he went, irritated at his difficulty with communication and irritated with Beth's constant emotional prodding. Why did human interactions have to be so complicated? Briefly he lamented the loss of his simple raptoid life, but in truth he didn't miss it all that much anymore. He couldn't remember most of it anyway. The memories were hazy as if that time, those near sixty years of his life by human reckoning, were just a dream.

His thoughts shifted to Talon and the other raptoids that had surfaced. When they'd tracked Talon from Pinewood and found the raptoid corpse in the forest, he'd been so confused. How was there more? Justan had told him that the wizard had lost his ability to travel to the desert. Then he'd smelled the moonrat mother's presence on it and a new possibility began to emerge. Why had Talon killed it if it were on the enemy's side? Had she changed perhaps as Beth had suggested?

Of course the idea had been ridiculous. Talon had resurfaced as the assassin that tried to kill Master Latva. But why had she killed one of the raptoids with a moonrat eye, then joined a group of others to attack the Mage School? He growled. It would have been so much easier if she had died during the attack, but she was still loose and there was another raptoid with her.

Deathclaw reached back and grasped Star's handle. It was eager to be used. *Would you help me kill them?* he asked. The sword's eagerness flared momentarily. While he was pondering the meaning of that response, he caught the scent he was searching for.

He crouched and picked up a brittle strand of dried troll slime. There were faint traces of a trail leading off to the east. Orcs and these new strange trolls had marched from that direction. He followed the trail for a mile or so and realized he was nearing the edge of the treeline. He looked up at the towering mountain ahead. There would be a lot less cover on the slopes.

Deathclaw grasped the whistle hanging around his neck and told Beth what he had found. Her reaction made him curious. Something about that mountain made her nervous.

He continued on his way and soon the smell of trolls

grew stronger. The trees thinned, interspersed more and more by sloping terrain and boulders. The troll scent intensified, but now it was different, more wrong somehow, almost virulent.

A terrible screech echoed out from somewhere ahead. It sounded like an enormous troll, no, a thousand trolls all screeching at once. Deathclaw nodded. The farm was nearby.

He caught his first glimpse of it from a distance. A large hulking shape on the mountain's slope, surrounded by dozens of orcs. He crept from boulder to boulder, getting closer without being seen.

It looked like a trash heap. A jumble of troll parts and limbs, glistening in the heat of the late summer sun. But it was moving. The limbs in the pile were moving. A slow flowing creek of slime rolled down the slope from the pile, gathering into a small pond at the bottom.

Deathclaw moved closer, sneaking past laughing orcs and gorcs, and saw that further to the south were clusters of trolls. There were hundreds of them, perhaps half a thousand trolls in all; the biggest farm they'd seen. Was the pile of limbs full of rejects, perhaps harvested from these trolls?

He didn't truly understand until he was much closer. He slid under an angled boulder, nearly gagging on the thing's stench at first, but then he forgot the smell and watched with astonishment. The mass of moving troll parts wasn't a trash heap. It was a single living thing, and bigger than he'd thought; as large as the mayor's house in Pinewood.

It had a large central body that had troll heads and torsos growing from it at random angles, and four long limbs that seemed to be made of a joined core of hundreds of troll arms and legs. It was lying on its belly. Deathclaw couldn't conceive of a way for the thing to stand and it was a good thing too. Something that big would be tall enough to simply climb over the walls of the Mage School. The gorcs surrounding the creature wielded axes and several of them were walking around hacking at it, chopping free whole troll torsos that grew from its side. The torsos would fall to the ground and suddenly become aware, screeching and dragging themselves away until moonrats appeared and took control of them.

As Deathclaw watched stunned, an orc climbed up the

slope with a green-eyed moonrat clinging to his back in some sort of leather harness. Following along placidly behind them was a large, bulky troll. It was one of the modified ones like Deathclaw and the others had encountered in the cave.

As the orc approached, the central mass of the troll pile quivered and an enormous gaping mouth opened up in the side. The modified troll approached the mouth and walked inside, letting itself be devoured.

Deathclaw understood now. This was why they hadn't seen any modified trolls around and it also explained why the new trolls weren't as flammable. He grasped the whistle around his neck.

Beth, we are going to need that pepper.

Chapter Twenty Nine

"Treachery!" Ewzad Vrill screamed as he entered the throne room. A few of the nobles gasped at the rudeness of the entrance, but were quickly hushed by others. Most of them had learned to keep their surprise quiet around the king. Ewzad swung his gaze around the room, looking for the gaspers, but what he saw were simpering smiles.

Ewzad's court was not like the Muldroomon courts of the past. A disdainful expression or even a laugh or witticism could get someone punished, perhaps killed on the spot if Ewzad was in one of his moods. And for the last few days he had been. Ever since the dwarf menagerie had disappeared.

Elise cleared her throat. "Would you like us to adjourn, dearest?"

"Adjourn Elise? Oh my. Do you think so!" He growled and turned to glare at the nobles and merchants assembled. Their numbers were far fewer than when Ewzad had started his reign, mainly because they had learned it was safer to stay away. "Treachery! Yes-yes. Treachery in my own palace. Mine! And you think to seek audience for your meaningless requests? Hmm?"

The crowd paled, but none replied or dare moved until told to.

Elise stood, wincing and grabbing her lower back as she did so. The Throne of Dremaldria had not been built for the back of a woman, much less a woman pregnant with twins. The birth mages told her that her children could come in a matter of weeks, but she couldn't imagine it being any more painful than sitting on the throne all day. The only reason she still did it was because Ewzad wasn't going to. She had to put up with the pain if there was to be any semblance of life as normal in Dremald.

She forced a smile onto her face and nodded to the speaker. The portly and heavily sweating man spoke out with a tinny voice, "This session is adjourned. You may depart." The man hadn't been so sweaty before Ewzad had shoved so much power into him. The way the speaker grimaced, Elise feared the man might pop.

As the nobles filed out, Elise stuck out her arms. Hamford and Arcon each took one and helped her down the steps. Ewzad had ordered the two men to stay with her while he worked in the lab that day. That had been a rarity. Usually he had the two of them following him around, insisting they grovel like whipped dogs.

She kept her smile pleasant despite the way her legs trembled. If Ewzad knew how much these sessions hurt her, he would force her to stop and she couldn't allow that.

The voice in the back of her mind agreed. Elise's one relief in the advanced stage of her pregnancy was that the voice wasn't gibbering in terror any more. It spent most of its time humming tuneless lullabies.

Ewzad tapped his foot impatiently as they descended and she saw that he held a crumpled piece of paper clutched in his hand. He glared at all three of them. "Well? Hurry it up, yes? Follow me!"

Ewzad muttered to himself as he stomped straight to the dungeon stairwell. Elise sighed when she saw where he was going. He used the main entrance freely now that he was king and no one dared challenge his comings and goings. At least this entrance would be easier for her use than the cramped secret passage from her rooms. Ewzad descended the stairs quickly, muttering 'treachery' the whole way. They followed as quickly as Elise found possible.

"What do you think he's found?" Arcon whispered. The mage used the tiniest bit of magic to assure that she alone would hear him. Even stone faced Hamford, who held her other arm, didn't hear. Arcon had assured her long ago that the magic was so faint that Ewzad wouldn't sense it. So far he'd been right.

"It could be anything," she whispered back, knowing that his spell would also direct her voice. She was somewhat surprised that he had spoken. He never spoke to her unless he was sure his mistress wasn't listening and when Ewzad was in one of his moods, she usually had something to do with it.

"Is it his raptoids, you think?" Arcon replied. Ewzad's exaggerated mourning over his dead assassins was the only thing that made him angrier than the disappearance of the dwarves the day afterwards.

She frowned. Arcon knew that discussions between them were to be saved for more important topics. "Do you know of something else?"

The young mage swallowed. "My mistress has been angry herself today, my Queen. I am simply preparing myself for pain."

She nodded sympathetically. The poor man had been caught between Ewzad and Mellinda a lot lately.

Ewzad stopped at the turn before the main landing and shoved aside the hidden wall to his laboratory. His glare was baleful as they descended and Elise's heart began to flutter. Ewzad never gave her that particular glare. Especially not after he had found out she was pregnant. What had he discovered?

This is bad! The voice inside her head began sobbing. *Protect the babies*!

It was nonsense, of course. Her dear Ewzad would never hurt them. Not on purpose at least. That last thought sent a shiver down her spine.

Ewzad led them past a row of cells. Elise heard horrible noises inside some of them, but many were empty. In the months since the destruction of the academy he hadn't spent as much time creating beasts as before. He was much too busy putting kernels of power into undeserving men that he could send to Sampo. Elise didn't like it. The creatures he made were horrible, but at least they were loyal. The men he chose for his army weren't worth the cost of the boots they wore.

The room he led them to was one Elise hadn't been in before. It was wide and spacious. Its walls were covered in odd sorts of rusty tools and a long bloodstained worktable ran down the center. In the corner, chained to the wall was the corpse of a man. At least she thought he had once been a man. His head was swollen and misshapen, while his lower body had been bent and twisted until his legs looked more like tentacles than legs. An ornate wooden handle protruded from a gaping hole in the side of his head.

"Yes, would the three of you stand apart from one another?" Ewzad said. He had pushed the anger from his face now and only disgust remained. Hamford and Arcon released her arms and took two steps away. Ewzad gestured to a chair next to the bloodstained workbench. "Elise, dearest, sit in that chair, hmm? We wouldn't want you to strain your poor feet, now would we?"

Elise did as he suggested. Usually she would have been relieved to get off her feet despite the filthiness of the chair, but there was no kindness in his voice and the chair put her two more paces away from the men. This could mean bad things for any or all of them.

Get away. Get away. Run! He'll kill us and the babies! the voice inside her gibbered. She shoved it away. Ewzad wouldn't harm her or the children. He wouldn't. He loved them.

"Well-well. Are you three wondering why you are here? Of course you are." He held up a sheet of parchment. "I received this today. Would you like to guess how I got it? So would I. Yes, I don't know who delivered it. No-no, it was on my desk. Here! In my laboratory." He grinned at them. "Would you like me to read it? I'm sure you would."

"What is this about, my dearest?" Elise asked, trying her best to sound uninterested. What did he know? What had he found out?

"Oh, I will read it to you. Yes-yes, I shall." He stretched out the page in front of him and smoke began to waft from the edges. Ewzad cleared his throat and as he read, flames sprouted from the parchment.

His tone was mild when he started, but with each word he grew progressively angrier. "King Vrill. At your request, we have departed. Please do not pursue our services again. We don't act kindly towards those who waste our dag-burned time. Signed, Blayne Cragstalker, Ringmaster."

As he finished, the last bits of parchment ignited and fell to the floor where it turned to ash. "Now, what does this tell us, hmm? That's what I wondered this morning, don't you think?

Yes-yes, I think you do. Someone told the dwarves to leave. Someone told them in such a way that they thought it was I who made the request. Me!" His face twisted in rage. "Someone did it in such a way that the entire smuggling world refuses to deal with me!"

Run! said the voice, but Elise was relieved. This wasn't about her. It couldn't be. *He'll think it was us*! The voice sobbed. She shoved it away again, this time far deeper where she couldn't hear it.

"I am so sorry to hear this, my king," she said, placing her hands on her swollen belly. "But must I remain here? I'm tired and this chair hurts my back."

"Yes-yes. You must stay, dear Elise. You must know what I found, yes?" Ewzad demanded. "You see, I realized that there were only three people. Three who could tell the dwarves to leave and be obeyed! Three who had the strength of my words behind them!"

Elise paled. That meant her, Arcon, and Hamford. What had he found?

"So, I had the royal guards tell me who my dearest associates had visited. Who had the three of you been speaking with? What do you think I found?"

Elise feigned outrage. "Even I?"

"Yes, you! Dearest, you most of all. I needed to know, yes? If my own queen was against me, I needed to know!" He walked up to her and placed one squirming hand against her cheek. For the first time since she killed her own brother in the council room, Elise shrank back from his touch. Ewzad didn't seem to notice. "Don't worry, dearest Elise. I know the truth. You wouldn't betray me, would you? No."

Elise glanced at Arcon and Hamford. The mage was quivering, but the guard looked relieved.

"I found this man!" Ewzad said, pointing to the tortured body in the corner. "Do you recognize him? No, I guess you wouldn't. Not like this, no. He's Fergus! My own; the king's own pigeonkeeper! Yes-yes, a perfectly reasonable person for any of you to contact. But do you know what he had with him when I called on him this morning? This!"

Ewzad reached over and grasped the handle protruding

from the man's swollen head. He lifted his leg and pressed his boot against the man's neck as he pulled. Slowly and with a sucking sound, he pulled what looked like a hand mirror out of the man's head. The glass was broken.

"You recognize this. Yes, don't you Hamford?" Ewzad shouted, glaring at the guard, the vein on his forehead pulsing with anger. "The mirror you used to contact the wizards, yes?"

Elise's eyes grew wider. That couldn't be right. Arcon had to be the one. But the guard didn't deny it.

"You shouldn't have done what you did to Kenn," Hamford said. He smiled for the first time Elise could remember. "You shouldn't have done it."

Elise leaned away, expecting the guard to pull his sword. But he didn't. He just smiled at Ewzad, completely unafraid.

"You . . ." Ewzad trembled, more angered by Hamford's ease than anything else.

"You want to know what I told the Mage School?" Hamford asked. "Everything. They know everything! How many monsters you have. Every troop movement! They know about your rings. They know how you and Elise killed the king! They know about the disgusting brood you placed in her and they know how you promised them to the Dark Prophet! They know it all!" Hamford chuckled. "All your secrets. So kill me."

"Enough!" Ewzad shouted and Hamford froze in place, his smile stuck on his face. Ewzad slapped the man. His arms had lost their form and become snake-like, but he slapped him anyway. Over and over he slapped him until Hamford's nose and lips bled, but no matter how many times he slapped him, Hamford's smile remained. "Enough!"

Ewzad stopped, breathing heavy. "Ohh, you want me to kill you, I know. Yes-yes, I can taste it. You asked me before. Begged me, yes. And I want to. Yes-yes I do. But no. No-no, you're my servant. Mine!" He slapped Hamford again then rose up and kissed him. When he pulled back, he had the guard's blood on his lips. "You will stay my servant."

Elise realized what was coming next. She knew what Ewzad was about to do and she didn't have the stomach for it. Not now. Not with Hamford. She'd spent too much time with him.

331

"Just kill him, dear," she pled. It would be a mercy. "Give me a knife. I'll do it."

"You know, Hamford," Ewzad said, ignoring her, a twisted smile appearing on his face. "Of all the times you failed me, one sticks out to me the most. Yes-yes, it was the time you let Talon free. The time you let her brother kill all my precious creations. Do you remember that? I do. Yes-yes, it still sours my heart." He caressed Hamford's cheek. "That's why I hurt your poor Kenn. Remember how I swelled his feet, yes? Stuck him in that cell? All because of you. It was your fault. Your fault he became my bandham. Your fault the wizards killed him."

The smile was still frozen on the guard's face, but Elise knew the tears streaming from his eyes were real. Ewzad was trying to be cruel, but Hamford already knew it. He'd always believed his brother's pain to be his fault. His guilt was likely why he had contacted the wizards in the first place.

"Of all my creatures that died that day, do you know which one I miss the most, Hamford?" Ewzad cooed. He threw a snake-like arm around the guard's shoulders. "I miss the Clench. Oh he was fierce. Huge, misshapen, yes, he was a baby giant when I found him, you know. I brought him up. Fed him whatever meat was handy at the time. I made a lot of mistakes making him, but when I was finished I thought he was perfect. Yes-yes, I was going to make him bigger and ride him into battle you know."

Ewzad pointed at Arcon and crooked a finger. "Dear Arcon, tell your mistress that it's time. I'm coming to Sampo and we will crush the wizards."

"But Ewzad," Elise said, struggling to stand. "You can't leave me now, dearest. The babies will come while you're gone. Our babies. Y-you can't."

Ewzad stuck out his bottom lip. "Oh!" he rushed over and hugged her. Kissed her, Hamford's blood still on his lips. "Dearest Elise, the children will be fine. Yes-yes, the Dark Voice won't let them die. Not even the one that's ours. He's promised. Our beautiful children will be fine, yes? The birth mages will see to it."

"Stay!" she begged.

"No-no, I must go. They know it all. They know too

much. Yes-yes, I must go. I'll kill them all and then, sweet Elise. Then I will return to you. Yes I will." He turned back to Arcon. "Since Hamford is unable, would you go to cell thirty three? There's a giant there. Yes-yes, I know he's dead. Bring me part of it. Something. An ear. A thumb. Whatever, yes?" He turned back to Hamford and gave him a cruel smile. "You'll make a great Clench."

Chapter Thirty

They waited until late in the night when Star's power would be at its fullest. The moon had risen and though it was only at half wane, it lit the mountainside with a soft glow. Deathclaw and Hilt were perched behind a boulder high above the creature, Hilt with a smile stuck on his face.

Beth had wanted to wait a few days and solidify their plan before they attacked, but the named warrior had pressed for them to attack that very night. The troll farm they had burned was far too close to this one. Mellinda would surely increase her troops in the area, but she wouldn't expect another attack within a day of the last one. They had never hit two in a row that fast before. But Deathclaw knew it was more than that. The man wanted to fight the beast; itched for it.

Hilt and Beth had encountered the troll behemoth once before, in a cave high on the mountain. Beth had hoped they'd killed it. They didn't know how Mellinda had gotten it out of the cave, but they were sure it was the same one.

"It's a monster of legend, Deathclaw," the man whispered. "You may never get another opportunity like this. Killing this thing will be hard, but once we've done it, we'll have done something only a handful of people have done in the history of the known lands."

Don't listen to him, Beth said sourly. She was hiding in a cluster of rocks higher up the slope, waiting for Charz' signal. *Him and his glory. He's never forgotten finding this thing. He's been talking about going back ever since.*

Deathclaw nodded, but said nothing. He didn't care about glory. He saw only the necessity of killing the thing. He still wasn't sure how they were supposed to do it. None of them knew. Hilt had explained to them what a troll behemoth was and how to defeat it, but it sounded impossible.

The behemoth's healing ability was so out of whack that it couldn't stop growing. It simply got bigger and bigger, sprouting more and more body parts, until it died of starvation. Sword attacks were useless. It healed too fast and any pieces of a behemoth that broke free turned into more trolls. The time before, Beth had set the thing on fire, but somehow it had survived. Now, if their suspicions were correct, it had eaten so many modified trolls that it had become like the trolls they had encountered the day before. Its slime would burn slowly and the fire would be even less effective.

Deathclaw shifted his weight, looking down on the beast intently. Star was letting out a low hum and he felt an itching at the back of his mind as if it were begging to be used against the thing.

The gorcs had stopped cutting at the behemoth once it got dark and had moved to camp near the orcs a short distance from the troll clusters. There were very few fires in the camp and those were carefully maintained to assure no troll slime got anywhere near them.

The Behemoth sat languidly, surrounded by four moonrats with green eyes. Every once in a while, one of them would let out a chittering moan that would be answered by the others controlling the troll clusters. Orc watchmen patrolled the area in pairs, scanning the trees below. The orcs watched the foothills intently, but none of them seemed to fear attack from the slopes above.

Charz is almost ready, Beth announced to both of them and then added for Deathclaw's ears only, *Listen, Deathclaw, I have a strong feeling and I need you to heed me.*

I will, Deathclaw promised.

Good. I need you to watch Hilt. She swallowed and Deathclaw could sense the fear in her thoughts. *Keep him alive. I have seen many visions of this moment, the time when Hilt would face this beast again, and in most of them he is killed. There are fluctuations . . . variables that could change the outcome, but I have never been able to see what would keep him alive. All I've known is that I would be here.*

335

I will try, Deathclaw said. Of course he would. A raptoid always protects the pack.

You must. Otherwise we will all die. She paused. *I think so anyway. Maybe it's just me and Hilt, or maybe even Charz, but I think this is why you are here. This night is your purpose for coming with us.*

I know, Deathclaw replied. He had understood when Hilt explained what the beast was. This was why he had come with them. This was the purpose for which Star was made. There was a certainty about it that sat on his shoulders.

"Tell Beth to stop telling you what a fool I am. She's been nagging me for a year about this thing," Hilt whispered. He loosened his swords in their sheaths and patted Deathclaw on the shoulder. "We can do this."

Oh, just tell him to shut-. Beth's thoughts intensified. *Charz is ready. He's making his move!*

Deathclaw looked down at the glistening pond of slime at the bottom of the slope and saw Charz slide quietly into it. He covered his body completely with slime and rolled out the other side. From this distance it looked like one of the boulders on the slope had just rolled out of the pond.

So far none of the enemy had noticed his movements. The giant crept up slope towards the troll clusters. The magic of his boots worked well, keeping his steps silent even when wet. He moved as stealthily as he could, knowing that the moonrats couldn't smell his scent under all that slime. His only worry was the orc guards.

Charz made it all the way up the slope to the first troll cluster before a guard saw him. Then as soon as the guard cried out, he set himself on fire. As before, the slime burned slowly, but the effect was impressive. To the orc guards, Charz waded into the troll clusters looking like a ten-foot-tall giant made of flame.

Charz made sure to set fire to every troll he could reach, spreading the blaze from cluster to cluster. Then the orcs arrived. He laughed as they charged and yanked the weapon out of the first attacker's hand. He grabbed the orc and as he lifted its struggling form over his head, Beth cut Mellinda's power from the area.

336

Screeches echoed across the mountainside as fiery trolls ran in all directions, some running straight for the orcs. Charz laughed. The flames against his rocky skin were little more than an annoyance. He charged the orcs, smashing them with his enormous fists, finally seeing some real action.

The moment Mellinda lost control of the behemoth, Deathclaw and Hilt attacked. Hilt threw a flaming branch onto its back and swung his swords, using the air magic in the blades to send a gust of wind to fan the flames.

Deathclaw drew Star and the blade was already glowing a dull red in anticipation. The feeling he was getting from it was something akin to joy. The behemoth let out a wail, hundreds of heads along its surface screeching at once. The sound hit Deathclaw's ears with deafening impact. He stumbled, but kept his balance and as he reached the creature, he had to wonder how they could possibly defeat it.

The behemoth's sheer size was overwhelming and as Deathclaw reached its enormous center, he had another problem enter his mind. Where should he strike it? Dozens of arms reached for him. Torsos stretched towards him with snapping mouths full of jagged teeth.

He ran as close as he could to the beast and swung his sword. Star ignited the troll pieces reaching for him and the side of the creature erupted into fire. The blade brightened and the behemoth let out another wail. At this range, the intensity of the sound nearly dropped Deathclaw to his knees.

The pepper! Use the pepper, Beth reminded.

Deathclaw backed away from the blaze and reached for the pouch tied at his waist. There was a ripple in the behemoth's central body and several large eyes opened in its surface. A vertical line appeared below the eyes and opened into a large fanged mouth, big enough to swallow him. A long tongue rolled out, reaching towards him, a pair of grasping hands sprouting from the end.

Deathclaw grabbed a handful of the pepper and threw it at the tongue. The powder hung in the air, much of it floating to the ground or sticking to the various troll appendages reaching for him, but a small portion did land across the tongue and where it landed, red welts began to swell.

Sir Hilt slashed with twin swipes of his swords, carving deep slices in the flesh of the beast. Wherever his swords cut, torsos and heads and grasping arms would grow from the wounds.

The fight looked lost before it had even begun, but Hilt knew this wasn't a sprint of a battle. This would be a long race. Every wound the behemoth recovered from meant more of its energy used. The more energy it used, the weaker it would get. Eventually it would begin to starve and its ability to regenerate would weaken.

That was the theory anyway. He had read a book on the ten legendary monsters in the Mage School library. Only two warriors had claimed to kill a troll behemoth and that was the technique they had used. The difference was that those men had attacked it with a team of skilled warriors and the battle had taken days.

Hilt didn't have days. He would be lucky to have hours. The mother of the moonrats definitely knew they were there now. She would be sending every goblinoid in the area after them.

How are you doing, Beth? he asked as he sent another deep cut into the beast, his swords' reach extended by sharp razors of air that extended from the blade.

She is confused for the moment I think, but she is already putting a lot of pressure on my magic, Beth said. *I don't know how long I will be able to hold her off before she breaks through.*

I'll try what I can, he promised, making another deep cut. Chunks of troll parts littered the ground around him and many were already forming tiny bodies. He wondered why the fire he had started on top of the behemoth hadn't spread to its sides.

Why aren't you idiots using the pepper? Beth complained.

I was waiting for the right moment, Hilt snapped.

The behemoth let out a screeching wail. Hilt winced. His ears ached. Much more of that and he might lose his hearing for good. He danced back and slashed again, putting more air magic into it this time. The wounds stretched longer and deeper than before and it finally happened.

Eyes opened up on either side of the cuts and the wound opened up into an enormous fanged mouth. It snapped at him and Hilt hurled the pouch of pepper inside. The moment it landed in the back of its throat, he slashed again, sending a blade of air to cut the pouch in two.

The troll's jaws slammed shut and the pepper disappeared within.

Charz hunched over and grabbed the unconscious orc by its feet, then swung it about him. He smashed several of its companions to the ground, using the orc like a floppy club. They screamed and died. Bones broke and blood gushed while he laughed uncontrollably.

This was the feeling he'd missed since leaving his cave; the power and dominance that battle gave him. These orcs were nothing to him. Even if one of their swords chipped his skin, the wound healed before they could take advantage of it.

A part of his mind warned him of the danger of this way of thinking. His conscience reminded him of the promise he'd made to put his bloodthirsty nature behind him. But Charz pushed the nagging thought aside. He remembered what Alfred had told him before he had left the school with Hilt and Beth. His hunger for battle was a weapon that, if honed, was a powerful tool. He could fight when fighting was needed. He just had to be able to let it go when the battle was over. He couldn't let the hunger control him.

As it was, he didn't know how much longer the fight would last. The flames covering his body had died down and the trolls that hadn't burned to death were fighting the orcs alongside him. Well, perhaps not alongside him really. They were just trying to eat the orcs while ignoring him. For some reason, he must not have smelled like food.

One of the orcs, a large and brutish beast, knocked a troll aside and got close enough to swing a greathammer onto Charz' foot. The weapon was four-feet-long and the hammer on the end wide and shaped like a wedge. Pain shot up Charz' leg as the skin on his foot cracked open. Blood seeped from the wound and he could feel the bones in his foot crunch. Charz winced and grabbed the orc by its ugly head. He squeezed, crushing its skull,

339

then shoved it aside and picked up the greathammer.

The hammer didn't look quite so great in his hands, more like a warhammer maybe, but he made good use of it. He swung it into an orc's chest, smashing its insides to jelly. The other orcs backed away and Charz threw the hammer, thumping one of them in the face.

The troll behemoth let out a screeching wail that jolted the mountainside. The fighting stopped momentarily as everyone staggered and Charz spared a glance over his shoulder.

Half of the behemoth's body was on fire and he could clearly see Sir Hilt dancing about the thing, swiping with his swords. The beast shifted and raised one of its massive limbs in the air, then brought it down in an attempt to crush the named warrior. Hilt dove out of the way just in time.

Charz let out a whoop of joy at his friends escape, then swore as something sharp pierced his side. He swung back around as a large orc sitting astride a giant spider pulled the tip of a trident from his side. From his perch on the spider, the orc was about at equal height to the giant. Charz couldn't believe the thing had managed to approach while his head was turned.

"Cheater!" he shouted. He took one look at the wound and knew that it was a bad one. He'd had a lot of those over the years. He shifted to mage sight as Master Oslo had taught him so long ago. The trident glowed a deep blue. Yep that was bad. He had seen that kind of magic before. Water magic on a weapon usually meant it was designed to either penetrate armor or slow healing. By the way this wound felt, this trident was made to do both.

The orc drew the trident back again and Charz got a good look at the weapon. It was finely made. The two outer prongs were sharpened like sword blades while the center prong was shaped like a spearhead. Intricate runes were carved into the metal. He wondered how the orc had obtained such a weapon.

The spider charged forward, its fangs dripping with poison. Charz knew he was in a pinch. Even if he was able to avoid the thrust of the trident, the spider's jaws could reach him. Giant spiders had the jaw strength to punch through skin even as thick as his.

Charz smiled. A century of arena fighting had taught him

that a mounted warrior was only as good as his steed. Instead of trying to grab the trident or backpedal to avoid the spider, he leaned into the spider's attack and brought his fist up in a stiff uppercut, smashing right into the spider's jaws.

The resulting crunch of chitin was so satisfying, he barely felt the prong of the trident pierce his neck. He brought his right shoulder up under the spider, lifted the creature with both arms, and shoved, upending the beast on top of its rider. He stepped onto the belly of the spider before it could flip back over and saw the moonlight glint off the shaft of the trident trapped under its body.

He ignored the blood flowing from the wound in his neck and tore one of the legs of the spider free so he could get at the weapon. He reached down and ripped the trident from the hand of the trapped rider. With a satisfied grunt, he thrust down with the weapon, piercing through the body of the spider and spearing the orc underneath. Then he stabbed a few more times, just for good measure.

When the spider's legs curled up, he stopped and took a step back. "Spiders are for eating!" he said, though it came out more like a croak. Not that the orc would have understood anyway. It was dead and that was an inside joke. Alfred would have found it hilarious. He yanked the trident out of his vanquished foes and looked around for another orc to crush. There weren't any around. Evidently they had all fled or were eaten.

Charz felt at the wound in his side. It had stopped bleeding, but the hole was still gaping open and it hurt like the wound was fresh. The crystal hanging from the iron chain around his neck glowed a soft white, showing that it was working extra hard to repair him.

He clutched the trident and turned towards the behemoth with a smile. The blood was still pouring from his neck, but he wasn't worried. He had plenty of blood and now he had just the right weapon to fight the thing.

The behemoth's enormous limb descended on Deathclaw, the arms and legs that made up its bulk squirming as it fell. His battle senses had slowed time around him and Deathclaw knew

341

he wouldn't be able to dodge. He thrust upwards with his blade instead and accepted the stinging scratches from the clawing arms as the tip of his white hot blade pierced the core of the limb.

The skin of the behemoth ignited on impact burning away as if it were made of paper. This time the fire didn't burn him. The flesh of the behemoth turned into coals all around him, but all he felt was a vague warmth as he swept the blade down to his right, cutting a fiery exit from the interior of the limb.

He dove out of the wound, shocked at what had just happened. The sword had never expended so much power before, yet Star was getting stronger instead of weaker. The sword was exultant and new aspects of its power were appearing. He should have been badly burned, yet he was untouched. Somehow the weapon was feeding on this battle.

Deathclaw looked back. The limb was ablaze and the glowing opening was closing very slowly but the wound was still there. Perhaps the pepper really was slowing the behemoth down. He hoped the barrel they had would be enough.

The battle had been going on for over thirty minutes. Deathclaw's pouch of the spice was empty and Hilt had gone back for more a few times. Charz had decided to make everything easier by bringing the barrel closer so it would be quicker to get to.

Deathclaw had exited the behemoth's limb on the side where Charz was fighting. The giant looked tiny compared to the thing, but you wouldn't know it by his attitude. Charz was laughing as he stabbed the behemoth's eyes with the trident he had found. Each eye burst in a shower of slime, leaving an open hole. A mouth opened in the body of the thing and tried to reach him with enormous fanged jaws. Charz stepped back and jabbed and slashed with the weapon, fighting off the long grasping tongue that came out after him.

Deathclaw noticed that the giant's two puckered wounds, one in his side and one in his neck, still hadn't closed. Neither were bleeding, but he had never seen the giant's body keep a wound like that before. They should have healed right away.

Hurry, Beth sent from her position huddled behind the rocks on the slope. Her eyes were closed and her hands over head as she bent all her concentration on battling the moonrat mother. *There is a large force approaching from the west. They have a lot of eyes with them and Mellinda's pressing me hard!*

How many? Deathclaw asked.

The behemoth wailed again, stunning them as it swung the two enormous limbs on either side of Charz and Deathclaw towards each other, intending to smash them in between. Deathclaw had been so focused on Beth's message, he couldn't react in time. The behemoth limb behind him slammed into his back. Troll arms protruding from the limb grasped him, latching on, their claws holding him in place as he was propelled towards the other oncoming limb.

Deathclaw tightened his battle senses further, his mind's eye slowing down the approach of the oncoming limb even more. He felt each individual claw piercing his skin. There were four arms clutching him; two wrapping around his legs, one grasping his torso, and one of them pinning his sword arm.

He rotated his wrist, flipping the sword blade up, briefly touching Star's white hot blade against the troll appendage grasping his sword arm. The appendage burst into embers and Deathclaw was able to thrust his blade towards the oncoming limb just as the two impacted.

The flesh of the behemoth burned away so rapidly that, with Deathclaw's slowed down perception, he could see the flesh vaporize around him in a cone extending from the blade, never touching his body. He saw a faint blue glow extending from the sword's hilt, protecting him from the heat as the force of the impact sent him hurtling through the limb and out the far side in an explosion of flame.

Deathclaw rolled across the rocky ground and came to his feet, looking back to see that the behemoth's massive limb had burned in two, the ends of each half glowing with enormous red coals. His eyes widened as the half of the limb he had cut free convulsed and rolled down the slope, trailing sparks and smoke behind it.

A sudden fear jolted him. What if the half of the limb he had burned free became a second behemoth? He shoved the thought away. If it was that easy to make multiple behemoths, Mellinda would have had her orcs cut off its limbs long ago and

343

they would be facing multiple behemoths instead of one. Hopefully there was enough pepper in it that the limb would just wither and die.

Hurry! Beth insisted. *Mellinda's force is just a few miles away. She'll break through my magic any minute!*

Charz roared as he tore free from between the two limbs, ripping several troll arms out of the behemoth's flesh as he did so. The giant stumbled towards Deathclaw and looked at the glowing embers of the severed appendage with an appreciative nod.

"That hurt," the giant said and Deathclaw saw that the giant was covered in troll scratches. Those wounds were already healing, but the wound in his neck had begun to bleed again. Deathclaw pointed at the wound and the giant reached up and felt the blood flowing. He chuckled. "Yeah, this trident is a nasty weapon! I think I might keep it."

Hurry!

Hilt ran over and pulled the two of them just outside the behemoth's reach. The named warrior was breathing heavy and there were two bloody and jagged tears in his scalemail vest, but he looked exhilarated. "I think the pepper is taking effect. Its wounds are closing much slower now."

Deathclaw thought on it. Justan had told him that regular trolls would die from pepper poisoning and modified trolls would just stop regenerating. But the behemoth was different. "Do you think it is . . ." Deathclaw wanted to say 'enough pepper'. Instead he said, "Will it die yet?"

"Who knows?" Hilt said. "No one has killed a behemoth with pepper before. We may have just made it sick. If we leave now, it could recover when we're gone and this will all have been for nothing. It's hard to know how much pepper is enough."

No time to stand there and talk! Beth chided. *They're coming. Hundreds of soldiers!*

"Let's be sure then," Charz declared. The giant rushed over and picked up the barrel of pepper. It was half full now.

"What are you doing?" Hilt said.

The giant smiled and ran towards the Behemoth's central body, the barrel tucked under one arm and the trident grasped in the other. As he approached, the behemoth wailed again. It hadn't recovered from their last attack. The eyes the giant had stabbed were still burst, the tongue a jagged stump, but the gaping mouth with its crushing jaws was still open. Deathclaw thought he knew what the giant was going to do.

Charz bent over and ran right through the behemoth's open jaws, leading with his trident held out in front of him. The behemoth's jaws closed around him.

Deathclaw watched as the behemoth wailed again. Half of its bulk was in flames. The stump of the limb he had cut through still burned with embers and its most recent wounds weren't closing. Its remaining limbs rose and fell as it tried to pull itself towards them.

"Charz'll come out any second," Hilt said. The warrior's voice sounded confident, but there was concern in his eyes. "He'll probably burst out its side, you watch."

He's in trouble! Charz is hurt! Beth sent, then a second later added, *She's through! Mellinda has broken through my magic. Her eyes can see*! A moonrat moan echoed from the rocks to their right and was joined by more further down the slope.

Deathclaw ran towards the behemoth, Star at the ready. He called out to the blade. *Don't hurt him, Star. Burn the behemoth, but not Charz*. He hoped that whatever spirit was in the sword was listening.

The behemoth kept its jaws shut, but Deathclaw made his own entrance. He slashed and Star burned the behemoth's flesh open around him. He held his breath and ran forward, the interior of the beast parting before him like curtains of coals being drawn back. He saw Charz then. The giant was motionless, his body pierced in multiple places by enormous teeth. The trident was clenched in the giant's hand, but the barrel of pepper was nowhere to be seen.

Deathclaw slashed the sword around them, burning the opening larger and larger, searing away the flesh and jaws surrounding the rocky giant. There was nothing he could do about the fangs piercing Charz's body, but he needed the giant to move. He kicked the giant in the head and Charz's eyes fluttered open in surprise.

"Go!" he shouted and the behemoth shuddered around him. Arms tried to sprout from the burned flesh around them, eyes tried to open, but the sword's power burned them all away. Deathclaw felt the sword surge with power and the glow around the blade seemed to grow.

Hilt watched from outside as the hole Deathclaw made in the behemoth's side smoked and belched flames. Coals poured out of the wound and fire crawled up along the surface of the beast, incinerating the limbs and torsos protruding from its skin as it went.

The body of the behemoth seemed to glow as if lit from within. It wailed one last time, then shuddered and went still. Fire exploded from the top of the beast. Charred chunks of troll flesh and burning coals rained down on the slope.

Beth shouted out, standing from her hiding place behind the boulder, slapping at a smoldering hole in the side of her bodice. She stared in awe at the destruction of the behemoth below.

Hilt ran up the slope towards her. "Are they okay?" he asked. "Are they alive in there?"

She gave a stunned nod and pointed as a hole burst in the rear side of the beast. Flames poured out and the opening widened as Deathclaw darted out, the white hot blade of his sword held before him. He tripped over a rock and fell to the ground, gasping.

Charz stumbled out after him. The giant's skin was blackened and in places glowed a dull red. The iron chain hanging around his neck had sunk into the rocky skin around it and the crystal pendant had fused to his chest. He fell to his knees next to the raptoid and took deep shuddering breaths, then coughed, spitting out black phlegm.

Hilt and Beth ran down to join them.

"Charz!" Hilt said reaching out to touch his shoulder. But the heat of the giant's skin made him withdraw his hand.

"I'll be fine," The giant wheezed. "Just a sec." The crystal in the giant's chest glowed as he stood and grasped at the stump of something piercing his side. Charz ripped a blackened fang from his abdomen, then pulled another one free from his leg.

Deathclaw stood and stared back at the collapsing center

of the burning behemoth. "Can we go now?"

"Please," Beth agreed. "They'll see us any second."

"Then lets run," Hilt said.

Chapter Thirty One

Star is silent now, Deathclaw sounded worried.

Silent how? Justan asked. Once again Deathclaw had contacted him just before dawn. In the week since the behemoth attack, they had been doing a lot of traveling during the night and this was the best time for Deathclaw to communicate. Fist had taken to calling him Justan's rooster. Not that he needed help getting up. Jhonate loved to wake Justan at dawn anyway. She was always eager to train.

It no longer hungers, Deathclaw replied. *The scar on my hand is still here, but I feel nothing from it.*

Maybe that's because it just ate, Justan suggested. The idea Beth had that it was a sword designed to fight trolls seemed likely from the descriptions the raptoid had given him. *I'm sure it will hunger again. When you get back here, we can have Lenny look at it for us.*

Perhaps, Deathclaw said, but Justan could tell it still worried him. He changed the subject.

Where are you now? Justan asked. *You feel a lot closer.*

We crossed the river Fandine today. We are west of the Mage School now. Hilt says we will circle around and approach Sampo from the plains.

That's good. We could use you there. We got word late yesterday that Ewzad Vriil arrived in Sampo. Valtrek's spies there are too terrified to scout the area and our own scouts are having difficulty getting an accurate count of his forces. Justan said.

Yes, Charz told us, the raptoid said and his anger poured through the bond. *I would love to be the one to tear out his throat.*

Please talk to me before you take that kind of chance, Justan said. He didn't like the idea of Deathclaw getting that close to the wizard. *Maybe since you're so close, you could even stop back in and visit us.*

I will discuss that with Beth.

Good, I will speak with you tomorrow then, Justan said.

Wait, Justan. Deathclaw hesitated and Justan could tell that something else was troubling him and whatever it was bothered the raptoid even more than the quietness of his sword. *I have . . . difficulty speaking with the others.*

Justan was aware of that issue. It was one of the reasons Deathclaw kept to himself so much. *Doesn't Beth's whistle allow you to communicate?* Justan asked. It had seemed a handy solution to Deathclaw's difficulties.

Yes, and that is fine with her, but when I try to speak to the others, I . . . Deathclaw struggled with his emotions for a moment. *Justan can you give me lips?*

Give you? Justan asked, stunned.

I have been thinking about the changes you made to Gwyrtha. Could you perhaps make this change to me as you did with her? Deathclaw asked.

But you aren't a rogue horse. You . . . Justan thought about it further. In some ways Deathclaw was. He didn't have the reserve core of power that came from multiple souls bound together as one, but Ewzad Vriil's changes to his body had made the cells of his body unstable like hers were. It would be more difficult than with Gwyrtha because he wouldn't have that core of power to draw on, but perhaps it could work if he pulled the power from somewhere else.

You sure you really want me to try this? Justan asked. *This wouldn't be like the changes I make with Gwyrtha exactly. It might take a long time to do and it could be painful. Modifying Gwyrtha's structures is different than adding something that wasn't there before.* He didn't add the fact that he was afraid he might make it look stupid.

I do, Deathclaw decided.

Alright. The more he thought about it, the more possible it seemed. *But not until after this siege is over. Or at least until I can have you here in person. I don't want to try this at a*

349

distance.

Very well, Deathclaw said and Justan could tell that he was kind of relieved he wasn't going to try it right away.

Justan got dressed, his mind whirring over the possibilities. The way Deathclaw's body adapted, he wouldn't need Gwyrtha's type of power to hold the changes together. If Justan added lips, Deathclaw's body would likely adjust and see them as a permanent addition.

It would be an uncomfortable thing for the raptoid to get used to, though. He would have to learn how to use them. Eating would be different. He might accidentally bite them all the time. Justan frowned. The way Deathclaw's upper teeth overlapped the bottom could affect the design. This was more complicated the more he thought about it.

Justan opened the door and heard soft voices. He stepped into the center room of the house assuming his parents had already woken. He froze in surprise.

The prophet was sitting at the table. Darlan was sitting next to him, smiling as if she had known the man for years. She was watching the prophet read the Scralag's book, Artemus' glasses perched on his nose.

John was wearing travel clothes. A plain woolen tunic and loose fitting pants that seemed to be cut for riding. Darlan was wearing robes Justan hadn't seen before. They looked formal, made of silk and equal parts red and black as befitted a magma wizard. It was as if she'd known the prophet was coming and dressed for the occasion.

"You're right, Darlan, that is a good recipe," John was saying. "Artemus made it for us once when we were on the road. He didn't have a proper oven, so he had Brevan reach down into the earth and fashion one out of the bedrock. Brevan thought it was a waste, naturally, but-." He looked up at Justan and smiled. "Ah, you're awake."

"You're here," Justan said, feeling stupid, but unable to think of anything better to say.

The prophet smiled. "Please join us, Edge. I hope we didn't wake you. I was just telling Darlan some stories about your great grandfather."

"Would you like some tea, John?" Darlan asked.

"I do suppose we have some time before the others arrive," John said thoughtfully. "That would be lovely, thank you."

Darlan walked to the small cupboard and pulled out a teapot. She made do without a stove by pouring cool water into the pot from a pitcher she had filled the night before and heating it with magic.

"We have more people coming?" Justan asked, taking the chair opposite the prophet.

"Not many," the prophet assured him. He picked up Artemus' book again, "I was quite surprised to see this when I came in. Artemus was always writing in the thing. It was in better shape back then, of course."

"You knew him well?" Justan asked. He had never thought of the prophet as spending much time with anyone.

"Yes, well during the war, we traveled together quite often. He was one of my companions," John said. "He was supposed to face the Dark Prophet with me. I was truly saddened when he didn't make it to the end."

"What happened to him?" Darlan asked. She sat some teacups in front of them. The slightly medicinal scent of strong herbs filled the air as she poured.

"I was hoping the book would tell me what he was up to before it happened. We had separated for a short time as we prepared the different forces for our assault." John shook the journal with an exasperated look. "I knew it the moment he died, but I've never known where he was or why he died. Unfortunately he had to choose this accursed thing to write in."

"It's been frustrating me too." Justan said with a frown. "It won't tell me anything useful. When mother reads it, it's just Artemus talking about family gossip and recipes. When Locksher reads it, he's talking about spells and mysteries. But when I read it, it's just stories from his childhood!"

The prophet chuckled. "It's called a 'living journal'. It was all the rage back when spirit magic use was at its height. I never liked the things myself. Artemus' mother gave it to him when he was young. I have no idea where she got it, since they had gone out of style by that time. Artemus used it all his life. Wrote in it every day, actually."

"He used that one book all his life?"

"Yes." He took off the spectacles and rubbed his eyes. He then took a sip from the teacup Darlan had filled and smiled. "Why thank you, Darlan, that's lovely."

Justan looked down at his tea with distaste. He'd never liked tea. The brown liquid swirled slowly in the cup and he could see tiny bits of herb in the bottom. His mother arched an eyebrow at him and he reluctantly took a sip. The hot water scalded his lips and he stifled a grimace. As expected, it just tasted like hot water with leaves in it.

"The journal is enchanted of course," John said. "Why with the way Artemus wrote, this thing probably contains an entire bookcase full of writings. There is a spirit bound to it. Yes, a deer I think." He flipped the book over, pursing his lips. "A miserly little doe the way she hoards his entries."

"Oh," Darlan said, sipping from her own cup. "So this spirit is deciding what we see."

"Unfortunately," the prophet said with a shake of his head. "When these things were created, the idea was that as you kept the journal, the spirit got to know you. It would come to understand your entries and the way you thought. Then when you passed away, your future generations could ask the book questions and the spirit would direct them to the place in your journal that would give them the advice you would have given if you were alive." He snorted and took another sip. "Unfortunately bound spirits are individuals, each one with their own personalities."

"Over the last week, it's just been showing me the same entry over and over again. On every page," Justan said. "He's talking about his awakening."

"Ah, yes." John said with a slight smile. "He always was a protective sort. When the wizards caught wind of what he'd done, they knew he would be powerful."

As bored as he was with the entry, Justan had to admit that it was impressive. There was a lightning storm one day when Artemus was twelve. The school house was struck while the children were inside. The building caught fire and before the teachers inside knew, they were trapped. Artemus had been stuck outside while his friends were trapped within. He blacked out

352

and when he woke, the building had burned. The mourning parents started clearing away the rubble, expecting to find nothing but bodies, but everyone was alive. Each child and teacher had been protected by an individual dome of ice while the building burned around them.

"But why does it bother showing me the same entry?" Justan asked. "I've already read it."

The prophet shrugged. "The spirit within must think that's what Artemus would want you to know. For me it keeps cutting between his recipe for pine nut corn cakes and the day I prophesied that he would be instrumental in destroying the Dark Prophet." He sighed. "I suppose it thinks he would be mad at me because he didn't make it there with the rest of us."

Justan blinked. The prophet had made a prophecy that hadn't come true? He opened his mouth to ask about it, but there was a soft knock on the door.

"Ah, our next guest," John said. "Darlan would you be so kind as to pour me another cup of tea?"

Justan answered the door as she did so.

"Justan," Jhonate said, cheerfully. "Are you ready to run?"

"Uh, sure, but would you mind coming in for a minute first?" he said.

She gave him a warning scowl that told him she wasn't going to let him get out of his training, but that scowl faded when she saw who was sitting at the table. The look on her face turned more expectant, almost eager. "Mister Prophet, sir."

"Please have a seat, Jhonate," he said. "I'm sure Edge wouldn't mind if you took his chair. Would you like some tea?"

"I would," Jhonate replied as she slid into the seat Justan had vacated. "Is it the same kind you made last time, Darlan? That was quite good."

Darlan beamed at the compliment. "Why no. It's similar, but I cut back on the mint and added dried honstule leaves."

Justan sighed. He hadn't thought it possible, but he was actually starting to get tired of honstule. The vegetable had grown quite quickly in the Mage School gardens and had been a hit with the elves. The cooks started putting it into everything after that. Nearly every meal Justan had eaten since awakening from the Scralag's world had some part of the plant in it.

The prophet gave him a curious glance. "Edge, if you don't mind me asking, may I see the famous scar that old Artemus has hid himself in?"

"Uh, yes sir." Justan fumbled with the buttons on his shirt and pulled it open, exposing the frost-covered rune. "Did you know he was here with me when we first met?"

The prophet leaned forward, peering at the rune. "No, I didn't. I knew there was a frost elemental with you, but I had no idea who it used to be. Quite an oversight on my part, actually." He reached out with his finger. "I hope you don't mind?"

At Justan's nod, John placed his index finger on the rune. A swirl of frost ran up the prophet's finger, stopping at the second knuckle. The prophet gave a slight frown and Justan felt a strange warmth in the rune that gave him a shiver. After a few seconds, the prophet removed his finger. Justan looked down but the rune seemed unchanged.

"It does appear that he was a bit upset," John said with a sad smile. "I explained myself and he feels a bit better about it. I was glad to see that you've jolted his mind. After two hundred years I don't know if he will be able to regain full control of the elemental he's become, but if you keep working with him, I think he may get better."

The flood of questions that filled Justan's mind were interrupted by another rap at the door.

"Oh, good," John said, rubbing his hands together. "We're waiting for just one more then."

Justan opened the door again, thinking how crowded the small room was going to be. His eyebrows rose at the identity of the visitor. "Alfred . . . good morning."

The gnome's gaunt face looked frantic with worry. "I heard a rumor that the prophet was sighted within the walls. Have you seen him? The guards said he went this way."

"Come in, Alfred," John said, turning in his chair to motion the gnome in.

Alfred stepped in quickly. "John, you must come with me. Latva is still ill. The wizards say they have taken all the poison out of his body, but they don't know why he isn't waking up!"

The prophet stood and placed a comforting hand on the gnome's shoulder. "I will go to him shortly. Please join us in the meantime. We are waiting for one more visitor and it shouldn't take long."

The door to Justan's parents' bedroom creaked open and Faldon poked his head out. The warrior looked bleary eyed. He had been up late at a council meeting the night before. Valtrek was fairly certain that the identity of their spy had been discovered and with the news that Ewzad was in Sampo, they had been furiously going over defensive plans.

"Good morning," Faldon said. "My, we have a lot of visit-." His eyes opened wide when he saw the prophet standing by the table.

"Good morning, Faldon," John said. "I am sorry to impose. I have something I want to discuss and we are waiting for one more."

Faldon stepped into the room. "But if you're here . . . then the attack is coming soon. How much time do we have?"

"I will discuss that later," the prophet said with an assuring smile. "This meeting is of a different nature." He paused and glanced back at the gnome. "Why Alfred, you're carrying your sword again."

The gnome's grip tightened on the cane that served as the sheath for his blade. "I have been . . . lax in my training. If I hadn't forsaken my sword, I may have been able to stop the beast before it struck Latva down."

"Ah, good, so you're training again as well," John surmised.

"Yes," said Alfred. "As I must."

"Perhaps then I could get you to reconsider standing before the bowl," the prophet suggested. "With your sword runed, your prowess would only increase."

The gnome stiffened. "That won't be necessary."

John shook his head, his smile amused as he sat back down and picked up his tea. He took a sip and glanced at Justan. "Being named wasn't always so rare, you know. And it shouldn't be now."

"Then why is it?" Jhonate asked cocking her head with interest.

355

"People come to the Bowl of Souls for the wrong reasons, mostly," John replied. "Most who come before the bowl to be named see it as the ultimate acknowledgement of their power or skill. The belief has spread that being skilled or powerful is the only requirement." He shook his head, taking another sip. "But while those things are usually true of people who are named, that's not what the bowl is looking for."

"It isn't?" Justan asked, confused. That's what he had been told.

"You of all people should know that, Edge," John said. "It's the Bowl of Souls, not the Bowl of Skills. When you stand in front of the bowl, it assesses you to see two things. First, are you the type of person that could be of use to the goals of the bowl, and second, are you the type of person that will do the right thing when it is asked of you?"

Justan frowned. "Then why is it so rare to be named?" Those requirements seem to fit most of the academy warriors he knew.

"People don't try as much anymore. There used to be a line outside the Rune Tower most mornings as people waited for their turn at the bowl. That's why we had to put in the rule that warriors could only stand before the bowl once. Some men would try every week!" The prophet sighed. "Nowadays, the bowl sees . . . how many, Alfred?"

The gnome shrugged. "A couple a week, unless the wizards are having a ceremony."

"Why do you think that is?" Justan asked, frowning.

"Some people, like your father," he said, glancing at Faldon. "Don't think they're worthy, and some people," He gestured to Alfred and Darlan. "Just don't want the responsibility."

Justan was surprised to see all three of them looked away. "You're telling me that if father, mother, and Alfred stood before the Bowl of Souls they would be named?"

"I am not the one who makes the decision, but I would think so. They definitely meet the requirement," John said.

"Father," Justan said, his expression perplexed. "Why don't you do it?"

"It's . . .." Faldon scratched his head. "I'm not as good a

person as people think I am, son, you know that."

"That's not true," Darlan said, glaring at him.

"The prophet knows how I used to be," he said.

"Faldon, that was eighty years ago. You put that life behind you," John said.

"Eighty years!" Justan exclaimed. Did he even know his parents anymore?

There was another knock at the door.

"I'll get that," Faldon said, avoiding Justan's eyes, and as he opened the door Justan knew he was hoping it was someone calling him away. Well it didn't matter. Justan would find out the truth soon enough. He was going to dig all their little secrets out so that this kind of thing didn't happen again.

Tolivar was standing at the door looking a little confused. "I-uh. I know it sounds a bit strange, but I just had a really strong feeling that I should come and visit you this morning."

"Good, Tolivar," said the prophet. "That means you are listening. Come in so we can get started. There is so much to do today."

"John, you're back!" Tolivar stepped in, looking unsure of what was going on. "Uh, good morning everyone."

"Now, John, can you finally tell us why you wanted everyone here?" Darlan asked.

"Of course," John leaned back in the chair and took another sip of his tea. "I have a story to finish. Before this battle begins I think it's important you understand the true nature of Mellinda."

Chapter Thirty Two

"Mellinda? Why are we the only ones here, then?" Alfred said. "We're missing several people that were here for the other story."

"All the people that most need to know this part are here," John explained. "And our time is short. The moment I walk into the Rune Tower there are going to be other demands on my time. You bonding wizards can relate the story to your bonded for me. Other than that, I trust your judgment as for who should know."

"Then tell us, sir," Jhonate said, leaning forward. She placed her elbows on the table and clasped her hands together. "I must know how the witch came to be buried under that tree."

The prophet chuckled. "Very well. When last we spoke of Mellinda she had left Stardeon to see what she could learn from the Dark Prophet. She left because she was frightened. She was frightened that she had lost some of the intelligence her bond with Dixie had given her and also scared to bond again. Considering how badly her last bonds had ended, she didn't trust another being to share her thoughts and even more, she didn't trust herself.

"When she arrived at his palace, I am sure that the Dark Prophet was happy to see this fear in her. Fear is one of his favorite tools to use, you see, because it is a great motivator. It's an emotion that overrides sense and reason.

"When Mellinda arrived, he fostered that fear in her. He fed it. He convinced her that a true bond was too dangerous for her; that the friendship and companionship the bond offers was an unwelcome prospect to someone as untrustworthy as her. Even more, he convinced her that the best way to get back what she had lost was to take it."

"And she believed him?" Jhonate asked.

"Not at first, I'm sure," the prophet said. He drained his drink and handed the cup back to Darlan. "Could you fill that one last time, dear? Thank you." He cleared his throat. "Remember that Mellinda had allowed herself to walk down that dark and selfish path before and falling into darkness is a lot easier the second time.

"When the Dark Prophet felt she was ready, he had his servants bring in a gnome. My sources were not able to tell me the gnome's name, but he was a scholar who had been in the Dark Prophet's service for some time. The Dark Prophet dragged this gnome before Mellinda in chains and began telling her a litany of the gnome's crimes. The gnome's focus had been in the dark side of spirit magic you see, and his sins were terrible I'm sure. So the Dark Prophet convinced Mellinda to hate this gnome; to despise this gnome more than she despised herself. Then he told her to reach out with her magic and bond with the gnome. She could do it quickly. He convinced her that she could take the gnome's intelligence, hollow him out and then leave him empty and harmless, unable to hurt another living soul."

Justan found himself wincing in distaste. "But could she even do that? Can the bond work that way?"

"Not with the Creator's power involved, no," John said. "But remember, she had removed the Creator's control over the bond. She could wield it as she wished. And that is what she did. She reached into the gnome and bonded with him. Their bond was as real as any bond of yours. Then, as the Dark Prophet instructed her, Mellinda absorbed his every talent, every scrap of his intelligence and skill. When she cut the bond between them the gnome was little more than a drooling husk."

John glanced around at the expressions of the faces of the people he had gathered and gave them a grim nod. "I see that you understand the gravity of what she did. Whatever her emotional state, no matter how foul the deeds of this gnome, the thing the Dark Prophet convinced her to do was the purest of evil. The bond is a sharing. A sharing of talents. A sharing of souls. She took that beautiful gift and turned it into thievery."

"But when she ended the bond with the gnome, wouldn't

the intelligence she had taken fade?" Tolivar asked.

"No. The Dark Prophet taught her how to accomplish a permanent theft of the gnomes intelligence. Mellinda felt the horrible nature of what she had done. But she had also increased her intelligence far more than she had dreamed. And to be truthful, it wasn't just her intelligence, but her capacity for thought that increased. It was an exhilarating experience for her; an addictive one.

"The Dark Prophet knew he had her then. She wanted more. So he brought her more prisoners and she sucked them dry as well. Together they went over a list of her weaknesses and found ways to overcome them. She roamed the countryside, doing the Dark Prophet's bidding as she searched for those whose powers she could steal.

"Over time she became stronger than a giant, faster than a horse. She went from species to species, looking for some aspect she could absorb. Her powers grew until she was truly god-like."

Alfred was wearing a deep frown. "But John, how could she do that with the bond? The talents and abilities we gain from the bond can't take us past the physical limits of our race. Sir Edge will never be as strong as Fist and I'll never be as strong as Charz."

"Those limits had been torn away by her perversion of the bond. Perhaps I've been unclear. She wasn't just taking their abilities. She was taking the aspects of their race she liked. She took the life magic from an elf. She took the toughness of a dwarf. She took the ability to breathe underwater from a merman. She took the power to exude heat from her very skin just like a bandham. Do you see now? Though she had human form, Mellinda was no longer human."

He shook his head. "Those were dark days. The average people in the populous had no idea who she was, but the leaders of every kingdom and Mage School in the known lands grew to fear her. None of them knew her as Mellinda of course. For them she was known as the Dark Goddess."

"The Dark Goddess," Darlan paled. "My mother used to scare me as a child with tales of her. She was a woman more beautiful than any other woman who could destroy any warrior, no matter how tough, and destroy any wizard, no matter how powerful. And if a child was bad, she would come at night and suck the living soul from your body."

The prophet laughed. "Well, the parts about her power were true, but of course, she had no need to steal the souls of children. It was the powerful that needed to fear her. At least that's the way it was in the beginning. After a while she grew bored. There were none who could challenge her. No one with a power she did not have. The only place she didn't dare attack was the Mage School and that's because she knew that it was under my protection.

"At one point, the Dark Prophet declared she was to be his bride. But that thought didn't please her. She began to ignore his wishes. After all, why did she need him? His powers seemed weak in comparison to hers. Instead she focused on a little thought that had festered in her mind for years. She thought of revenge. There was one group of people that had wronged her in the past and she wanted them punished."

Jhonate's hands flew to her mouth. "The Roo!"

The prophet nodded. "She decided to destroy the people that had rejected her. She decided to conquer Malaroo. But to do it alone would have been tedious. So she bent her mind to building an army."

"She became the Troll Queen," Jhonate said through clenched teeth. "All this time I thought she had been destroyed." Justan placed a comforting hand on her shoulder.

"You understand now," John said. He looked around at the rest of them. "Mellinda built an army of trolls, creatures that were barely a nuisance back then. But she infused them with her magic to make them stronger and hungrier and less intelligent. Then she farmed them until she had hundreds of thousands of the creatures, all of them under the control of her vast mind. She brought them out of the mountains of Razbeck and invaded Malaroo."

"But the Roo fought her," Jhonate growled. "They were a proud people, strong with the gifts of the spirit. They drove her back."

"You know your people's history. That's good, because I told them not to forget," John said. He picked up his cup, but the tea was no longer hot and with a somewhat regretful look, he set it down.

"Would you like me to heat it for you?" Darlan asked.

"No, that's fine," John said with a shake of his head. "Sipping tea will just slow me down and there are too many things I must see to." He put his hands to his head and began to massage his temples. "Let's tell this story a bit faster."

Justan felt a strange but familiar buzzing in his ears and he knew that everyone else in the room was feeling the same thing. His vision shifted and he saw a lush green landscape full of leafy trees and shifting waterways. The Roo people were a large and proud nation, just as Jhonate had said. They had built massive, sprawling cities within the swamplands at the end of the Wide River. They had a formidable army as well. Their warriors were strong and used light weapons and armor enchanted by binding magic.

They eschewed elemental magic and would have nothing to do with the nations that used it, but they were not a threat to other nations either. They were a people that wanted no more than to keep to themselves. Unfortunately, this was also why they had no allies when the Troll Queen attacked.

Hundreds of thousands of screeching trolls invaded the swamps under Mellinda's power. The leaders of the Roo didn't understand the threat at first, not until entire cities had been overcome. Then their most powerful spirit wizards combined in a counter attack and drove Mellinda's power from the mind of the trolls. Without her control, the invading army lost its purpose and though the sheer number of trolls was a scourge of its own, the kingdom no longer felt itself to be under threat.

"But while the Roo thought themselves victorious, Mellinda was hard at work on the second part of her plan," said John. The scene shifted again. "She was hard at work changing the nature of the swamps themselves."

Justan saw KhanzaRoo, the capital city of the Roo people, an immense floating city made of wood and stone that covered the center of the swamps like a living blanket, moving and flowing in concert with the water itself. But something Mellinda had done changed the waterways. The entire landscape shifted as though moved from underneath. Rope bridges were tangled. Barges bottomed out. Entire warehouses sank into the water.

A strange haze filled the air, a stinking mist that caused torches to spark and flare out of control. A thick film floated to the top of the water. Fish began to die. Their swollen and rotting bodies clogged the waterways.

Clean water became a rarity. People got sick. They became weak with hunger as the industries they used to rely on withered and died. Then the troll army resurfaced.

Regions of the swampland had become infested with the creatures and Mellinda took control of all of them. The people fought valiantly, but their one weapon against trolls was now their weakness. Fires swept through the swamps, carried by the pockets of flammable mist and the oily slime in the water. Though the fires killed many of the trolls too, cities burned and the Roo were forced to abandon their homeland for the dryer forest lands.

The swamps of the Roo became known as the Troll Swamps, a vile place too dangerous to travel through. But Mellinda wasn't satisfied with uprooting the people. She wanted the Roo destroyed and that burning vision was all that interested her. She drove them further and further to the north and east; to remote parts where only the hardiest of the Roo had chosen to live in the past.

"That was when she became aware of the Jharro Grove," John said and Justan's vision shifted again.

The Jharro Trees were enormous. Their gray trunks were as wide as four large houses stacked side-by-side. The elves that were the caretakers of the trees were short and looked like Yntri Yni, with dark brown leathery skin and stubbly hair on the top of their heads.

"Mellinda wanted to harness the power of the Jharro trees to help her finally end the Roo, but she did not understand the way their power worked."

She drove her troll army to the grove, but her power was useless there. The trees rebuffed Mellinda's mind and her army fell apart. Yntri's people came out of the grove to fight them and the trolls scattered. Mellinda, seeing how small the elves' numbers were, decided to defeat them all by herself.

Sure of her god-like power, Mellinda walked into the

grove and attacked. The elves fought back as did the spirit magic of the trees themselves. Their losses were high, but they managed to injure Mellinda, disrupting her power. Finally the prophet arrived.

"When I came to the grove, I was saddened by the damage." John's voice was filled with sorrow as he spoke. "The Jharro Grove was a sacred place, a place I was charged with protecting. I brought the high Priestess of the Roo with me. Her name was Jeanene and she was Mellinda's younger sister. Jeanene had been a small child when Mellinda had been expelled from her people but she had grown beautiful and strong with spirit magic."

Justan saw her visage raise before him then and she was the spitting image of Jhonate. She had the same hair and her striking green eyes were fiery with determination. With the power of the trees to assist her, she joined with Yntri's people and turned the battle against Mellinda. They drove her back to the edge of the grove and when the witch saw the prophet appear by their side, she ran into the mountains to the east and crossed the border of Malaroo into the land that would become Dremaldria.

"We followed her. Jeanene and the leader of the elves and I," John said. "We chased her over the mountains and into the forests near the Mage School. I sent two powerful spirit wizards and one elemental wizard to join them and they finally caught up with her in the center of the forest that became the Tinny Woods."

Justan caught a glimpse of the epic battle in the forest that day. Much of it was only watchable with spirit sight, but even with the combined strength of the mighty heroes, Mellinda nearly won. It was a blow to the head that downed her in the end. Jeanene silenced her with a blow to the temple as Mellinda was focused on fighting the others.

The elemental wizard unearthed a deep grave and they placed her deep within. Then the elf planted a Jharro sapling in the spot above her. With the prophet's help, they used their combined magic to grow the tree around her, imprisoning her in its mighty roots.

The vision faded away and everyone took a deep breath.

The room was filled with silence for a few moments and the prophet took a drink from his cold tea. Jhonate was the first to speak.

"So how do we destroy her?" she asked.

The prophet smiled. "You are much like your ancestor, Jhonate." He bent down and reached into a small pack sitting next to his chair. He pulled out a small velvet bundle. "It will not be easy. Her body is withered and dead, but the core of her being is very much alive. Mellinda is trapped in that place, her spirit bound to the dagger she plunged into the Dark Bowl so many years before. It is the rune that holds her there."

He began to unwrap the bundle. "But I fear she is close to finding a way to get free on her own. In fact I fear that we may be too late already. This will be your way to destroy the dark binding magic that keeps her there."

Within the bundle was the ruby dagger he had purified the day they had arrived at the Mage School. The metal of the dagger was now a pure white and the rubies in the hilt sparkled. "This dagger was once named Tulos. I have taken it to my master's altar and sanctified it there. I have renamed it Palos. It has the power to destroy dark and foul magic."

He looked at Jhonate. "Though you may not have Jeanene's power with spirit magic, you truly are the heir of her strength of will. I believe you can use it to destroy Mellinda's dagger." He held it out to her hilt first and when Justan saw her pick it up, a shiver went up his spine. This dagger truly belonged in her hands.

Jhonate stared at the blade, her mouth hanging slightly open. Then she swallowed, shaking her head slightly and turned her gaze to the prophet. There was gratitude in her eyes. "Thank you."

He smiled at her and stood. "Listen now. Each and every one of you in this room will be needed if Mellinda is to be destroyed. If any one of you are killed in the upcoming battle we very well may fail and Mellinda will slip free."

While everyone in the room tried to digest what he had told them, he turned to Alfred. "The same goes for Latva I'm afraid. He knows things about this situation that I do not. So now that the tale is complete, we must go and see if we can't wake him. There is so much to do and the battle starts tomorrow."

"Tomorrow?" Faldon said, his brow furrowed in concern.

"Gather the leaders of all factions within the walls. Have them meet me in the Hall of Elements in one hour." John sighed. "Like I said, there is much to do."

Chapter Thirty Three

"My queen, what are you doing?" asked the Royal Speaker, his sweating face white with panic.

"I am joining my husband," Elise snapped, giving the speaker a glare. She felt the twins kick in unison. The small voice inside her hummed a tuneless lullaby. Servants hustled around the royal carriage, loading Elise's things. The royal guard spread out, clearing a wide space for them to work in and eyeing the crowd for weapons.

The first thing Elise had done after Ewzad left was to outlaw weapons within the palace walls. She had argued for the law before, but Ewzad had resisted issuing that decree because he felt it would make him look weak. Elise's one concern was for the babies. Someone could try to assassinate her while he was gone. In fact, with the glares that the nobles were giving her, she was sure of it. For the first time in a long while, the small voice inside of her was making sense!

"B-but my queen, you shouldn't be traveling in this state," the speaker blustered.

"He is right, my queen," said Mereld, the head birth mage. She was a kindly old woman who had overseen the births of over a hundred noble children in her years of service. Better yet, she was from the mage school in Alberri. Elise had ordered all the Dremaldrian birth mages away from the palace in case they felt their ties to the Mage School were stronger than their loyalty to their queen. "You mustn't leave now. You could have these children any day. Sampo is a week's ride from here."

Elise growled and swung her arm, delivering a stinging slap to the gray-haired woman's face. "That will not happen! You will see to it. I will give birth at Ewzad's side!" She whirled back to the Royal Speaker. "I didn't summon you here to ask for permission. I brought you here to give you instructions for handling the nobles while I'm gone."

The man paled but had the sense not to argue. Elise pulled him in close and began delivering her instructions in his ear. She had to force herself not to gag on his odor. She had ordered the man bathed daily and his clothes cleaned and, from the disgusted looks of the maids that had to bathe him, it had been getting done. Still, the man reeked from whatever Ewzad had put in him and all the powders and scented oils in the palace wouldn't keep the smell away.

As she was issuing her final instructions, a wave of pain rippled across her swollen belly. Elise doubled over, gasping, and Mereld placed her hands on her stomach, sending cooling tingles of magic to soothe the pain away.

Get that old woman away! No magic near the babies! shouted the voice inside her.

"That was a contraction, my queen," said the mage, her voice composed despite the red handprint on her cheek. "It doesn't mean your labor is starting now, but it does mean that you are close."

Elise forced a smile on her face. She reached up and grasped the woman by the back of the neck. "This is why I am glad you're here, Mereld. I am sure that you and your excellent staff will make sure my babies and I arrive safely at my husband's side."

"That is our duty, my queen. For you or for anyone," Mereld said with a short bow of her head.

"I am not just anyone," Elise reminded gritting her teeth. "I am queen and if anything should happen to us, I will have my husband turn you inside out! Understand?"

Yes. She must die! Kill her now. We must protect them! The voice broke down into sobs.

The woman's composure didn't alter one bit. She bowed her head again. "I understand, my queen."

The servants finished loading the carriage and the royal guard mounted horses to escort her. Elise rested inside on a dozen pillows embroidered with runes and fashioned in various shapes to alleviate soreness in her back and legs. As she rode, five birth mages and her personal maid sat on the other plush benches around her. The royal carriage made it all the way to the outer gates of Dremald before the Dark Voice let its displeasure known.

"Elise, what are you planning?"

She didn't answer. Dread boiled in her stomach. The Dark Voice so rarely spoke to her anymore. Maybe it was growing weak? She refused to listen. *Run! Get away!*

"I will not be ignored." A bolt of pain stabbed through her brain.

She cried out and Mereld was there, placing her hands on Elise's head, easing the pain.

"I am . . . joining my husband," Elise gasped.

"I know, dear," the old mage said. She glared across the carriage and two other birth mages joined her around Elise, sending cooling and soothing tingles through her body.

"You are not needed there. Turn around. Return to the palace," the Dark Voice commanded.

"I will not," she growled.

"She's delirious," said one of the birth mages with concern. "We should go back. This is a bad idea."

"You will do nothing of the sort!" Elise shouted. She clawed at the woman, but her hands fell short.

"We will follow the queen's commands," Mereld said coolly. The red print was no longer on her face. One of the other mages must have healed it. She looked at the others. "The queen has conversations we cannot understand at times. Do not be frightened. Like King Vriil, she has sensitivities to other worlds."

The mages went slightly pale and nodded.

Elise wondered what the old woman was doing. Was this a code of some kind? Was she implying that Elise was crazy? She had half a mind to slit the woman's throat. *Yes, we must kill her. Protect the babies!* But perhaps not. The woman may have just been easing the others' distress. She would wait and see.

"Turn around now," the voice commanded. Another bolt of pain seared her mind.

"I refuse," she snarled, shoving the pain away.

"The heir is mine," the Dark Voice said.

No! They're ours!

"You will have it," she said. "But the other is mine."

"Your journey puts the heir in danger. If I must, I will continue to punish you until you return."

"You won't!" she shouted, startling the other women. "Hurting me could hurt the heir and you can't have that." She laughed. "I tell you now I will not back down no matter how much you torture me. I will reach Ewzad's side, so hear me now and LEAVE ME ALONE."

"Punishment can take many forms, Elise," the Dark Voice said. There was no anger in the voice. Just certainty. **"Your insolence will not be forgotten."**

"Leave me then. Remember what you wish," Elise said.

Amazing. We won, said the voice inside her.

Elise smiled. Yes she had won a small victory against her master. But she had no doubt he would remember.

It wouldn't matter, though. Once the babies were born, Ewzad would see them and fall in love with them and then she could tell him her plans. She could tell him she had discovered a way they could keep both babies.

No. He mustn't know. Him least of all! The voice began singing again.

Elise shoved the voice aside. Ewzad would understand. With the Mage School and academy gone and no one to oppose him, he wouldn't need the Dark Voice anymore. She would convince him and he would agree. Both babies would be theirs. Theirs alone.

*   *   *

"While I have been away from you, I saw many things," John said, his voice carrying clearly throughout the domed Hall of Elements. He had changed from his travel attire and now wore a set of white robes with silver trim. "I traveled first to the Palace of the Dark Prophet. It had been blasted to ruins at the end of the war two hundred years ago, yet I saw signs of life. Goblinoids have been clearing the place of rubble and I saw repairs being made. Excavations have been underway for some time I'm afraid, and I saw something even more troubling. One of the Dark Prophets' weapons had been unearthed. They found a crysalisk."

Justan had no idea what the prophet was speaking about, but there were a few murmurs among the leaders assembled at that statement.

Faldon spoke up. "For those of us who don't know, what is a crysa- . . ?"

"A crysalisk was a defensive weapon of great power," said a shaky voice.

Everyone turned to listen to Master Latva, looking pale and weak, who sat in a chair not far away from where the prophet stood. Alfred stood behind him, one hand on Latva's shoulder, the other grasping his cane. Justan had been relieved when the prophet had brought the man out of his sick bed. The healing wizards were calling it a major miracle. Most of them had felt he was too old to recover. They had expected his heart to give out after all the strain the poison had put him through.

The master cleared his throat. "It has the ability to throw up a barrier that can deflect both physical projectiles and elemental spells. I believe that is what the enemy used to foil our attack on the road to Sampo."

"The Dark Prophet had intended to use them against the Mage School two hundred years ago, but we took the battle to him before he had the chance." John shook his head. "I had hoped them all destroyed. Nevertheless, preparations must be made. They will be able to attack you from within the barrier, but your attacks will be useless unless you can get inside it first."

"I suppose the real question, if I may ask, is can it be destroyed?" asked Wizard Randolf with an irritated air. He had been the council head while Latva was down and he wasn't quite happy about relinquishing the role. Justan wished the man would let go of his attitude until the siege was over.

"It can," said the prophet. "We shattered two of them during the war. The key is getting close enough to smash through the metal casing."

"I have a drawing of one back in my rooms," Latva said. The old wizard looked so frail. Justan had never thought of him as frail before. Even the youthfulness in his eyes had faded. "I can show everyone later and we can plan out how to destroy it. Our first problem will be getting a force inside the shield. We can be sure that the enemy will keep behind it themselves."

The hall erupted in discussion as the various leaders discussed certain ways it could be done. Justan was considering Hugh the Shadow's plan for placing assassins high in the trees armed with explosive arrows when the prophet raised his voice.

"There is more!" John said and the hall quieted. "I was concerned about the increase in activity at the palace, so I entered unseen. I made my way to the throne room where we destroyed the Dark Prophet. As I stood over his remains I must say I was pleased to see that he hasn't yet found a way to return. However, though his physical form is gone, his voice is still very much alive."

"What did he say to you?" Fist asked. Wizard Randolf and a few of the others frowned at his interruption and the ogre looked down apologetically.

Ignore them, Fist, Justan sent. *That was a good question.* There had been some dispute about whether Fist should be allowed into the meeting, but the prophet had said all the bonding wizards were welcome, as were their bonded. Justan had brought Gwyrtha in as well, just to irk them. Squirrel sat on the rogue horse's head shelling seeds as the meeting went on, cocking his head any time Randolf gave him a cross look.

"The Dark Prophet does like to taunt," John said wryly. "The worship of the goblinoids has renewed his strength and he declared that he has a plan in place to return to us soon."

"How soon?" Lenny asked. The dwarf was standing not too far from Justan. Bettie was at his side, his brother Chugk behind him.

"That is yet to be determined," John said. "And we mustn't forget that he is a master of deception. But I can tell you this. His threats were real. I left his palace to commune with my master and I saw many things. If you lose the battle here against the Dark Prophet's servants, his rise will be very soon. If you are victorious, we should be able to delay it for some time. However, either way, he will return."

There was a troubled silence in the hall at this statement.

"I tell you this because I want you to understand what I say to you next," the prophet said. "You are crucial to our success. Don't misunderstand me. I'm not just talking about the people in this hall, but everyone within the walls of this school. You are the premier warriors and magic users in the land and each of you will be instrumental in fighting the Dark Prophet off when he does return. Every single one of you who dies here will be a major blow to that effort. And if you should be defeated, that war will be close to impossible to win."

Justan felt chills as the gravity of the moment set in. He hadn't been thinking past the immediacy of this fight. For the first time, he realized that this war could be the first of many.

"So what yer sayin' is . . ." Lenny rubbed his chin as he thought how to phrase what he wanted to say.

"Don't die," Bettie finished.

"Yes," the prophet said with a laugh and the tension broke as the rest of the room laughed with him. "Please don't die. I am counting on you all to survive this."

"Then fight with us," said another voice. Everyone turned an uneasy glance to Wizard Nikoli. The council had decided to free him the night before. He had finally broken down and admitted his dealings with Mellinda after the raptoid attack and had been pleading to be allowed to help. With Wizard Munsey and Wizardess Landra dead, they needed someone of his power and experience helping in the fight, but it was only after the prophet spoke with him and gave his okay that Nikoli was allowed to be in the meeting.

The prophet shook his head sadly. "I wish that I could, Nikoli. But I am only allowed to do so much. I am here to balance out the damage that the Dark Prophet has done. I cannot take a direct part in the battle unless he does."

There were several frowns at this statement and Justan couldn't blame them. Surely if the prophet joined the fight, there was no way they could lose. It was hard to accept his speech about how important they were when he refused to fight along side them.

"What I can do is give you a warning," John said firmly. "I saw a vision. Ewzad Vriil's army will march here tomorrow and this siege will end one way or another. You have a day to prepare and you must be ready."

The men nodded grimly. Faldon had already informed them of the deadline and they had been expecting this information. The prophet then turned the meeting over to the rest of the leaders. As they began discussing how to overcome the enemy's new weapon, Justan saw him head quietly towards the back of the hall and slip out the door.

Justan made his way around the others and went through the door after him. It led into a small changing room, unadorned except for a privacy screen, a wardrobe and a few chairs. Justan was afraid the prophet would have already left through the door in the back, but the man was standing there, his back turned to Justan. He was trembling, his hands clenched into fists.

"I'm sorry to bother you, sir," Justan said hesitantly, concerned that he had angered the prophet.

John's hands unclenched and he took a deep breath. When he turned to face Justan he was composed. "Please don't mistake my frustration for anger, Edge. Even after thousands of years following a rule, it's not easy."

"You wish you could fight with us," Justan surmised.

"Oh I wish I could do a great many things, Edge," John said. "I have spent so many years guiding all of you to this point . . . If the creator wished it, I could fight by your side. If he wished it, I could cause the very earth to swallow your enemies whole. But that isn't my role to play." He sighed and placed a hand on Justan's shoulder. "I must trust you and the others to handle this situation without me."

"Are you leaving?" Justan said with concern. "But even if you can't fight, just having you here with us would give the men courage."

"I know it is difficult to understand, but I must go. Please believe me when I say that what I go to do now is every bit as important as this battle. In fact your success depends on it."

"Then you are fighting with us," Justan said, giving him a reassuring smile. "You're just doing it in your own way."

The prophet smiled back at him. "I'm glad you can see it that way, Edge. For me it isn't so easy." He dropped his hand and turned to leave.

"Wait," Justan said. "Before you go, can I ask you one more question?"

He paused. "I'll answer if I can."

"Why didn't your prophesy about Artemus come true?"

Justan asked. The question had been burning in his mind ever since that morning and for some reason it seemed crucially important that he know. "Why wasn't he there at the end?"

"A lot of things didn't turn out the way I expected at the end of that war. Some of it I didn't discover until recently." He gave a humorless laugh. "Think on this. Is the Dark Prophet truly destroyed? Is Artemus? I am afraid that prophecy now includes you."

As John left the room, the ramifications of that statement weighed heavily on Justan's mind.

Chapter Thirty Four

Months' worth of defensive plans were put into motion during the night. Assassins Guild troops and wizards were sent around the outside perimeter of the school. The wizards dug trenches with earth magic, filling them with stone spikes and assisted as the assassins set traps, both physical and magical all through the forests and along the main road leading up to the gates.

The dwarves' exclusive contract with the academy finally bore fruit. The other council leaders had been angry with Faldon's decision, but they began to understand how good a thing their alliance would be, as under Lenny's direction, the dwarves handed out the magic weapons they had been making in the forges since they had arrived at the school. Elementally charged swords, axes, and bows were given out according to rank, skill level, and need, while explosive arrows were passed out to the archers on the wall.

At dawn, the elves joined the academy graduates, advanced students, and retirees manning the walls. Interspersed with them were the mages and wizards that could use ranged attack spells. The newer students and trainees were kept back in reserve in case the ranks were thinned.

Healers were stationed all along the base of the wall under Matron Guernfeldt's command. Captain Demetrius and his cavalry were mounted and ready to charge any creatures that should make it over the wall.

Lenny and his dwarves were also kept in reserve at a fall back defense post. If the walls were overcome, their job was to hold the enemy off while everyone else escaped to the safety of the Rune Tower. In the meantime, they would continue to fashion arrows and repair weapons and armor as needed.

Enormous trebuchets and catapults and other anti-siege weapons were brought up from storage deep in the bowels of the Rune Tower. Most of the weapons hadn't seen daylight since the War of the Dark Prophet and some of them were so strange that wizards had to go into the library to look up how they worked.

The command center was placed on the school's main road, half way between the main square and the outer gates. The leaders of the defensive effort stood behind a high table reading reports off large message stones and issuing orders via runners. Faldon, Oz the Dagger, Hugh the Shadow, and Stout Harley were there, along with Wizards Valtrek and Beehn and Elder Toiynt, speaker for the Silvertree Elves. Master Latva, feeling too weak to take part, was in the Rune Tower by an observation mirror where he could see the action happening all over the grounds and issue orders to the command center via message stone.

Justan was stationed on the front wall next to his mother and Fist. They watched as a large anti-siege machine was put into place over the main gate. Darlan had called it a lava bucket. It was attached to the outer edge of the wall and hung over so that it didn't get in the way of the defenders while at the same time offering some protection to those directly behind it.

To Justan's mind, it looked like a huge horse trough made of rock and black iron. Runes had been carved into nearly every piece of it and the thing was wide enough to cover the entire front gate. It had been designed to be run by two wizards, an earth wizard and a fire wizard, who had to charge it with their magic to get it going.

"Can I help make it work?" Fist asked. His fingers twitched and Justan knew he ached to try it. The ogre was wearing his latest gift from Bettie: a steel breastplate and chain greaves, runed with earth to make them strong and air to make them light. It made the already imposing ogre look truly frightening.

"It takes a subtle touch, dear," Darlan replied. She placed her hand on a metal plate on the back of the machine and sent a tiny flow of fire magic into it. It made a clanking sound, as if a series of gears were turning inside. "It seems to be working fine.

That's good."

"I can be subtle, Mistress Darlan," the ogre pleaded.

"Fist, if one of the wizards operating it dies, you may get the chance," she said, giving him a look that said she would have no arguments. "Let's hope that doesn't happen."

"Please," he said, trying to give his best winning smile.

"Can you at least show him how it works, mother?" Justan asked. "I don't see how it could hurt."

Darlan sighed. "Fine. Come here, Fist. Now place your hand on that metal plate." The ogre had to hunch over a ways to do so. Darlan moved down to a similar plate a short distance away. "Justan, make sure the way is clear. I don't intend to fire this thing off, but just in case, I don't want to kill any of our people below."

"Now what?" Fist asked.

"Focus on sending pure earth magic into the plate. Don't try to form any particular kind of spell or anything, just pure earth. Understand?" she said. Fist smiled and the machine began making that clanking noise again. "Good, don't try to use too much, just a slow steady stream. The machine will do the rest. Now when I add some fire from this plate . . ."

The clanking turned into whirring and a deep red glow began to issue from within the trough. Darlan let go and the whirring stopped, returning to the clanking sound and the red glow faded. Fist followed her lead and let go of the plate, though he did so somewhat reluctantly.

"There you are," she said, giving the ogre a satisfied nod. "You did a fine job."

"What would have happened?" Fist asked.

"The machine would have issued a steady flow of hot liquid rock onto any enemies below, stopping battering rams or just about any other attempt to break through the main gates."

"Ooooh," Fist said, grinning and Justan knew he wanted to put the thing into action.

I want to see. Gwyrtha complained. *Can I come up?*

"She can't see what's going on from down there," Fist pointed out.

"I'm well aware of that, but it's not a good idea," Justan told him, then told Gwyrtha, *I'm sorry sweetie. There is not*

378

enough room on the wall for you to come up here. You're too big.

    Fist is big, she pointed out.

    Fist stands and can get out of the way easier if people need by, he explained.

    I can be small. I can be fast.

    "Thanks a lot for encouraging her, by the way," Justan said, giving Fist a frown. The ogre shrugged and Justan sighed. *Please understand. I need you down there, Gwyrtha. If something gets over the wall, we will need your help to fight. There's not much you could do from up here.*

    I could fight, she insisted.

    I need you to stay down there for now. Justan insisted.

    "Justan, look!" Fist said pointing down to the command center below. Runners were streaming away from the table in all directions and the leaders were talking back and forth urgently.

    Justan felt a vibration from the stone in his pocket. He fished it out and saw the message in his father's terrible handwriting. *Here they come!* Justan couldn't see anything to show the army's approach. He focused his hearing to the outside of the wall and when he shut out the shouting and bustle of activity within the Mage School, he could hear the distant sound of falling trees. Ewzad was coming and he was bringing something big.

    Justan shouted, his voice echoing along the wall. "They're coming!"

    "No-no! Send her back. I don't want her here!" Ewzad Vriil shouted from his position high above his army. He swayed back and forth slowly as the giant crawled forward beneath him. His luxuriant chair had been mounted on the back of the Clench's neck. The enormous giant that used to be Hamford crawled on its hands and knees at the rear of the army, its body too heavy for it to stand and walk. Ugly, with spiked protrusions on his skin, the guard looked nothing like his former self.

    "She disobeys me, Envakfeer," the Dark Voice said. **"Once the heir is born I will have to punish her."**

    "Please, Master," Ewzad pleaded, "Yes, please forgive her. The children inside her make her rash. Yes-yes. Mellinda, she must be turned back to Dremald. Make her go."

"*She refuses to listen to anyone*," Mellinda said. "*My mage has tried to stop her, but still Elise demands they come. They are already a day outside of Dremald and her labor could start at any moment.*"

"A day? Blast! And why did you not tell me this sooner? That is not acceptable. No-no, it isn't!" Ewzad fumed. If he didn't need her, he would have destroyed Mellinda then and there.

"*I tried to tell you, but you had set your attack plans in motion and you refused to listen. You even punished dear Arcon when he tried to tell you,*" she said. "*She should be okay. My mage assures me she is well protected. The royal guard is with her.*"

"Good-good. If she will not return, make her safe, yes?" he demanded.

"**The heir must not be harmed**," the Dark Voice agreed.

"Both children," Ewzad added.

"*Yes, masters,*" Mellinda purred. "*I will see to the children. I have already sent someone else to make sure they both survive.*"

"Good-good, yes. See that they do." Ewzad snarled. He looked down at his forces below. The creatures of his own creation moved all around him, some of them small and quick, others enormous and ready to climb the Mage School walls if needed.

The Clench was big enough to stand and reach the top of the walls by himself. His thick skin would repel arrows and resist fire, but Ewzad didn't intend for him to get that close. The giant was his steed, a fitting role for the thing that used to be Hamford. Its face was malformed and drooling. Its bulky body wore nothing but a loincloth, and only that because Ewzad tired of its nakedness.

The Clench hadn't been that large when they started their journey, of course. It would have slowed them down too much. Hamford's form when they left Dremald had been small enough to ride in a flat wagon. But once they arrived in Sampo, Ewzad had increased its size, wanting a truly awe inspiring mount. The sheer amount of power required to keep Hamford in his massive form was formidable, but Ewzad felt it was worth it. Once the Mage School was destroyed, he would give Hamford his wish and let him die. But not until he had crushed many wizards under his enormous hands.

"What of you, Kassy? Are you eager? Hmm?" he asked.

The black-skinned raptoid twisted her head to look back at him from her perch on the top of Hamford's head and smiled, her full lips parting to expose her mouthful of razor teeth. She was the most beautiful of his new raptoids, the one he had patterned most after Talon. It was too bad that she was the only survivor. "Yesss, King Ewwie."

"Well you shall get your turn soon enough. Yes-yes you will." He would keep her at his side for now. But once he had broken through the walls and entered the mighty Rune Tower, she would lead the first wave of assassins to hunt down the survivors.

"*Your men are approaching the gates,*" Mellinda said. "*My eyes show the glow of magic in the ground.*"

Ewzad raised a writhing thumb and the air above it blurred until an image appeared. He could see the ground surrounding the Mage School now and Mellinda was right. There was a myriad of magical traps scattered about.

"Halt the men, yes?" Ewzad said. He giggled. "It's time I gave the wizards my demands."

He leaned back into the chair and closed his eyes. The other Envakfeers had given him this idea. He enacted the spell as they had shown him and felt a gut-wrenching lurch. Then he was floating above his body. He giggled as he looked down at himself.

He could see Hamford's massive form and the breadth of his army around him. He could even see the mage Arcon, riding on his horse down below. The vision was so clear and detailed that he wondered how real it was. He looked at Kassy sitting on the top of the giant's head and decided to try out his technique.

"*Kassy!*" he said.

Her red slitted eyes blinked and she whipped her head around to look at his body slumped in the chair. "King Ewwie? You iss awake?"

Ewzad concentrated and formed a shadowy figure in the

air in front of him. He transformed the face of the figure into his image, crown and all. "*Kassy.*" He commanded. "*Watch over my body.*"

Her jaw dropped. "Yess, King Ewwie."

Ewzad giggled and dissolved the figure, then soared through the air towards the Mage School. His troops were spread out below him. Thousands of men, most of them marked with a kernel of power. He looked back and saw the silvery cord connecting him to his body.

"*This is a dangerous spell,*" said Mellinda.

"*Dangerous? No-no. No one can reach my body, witch,*" he said. It irritated him that she could still communicate with him when he was separated from his body like this.

"*Many of them have spirit sight,*" she reminded. "*If they see your spirit, they will know you are vulnerable.*"

"*Ah, but I'm not. No, you see, Stardeon's rings allow me to bring my power with me.*" If he had a face to smile with, his grin would be stretching from ear to ear. "*Watch, dear Mellinda. Yes, watch.*"

He soared to the great gates of the school and climbed through the air until he was high above them. The warriors and wizards scurried around on their wall and on the grounds behind it like insignificant bugs. He longed to squash them and he would, but for the moment he stared up at the Rune Tower and seethed. Oh how he loathed this place.

He had seen it first as a child. When he was twelve, his father took him on a tour of the kingdom, showing him every major city, introducing him to every noble. So many of the places were impressive. So many were grand. But this place, the Mage School, was glorious. He gazed in awe at the clock tower and the fountains. The wizards let him come inside and see the great library. He had laughed in excitement. All the knowledge he would ever need was there at his fingertips. And all the time, he had known they were his enemies.

His Uncle Larvitus had taught him of the evils of the Mage School the day Ewzad had his awakening. It had been the year prior. Eleven was an early age for an awakening. For most children it didn't happen until puberty, but that summer spent at his uncle's house had been full of revelations.

His father liked to visit his brother's spacious house often. It was a lovely place, set on a lake with a small town full of peasants to wait on them. They spent many a week there as Ewzad was growing up and all that time, he'd had no idea his uncle was a dark wizard.

Ewzad was nearing his teenage years and it was expected that he would spend most of his time at the palace in Dremald learning the courtly arts. Uncle Larvitus knew Ewzad wouldn't spend much time with him in the future, so he forced the awakening on him.

Larvitus had grabbed him by the neck and sent some kind of strange tingling deep within him, then locked him in the dark chicken house. Ewzad had been frightened, but chickens were harmless creatures really. Then Larvitus let a weasel loose inside. The chickens erupted into panicked squawks, buffeting him with their wings, pecking at him, and that tingling sensation grew into a burning. One minute later Ewzad had blown the house to pieces with an explosion of steam, cooking every living thing within.

Ewzad stumbled from the wreckage, terrified at what had happened and Larvitus was there waiting. He grabbed Ewzad then and asked him an important question. What did he want to be? Ewzad didn't have to think about his answer. He wanted to be king. That was the only way he would be able to marry Princess Elise.

Larvitus told him then that wizards aren't allowed to be king. Wizards aren't allowed to rule anywhere. They aren't even allowed to be nobles. Ewzad's uncle stood with him in the wreckage of the chicken house, the stench of cooked feathers in the air, and told him he had two choices. Admit that his magic destroyed the place and go with the wizards to the Mage School where he would be taught magic, but stripped of rank. Or he could leave with Larvitus and blame the coop's destruction on a sudden lightning strike. Larvitus would teach him to use his magic, but he would have to keep his powers secret or the wizards would take him away.

The wizards' rules were unfair. That's what Ewzad had understood the day he'd first visited the Mage School. This was a place he had deserved, full of the knowledge he'd craved. He

383

should have been taught by true teachers instead of the smelly uncle he'd been forced to kill two years later. But the Mage School was never to be his. Not until now.

As he hovered above the wall, staring at that magnificent tower, his plans solidified. Once the wizards were gone, he would claim the Rune Tower to be his and his alone. He would raise the bridges and close the gates and use one of the Mage School's mirrors to travel from Dremald palace to the tower and back again. He could rule Dremaldria and mine the tower's secrets all for himself.

He giggled at the notion and shifted his attention back to the insects milling about below. It was time to give his speech. He gathered air magic to amplify his voice.

"*Citizens of Dremaldria!*" he said, his voice echoing throughout the grounds. He glided back a short distance from the gates and built an image in front of him. To the shocked people on the wall it looked like Ewzad's face floated in the air, a hundred feet tall, a sparkling crown upon his brow. "*It is I. Yes-yes, your king. I come before you now to ask you to rejoin your fellow citizens. Come into my arms and avoid this folly. Yes, wouldn't that be better? Surrender now and you live.*"

"Do you wish to negotiate?" shouted a wizard wearing a golden robe. Ewzad didn't recognize the man's face.

"*That's Air Wizard Randolf of the High Council,*" Mellinda said. "*With Latva ill, he is their speaker.*"

"*Oh, good,*" said both Ewzad and the giant face in the air. "*No-no. There will be no negotiations, Wizard Randolf. Just surrender.*"

The wizard, unused to such a start, continued on as if Ewzad hadn't already stated his terms, "What are your demands?"

"*My demands?*" Ewzad scoffed. "*Your surrender. I said it, didn't I? Yes-yes, I did. It's surrender or death. I don't see how I could be more clear, do you?*"

Randolf cleared his throat and Ewzad decided he hated the man. "We need to know more. What are the conditions?"

The people around Randolf didn't like the idea of negotiation any more than Ewzad did. Some of them began to shout him down.

"Yes, my conditions are simple. Oh-oh so simple. You must surrender to my army and turn over your leaders for execution."

"Our leaders?" said Randolf, obviously aware that he was one of those leaders.

"Yes indeed. The rest of your men will be spared as long as they swear fealty to me. Your king and protector, yes. Then the Mage School will be dissolved and I will take possession of the Rune Tower. Nice, yes?"

"Swear fealty to you?" Randolf scoffed. "Your legitimacy as king is still very much in question. Come back to us when you are ready to talk."

"In question?" Ewzad's enormous visage snarled. He reached out with the rings' magic and pierced the wizards's body, then ignited an explosion of steam from deep within the man. Randolf burst into pieces with a loud pop. Ewzad's visage frowned. A pop? What an unsatisfying sound. He added a loud thunder roll so that the entire school could hear what had happened.

"Who wishes to speak next? Hmm?" he asked. The shocked expressions of the tiny people told him that his point had been made. He began to think that this might perhaps work after all. He could keep blowing them up one by one until they surrendered. What a delicious notion. Yes, and his army wouldn't be wasted.

"I will speak!" shouted a brawny brown-haired man. He had two strangely shaped swords on his back and a gray bow in his hand.

Ewzad recognized the speaker's face. This was the proud bonding wizard Mellinda had told him about. He was bigger now, but this was the young Sir Edge that had released all those prisoners in his dungeon. This was the man that had defeated his precious Bandham.

"I don't think your magic will work," Mellinda warned. *"The bond may protect him from the rings."*

"Ridiculous." Ewzad said, his visage forming a sneer. *"Oh, speak will you? Sir Edge, is it?"*

"I am!" the named warrior shouted. The people around him, including one ugly ogre, were clutching at him, trying to

385

talk him down.

"***Do you wish to surrender, Edge?***" Ewzad asked. Not that it mattered. He intended to kill the man one way or another.

"No! We won't surrender!" Edge shouted. He drew an arrow and pulled it back on his gray bow. "We will fight! We will destroy your army! And we will destroy you!"

The man fired, his arrow flying faster than an arrow should. It passed between the eyes of the visage and continued right through the center of Ewzad's invisible form. An agonizing shock spread through him and Ewzad knew that, back in his chair on the back of Hamford's neck, his body had just convulsed.

"***How dare you***?" Ewzad growled and he reached for the man, intending to inflate him like a sheep's bladder balloon. But he couldn't. The man was slippery. It was like there was nothing for Ewzad to grab hold of. Ewzad's visage showed his confusion.

"*Just leave,*" Mellinda said. "*Or kill one of those near him. Your monsters can kill him well enough later.*"

"I see your true form, Ewzad Vriil!" said Edge. "Would that I could reach your body with this arrow." He fired again and this time, the arrow was surrounded by a faint glow.

It passed through Ewzad before he could move out of the way. This shot was more painful than the one before. Back on his throne, his body bit through its tongue. His visage winced. The people cheered.

"***Then die all of you***!" Ewzad shouted.

His visage faded into the air and Ewzad fled, full of fury. He followed the silvery line connecting to his body. He could see Kassy perched over his spasming form, trying to wake him. Once he was inside, he shoved the concerned raptoid away and spat out the tip of his tongue. A simple writhe of his fingers healed the wound and he shouted out to Mellinda.

"Witch! Have your spies planted their surprises?" he asked.

"*I told you not to stay,*" she said.

"I asked you something, you horrible hag! Didn't I?" he asked, aching to reach through their connection and throttle her. But he needed her and she knew it. He could not afford to damage her now. Not yet. Perhaps when this battle was over he could indulge himself. "Have they planted their surprises?"

"*Yes, Master. They have,*" she said smugly. "*All but two, but that will be more than enough.*"

"It had better be. Don't you think?" he snapped.

"*It will,*" she promised.

"Yes-yes. Good, and the wizards don't know?"

"*They do not,*" she claimed. "*Your raptoid killed the captured ones before they revealed what they had done for me. Shall I have your packages activated now?*"

"No-no. Send in the fodder," he smiled. "Yes, let them think their defenses were effective. Then, when I give the word, activate our little surprise."

The defenders cheered. A chant of 'Edge! Edge! Edge!' began to run down the wall.

The people around him clapped Justan on the back and Fist wrapped him up in a hug. His mother grasped his arm and said, "Never do that to me again."

Justan's hands were still shaking. Ewzad's show had been impressive and he'd been afraid, but he'd seen the way Ewzad had pierced Wizard Randolf with spirit magic and knowing it to be the power of the Rings of Stardeon, he had hoped that the bond would protect him.

He'd also known that his father or mother, or one of his other friends would have spoken up if he hadn't. So he'd taken Ewzad's fury upon himself. He'd half expected his gambit to fail. Fortunately, he had been lucky and Ewzad's power hadn't been able to hurt him.

Perhaps more importantly, he'd noticed that his first arrow had hurt the wizard. That was why he had wrapped a small piece of the bond around the arrow on his second shot and that had been enough to drive the wizard away. It was too bad he hadn't been given a third attempt.

The stone in Justan's pocket vibrated again. He pulled it out and saw the words, 'Good one son'. Followed quickly by, 'Incoming!'

"Incoming attack!" Justan cried.

They heard the shouts of crazed goblins long before they saw them. Thousands of the stupid creatures ran down the main

387

road and streamed from the forest around the school. The traps worked well. Explosions rocked the ground, launching their little bodies in the air. The earth opened beneath them, dropping them onto rocky spikes. Blades of air spat from the trees, hewing them to pieces. It was a slaughter.

"He saw the traps," Fist said, shaking his head at the destruction below. "He doesn't care about goblins."

Justan looked down on the torn goblin bodies. Of course. Ewzad had mage sight. He had seen. This was how he handled obstacles; as calculating and cruel as if he were only playing strategy games. Or perhaps crueler, he thought, shivering as he glanced at the bloody splatter where Wizard Randolf had been standing.

Justan! I smell one, Gwyrtha sent.

What? he asked.

An eye! A moonrat eye! she said excitedly.

Where? Suddenly he felt a sense of foreboding.

In here, Gwyrtha sniffed at the air. *By the wall! By the pasture!*

Go. Find it and stop whoever it is. Show me as soon as you see them!

"Mother," Justan said, grabbing Darlan's arm to get her attention. She was busy watching the destruction below, readying herself to activate the lava bucket if needed. Her eyes swung to him, his tone of voice concerning her. "Gwyrtha senses a moonrat eye down by the wall, near the pasture. She's heading there now, it's-."

Justan closed his eyes and concentrated. Gwyrtha was nearing the wall. A woman wearing a mage's robe was kneeling down at the base of the wall doing something. Gwyrtha's mage sight showed a steady flow of earth magic coming from the woman.

Gwyrtha, knock her over. See what she's doing!

The woman screamed as Gwyrtha bowled her aside. Justan didn't recognize the mage, but she was wearing a black robe with blue trim. An earth mage. Gwyrtha sniffed at the spot where the woman had been kneeling. There was a tiny round hole in the grass. *An eye! Down there!*

Gwyrtha began to dig, but the mage cried out and a block

of earth shot up from the ground underneath the rogue horse, blasting the air out of Gwyrtha's lungs and sending her tumbling to the side. The woman ran to the hole and earth magic flared again.

Get her, Gwyrtha! Justan sent.

I am fast. I am hard. I am strong. Gwyrtha said. She climbed to her feet, the changes in her body already beginning to take place. She leapt at the mage, but another block of earth shot up, shoving her to the side.

I am fast. I am hard. I am strong. She darted forward, dodging the next block of earth, and collided with the mage, slamming the woman into the wall and knocking her unconscious. But it was too late.

A great tremor rocked the school. The wall began to shudder under Justan's feet. He looked over the edge and saw the ground slowly rising towards him. Darlan's eyes widened.

"We're sinking!" Fist declared.

Chapter Thirty Five

The devices were cunning things. Ewzad's goblinoid troops had found them in the Dark Prophet's palace along with the crysalisk. They were runed cubes made of steel and filled with crystals, each one only about the size of a fist. Their purpose was to reverse a magic spell. The process was rather simple. Place the cube next to a spell. Activate it one time for it to learn the spell's pattern. The longer you let it learn, the more effective it would be. Then activate it a second time and it would unweave the layers of the spell it had learned.

Ewzad had come up with the idea of creating a little crab-like creature that grew around the cube and when instructed, it would burrow down deep into the earth only to disintegrate and die two weeks later when Ewzad's power ran out. Over the last year, Mellinda had been sending servants into the school in one guise or another. They would leave the cubes in various places for her spies to find.

There had been thirty of the devices in all and twenty eight of them had been placed along points at the base of the wall and linked together with a low level spell. Deep in the earth, the devices were all but undetectable. They learned the spell's pattern and waited to be activated.

Ewzad's plan could not have been executed better. When the mage finished her spell, the cubes came to life at once and began unraveling the centuries-old spells that had raised the walls from the bedrock. The walls descended at roughly the same pace in which they'd been raised. Within a few short minutes they had been reduced from fifty feet tall to forty.

The defenders scrambled, gathering their strongest earth wizards to combat the wall's descent. Thirty of them, anchored by Wizard Nikoli, worked to keep the walls from failing. The amount of magic they wielded was immense.

The wall sank further and further despite their efforts. They tried to work directly against the descent with sheer force. They drew up enormous supports from within the earth. They tried to firm up the bedrock underneath it. But the cubes' work was inexorable. The wizards didn't know the nature of the devices they were fighting against and none of them had been around at the creation of the original wall raising spell to know how it had been executed in the first place.

As the earth wizards tried to halt its descent, the wall shook more and more violently. The defenders on top of the wall didn't know what to do. Many of them were knocked off their feet and one retiree archer dropped an explosive arrow resulting in a blast of air that knocked ten defenders off the wall. Eventually when the wall was only twenty feet high, the leaders made the decision to abandon the wall and regroup.

Getting off the wall was a more difficult prospect than it seemed. The ground around the descending rock was churning and anyone who stood too close would be sucked in. When the top of the wall finally sank into the earth, the ground closed around it, swallowing the few who hadn't managed to get off in time. All in all, over a hundred died during the wall's collapse.

Ewzad didn't give them time to build up new defenses. His army of scruffy men surged forward, roaring and bloodthirsty. The academy archers launched volleys of arrows and the wizards sent out lightning strikes and fireballs, but the protective bubble generated by the crysalisk surrounded the army. The men began to change, swelling and transforming into monsters.

Justan charged forward, swords in hand, Fist and Gwyrtha at his side. He fell into the calm of battle, the world slowing around him, and danced among the monsters. Peace drained their emotions. Rage blew them to pieces.

Fist kept pace, his enormous shield in one hand, his mace in the other, enhancing his speed. He charged both shield and mace with electricity, swinging with all his strength and knocking down beasts far larger than him. All the while, Squirrel sat in the observation room with Master Latva, cheering him on.

Gwyrtha had transformed herself into a form similar to the one she had used to fight the raptoid, her scales enlarged and hardened into armored plates, her mane sticking up like stiff bristles, her claws and teeth lengthened, the scales on her tail turned to spikes. She leapt on the transformed men, the weight of her body bearing them down as she tore into them with claws and teeth, whipping her tail at reaching arms and tentacles.

The berserkers charged into the men, led by Zambon wielding the sword newly renamed Efflina. Zambon howled with the rest of them, letting the sword build him into a terrible rage. The Howlers were sorely pressed, but Riveren and the Mage School guard joined with them, driving the changed men back; Zambon with his blade of fury and Riveren with wide swipes of his double-bladed axe.

Captain Demetrius and his cavalry were forced to deal with a wave of orcs and gorcs. The enemy was armed with miss-matched armor and high quality weapons mainly purloined from the wreckage of the academy and other human settlements, but the cavalry was ready. Each horse had been fitted with a blast plate on the front of the animal, runed with air magic to shove enemies to the side upon impact.

The cavalry charged through the center of the goblinoid forces with Demetrius at their head. The captain wore a new suit of armor dwarf-forged and runed with earth magic and a dual-chained flail gifted to him by the wizards. The two balls on the tips of the chains were covered in runes that would send spikes of air into the enemy on impact. Samson rode beside him, his skin altered to armor-like thickness and wielding a runed spear in each hand.

On the far side of the school, a mix of regular and modified trolls poured out of the forest, running and screeching. The elves fought them back with arrows, swords and pepper, assisted by wizards and mages with fire and lightning spells. Antyni fought valiantly with her brother's runed steel bow. She was a rare talent, shooting the beasts through their eyes and open mouths with pepper-laced arrows.

Despite the ferocity of their counter attacks, the enemy army pushed forward, the crysalisk moving with it. The leaders of the defensive effort abandoned the command center to lead a charge of their own. Faldon the Fierce, Tolivar, Oz the Dagger, Hugh the Shadow, and Stout Harley, along with Darlan and Wizard Beehn gathered a group of graduates and retirees and made their own push into the enemy ranks.

Faldon's great sword, The Monarch, whose enchanted blade parted steel as easily as parchment, cut swath's through the mutated ranks, cleaving great beasts in half at the waist. Tolivar danced through them, a whirlwind, slicing and dodging.

Oz the Dagger's attack style was more precise. He slipped between the enemy, striking at critical points, cutting hamstrings and tendons, incapacitating them, while Stout Harley followed, bashing in the skulls of the fallen enemies with his hammer, his armor protecting him from the most frantic of blows.

Darlan followed behind her husband, using her decades of experience as a war mage to enhance his attacks and protect the rest of their forces. She staggered enemies with fireballs, threw stone spikes up from the ground to impale them, and even pulled a great gout of molten rock up from the earth below. Professor Beehn, in his wheeled chair, floated just above them, providing a moving shield of air that thwarted projectile attacks and sending blades of air into enemies that the others missed.

Hugh the Shadow darted about between them all, assisting with cunning throws of his seemingly inexhaustible supply of magic throwing weapons, potions, and assassins devices. All the while, complaining about the difficulty of retrieving them when he was done.

Jhonate led a charge of advanced students and graduates, her goal to find and destroy the crysalisk. She wore a new breastplate fitted and designed by Bettie, made of firedrake leather and runed to make it as resistant as the hardest iron. With her was Poz, son of Weld, whose sword, Limber, lived up to its name as he carved through great monsters, his blade shearing through bone like it were butter.

Qenzic, son of Sabre Vlad ran beside them, wielding his father's magic blade and a new shield made of earth-runed steel. With him was Lyramoor, who hadn't left Qenzic's side since Sabre Vlad's funeral. The elf, fully healed from his injuries, was as deadly with his dual blades as ever and, to Qenzic's tastes, far too overprotective.

Willum ran next to them, eager to use his new weapon, a scythe with an air-enhanced blade that cut enemies farther and deeper the quicker he sliced with it. Theodore didn't like this new acquisition and spent the battle belittling its abilities even though it was obvious his axe was still the main weapon.

"It's really quite a puny thing, Willy. Though it's good for cutting tall grass, I suppose," said the imp.

Shut up, Willum said as he dodged the swipe of a tall black beast with a bladed pincer for an arm. He swung the axe at the creature's knee. *Force!* A deep bell rang out and the lower part of the beast's leg disappeared from view as it shot into the crowd. The black beast toppled over and Kathy the Plate chopped its twisted head off its body.

You should be happy, imp, Willum thought, jumping over the smoldering body of the fallen beast as he tried to keep up with Jhonate and the others. *You're lapping up plenty of energy from these things.*

"Ho-ho, that's true, Willy. That wizard's power is quite tasty, but you really must remember to speak properly. Call me Theodore."

Imp is faster, he sent.

"You're the one that named me," the imp reminded.

You're right. I should have named you Teddy, he said, watching as Jhonate changed the end of her staff into a thick spiked ball and swung it with two hands, catching a red-skinned beast right in its ant-like head, knocking it down.

"That only saves you one syllable," the imp pointed out.

The ant beast fell in Willum's way. He swung the axe. *Force!* And blasted the beast to the side, tripping another beast that fell into Kathy's waiting axe. *That's right. I could save just as much time pronouncing it 'Theedore'.*

"Hey, Odd Blade," shouted Kathy the Plate, smacking his rear with a gauntleted hand. "Do you really need to make that gong sound every time you hit somthin'? Sounds like you're announcing it's time for dinner!"

"I'm . . . not sure," he replied. "I'll ask!"

"Good," she said and the way she cocked her head, it was possible she thought he was crazy. It was hard to tell with her full helmet on. She smacked his butt again and ran over to slice the eyestalk off of a hovering beast with razor-like antennae.

Do you have to make that bell sound, Theodore? he asked, wondering why she had smacked him. Her gauntlet had likely left welts.

"*I like it. Ho-ho, the bell tolls letting you know a debt has been paid.*"

We aren't keeping that ledger anymore, Willum reminded.

"*You might not be,*" the imp mumbled. It changed the subject, "*I think the dishes lady likes you.*"

Don't be ridiculous. That was more of a . . . you know, fighting slap. And her name's Kathy the Plate.

"*Oh-ho, you like her too, don't you?*" the imp taunted.

Willum slashed out with the scythe in his left hand, splitting the grasping claw of an insectoid creature. *Now's not the time for this discussion.*

"*Hmm, true. All you've ever seen is her face since she never takes that armor off. For all you know, she's got a pot belly under there.*"

You're changing the subject. No more bell sound.

"*You disappoint me, Willy.*"

Force! Willum sent as a furry wolf-headed monster with tentacle limbs climbed into his path. The axe blew its head off its body and there was no bell sound. As the creature's body deflated, the imp gave out a sigh.

"*See? It's just not right.*"

I like it better this way, Willum decided.

The imp grumbled. "*I miss the sound already.*"

Willum saw the others pause ahead. They had found the crysalisk. It was sitting on top of a wooden wagon being pulled by a team of heavily armed ogres. It was a tall cylindrical object made of two large crystals stacked on top of each other that had been charged with elemental magic and held in a metal frame. The shield was generated at the point where the two crystals touched.

Latva had told them the crysalisk could be destroyed by smashing either crystal. The problem was that they were encased in a thick iron sleeve covered with protective runes. They were going to need a lot of force to break through that sleeve. Willum hoped his axe would be enough.

"*I don't know, Willy,*" Theodore said. "*That is some major protective magic.*"

"I-!" A sudden wave of pain swept over Willum, gnawing deep in his chest. He cried out and fell to his knees behind the others. Had he been hit?

"*What is it, Willy?*" the imp asked in concern.

"Shield!" he cried and a dome of air interwoven with fire surrounded him.

Kathy the Plate knelt beside him, tapping at the shield, but he couldn't hear what she was saying. Tears streamed down Willum's face and he realized it wasn't a physical pain he was feeling. This was grief.

"*What is it?*" the imp demanded.

"It's Tolivar," he gasped. "Something's happened. Something horrible."

Tolivar saw Zambon fall.

It was a bear that felled him; a bear twelve-feet-tall that breathed fire from its mouth and had eyes like a spider. Zambon took out its leg at the knee with one swing of his sword, but as the beast collapsed, it swung down with its enormous claws and tore him from shoulder to hip.

Zambon collapsed and Tolivar disappeared.

It was Tamboor who ran to his son's side; Tamboor who shoved Riveren away from his son; Tamboor who thrust the healing sword into Zambon's hands, ignoring the battle around him.

"Live!" Tamboor shouted.

The berserkers surrounded them, protecting their former leader while the battle raged around him. Tamboor didn't notice. He could see only his son's lifeless eyes. They were Efflina's eyes. He blew air into Zambon's mouth. Tamboor tried again and again, but it didn't matter. The bear had torn his lungs.

Zambon had hunted bears with Tamboor the year he went to the academy. It was Tamboor's first year in Jack's Rest and he was just getting used to retired life. Zambon had been excited when they found one of the beasts on their property. It had been a big beast, but Tamboor had let Zambon use Meredith and Zambon had struck the killing blow . . .

Tamboor grasped his sword and stood. But the sword in his hands wasn't Sadie. He shoved the berserkers aside and launched into the beasts around them. Tamboor dodged their attacks and struck them down. Meredith found their hearts. Meredith found their throats. The only reason he didn't let them land a blow on him was because he could not die yet. He could not die until he killed them all. The mutated men, the goblinoids, all of them, and once they were dead, then he could die. Then he could see his family once again.

Justan saw Jhonate and the others from a distance. They were fighting in a circle around someone who'd fallen. He ran towards them, blasting aside any beasts that got in his way.

Fist was having difficulty keeping up. The combination of using the mace and his elemental magic was taking its toll on the ogre. Justan reached into Gwyrtha and siphoned some of her energy stores, giving Fist what he needed.

Thanks, Fist said, his steps picking up. He saw Jhonate now. *What are they doing?*

I'm not sure, Justan said. He sped up, ignoring the beasts he didn't have to fight. They moved so slow in his mind's eye that it wasn't too difficult. As he got closer, he saw that Jhonate and the other advanced students were fighting around a small dome shield made of fire and air. *It's Willum.*

A large beast that looked like a centipede with gelatinous segments for its body reared between Justan and the others. Justan tightened his concentration and threw Peace in front of him. The heavy sword spun end over end and pierced one of the creature's segments. The thing turned and looked at him in confusion and he buried Rage between its insectile eyes, blasting it into nothingness.

He retrieved Peace and reached Jhonate's side. She pointed towards the wagon. The ogre handlers continued in their forward march, but several of them paced by it protectively, keeping their eyes on Justan and the others.

"The crysalisk is there," she said.

"What's wrong with Willum?" Justan asked.

"We do not know," she replied, her brow furrowed in consternation. "He just fell and that shield appeared around him."

"It's that axe of his," said Kathy the Plate. He couldn't see her face through her visor, but her voice was filled with concern. "It won't let us touch him, but we don't dare leave him here alone."

"You go," Justan said. "Take out the ogres and destroy the crysalisk if you can. I'll take care of him. Fist, go with them. Gwyrtha, stay here and watch me.

The others ran off, but Kathy didn't move. "I'll stay. You help him and I'll help your monster horse keep these other beasts off you."

He nodded and reached out to touch the shield. It sparked and he drew back his hand, his fingertips singed. "Imp! Listen to me. Let me through!"

The shield faded. Willum was curled into a ball, his hands over his head, sobbing.

"Willum!" he said, but the academy student didn't answer. He reached out and touched the axe. *What's going on, imp?*

"It's Tolivar. He's gone crazy with grief. His son died."

Justan's stomach lurched and he told the others, *Zambon's dead.*

Gwyrtha growled, launching herself at a beast that came too close. Fist yanked the point of his mace out of an ogre's skull. *Poor Tolivar.*

Justan grasped Peace's hilt, letting the sword take his grief away for a moment. Then he pried Willum's scythe from his left hand and replaced it with Peace's handle.

Willum gasped and his eyes opened. His brow furrowed in confusion. "Sir Edge. Wh-what's going on?"

"It's my sword. It's draining the pain." Justan said. "What happened?"

"Tolivar's gone from the bond," Willum said. "The only thing in there is anger and sadness."

"What about the others? What about Bettie and Samson?" Justan asked, worried that they could be somewhere prostrate on the battlefield with monsters all around them.

"I-I'm not sure. Tolivar doesn't keep the bond open between us quite like father did," Willum said.

"Alright, listen to me," Justan said. "Keep holding on to my sword. Go through the bond and let it draw Tolivar's pain away until he will listen to you. Talk to him and make sure the others are okay. Imp! You help him."

"His name is Theodore," Willum said numbly.

"Just go and do it."

Justan stood. Sorrow over Zambon's loss filled him again. He turned it into fuel. Rage buzzed in his hands, aching to release the power of Tolivar's pain. Justan turned his eyes on the crysalisk.

Willum's mind swam through the bond, heading towards the source of pain and anger. With the imp's help, he was able to drag the power of Sir Edge's sword with him.

"*This isn't easy, Willy,*" Theodore complained. "*We need to do this quick.*"

They came over a form in the darkness, but it was Samson. Willum reached out and touched the rogue horse with the power of Edge's sword. Samson stirred.

Are you alright? Willum asked.

I fell in the middle of a charge, Samson said. *I think I broke some ribs, but a healer's working on me.* Samson's mind was uncertain. *All this pain . . . It's worse than when Coal died. I-I don't know how to handle this, Willum.*

Just hold on with me, Willum said. *We need to find Tolivar.* He shared the sword's power with Samson and the centaur calmed. They found Bettie next. She recovered quicker than the rest of them, needing just a light touch of the power.

Why'd Zambon go off and get himself killed like that? Blasted fool! She sighed. *Let's wake Tolivar up. Lenui's about to crap himself worried about the baby.*

Is it okay? Willum asked.

Yeah, the battle ain't reached us yet. I just fell on my backside. Come on.

She grasped the power and together they surged through the pain and anger, reaching with the sword's power to suck it all away. They headed towards the source of the pain and finally they found him.

In Willum's mind, he was a solitary figure all in black, holding a sword in his hands. The sword was made of fire and the flames licked up his arms and disappeared into a gaping hole in his chest. On the ground next to him, discarded, was a white sword and robe. Both of them had a shining naming rune embossed in them.

Tolivar, Willum called. *Tolivar, please listen.*

While he spoke, Bettie picked up the sword and Samson picked up the robe.

Tolivar didn't respond. His face was fixed in a soundless scream. Willum understood. This wasn't Tolivar, not really. This was Tamboor. Or . . . No, this was the thing Tamboor had become when his family died.

"*Hurry, Willum,*" the imp said. "*Ho-ho, this power is slippery! It doesn't belong in here. Do this quick before we lose hold.*"

Willum wrapped his hand in the power and grabbed Tamboor's shoulder.

The power of Edge's sword didn't have a color. It was more like an absence of color, and when it touched the flames, the fire in the sword was sucked away. Once that was gone, Tolivar's face relaxed and the blackness that covered him began to be sucked away as well.

He blinked as the blackness faded. *What is this?*

It's me, Willum said. *And Bettie and Samson. We're so sorry about Zambon.*

He's gone! Tolivar's face twitched and the blackness started to return, but the power continued to suck it away. He sobbed. *He was the real reason I stayed alive, you know. Not the revenge. He was the only part of Efflina I had left. Now . . . now the only way to see them again is to die myself.*

"*I'm losing hold, Willum!*" the imp shouted.

Samson placed the robe about Tamboor's shoulders. Bettie pried the black sword from Tamboor's hands and replaced it with the white one. A silvery glow flowed from the sword, but it was sucked away by the power as easily as the fire had been.

Then the power left, ripped away from them, and the darkness returned. Tamboor began to sob. Willum wrapped his arms around him and he felt Bettie and Samson join in the embrace.

Tolivar, stay with us. We need you, he said.

If you die, we die, Bettie added. *And so does my baby.*

Please, Tolivar, said Samson. *We can't replace your family, but we are here.*

Tolivar let out a sigh. *I . . .*

The figure in their arms turned from black to gray. The glow of the sword poured into the hole in Tolivar's chest.

They embraced for a moment more, sharing in Tolivar's loss. Then he pushed them away. *We have a battle to finish.*

The sound of the explosion reached all the way to Ewzad's ears. He saw the glow of the protective bubble overhead fade.

"What was that?" Ewzad said.

"*The crysalisk is ruined,*" Mellinda replied, fear in her voice. "*Sir Edge destroyed it.*"

Ewzad swallowed. How could he have destroyed it? That thing had been so wrapped in protection it could have been thrown off a cliff and survived. "N-no matter. Yes, we must press forward."

"*I suggest we withdraw for now,*" Mellinda said and he could sense her trembling. "*The loss of the crysalisk is emboldening the wizards. We should return to Sampo.*"

"Return? Withdraw?" Ewzad sputtered. "Nonsense! Impossible!" He raised his thumb and brought up the image of the battlefield. Lightning strikes and fireballs were pounding his changed men. Their hulks were losing form and melting right and left and his standard troops were falling back in fear.

"*You see?*" she said. "*Withdraw. Put power in more troops. Attack again while they are mourning their losses. We'll send in more assassins, weaken their resolve!*"

"No. We can't back down. Not now. The wall is down. Yes! Send everything! Yes-yes, end this now while they are weakened!"

"*But Master . . . there is something else you must know,*" Mellinda said and Ewzad could tell she was mulling how to say the next part. "*Elise has gone into labor. Your babies will be here soon. They will be in Sampo in another day or two."*

"My . . . babies?" Ewzad said, his thoughts numb.

"Yes. So let's withdraw. Build our strength. We have infinite resources if you allow us the time to build more troops. The school does not. There is no way for help to come for them. They will grow weaker while we-!"

"No!" Ewzad reached through their link and slapped her with all the power he could muster. Scores of moonrats fell over dead. Trolls screeched and ran free. Several commanders felt their connection with their mistress fade as the eyes they held lost their power.

"You fool," she growled. *"Do what you wish. I send all your forces forward."*

Ewzad felt her withdraw from their connection with satisfaction. The babies were coming. He had to have this finished before they arrived. If there was any chance that he could keep them both, the fight had to end now. With the Mage School gone and Dremald his, he wouldn't need the Dark Prophet anymore.

"Arcon!" he shouted, walking to the edge of the giant and looking down.

The mage jerked in his saddle and peered up at Ewzad from below. His face was pale and he was clutching his chest like he was in shock. "Y-yes, my king?"

"Go with them! Go! Kill as many as you can with your magic!" he demanded. Let the mage fight. If Mellinda wanted Arcon to live, she would have to assure Ewzad's victory.

"Y-yes, my king," Arcon repeated and started his horse forward at a gallop.

Ewzad sent most of his prized creations surging ahead with the mage and had Hamford follow behind them. He kept only a few beasts around him just in case. By the time he arrived, the battle should be finished. Ewzad pulled the image up again and saw that the destruction of his forces was continuing. Mellinda had been right about one thing. Even with the reinforcements he sent, he could still lose.

Ewzad smiled as a plan formed in his mind. "Kassy! Come here, yes?"

She sauntered over to him. "Yesss, King Ewwie," she

purred.

"Closer," he said and she slithered up to him, mere inches from his face, her full lips slightly parted. Mellinda was such a good teacher. Too good a teacher. He reached up and touched the eye in the center of her chest. "Do you want this eye gone?"

She swallowed and her eyes widened in fear. "Th-the misstresss is kind, King Ewwie."

He smiled and plucked the eye out. She winced and the claw on the back of the eye writhed and clutched blindly at the air. Ewzad burst it with an explosion of steam. "You are loyal to me, yes?"

"Yesss, King Ewwie!" She lifted one of his writhing hands and began kissing it in gratitude. Tears came from her eyes. "Thank you, King Ewwie!"

"Good-good," he said. "Watch over me while my body sleeps, would you, my dear? Don't let anyone come near me, yes? No one."

"Yesss, King Ewwie," she purred, kissing his hand again.

"Good." He enacted the spell once more and slid free of his body. Ewzad soared over his army and past the wreckage of the crysalisk. He would destroy them. Destroy the defenders of the school one by one if he had to. Pop! Pop! Pop! He would kill them all if he could. And if there were any more like that Sir Edge that he could not destroy, he would leave them to fight his monsters alone.

Chapter Thirty Six

Deathclaw hissed in frustration. *They are fighting now*!

"I know!" Beth said, running alongside him, a scowl on her face. "I'm pissed too! I was sure my instincts were right about this!"

They had arrived in Sampo hoping to find a way to sabotage Ewzad from behind or perhaps assassinate him, but the wizard hadn't been there. His army had marched on the Mage School and he'd gone with them. While they'd been arguing about what to do next, Charz told them the attack had begun.

"Alfred says that the battle has turned slightly in their favor," Charz said. "They destroyed that shield making thingie."

"Justan destroyed it," Deathclaw added. He had been pleased to hear it, and yet Justan had seemed so sad when he told him.

"Good!" Hilt said in relief.

"But right now," Charz added. "He's mostly worried that Vriil might decide to retreat."

"Why does that worry him?" Beth asked.

"Because Ewzad Vriil can always regroup and make more monsters." Hilt said. "The Mage School can't make more wizards. I doubt they can even raise the walls again, at least not any time soon."

"Then we kill the wizard now," Deathclaw declared.

"Good idea," Hilt said, nodding.

"Charz, carry me!" Beth said. "I need to focus on the road ahead."

The giant picked her up in his arms and kept running while she closed her eyes and sent her senses ahead. Beth ground her teeth in frustration. The instinct to come to Sampo first had felt so right. Her feelings were never wrong. What had happened?

"They're not far!" she said. The rear of the army was a few hundred feet ahead around a curve in the road. There were several big monsters glowing with spirit magic in the back and then a bit further something else; something enormous, and riding on it . . . "It's him! It's Ewzad Vrill and better yet," Her eyes popped open and a grin spread across her face. "He's traveled! That idiot has traveled!"

"What do you mean, he's traveled?" Hilt asked.

"He's not in his body." Charz said. The giant laughed. "Idiot left himself wide open."

"There's some monsters ahead, between us and him," she said. "Also, he's riding some sort of huge thing, but if we can take it down . . ."

"That?" Deathclaw asked, pointing. They could see it moving just above the top of the treeline now.

"That big set of arse cheeks is his ride?" Charz said in awe. Indeed that's what they could see. The rear end of a beast so big it towered above the trees, even while crawling.

"I thought the behemoth was big," Hilt said, wide-eyed. "That'll be hard to kill."

"Then I'll . . . scale it," Deathclaw said, refusing to be intimidated by the sheer size of the monster. "I'll scale it and then I'll kill the wizard."

"Scale?" Charz said.

"He means climb," Beth said. "Not like scaling a fish."

"I knew what he meant," Charz snapped.

"We'll have to get past them first," Hilt said, grabbing the hilts of his swords.

In the road ahead, their backs turned to them, were four giants, each one of them around twelve feet tall and wearing heavy plate armor. They were carrying large weapons. One of them carried a sword and the other three had spiked clubs.

"Uh, you'll have to get down for this one, Beth." Charz set her down and pulled the trident from the harness on his back. He smiled. "This'll be fun."

Beth pulled Viper off her back and drew an arrow. "I can get two of them before they see us."

405

"Then shoot," Deathclaw said. Justan was in a pitched battle. The calm of the man's sword didn't mask his exertion. Deathclaw darted down the road towards the giants and sent to Beth, *You fight them. I'll kill the wizard.*

"What's he doing?" Hilt asked her.

"He has to do this. Blast it, I can feel it." Beth fired. The arrow zipped ahead with a hiss. The giants were well covered by their armor, but Viper sank its fangs in the exposed neck of one giant. It stumbled, swearing as it reached back at its neck. Beth pulled back another arrow. "We should get to killing these giants so he can do what he has to do."

Deathclaw ran up behind the giants and as they were turning around in alarm, Beth's second arrow struck, slipping through the eye hole of one giant's helmet. It reached towards its face in shock and Deathclaw dove between its legs. He rolled to his feet and kept running, not looking back. There were a few other beasts nearby, but he ignored them and kept going. The enormous crawling giant ahead of him was his only target.

As he got closer, Deathclaw saw that its thick hide was covered in protruding spikes. It was obvious that the beast wasn't made to move this way. The crawling was hurting it. Its hands and knees were torn and it left bloody prints behind it as it moved. The stench of the wizard's power was strong. Deathclaw switched to mage sight and saw that its body was pulsing with energy. It was barely being held together and it was taking a massive amount of magic to do so.

Some of the monsters around him saw his approach, but none of them did anything. They watched as if his arrival was nothing new to them. Perhaps they had seen the other raptoids before or perhaps they smelled some trace of the wizard's stink on him. It didn't matter. They were letting him pass and when the wizard died, so would they.

Deathclaw caught up to the giant's huge foot and jumped on. Its skin was thick and tough and it didn't seem to notice as he ran across its calves. He jumped and latched onto its thigh, digging in with his claws to help him climb. He scaled the leg quickly, using the spikes that jutted periodically from its skin to help him climb. He reached the top and found himself staring into two red slitted eyes.

"Hello, brother," the black-skinned raptoid said and slashed out in an uppercut, her claws catching him under the chin and knocking him back.

Deathclaw fell backward, but dug in with his rear claws. He dangled upside down, hanging by his feet, and Star slid from its sheath. The sword bounced off a spike and struck the giant's calf, point down, sinking in nearly to the hilt. The giant roared in pain. It was a pitiful sound.

Deathclaw hunched over, grasping its skin to pull himself up, but the black-skinned raptoid dove off the giant and wrapped her arms around him, digging in with her claws. The impact tore Deathclaw free and they tumbled off the giant together, striking the back of the giant's leg and rolling to the ground.

Deathclaw kicked out with his claws and tore free of her, then rolled to his feet. His throat was bleeding and torn and his chin had been cut down to the bone. His back was covered in deep gashes from her claws and the wounds stung, but no major vessel had been struck. She hadn't altered his ability to fight. He focused in, slowing time around him.

The other raptoid was a bit more damaged. She had landed on one of the giant's spikes as they fell and the force of the collision had torn the spike free, leaving it inside of her. He could see the pointed tip of it protruding from her stomach. There was also a strange circular wound in the center of her chest, but it wasn't bleeding. He was pretty sure he hadn't caused that. She ignored the wounds and stood in attack posture, claws extended.

Deathclaw cocked his head at her and chirped questioningly. She reminded him of Talon. Ewzad had given her much the same shape except for the ridges on her arms and her spiked tail.

"We do not use the old sspeech, brother," she hissed, crouching and circling him slowly. "We are better now, yess?"

Deathclaw matched her posture and movement so that they were circling each other. "Where is Talon?"

"Talon?" she gurgled a laugh and her eyes narrowed. "Talon iss dead."

Deathclaw hissed. Was this true? "How did she die?"

"I killed her! Yess, I tore her throatss and ate her

heartss." Drool poured down her chin as she spoke. She licked her lips with a black tongue. "It wass a mercy."

"Was it?" he asked. Could this thing have done what he and Justan couldn't?

"The Misstresss had taken her ssoul. King Ewwie wanted her killed," it said.

Deathclaw didn't know whether to believe her or not. He wasn't even sure that tearing Talon's heart out would kill her. The raptoid moved as though to attack and he adjusted his stance, but she seemed to think better of it and continued to circle. He hadn't expected this. If she had killed Talon, he was grateful, but was she loyal to the wizard? He didn't have time to figure it out. Ewzad Vrill was helpless at the top of the giant!

"What is your . . ." He wanted to say 'name'. Instead, he chirped a command, telling the strange raptoid to identify herself.

She understood, though her face twitched. "The old ways are old, brother," she chided. "I am Kasssy. You are Deathclaw." She hissed. "King Ewwie sspoke of you."

"I will kill the wizard now, Kassy," he said, then added. "We can kill the wizard together. Then you can join us." He chirped the sound offering for her to join the pack. If she accepted and helped him kill Ewzad there was a chance she could be saved.

"No." Her face twisted in derision. "Come to King Ewwie. He will lovess you. He will changess you. He will makess you better."

"No," Deathclaw growled and ran for the giant. He had wasted enough time with her already. He would kill the wizard first and then see if she could be saved.

Kassy was faster than he was. Even with the spike in her body slowing her down, she caught up with him. He glanced back and saw her at the last moment. She leapt at him and he turned to meet her, claw-to-claw.

Justan stood amongst the shattered pieces of the crysalisk and watched Willum approach, still in awe of how much destructive power Tolivar's rage had unleashed. Willum handed Peace back to him. The moment Justan touched it, his sadness over Zambon's death was sucked away and he let out a slow breath. Somehow he resented the sword at that moment. It didn't seem fair that he could escape his grief so easily.

"Thank you for lending me your power, Sir Edge," Willum said.

"I am glad you were able to reach him," he replied.

"It still hurts, but he's regained his mind," Willum said. His face was drawn and sad. "It's, uh, going to be difficult for awhile."

"Tell him that his pain is what destroyed the crysalisk. Maybe that will help somewhat," Justan suggested.

Before Willum could answer, a roar came from up the road towards Sampo. The enemy had regrouped. Hundreds of reinforcements were pounding towards them, misshapen monsters and men.

"We should fight," Jhonate said, her staff at the ready. "We can delay them reaching the school."

"Our numbers are small. They'll go around us or overwhelm us," Justan said.

"I don't fear them," said Lyramoor. The elf had been disappointed when the enemy had scattered after the crysalisk's destruction.

Justan felt a chill and looked up in the air just in time to see Ewzad Vriil's spirit form soaring through the air above, trailing a silvery thread. "We must go back." He turned to the others. "We must go back! Ewzad is headed to the school!"

They turned to run. "Gwyrtha!"

Gwyrtha came to him, her body already in the process of changing back to her regular form. *We ride?*

Yes, he said and swung onto her back. "Fist, stay with Jhonate!"

"Okay," the ogre said, running to keep pace with her.

He spurred Gwyrtha towards the school and soon they caught up with the invading army's forces. *Just go past them*, he urged, and she ran through, weaving between the men and beasts. When there was a point too cramped, he would swing Rage and blast an opening.

The scene around the Mage School was chaos. Lightning bolts and fireballs crashed into the monsters all around, intermixed with volleys of arrows and boulders hurled through the air.

Justan threw up a shield around him and Gwyrtha as they ran through, hoping to avoid being struck by a stray magic attack. He did it just as a bolt of lightning struck the ground right by him, felling several beasts in the vicinity. Even with his shield up some of it got through.

Hurts! said Gwyrtha, but she didn't let it stop her. She kept on running and then Justan saw him.

Ewzad Vriil had once again created a giant image of his face that hovered over the defenders, laughing as he reached at them with his magic. People died one by one, some of them exploding into pieces like Randolf had, others swelling up and falling over, their heads or guts bursting. Ewzad didn't seem to have particular targets in mind and was just selecting individuals randomly.

Wizards hurled fireballs and lightning bolts at him, but they passed right through his face to no effect. Justan knew why. Ewzad had no physical form here for them to hit. He drew his Jharro bow. It made sense now. When he'd fired with Ma'am, his arrows had been enhanced with spirit magic.

He brought Gwyrtha to a stop and wrapped the bond around an arrow, thickly this time, pouring his intention into it. He wanted this arrow to strike Ewzad Vriil down. He pulled back and felt Ma'am surge with eagerness. *Get him, Ma'am. Destroy him*! He released the arrow and it sped towards its target faster than usual, almost as if the golden string had been attached.

Ten feet before striking him, the arrow shattered to pieces.

Ewzad's huge face turned his way and its eyes glowed red with flame. "***Sir Edge, you return!***" His voice reverberated throughout the grounds. "***Yes-yes, I didn't like your little arrows last time, so I decided to stop them***!" Justan saw it then. A shield of solid air around Ewzad's spirit form.

A squad of archers lined up, led by Mad Jon himself. A volley of arrows arced toward the wizard. Some of them passed through his insubstantial face, while others clattered off of his shield. Justan knew he could break the shield with defensive magic if only he were close enough.

"*Arrows? No-no! Do you not learn?*" Ewzad reached out with his magic and grabbed Mad Jon, lifting him into the air.

"Stop!" Justan cried, but it was too late.

Ewzad caused the archery teacher's legs to swell and harden. Caused his head to turn green and shrivel. Justan swallowed. He hadn't liked Mad Jon's class when he was in Training School, but as he'd learned more about the bow, he'd learned to respect the man. Ewzad dropped Mad Jon and looked around for his next victim. Justan swallowed. Anyone could be next. Anyone!

"Ewzad Vriil!" came a voice loud and clear and Tolivar strode into view. The bonding wizard was soaked in blood, but looked to be free of wounds. He lifted his healing sword and pointed it at the wizard. "Try me!"

Ewzad laughed and went to him. Justan was grateful for the distraction. Ewzad couldn't hurt Tolivar with the Rings of Stardeon since they wouldn't be able to penetrate the bond.

An idea came to him. *Gwyrtha, find Professor Beehn.* She ran forward and Justan hoped dearly that his friend was still alive. He didn't know if anyone else could do what he wanted to ask.

She found him quickly. He was next to Darlan, sitting in his chair gazing at the scene in horror. Justan leapt from Gwyrtha's saddle and grasped the man.

"Wizard Beehn, I can stop Ewzad Vriil but I need your help!"

"He's-he's killing everyone, Edge," the wizard said, looking dazed. "He killed Auger. Ripped the old man in half."

Justan grabbed him by the front of his robes and shook him. "You've got to focus!"

"What is it?" Darlan asked, her hand to her mouth in horror as she watched Ewzad attacking Tolivar.

"*Running? That's your plan?*" Ewzad shouted with laughter.

Justan glanced over and saw that the wizard had given up trying to use the rings' power and was now hurling fireballs. Tolivar ran and jumped, avoiding most of them, but his clothes had caught fire.

"Listen, Beehn!" Justan snapped.

411

"What?" His improper use of the wizard's name seemed to break through the fog in Beehn's mind.

"I need you to hurl me at him!"

"Hurl you?" Beehn said, aghast.

"Yes! Throw me at Vriil. I need you to aim right behind the nose on that ugly face he is projecting!"

"But what if I miss?" Beehn asked, his eyes wide with concern.

"For the sake of all of us, don't miss!" Justan said. He turned and drew his swords. A calm enveloped him. "Do it!"

"But you'll fall!" Darlan said.

"Beehn will have to catch me with his magic." He didn't look at her, just focused on the task ahead. "Or you'll have to heal me if I survive the fall but we don't have time. Just do it!"

Justan, Gwyrtha said in concern.

Justan felt a tightening around his waist and he shot up from the ground as if he'd been picked up by a large invisible hand. Then he was hurtled through the air towards Ewzad's giant floating face. The wizard laughed as a fireball struck Tolivar, but Justan didn't dare watch.

He focused and the world slowed around him. He saw Ewzad's spirit form and the shield of air around it. As he inched towards it, he reached out with his defensive magic and started picking the shield apart.

Ewzad felt the intrusion and his visage started to turn. But the wizard was too late. The shield disappeared. Justan held out Peace and Rage, ready to strike.

Then Ewzad moved. Impossibly, he moved his spirit form out of the way and Justan swung past him. In desperation he reached back, swiping down with Peace, and the sword touched the silver wire that stretched behind Ewzad's spirit.

Justan felt a surge of emotion. For a brief moment, he felt the wizard's sense of triumph. He was invincible! Untouchable! Then his emotion turned to horror as he realized that Justan's sword had landed. He panicked. This couldn't happen! What about the babies?

Then Justan's sword sheared through the silver cord and he fell, watching Ewzad's form speed out of view.

Ewzad felt the cord snap. His awareness of his body disappeared. The cord darted away, receding into the distance and Ewzad followed after it in a panic. He couldn't let it get away. He had to grab hold! Had to reattach himself! He burned the energy he had brought with him, soaring after the silver line, reaching for it, inching closer and closer!

He sped past the fighting, sped past his advancing armies. He'd almost reached it. Just a few more inches. He saw the Clench stir. It was holding something in its hands.

Hamford awoke from what seemed like a long sleep. Something was wrong. He hurt. His very bones hurt. All of him hurt. He felt swollen and hungry. Where was he? He was kneeling. He looked down and saw some trees and a road below. How was he so high up? Was this a dream?

There was something on the back of his neck, scratching him. He reached up and grabbed it with his raw and bloody hand, then lifted the thing in front of his face.

There were two things. A tiny chair and a tiny man. The tiny man was wearing fine clothes embroidered in black and gold and wore a tiny crown. He was like a little living doll. He started to smile but there was something about the man's face. What was it? There was something he didn't like.

Then he remembered. Visions flashed before his eyes. This man hurt him. This man enslaved him. Then one more vision flashed before his eyes and he remembered the most important thing. He remembered his brother.

Ewzad grasped the silver cord just before the Clench slammed his open palm into the ground.

Ewzad felt a brief flash of pain and then the silver cord vanished. The Clench moved its hand and looked down at Ewzad's crumpled body. The giant smiled and crashed to the ground as its enormous body began to deflate and melt away.

Ewzad flew down to his body. His crushed remains. Luckily, his head was still intact. Hopefully the brain wasn't damaged. He reached into his broken form with his magic and began rebuilding the tissue. He felt dizzy. His thoughts were losing cohesion. The rings were starting to reappear on the

413

broken fingers of his hands.

He worked harder, focusing on the vital organs. He fixed his skull, rebuilt his lungs and heart, reformed his ribcage, got his heart beating.

There was more to be done but he had no time. He would fix the rest once he was inside. He climbed into his shattered body, forced his spirit to fall in place. He willed the rings to obey him; reconnect him.

It started to work. He could feel his chest rising. He could feel the agony of his mangled limbs. Oh how it hurt, but pain was sweet because he was alive. He was alive! He pulled at the power of the rings, turned them inwards. He worked on his intestines and liver and kidneys.

A shadow passed over him. It was Arcon. The mage looked down on him. Ewzad blinked, worked his jaw. "A-ar . . . Arcon. H-heal me . . . Yes?"

The mage bent and pulled at something. Ewzad couldn't see what it was. But it hurt. His shattered arms jerked and he cried out. The mage took one last look at him and shuddered. Then he left. Ewzad forced his attention back on his body. He reached out with his power . . . Where was it? He couldn't feel his power. He couldn't feel it! All he could feel was the pain. The pain was horrible and throbbing.

Arcon had taken the rings. He had taken them! That was the only explanation. He wanted to kill the mage, throttle him, burst him to pieces, but how could he? He was going to die. He, the King of Dremaldria was going to die and Elise . . . Poor Elise would have to raise the babies herself.

"You have failed me, Envakfeer," said the Dark Voice. **"Pity."**

Envakfeer? What a stupid name. He'd never liked it. Still, perhaps there was a chance. Surely the Dark Voice could do it. He forced his jaw to move. "S-save me . . . Master."

"There has been a change of plans, you imbecilic fool," said Mellinda, her voice angry. *"We're keeping both of them. We'll rule without you."*

Ewzad screamed in frustration. He screamed from the pain. He screamed for his babies. Then another shadow passed over him. It was a demonic face. A beautiful face. After all this time searching, it was there. "Y-you. You came."

Deathclaw cocked his head at the wizard. "Die," he said and tore out Ewzad's throat.

Chapter Thirty Seven

When Ewzad died, his power died with him. All across the battlefield, his monsters, and the unfortunate men who had been in mutated form at the time of his death, smoldered and collapsed. Of Ewzad's changed beasts, only the modified trolls survived.

Any of his men that hadn't yet turned into beasts felt the kernel of power inside them disappear and ran. Mellinda withdrew her forces, taking the goblinoids and trolls back to her forest, leaving their dead where they lay.

For the defenders there was no time for celebration.

Wizard Beehn and Darlan organized the wizards and mages into groups and set about healing the injured. Matron Guernfeldt herself took charge of the worst cases. Organs were mended, limbs reattached. As long as a soldier was still alive, their bodies were repaired. Only severe damage to the brain or spine was irreparable.

Despite these efforts, their losses were palpable. Once the wounded were found and taken to the healers, the sad work of reclaiming their dead began. Record keepers and scholars went about with the soldiers and identified the bodies of the slain. Later, records of their deeds would be written and families notified.

Justan's injuries were not as bad as they could have been. Professor Beehn's attempts to halt his fall had slowed his descent, but his hip had been dislocated and one leg broken when he struck the edge of the lava bucket. The wall's collapse had left the anti-siege device sticking partially out of the ground.

Darlan saw this as a teaching moment.

"But I can't heal him!" Fist objected.

416

"You can and you will," Darlan said firmly.

"Do I get a say in this?" Justan knew that if he hadn't been holding on to Peace, he would be screaming in pain. As it was, the way his leg sat outside of his hip joint was extremely unnerving. "What if he does it wrong?"

Darlan's glare told him she was a hairsbreadth from slapping him. "Fist needs the experience and you are going to be a responsible bonding wizard and help me teach him."

"What if I do it wrong and his leg is wrong forever?" Fist asked, his face white with anxiety.

"Nonsense," Darlan said. "I am here to help and Justan can observe within the bond like he does. Right, Justan?"

Justan forced himself to admit she was right. This was a good learning opportunity for the ogre. "Fist, it's okay. I'm alright with it, really."

"Besides," Darlan added. "If you get it wrong, we can always re-break it and have you try again."

She had Fist take off his breastplate just to be sure that the runed metal didn't get in the way of his spellmaking and set him to work. The ogre's ministrations were clumsy at best. Justan tried to guide him from within the bond while Darlan barked instructions from without. The two of them had the poor ogre frazzled by the end, but the ogre was successful. Justan was whole and on his feet when Deathclaw arrived.

Gwyrtha tackled the raptoid and licked him over and over despite his protests, calling Deathclaw's name repeatedly, until Justan was able to pull her off him. Justan helped the flustered raptoid to his feet and wrapped him in a hug.

"I'm glad to see you," Justan said.

It is good you survived, Deathclaw replied.

He examined Deathclaw's wounds. The raptoid was covered in scratches and punctures, but they were mostly healed. "Looks like you had a good fight of your own."

"I killed the wizard," Deathclaw said. There was no joy in the statement. Just cool satisfaction.

Justan pulled back, a little disappointed. "I thought that I killed him."

Deathclaw cocked his head. *He was still alive when I got there.*

417

"You're the one who killed him?" Fist said with a grin and wrapped Deathclaw up in a hug of his own. "That's great!"

"Let go, ogre," Deathclaw complained. *There's more.*

The raptoid pointed and Justan waved as he saw Beth, Hilt, and Charz coming down the road towards them. Gwyrtha darted over and Beth greeted her enthusiastically, laughing and putting up with her licking.

"Gwyrtha! Yes, I know. I've missed you, too. Oh what a good beautiful girl you are! No, I can't ride right now. Later, though, I'd love to!" Beth said, then ran up and threw her arms around Fist. She placed her ear over his heart and sighed, a contented smile spreading across her lips. "Mmmm. You good boy, I missed you too."

"Uh, hello, Beth," Fist said, patting her back. When she didn't let go, he looked to Hilt for help, but the warrior didn't seem to notice.

"We have a problem," Hilt told Justan. He gestured to Charz. The giant was carrying two bloody bundles under his arm.

"We brought gifts," the giant said. He dropped both bundles on the ground.

They gathered the leadership and stood around the two bundles as they were opened. The first one contained the remains of the black-skinned raptoid. It had been slashed and stabbed multiple times and its head had been caved in.

"That's the one that got Vlad," Lyramoor said coldly from the side, relieved that it was gone, yet upset that he hadn't been the one to kill it. "You do it?" he asked Deathclaw.

Deathclaw shook his head. "Charz killed her."

"Well, I can't take all the credit," Charz corrected. "Beth shot her with a paralyzing arrow. I just stomped on her head."

"What's in the other one?" asked Hugh the Shadow.

"Ewzad Vriil," Hilt said and there was a hush from those assembled.

"Show it to me," said Tolivar. His face was grim, his clothes bloody and half burned away, but his skin was whole. They withdrew Ewzad Vriil's corpse from the bag along with the crumpled crown that had been on his brow. Tolivar gave a brusque nod, then looked away.

"I don't think he's coming back this time," Fist said,

wrinkling his nose at the mangled remains.

Wizard Locksher knelt down by the body and examined him. "Where are the Rings of Stardeon?"

"That's our problem. The rings weren't on him when Deathclaw killed him," Hilt said.

"We must find them," Locksher said, concern creasing his brow.

"You killed him?" Hugh the Shadow said, eyeing Deathclaw with interest.

"He was . . . dying when I got there," Deathclaw admitted.

"Describe it to me," replied the Assassin's Guild master. "What did you see when you arrived there?" Locksher came closer to focus on his every word.

The raptoid swallowed. *Justan, you may have to help me.* "I was fighting the other . . ."

"Raptoid." Justan came over and stood next to them.

"Yes, and the giant that carried the wizard died. It . . . crashed down." This next part was more difficult to say so he passed the information on to Justan.

"But the raptoid's attack was too fierce for him to get there right away," Justan said as the memories flowed over to him through the bond. The sheer size of the giant that had melted was staggering. Its gelatinous remains stretched across the road and far into the trees off to the west side. It was going to take a lot of cleanup. "Once the raptoid was dead, he ran over and . . ." The image of Ewzad's condition when Deathclaw had arrived was disturbing. They way he had looked into Deathclaw's eyes with such a strange expression of hope made Justan pity the man. But Deathclaw hadn't. Justan shook his head as the images faded. "I'm not sure how he was still alive. But there were no rings on him."

"Maybe he hid them before he was struck down," Hugh suggested. "Or gave them to one of his men."

"That's a possibility," Locksher mused. "But he didn't seem like the type of man to trust others with something that important. Besides, if he had the rings on him, he may have been able to heal even the immense damage he had suffered."

"Perhaps Mellinda took them," Justan suggested.

"A power play?" Hugh said, rubbing his chin as he thought about it. "During the middle of the attack seems like odd timing for such a thing. Especially when it leaves her vulnerable. If that was her plan, she should have waited until his forces killed as many of our men as possible, then kill him while he was celebrating."

"Locksher!" Vannya called, kneeling by the raptoid's remains. She had a notebook in her hand and was furiously jotting something down.

The wizard ran over to her and she whispered something in his ear. He reached out over the raptoid and sent flows of magic into its body, then nodded. He started wrapping it back up. "We're taking this back to my lab for further study. Vannya found something interesting."

No one objected and together, he and Vannya carried it back towards the rune tower. Justan found it oddly concerning, but then, Locksher had examined the bodies of the other raptoids so he didn't see how it mattered. He again reminded himself he needed to have a talk with the wizard when this was all over.

Perhaps it would be better if he told Locksher the secret of the rogue horse's creation instead of letting the wizard discover it for himself. Locksher was a good man, but could he be trusted not to say anything or write it down somewhere where it could be discovered? Justan would be more comfortable if the rings were destroyed before such knowledge got out. Otherwise, some future bearer of the rings could do something even more horrible than Ewzad had done.

"I want this body displayed," Captain Demetrius said, staring at the wizard's corpse. "I want everyone who fought today to see this and know that he is truly dead this time."

"Wait a minute!" said Beth, stumbling towards them. Her eyes were unfocused, her speech slightly slurred. "We don't have time for looking at bodies. We need to march on Mellinda now."

"What's with her?" asked Stout Harley. "Is she drunk?'

"No, it's Fist," Hilt said. "She has this reaction with him."

"I didn't do nothing!" Fist said, raising his arms in the air. "I was just standing there."

"Stop it! Everyone listen to me!" Beth said, stomping her

foot. She swayed a bit, her brow furrowed as she tried to focus. "We need to march now. She has been weakened by this battle. I had a vision-."

"I think she's drunk," Hugh the Shadow said.

"Damn it, listen to me!" Beth fumed.

"Everyone, shut up!" Darlan commanded. "We should listen to her. She has some kind of spirit magic we don't understand."

"Thank you, Sherl," Beth said. She rubbed her face with her hands and shook her head, gathering herself. Justan wondered why listening to Fist gave her this kind of reaction.

Fist is nice, said Gwyrtha.

"Alright, so as I was saying, I had a vision," Beth continued. "Something really important is happening today. Right now, in fact. Things are being set in motion and if we don't invade Mellinda's forest and destroy her soon, she's going to get away."

"But I thought she was trapped there." Justan said.

"Not for long," Beth said. "We have maybe a few days at the most and she'll be able to escape."

"She's right!" Master Latva walked towards them, staff in hand. The wizard looked much more vigorous than he had the night before, but Alfred still looked concerned. "Mellinda's had a plan underway for a long time. We must go now. And on horseback, I'm afraid. There isn't time for anything else."

"Horseback?" Faldon said. "But we don't have nearly enough horses."

"We'll need to put together a small group," Latva replied. "A strike force, to use academy terms. It's unfortunate, but necessary. I know where Mellinda is. I've been there before, and if we hurry, we can get there in just over a day. Pick your men well."

"You'll need some of our horses then, I'd expect," said Captain Demetrius. The commander chewed his lip. "The men aren't going to like that."

"Good!" said Beth. She strolled over a bit unsteadily and leaned on Sir Hilt. "While you guys are figuring that out, I have just enough time for a bath." She grabbed Hilt's arm and headed towards the tower, pulling him with her. "You're taking one with me."

* * *

The royal carriage stood alone. The supply wagon was knocked over and burning and the corpses of thirty royal guards littered the ground round about, their horses dead or scattered. The trolls had done most of the work before the guards managed to set them on fire. Talon had been forced to kill the eight remaining men on her own.

Talon pulled an arrow from her breast and threw it down. Their leader had been particularly fearless, but he had been an archer, not used to close combat. She yanked another arrow from her thigh, saving the one in her throat for last. She broke the arrowhead off of that one and pulled out the shaft.

Blood spurted from the wound at an alarming rate. But Talon wasn't concerned. She didn't even enjoy the pain. Not now. Just a few hours ago Ewwie had died. Killed by her brother and his bonding wizard. The moonrat mother railed against them, but Talon wasn't fooled. This was Mellinda's fault. She had forced Talon to leave Ewwie behind. Now Ewwie was dead and Talon was here. She wished she was dead with Ewwie.

"Now –now," Mellinda said. *"That attitude doesn't suit you."*

"Yess, misstress," Talon replied automatically. She had no choice really. Not now. The blue eye gave the witch full control over her. Punishments were worse than simple numbness. When she didn't obey, her mind was shut away in a little place that wasn't light or dark and wasn't cool or hot. She couldn't feel her body. She couldn't hear. There was just nothing. And the time in this place stretched on forever.

"That's what death feels like," taunted the mistress. *"You don't really want death."*

Talon didn't believe her. She had touched death enough times to know that there was something there afterwards, something else. More than the nothingness the mistress punished her with. But now that Ewwie was dead, there was no hope for rescue. There was just endless servitude.

"Nonsense," Mellinda said. *"Curb those thoughts unless*

you wish to be punished."

"Yess misstress," Talon said.

"If you are a good girl and obey me, I'll let you have your body back. Once I'm done with it, of course."

"Yess misstress," Talon said. She forced her mind not to think of how big a lie that was. There was no escape. Never.

She approached the door of the carriage where the old mage woman stood, wringing her hands. The blood had stopped spurting from Talon's neck, not that she had worried. It was just something to notice.

"She's inside," said the woman. Her hands were trembling, but her wrinkled face was composed. She had killed the other four birth mages and the queen's maid herself during the confusion. A sleeping spell and poisoned dagger had done the job.

This one had been in Mellinda's service for a long time. But there was no eye in her. She thought youth would come from this. Eternal youth like the moonrat mother's. Talon would have hissed with laughter had she been allowed. That wasn't youth. Talon had seen what the witch was.

"Do you wish to spend time in the quiet, Talon?" Mellinda warned, anger tinting her thoughts.

"No, Misstress," Talon said.

The old woman didn't blink at Talon's words. She knew what they meant. "The queen has gone quite insane, I'm afraid. She made us all leave during the attack."

"And the babiess?" Talon asked.

"Th-they are fine. They are well. Quite healthy actually for being born this early, why I would have thought they were each full term." When Talon didn't respond right away, the old woman licked her lips. "I-I would have told the mistress about this earlier, of course, but the eye stopped working. I-I would like another one, if the mistress pleases."

That had been Ewwie's doing. Talon had felt the blow even in her blue eye. He had hurt the mistress, but he was dead now.

"Indeed," Mellinda said. *"He didn't listen, now did he?"*

"You havess the case?" Talon asked.

"Yes. Right here," said the old woman, indicating a black

bag by her feet. "Where are you taking the queen anyway? Might I be of help?"

"Comess with me," Talon said. She opened the carriage door and stepped inside.

"You!" Elise said. The queen was sitting on the rear bench. Her babies cupped protectively in her arms. Her eyes were wide, her face covered in sweat. The sounds of the battle had scared her; increased her madness. "Did my husband send you? Is this our escape?"

Talon could smell the babies. One was a boy, one a girl. They smelled fresh. They smelled sweet. They smelled slightly of Ewwie. Their skin would be soft. She loved them already.

"Ewwie iss dead," she said.

"No! You're lying!" Elise shouted.

"The king is dead?" said the old woman.

"Silence!" Talon hissed. Mellinda told her what to say. "Ewwie failed the misstress. He failed the Dark Voice. And now it iss time for your punishmentss. We will have both childss."

"No!" Elise held them tight to her. Too tight, Talon could tell. They wouldn't be able to breathe. "They are mine! Both of them!"

"My queen, you'll hurt them!" the old lady said. "Be gentle."

Elise's eyes cleared for a moment and relaxed her grip. They started to cry and she sobbed, kissing both of them.

"You can havess them back if you can keepss your kingdom," Talon said. "You can be queen motherss to the new Dark Prophet and the new Dark Misstress. Otherwise, you lose them both."

"You can't have them! You can't!" Elise turned her eyes on the old woman. "Mereld! Help me! Don't let them take the babies!"

The old woman's eyes were troubled.

"Makess her ssleep, woman," Talon instructed.

Mereld tightened her jaw and cast a spell. When the queen slumped back, she shuffled in and picked up the two screaming infants. Talon smiled. She found their sounds quite entertaining. The old woman swaddled them up and placed them in a basket side-by-side.

"*I tire of their squalling,*" said Mellinda. "*Give them the eye.*"

Talon pulled the pouch Mellinda had given her off of her shoulder and plucked the blue eye from within. It was the twin to the one inside her. She placed it in the basket between the two infants and both of them calmed and fell to sleep.

"A blue eye?" Mereld asked in interest.

"*I don't need this one anymore, dear.*"

"You are lucky, oldss one." Talon thrust upwards with her tail, striking the old woman under the chin and pumping poison into her brain. The old woman was a possible voice that could spread word of the day's true events. Mellinda thought that unnecessary.

Talon lifted the basket and opened the door. She took the black bag the mage had packed and carried it and Ewwie's twins out into the night.

Suddenly Talon was nervous. The babies were so small and so fragile and so soft. How could she touch them? Her hands were for killing. Her hands were sharp, her voice frightening. Would they fear her face?

"*Don't worry, Talon,*" said Mellinda with a soft laugh. "*I have given you all you need.*"

Goat's milk and bottles were inside the bag, treated magically to provide all the nourishment the babies needed and keep for a long time. There was enough for a week's travel. Enough for Talon to get the babies to a place Mellinda had prepared. The blue eye would keep the babies quiet. The blue eye would make them sleep. The blue eye would make them eat when Talon tried to feed them.

"*All will be alright,*" Mellinda cooed.

Talon would protect them until the day the Dark Prophet was ready for the male child. Then she would take the boy to him and the Dark Prophet would become the boy. Then when the girl was ripe, perhaps sixteen or seventeen, Mellinda would become the girl. Then Talon would be released. While Mellinda and the Dark Prophet ruled the known lands, Talon would be free again. At least that's what the mistress said.

"*All will be alright.*"

Chapter Thirty Eight

Convincing the cavalrymen to lend their horses to the others was less difficult than Demetrius had thought. Master Latva's plans for a strike force only required thirty horses and there were already over a dozen horses that had lost their riders in battle. Justan thought it fitting that Albert and Stanza should come along and the rest of them were borrowed with assurances that they would see very little battle. The truly dangerous part of the journey would be done on foot.

Latva outlined his plan. The cavalry would accompany the thirty hand-picked members of their strike force to Sampo. From there, they would cross the bridge and ride down the main road through the Tinny Woods. He expected to meet only token resistance there. When they reached the darkest part of the woods, the strike force would depart and travel to Mellinda's tree on foot.

Once they had left, the remainder of the combined academy and Mage School forces would travel east of the school where they would ford the Fandine River and help the elves retake their homeland.

It was a sound plan considering the time frame involved. The only major sticking point was the size of the force. Thirty seemed an insignificant number to deal with the amount of creatures Mellinda had at her disposal. However, Master Latva was adamant that the force remain small to keep casualties to a minimum in the terrible terrain. He assured them that the prophet himself had signed off on the idea.

In the end only a few minor changes were necessary, including one additional plan of Justan's that caught everyone by surprise.

Picking the strike force was the next difficult part. The prophet had already told them the necessary members of the group. Justan, Beth, Tolivar, Jhonate, Darlan, and Latva were the key members as were their bonded. Alfred argued against Latva going, but the old wizard was adamant that he needed to be there. The rest of the group was divided up between Faldon's advanced students and several of the academy elite, including Stout Harley, Kathy the Plate, Lyramoor and Swen, and the most experienced wizards, Darlan and Nikoli included.

There was a bit of a stir when Lenny demanded to be included. The dwarves hadn't seen much of the battle against Ewzad's forces and he wanted to have a part in taking the witch down. Bettie argued with the dwarf, telling him to stay behind and watch over his unborn child. He put his foot down and left anyway and Fist made Squirrel promise to stay behind and watch over Bettie while they were gone. Despite all her hollering, Justan was pretty sure he saw a satisfied smile on her lips when Lenny climbed up on Stanza's back to leave with the others.

The wizards provided a supply of magically enhanced oats that would allow the horses to maintain a faster speed without tiring. Despite the protests of the kitchen workers, they also brought up the majority of the school's pepper reserves. By the time Beth and Hilt emerged from the tower freshly bathed and dressed, they were ready to leave.

Captain Demetrius and his cavalry led the way with the strike force taking the rear. Justan had to increase Gwyrtha's size so that she could handle taking him, Deathclaw, and Fist as riders. Jhonate had taken great pleasure in telling Justan how ridiculous they looked. Justan sat in the front at Gwyrtha's shoulders, Fist in the middle on her saddle, and Deathclaw was perched on her hindquarters facing backwards.

Fist lent his mace to Charz so that the rock giant could keep up with the rest of them. Charz enjoyed the burst of speed and due to his enhanced stamina, he barely noticed the extra stress the mace put on his body.

Fist watched glumly from Gwyrtha's back as the giant ran from the front of the party to the rear and back again. "Why is it so easy for him?"

"Let him have his fun," Justan said. "You know how it

was for you. He'll be bored of it by the time we reach Sampo."

"Dag-blasted rock-biter's a friggin' nuisance is what he is," Lenny grumped from his seat on Stanza's back just ahead of them. He'd had to move Stanza aside a few times already as the giant ran by.

"It's never boring being fast," Fist grumbled. "It's just tiring."

Can I run with him? Gwyrtha asked, excited.

"No," said Deathclaw.

"There's not enough room on the road for both of you to be cavorting around," Justan said.

"And we need to ride you," Fist reminded her. The ogre sighed. "My back hurts already."

Justan soothed his pain through the bond and they arrived in Sampo quite quickly. They stopped briefly to raid the city's stores of pepper, then headed across the Sampo Bridge. The forested shoreline was strangely quiet. When Justan had last been to Sampo, the opposite bank had been crawling with moonrats.

They encountered their first difficulty at the forest's edge. Mellinda's forces had been busy and trees were downed across the road at regular intervals. Beehn and Nikoli moved to the front of the column and, working together, used a mix of air and earth magic to move the trees from the road as they traveled.

Despite the obstacles they were able to make good time. With the pace they were setting, they expected to reach the dark forest's center within half a day barring major attack and there had been no sight of threat. Not so much as a moonrat moan.

Justan spent most of this time thinking on his bonded and what they would do once the battle was finished. Fist was an apprentice now and Justan's contract with the Mage School would be up in a few weeks. Would the ogre stay behind and study? What of Deathclaw? What would his role be? For that matter what would Justan himself do?

Jhonate was under contract with the academy for another year. She had already told him she wanted to finish that contract out before going to see her father. Should he go and help rebuild the academy and train along side her or stay at the Mage School?

Eventually his thoughts wandered to the Scralag. Artemus' book would only show him the one entry. Why did the spirit in the book think that Artemus' awakening was so important? What he really needed to know was how he could call on the Scralag if he needed it. What if it could help during the fight with Mellinda? A thought occurred to him. There was someone he could ask.

Fist, keep an eye on me. Make sure I don't fall off, he asked

Okay, the ogre replied, and Justan felt his large arms wrap around him.

Justan delved into the bond and reached for the frozen blockage that led to the Scralag. He could see it clearly, the solid web of blue and gold strands. He pressed his thoughts up against it and this time, instead of picking the woven magic apart, he sent his own magic into the blockage. He began altering the magic, making new connections until he had formed a tiny hole. He sent a tendril of thought inside.

Artemus. He waited for a few moments. *Artemus, I need you.*

There was a stirring beyond the blockage. A rush of coldness blasted through the tiny hole, chilling the bond, and Justan saw a flash of razor teeth. A beady black eye appeared on the other side of the hole.

"*Whaaaat isss thiiiis?*" said the Scralag. Its voice was like the coldest of winter winds blowing through cracks in the wall; high and airy.

Artemus, it is me, Justan.

"*Iiiii knoooww yyouuu.*"

Justan shivered. He reminded himself that he had nothing to fear. This was his great grandfather and the Scralag had never tried to hurt him. *Artemus, I have a question. I've been trying to read your book, but the only passage that will come up is about your awakening. I need to know why that's so important.*

"*Aaawaaaaake?*" It sounded confused.

Yes, it's a passage from when you were young and the school burned down. You protected everyone inside. That was the day you first discovered your magic. Do you remember?

"*Thhhhe chiillldreeen. I saaaaaved theeeem.*"

Yes. But what I need to know is what to do if I need you. What if I need your help to fight?

"Fiiiight? IIIII saaaaaaved theeeeem . . . IIIII saaaaaave . . . IIIII saaaa . . ."

Justan! We're here, Deathclaw said.

Wake up! Gwyrtha added.

Justan withdrew from the bond, a bit frustrated. He hadn't accomplished what he had wanted, but at least Artemus had spoken to him. When he opened his eyes, he saw that it was dark and everyone was dismounting from their horses. The air smelled bad. How long had he been out?

"Justan, are you alright?" Jhonate asked, tugging on his leg. He slid down from Gwyrtha's back and put his arm around her. He liked her new leather breastplate. It wasn't as bulky.

"I'm fine," he told her.

"You are shivering," she said and in the dim light he could see her brow was furrowed in concern.

He kissed her forehead. "I was speaking with the Scralag. It's cold in there. Where are we?"

"We are in the center of the dark woods," she replied. "Can you smell the rot?"

"Smells like the south side of a dag-blamed beached whale," Lenny said, his nose wrinkling.

"I smell it," Justan said. It smelled like mold and rotten fish. But there were no fish in this place. The creeks that flowed through the forest were too small and the water that flowed out of the dark side of the forest was undrinkable. Justan looked up at the canopy overhead and saw pinpricks of light. It was still daytime.

This land is dying, Deathclaw sent. *It smells of death.*

Stinks! Gwyrtha agreed.

"I've only been in this place once before and that was with Gwyrtha when I first traveled to the Mage School," Justan said. "There were moonrats everywhere then."

"We have not seen a single one," she said. "Not a moonrat or a troll or anything."

"Sir Edge," called Master Latva and Justan ran over. The wizard was standing with the leaders about half way down the line of horses and barrels of ground pepper were being unloaded. There were over twenty of them in various sizes. The ones pulled up from the Mage School's storage had been as large as wine

430

barrels. He hoped they had enough.

The old man smiled at Justan and a bit of that familiar blue twinkle in his eyes was back. "We're ready to try your plan."

"Good. What do you think, Professor Beehn?" Justan asked.

"I don't know," said the air wizard from astride his horse. It had been fitted with a special saddle that tied him in place so that he could ride despite his paralysis. "The trees are pretty thick here, but I understand they thin out the further in we go."

"The air is foul and full of mist at its center," Latva said. "That might help to keep it in the air."

Beehn nodded. "Well there's still a lot of forest to cover, but I suppose there's nothing to do but give it a try." He motioned to the four other air wizards they had brought with them. "Alright, I'll get a current going. You start feeding it up to me when I give the signal. Then your job's just to help me keep the air flowing, understand?" The wizards nodded. "Okay, then, everyone else will want to keep their faces covered as a precaution in case some of this blows back on us."

The word went down the line and everyone placed handkerchiefs or cloths over their mouth and nose. Beehn concentrated and there was a stirring in the trees. A breeze blew past them, pushing towards the depth of the forest. The air was sweet compared to the foulness. Then the wind increased until leaves and twigs were flying past them, lifting up into the air.

Wizard Beehn gave the command and the barrels of pepper were opened. The wizards fed clouds of the black powder up and into the wind. The spice was carried through the tops of the trees and rained down like a fine mist. They began to hear screeches and moans from the darkness. Lesser trolls would be killed and modified trolls would be weakened and unable to regenerate. For anyone else, be it moonrat or goblinoid, the effect would be uncomfortable to say the least.

The last of the barrels was finally emptied. The professor continued on for a few more minutes, then stopped and let his arms down, slumping forward in exhaustion. "That's all we have. Frankly I'm surprised it worked so well. I don't know if we covered the entirety of the Dark Woods, but we got most of it."

431

"Thank you, Professor Beehn," said Master Latva with a smile. "You have performed admirably."

"I only wish I could come with you, sir," Beehn said.

"You have done more than enough here," said the head wizard. "Now I need you to take charge when you get back. We'll need Valtrek and Locksher to take Ewzad Vriil's body and accompany Captain Demetrius back to Dremald. Then I want you to do a review of the wizards. We need to start the selection process for new High Council members right away."

"What about Nikoli?" Beehn asked, eyeing the wizard who had once been Master DeVargas.

"I won't be on the council again," Nikoli said, his face tinged with embarrassment. "I'm content just being a wizard."

"Well," said Latva. "We can sort all that out later, can't we?"

The cavalry took the horses and returned the way they came. The members of the strike force were left alone on the road, the stench of the Dark Forest only somewhat muted by the smell of pepper. It was expected that they would return by foot or not at all, meeting the rest of their men in the elf homeland when it was all over. If they did not return within a week's time, it had been agreed that the remaining forces would come through and burn the dark forest to the ground.

Latva gathered them around and had everyone light their glow orbs. The devices were designed to imprint on the person who activated them and hover one foot over their heads and slightly forward, lighting the area around them. It had been agreed that, in this place, night vision wouldn't be of much help because the creatures here had much better night vision than a human ever would. It was more important to be able to see where they were going.

The second thing Latva did was to have all of them clamp metal straps around their upper legs. He had brought a pair for each of them. The straps were runed to surround the legs of the wearer with a shield of water magic. He explained that the most perilous part of the Dark Forest was the danger of stepping on the venomous snakes and insects that inhabited the place. The shields the straps provided were strong enough to protect them against bites from any of the creatures they were likely to face.

432

Lenny cursed as he tried to put his on. The runes on his plate metal greaves were interfering with the magic in the straps and he couldn't get them to stay on. Finally he just gave up. The armor would just have to be enough.

"It's almost as if you've been planning this attack for years, Master Latva." said Faldon, one eyebrow raised as he snapped his second leg band into place.

"Isn't it?" Latva replied with a smile. He pointed into the forest. "She's not far from here."

They started off the road southward, into the bowels of the place. Master Latva insisted on taking the lead since he had been there before, but allowed Deathclaw and Alfred to scout ahead. The two of them hadn't bothered with the glow orbs. Deathclaw's natural eyesight was as sensitive as the beasts of this place, while Alfred wore some kind of dark-lensed spectacles that allowed him to see.

The two scouts sped ahead through the darkness completely at ease. The gnome was every bit as agile as Deathclaw and Justan couldn't believe he had thought Alfred a scholar all these years. Justan walk next to Master Latva. The wizard kept a steady pace, quite quick for an old man, and sent a steady stream of earth magic ahead, opening up a path before them. Leaves and sludge and detritus fell away, replaced by smooth hard packed earth.

"Your father was right," Latva said to Justan as they walked. "I've known this journey was going to come for a long time. It's been one of my greater purposes you might say."

"What do you mean, sir?" Justan asked. The light of his glow orb reflected off tiny eyes and slithering bodies in the darkness around him and he was grateful for the wizard's precautions.

"It's something I learned fifty years ago when I was called as head wizard," he said. "Have you heard of the ceremony?"

"Yes, sir." The High Council gathered around the Bowl of Souls and beseeched it to tell them the identity of their new leader. Then they projected their magic upon it until it chose one of them. Usually it was a wizard that had already been named. Sometimes in the past, it had named one of them on the spot.

433

"I had a vision granted me by the bowl that day. I saw a woman all in black standing before an enormous rotted tree. Orange-eyed moonrats clustered around her and she was holding a pair of blue eyes in her hands. A battle raged around us."

"Blue eyes?" Justan said. A moonrat moan echoed from the forest ahead of them, echoed by many more throughout the forest. Justan saw tiny dots of light blink into existence all around. He saw the corpses of trolls killed by the pepper, their slime intermingling with the black rot on the forest ground.

"Yes, I've known this day was coming a long time. I researched the forest. Found out everything I could about its past. Finally I found who she was in the records. It was in an ancient book called, 'The Sealing of Mellinda, the Troll Queen'." Latva didn't stop or acknowledge the trolls or the lights in the forest ahead. "Finally one day Alfred and I came here to see the place for ourselves. It wasn't quite this vile then. The dark part was much smaller."

"What did you see?" Justan asked. The troll bodies were much more numerous now. Many of them had fallen on top of each other.

"I saw the tree and the nastiness and I saw Mellinda herself, or at least the form she chose to show me." He glanced at Justan then. "Listen Edge. She tries to be graceful. She tries to be alluring and seductive. But what you see isn't really her. Remember that. What she really is withered away long ago."

Justan nodded, and tried to ready himself mentally for the encounter. "What happened?"

Moonrat eyes glowed in the darkness all around the trail now. Most of them were green, but a few orange ones began to pop up amongst them. Justan found it strange that they weren't trying to eat the troll carcasses.

The old wizard snorted. "She teased me. She tried to tempt me. In the end I was forced to be rude. I told her that one day I would return and when I did, I would bring her destruction. I told her I knew about her moonrats and their eyes. She attacked us then. We were able to fight her off, but I assume she is much more powerful now than she used to be."

"So you knew about her all this time?" Justan said. The pairs of moonrat eyes were much thicker now. They hung in the trees all around. Troll corpses were piled up in the dozens all around them now and Master Latva's magic lifted and rolled them aside to make room for their path they forged ahead. Deathclaw and Alfred returned to their sides.

Scouting ahead is useless now, Deathclaw said. *The moonrats leave us a path all the way to a large tree. They are so thick there we will have to fight.*

Alfred must have been communicating the same thing because Master Latva nodded. "I need to wrap this story up, so no more interruptions, please. I knew this day would come sooner or later, but I knew certain conditions had to be met before it happened. Mellinda needed to be a threat to the lands and she needed to have moonrats with orange eyes.

"I tried to slow down her progress as much as I could. I raised the wards around the road. I brought in the elves and gave them the land east of this place so they could combat her rot. When I first heard reports of green-eyed moonrats I knew the time was near. I hadn't heard of the orange eyes until the day you returned through the Mage School portal. Now all we're waiting for is the blue eyes, and to tell you the truth, I think it's happened. I think it's why she's letting us in. So, be ready. I'll do what I can, then it's all up to you."

"What do you mean, master?" Justan said. It sounded like Latva didn't expect to be there for the whole battle.

Why did he say it like that, Justan? Fist asked.

You heard? Justan replied.

Everyone heard. Master Latva was letting all of us hear with his air magic, Fist said.

The corridor of moonrat eyes opened up and the old rotted Jharro tree came into view. It stood at the center of a small clearing, its great roots stretching into the forest around it. Black sludge and rotten leaves covered the ground and hundreds of moonrats circled the clearing. At least a third of them had orange eyes.

There, lounging in the roots, surrounded by moonrats was a female figure all in black. She pushed up to her knees and looked at them. Then slowly she stood, rubbing something between her fingers.

"*What is this stuff you found that kills trolls and hurts my babies' eyes?"* she asked, walking towards them with a sultry swing to her hips. Mellinda seemed to grow as she approached, going from the size of a woman to the same height as Charz in just a few steps. She blew a small cloud of pepper off the tip of her finger. *"It seems familiar to me somehow, but it's been so long since I've been away from this place that I can't quite figure it out."*

"Does it matter?" Latva said. "We're here. This is the end. I've come to destroy you just like we talked about long ago."

"Long ago?" She laughed. *"What are a few decades? I suppose if you won't tell me, I'll just have to have some slaves come in and test it for me after you're dead."*

"It is you that will die, witch!" Jhonate shouted, twirling her staff.

"Stay on the trail!" Latva shouted.

"Ah, Jhonate Bin Leeths," Mellinda chuckled. *"You're a Roo. You should know that being a witch isn't a bad thing."*

"I am Roo-Tan!" Jhonate snapped.

"This ends now!" said Stout Harley.

"Ah Harley. I was so disappointed when you betrayed me." She clasped her hands together and smiled, showing them a row of even white teeth. *"Oh all my enemies are here. It's so sweet. The thing is, you're too late."* She laughed and grew in height until she rose above them all. She leaned forward, hanging over them. Her arms raised.

"Oh, I think you're wrong," Master Latva said, and he plunged his staff into the ground. The black sludge parted, flowing away from the tree, pushing Mellinda's form with it, until the clearing was dry and clean.

"Now we have room to fight!" Lenny shouted.

Everyone began moving into the clearing. They formed a circle, the warriors staying to the outside while the archers and wizards kept to the middle.

"Stay out of the sludge and don't let her touch you if you can avoid it," said Latva.

Mellinda laughed. *"Oh, I suppose that should have made me angry, but can't you see? That's why I haven't tried to stop you. Nothing you do here will matter."*

436

"I dreamed this part, you know," Latva said, smiling. "Your end begins moments from now."

Mellinda reached one enormous black hand towards the wizard. Alfred darted forward, slicing through her hand with his gnomish blade. Her hand fell to the ground and deflated, releasing a swarm of insects, but another hand formed from her stump and grasped the wizard.

"Dream? You must have been mistaken. This is your nightmare."

Chapter Thirty Nine

Talon hurried to the southwest, weaving her way through the forest, careful not to jostle the babies. She wanted to get to the Wide River, and the small farm on its shore that Mellinda had prepared, as quickly as possible.

It wasn't the babies' fault. Caring for the babies wasn't as hard as Talon had feared. The blue eye kept them calm. The blankets protected their soft skin from her claws. And she could kiss their tiny faces and smell Ewwie on them without cutting them with her teeth. Feeding them was tiresome and changing their filthy rags a chore, but she didn't mind.

The reason she ran was the battle. The mistress would be fighting soon. She had shown Talon. The Mage School and academy people had entered her home. Her brother was there and his wizard. And many other foes. All the foes the mistress feared the most were there.

"*Don't fear, Talon,*" Mellinda cooed. "*I will destroy them. The closer they get, the more I have them where I want. I will kill them all. All my enemies in one attack.*"

That's what the mistress thought. Talon kept her worries quiet, but she knew. She was sure of what would happen if the mistress lost. If her enemies defeated her, the mistress would escape into the blue eye. The mistress would become Talon and Talon would be shoved into the quiet place forever, kept there unless the mistress found a new host for the blue eye. But if Talon could find the farm, maybe she could find someone Mellinda would rather be. A beautiful farm girl, perhaps.

"*Don't be silly, Talon,*" Mellinda purred. Talon saw her pick up the old wizard. She saw Mellinda squeeze him, saw her bugs sting him. "*They are mine. See? They-.*"

Talon froze. "Misstress?" There was no answer.

The babies began to cry.

She spun around. What had happened? Where did the mistress go? A smile parted her lips. Did she dare believe? Was the mistress gone for good? Destroyed? Talon laughed along with the babies' sweet cries.

"Hello, Talon," said a voice behind her.

She spun again and saw a man sitting on a rock. He wore brown clothes and a traveler's robe, and had brown hair and a fuzzy face; a blurry face. He hadn't been there before. Where had he come from?

Behind him stood a great beast with a large face. The front end of it was that of an enormous gorilla with dark gray fur, while the back end was like a mountain cat. Yet it wore a saddle and smelled much more like a horse than either of those animals.

Then there was what the man had said. He had called her by name. How did the man know her name? "Did the misstress ssend you?" she asked.

"Your mistress?" he folded his arms. "Mellinda?"

She nodded hesitantly.

"Most definitely not," the man said with a chuckle. He stood and walked towards her. "Do you love your mistress?"

Talon didn't know how to respond. Her heart beat quickly in her chest. This man was an enemy! This man was a foe of the mistress! She had to leave! She had to leave or she would be punished!

"You will not run," the man said and he was right. Talon couldn't run. She could only stand. He bent over and peered into the basket she held in her right hand. "Shh," he said and the babies quieted. "Sweet little things, aren't they?"

"Yess," Talon said. No, this wasn't good. The man would take them! "Go away or I will . . ." What would Ewwie have her say? "I will killss you."

"No you won't," the man said, still smiling at the babies.

He was right. She wouldn't. She didn't know why but she couldn't. She couldn't will her tail to strike the man. "I will eatss the babiess. I will kills them!"

"No you will not," he said and this time his voice was a bit firmer. But he did not look up at her. He reached down into

439

the basket and picked up the blue eye from between them. He rolled it in his fingers, a frown darkening his blurry face. "What a truly horrible thing to give a child."

He looked at Talon now and his eyes were kind. Why were they kind? She blinked. "Who are you?"

"I am the prophet," he said, still gazing into her eyes. "But you may call me John."

"The prophet?" What did that mean? He was not the Dark Prophet. Of that she was fairly sure. He was not Ewwie's master. Ewwie's master would not be like this man.

"Would you like me to destroy this?" the man asked.

"Y-you destroyss it?" Talon asked.

"If you wish," he replied.

She licked her lips. If that blue eye was gone, then the only one left would be the one in her. The mistress would always live in her. Still, for some reason, she said, "Yess."

"Very well," the prophet said.

He held out the blue eye and it quivered and shook. A little grasping claw sprung from the side. He grasped it in his other hand and tore it out. Then the eye began to change color. It was no longer dark blue, but light blue, then lighter still until it was a bright white and held a soft glow.

"There then," he said and placed the item within his robe. "I will be taking the children now." He reached out and though she didn't understand why, she handed him the basket and the black bag. He nodded at her and took them over to the beast. He lifted the basket and the beast sniffed them with its wide nostrils and smiled, showing a huge mouth full of yellowed teeth and making a huffing noise that sounded something like laughter. The man laughed. "Babies do smell delightful, don't they, Rufus?"

Talon realized that the man was going to leave. He would leave her and the mistress would return and she would be angry. "Wait! John! The prophetss!"

He turned his kind eyes back on her. "Yes, Talon?"

She walked up to him hesitantly. "Will you . . . kill me? Please?"

He raised his eyebrows. "You wish to die?"

"Yess. I . . ." her jaw quivered. "I am . . . broken."

"I'm sorry, Talon," he said and his eyes really did look sad. "I am not the one who is to kill you."

She looked down. There was no hope then. Just endless nothingness.

"Would you like me to remove the eye from within you?" he asked.

She shuddered, and looked up at him. Did he mean it? Tears welled up in her eyes. "Yess! Please!"

He smiled. "Very well." He moved closer and placed his palm just under her ribcage. "Hmm. She did make this hard to get to, didn't she?"

He closed his eyes and flattened out his hand, then pushed his fingers inside of her. Talon felt his fingertips push through her skin and muscle. It did not hurt, but he pushed through her inside parts and she felt a tingling as he clenched something within her. When he withdrew his hand, he held the blue eye. His fingers were not bloody and he did not leave a wound in her flesh.

"Would you like me to destroy this eye?" he asked.

"Yess!" she exclaimed, clapping her hands together. And in a moment, this eye was as white as the other one. He placed it in his pocket and turned to leave again.

"John!"

"Yes, Talon?" he asked, smiling kindly at her again.

"I-I . . ." She feared to speak it. Part of her adored this man now. Yet inside of her was another part that wanted to kill him. That part was being held in check at the moment, but it was snarling in the darkness within her. It wanted to rend his flesh, to tear him, to string his inside parts around the clearing.

"Can you . . . fix me?"

"Is that what you wish?" He asked and his face seemed to glow.

"Pleasse."

He reached out and placed his hands on her head and the dark part inside her screamed. Now! Now was the time. He was vulnerable. He would not stop her. Rend him! Tear him! Eat him!

Then a warm glow spread over her body and the dark part shrunk back. This was a new feeling for her. It was a new

441

sensation and was very interesting. It felt good. Far better than pain. Far more than pleasure. This feeling was different.

Then he let go and the feeling faded. The darkness inside her growled and screamed, but it was weak.

"It is not for me to fix you, Talon," said the kind man. "But perhaps that will make it easier."

"Pleasse!" Talon said. Ewwie would have had her caress him, grasp him as she begged. But not this man. She fell to her knees at his feet. "Pleasse, John, try again!"

"Talon, do you know what it is to be good?" he asked. She blinked. "Good?"

He sighed and his smile turned sad. "If you want to be fixed, go east, the direction the sun rises. Travel through the forest. I believe you have a friend there. Take her and continue east. Go over the mountains."

"Friend?" She thought on his instructions. How could she go? She wasn't allowed. If she left . . . there was no more Ewwie and the mistress could not touch her now. She smiled. She could go east and she could get fixed because she was free!

"Another thing, Talon," John said. He held out the two white eyes. They glowed softly. "Take these. You may need them."

Mellinda froze. She held Latva in her fist, high in the air, surrounded by stinging bugs. But she looked like the one who had been wounded.

"You see? We're not the ones who are too late, Mellinda. You are." said Latva his voice pained, yet full of satisfaction. Alfred shouted his name and ran to the base of the witch's form, slashing repeatedly with his sword, but there was no effect.

Latva smiled through the pain. "You gathered all your moonrats around us, didn't you? You wanted them all to see." He turned his head to look down at the others. "Remember the orange eyes! Don't let them-!"

"*Enough!*" Mellinda roared. The wizard disappeared into her hand. Moonrats poured in from the forest all around, snarling and biting. "*What did you do?*" she demanded, glaring down at them. "*What have you done!*"

"Her real body's under the tree!" Wizard Nikoli shouted.

He shoved his way past the warriors and reached his earth magic into the ground. He strained. The great tree shuddered. Its roots began to pull up from the ground.

"*No!*" Mellinda cried and slammed her black hand down over him. When she lifted it again, he was gone, disappeared inside her black form.

The warriors and wizards fought in the clearing, slaying moonrats as quick as they could, but the sheer numbers were overwhelming. Fist knocked them aside with great swings of his mace and electrified his body, frying any moonrat that reached him. Gwyrtha in her armored form tore into them, biting and slashing, while Charz stomped them and smashed them and tore them apart, immune to any kind of damage they could inflict.

Modified trolls screeched as they ran into the clearing, but they were weakened by the pepper and few in number. Willum blasted one into pieces with his axe and Lyramoor lopped the head off another. Kathy the Plate tore one in half with a swing of her axe and Lenny caved in its skull.

Tolivar and Faldon fought side-by-side as they had in days gone by, leaving quivering pieces of moonrats in their wake. Samson ran around the outside of their circle, trampling and spearing them. Swen stood in the center of the circle, each of his arrows piercing a skull, while Darlan hurled fireballs into Mellinda's form, knocking her back and trying to keep her from grabbing any more of them.

Despite their efforts, black sludge crept back into the clearing, flowing steadily over the dirt. Wherever the sludge was, Mellinda was in control. It rose up, forming grasping hands, and her form rose above it all. She swung her arms, knocking people down and at times, swallowing them whole.

Justan fought, the world slowed down in his eyes. He slashed about him with his swords, slicing and blasting the moonrats away.

Where are they? Deathclaw sent as he speared a moonrat through the eye with his tail barb. *Where are the orange eyes?*

Justan blasted aside a group of moonrats, blowing them to pieces, and glanced around. Deathclaw was right. All the moonrats they fought had green eyes interspersed with a few yellow ones. Latva had thought the orange eyes important. Why had they disappeared? Was Mellinda protecting them?

He ran to Beth. The witch was standing in the center of a circular area about ten feet in diameter that was free from black sludge. Her eyes were closed and she was grimacing.

"Beth, where are the orange eyed moonrats?"

She flinched. "I don't know. Scattered. They're running away."

"Stop them! Cut her off." Justan said.

"I've been trying but she is too strong here," Beth said. "I can barely slow them down!"

"Fight her!" Hilt said.

"I'm going to collapse any minute!" Beth shouted.

"She needs . . . Fist!" Hilt shouted. "Fist come here!"

The ogre slammed out with his shield, shocking moonrats and knocking them aside. He ran over to them.

"Hold Beth," Hilt said. He slashed out and a blade of air sliced through three moonrats at once. "Hold her to your chest!"

"But why?" Fist said.

"Just do it!" Justan said. Mellinda reached a great black arm towards him and Justan swung out with Rage, blasting it and all the insects within to pieces.

Fist grabbed Beth and pulled her in against him. Beth struggled for a moment, then she sighed and suddenly it seemed as if the air thickened around them. The sludge flooded back. Moonrats fell, jittering on the ground and Mellinda screamed.

Fist staggered and Justan felt the ogre's energy fade. Desperately, he pulled energy from Gwyrtha and fed it into him, but Beth was pulling it in as fast as he could draw it. Justan ripped at the magic blocking the Scralag, yanking at the threads until finally he tore it free.

Come out, Artemus! Come out and fight! Coldness leeched through the bond, but there was no reply. Why was there no reply? He needed him now! He blasted out with Rage again and thought back to what Artemus had said when they spoke. Suddenly he understood. The Scralag wasn't going to attack for him.

The warriors kept hacking away at the flailing moonrats, but more tumbled into the clearing. Mellinda slowly reached for them.

Beth cried out. "She's too strong!"

"Mother!" Justan said. He grasped Darlan's shoulder. She shot fireball after fireball into Mellinda's figure, knocking it back. "Mother. We need you here!"

A fireball went awry, blasting to the side as he dragged her over to stand by Beth. She turned at him, her face enraged. "Are you crazy! I could have fried you!"

"I need you to fry everything!" he said emphatically. Beth's sphere of influence was shrinking again. The warriors backed in, tightening the circle.

"What?" she demanded.

"Do your huge spell. The one you're famous for. The Sherl spell!" The moonrats were getting to their feet now, sluggishly, and Mellinda was leaning forward again. "You have to do it. The orange-eyed moonrats are getting away. It's the only way we'll reach them all."

"But I'll kill everyone," she gasped.

"No. No you won't. I will protect them. You must trust me," he said. "How big can you make the spell?"

"I-I don't know. I've never put all my energy into it," she said.

"Make it as big as you can. Destroy the whole dark forest if possible!" he said. "Just kill all the orange eyes!"

"But-!" The moonrats began streaming from the trees again. Mellinda picked up Stout Harley. Jhonate charged into the blackness after him, but Justan could do nothing to help her. He had to trust on the ring to protect her. He looked to his mother.

"We'll live! Do it! Otherwise she'll get away!"

She grit her teeth and began to gather her energy.

Justan reached back through the bond, reaching his thoughts into the Scralag's place. This had to be what the book meant; what Artemus meant. It had to be! *Artemus! Protect us. Please! Protect my friends from the fire. Artemus save us!*

"It's gettin' friggin' hairy here!" Lenny shouted.

Mellinda's sludge rose up like a wave, swallowing Faldon and the dwarf. Gwyrtha jumped in after them.

"Faldon!" Darlan shouted.

"Do it, mother!" Ice flowed from Justan's chest. Black talons burst free from his chest, followed by a white arm . . .

445

Darlan screamed.

Flames erupted in a circle from where she stood, filling the clearing in half a second. It flowed past the enormous tree with a deafening roar, shooting through the dank and damp places, consuming huge hornets' nests and hives of biting ants, incinerating pits of venomous snakes as it went. It surged outward, covering the trail Latva had made, and blasting across the road into the forest beyond. The inferno's intensity rose and molten rock bubbled up from the earth.

The creatures within the radius of the spell disappeared with little more than a sizzle to designate their passing. The black sludge bubbled to ash. Trees burned away in seconds. Not a single orange-eyed moonrat escaped.

Darlan stood alone in a molten sea and sobbed as the last of her magic faded. The ground began to cool to black and she fell to her knees. "Justan!"

There was no trace of anyone.

"You promised!" she cried. "You promised . . ."

She felt a chill and turned. There had been nothing behind her a moment ago, but now there stood a tall white figure. It had a mouth full of razor teeth and its claw-tipped arms stretched nearly to the ground. It reached out and touched her shoulder and she heard it speak in a hissing whisper, "Graandaauughterr."

It raised its hand and a wave of frost radiated outward from it, rolling across the fiery landscape. The flames went out. The ground cooled and the rock settled. A wind flowed across the baked landscape, blowing the ash away and Darlan saw domes of ice scattered all about her, bulging up from the blackened ground.

"Thank you," she said, turning back to look at it, but the creature was gone.

The icy domes cracked. Then one-by-one, they burst apart. People stirred in the space beneath, then stood and looked around them in awe.

"That was cold . . . holy hell," Charz said his eyes wide as he looked at the destruction around them. "I believe that would have killed me."

"You ain't blasted kiddin'," Lenny agreed.

The forest was gone. For hundreds of yards in every direction there was just flat blackened earth.

Justan stood in awe of the destruction around him. He laughed. It had worked! He hugged Darlan. "Thank you, mother. Thank you for believing me."

"How did you know it would work?" she asked.

"It's Artemus' nature. That's what the stupid book was trying to tell me," Justan explained. "He's a protector, not a fighter. I should have seen it before. He needs my magic in order to survive, but he has always let me use it for defensive purposes. When he appeared while I was fighting the bandham, he only came when it had me in its hands. Then he froze it, but it was my sword that destroyed it. When I realized that, I knew he would protect us."

"I had forgotten how powerful you are, Darlan," said Faldon. His face was swollen and he was covered in welts and insect bites, but the warrior walked towards them with a smile.

She ran and embraced him. "I wish I could heal you with a kiss, dear, but I'm too tired."

"I'll settle for a kiss," Faldon replied. She kissed him hard and he didn't mind that it hurt his lips.

Justan looked around the clearing. He saw Fist and Deathclaw and Gwyrtha. But where was . . .

"Justan."

He felt Jhonate's hand on his shoulder. He turned around and hugged her, and her wonderful scent filled his nose despite the charred earth around them. She kissed him and he pulled back and looked at her. She didn't have so much as a single welt on her. "When I saw you swallowed up, I thought you were gone."

She frowned. "Why? You were always protecting me."

"It's the only thing I want to do," he said.

Justan, Fist sent sadly. *Look.*

Not every dome of frost had contained a live body. Alfred knelt by Master Latva, weeping and Charz knelt beside him, a hand resting on the gnome's back. Not far from them was the body of Wizard Nikoli covered in welts. Several others did not stir.

"We're not done," Beth said, pointing to the spot where

the tree once stood. Now it was little more than a lump in the ash. "She's still under there."

Darlan gathered the wizards that could stand and together they finished what Nikoli had started. They ripped up the burnt remnants of the dead Jharro tree.

There, deep in the ground, was a withered husk of a woman, her body dry and pierced by remnants of tree roots. In her hand was a black dagger with a rune carved into its blade. The dagger made Justan sick just looking at it and when he switched to Mage sight, he saw a black nimbus of dark magic swirling around it.

Jhonate drew the white dagger the prophet had given her, the rubies on its hilt sparkling as she slid into the hole where the tree had been. Beth and Tolivar followed her, but Jhonate did not wait for them. She was ready for this to be over. She raised her dagger and stabbed Mellinda's runed blade.

A flash of light exploded in Jhonate's skull. Then the dirt around her was gone.

Jhonate stood in the dark, a white glow surrounding her figure. She was wearing a white suit of armor. In her left hand she held her Jharro staff and in her other hand she held the white blade.

Jhonate nodded to herself. She knew what this place was. She had been there once before. She soared forward into the center of the place until she saw a creature stir in the darkness.

She recognized the form of Mellinda's mind immediately. It was bulbous and black, but it wasn't as large as it had been the last time she'd seen it. The sky in this place had once been full of pinpricks of lights that looked like stars, but were really doorways to Mellinda's eyes. Now the sky was black but for a few tiny dots.

"Gone!" wailed the black blob. "Gone! All my babies. My sweet-eyed children . . ."

Jhonate knew what she had to do. She took the white blade in her right hand and pushed it into the shaft of her Jharro staff, willing the staff to melt around it and for them to join together. The wood sizzled until they had combined into one weapon. She now held a shining white blade ten-feet-tall.

The light from the blade illuminated Mellinda's

misshapen mind. The black matter stirred and a feminine figure rose from the midst of it, but its creation was clumsy, as if she could not quite remember how to form it. One arm was longer than the other and half of its face a lump.

"*Y-you . . .*" It pointed at her with a melting finger. "*You are marked . . .*" It shuffled towards her.

"You will be destroyed," Jhonate swore.

The black thing rose up before her, its slouching female form high overhead, and Jhonate realized the sword wasn't quite big enough. She willed to grow. She willed it to become longer, and it did, but still not enough. Mellinda's blackness rushed forward to swallow her up.

Jhonate felt hands fall down on her shoulders. On her right side was Beth standing in bristling white armor. On her left was Tolivar wearing a white robe and the hilt of a sword protruding over one shoulder.

The black form overshadowed them all but Jhonate focused her will and added the willpower of the people beside her. The sword grew, rising to twenty feet, thirty, then a hundred feet in the air. She cried out and brought it down on the blackness with all her might.

Mellinda screamed as her form was hewn in two.

Jhonate gasped. Her eyes opened and she was kneeling in the dirt under the tree again. Beth and Tolivar at her side. The point of the white dagger had pierced Mellinda's blade, shattering it. To the side, the withered husk of Mellinda's body crumbled.

Chapter Forty

The elven homeland was a mess. Mellinda had turned the place into a moonrat breeding ground, hoping that it would strengthen her children and bring their evolution about more quickly. The ground had been torn up, the soil scattered. Bark hung from the trees in shreds.

When Mellinda had been destroyed, many of the moonrats had died. The rest of them lost their direction and reverted back to pure instinct, most looking for darker places. By the time the elves arrived, there were few remaining and the battle to reclaim their land was much easier than they had feared. A few of the moonrats attacked on sight, but most of them ran, all their will to fight gone.

Academy troops ran into several groups of goblinoids, but without the witch to keep them there, they fled, offering very little resistance. The largest problem was the trolls. Without Mellinda to control them, they scattered, looking for food. The forest was infested with hundreds of them and it would be a long time before the elves destroyed them all.

When the survivors of the strike force arrived at the homeland, the elves were already hard at work repairing the damage as best they could. Justan and his bonded stayed there for a few days helping Antyni and the elves plant the first honstule seeds using soil made from Qyxal's remains.

The foulest portion of the Dark Forest had been destroyed by Darlan's spell. Fire was a cleansing force as well as a destructive one and the elves were confident that the place could be regrown and beautified in time.

The Sampo refugees returned home shortly after the elf homeland was freed, but the Reneul and academy people stayed behind. There were a lot of decisions to be made. Would the academy be rebuilt in the same spot or moved somewhere else and what would that mean for Reneul? The dwarves and wizards pledged their help in the rebuilding process and it was hoped that some of the academy's larger clients would pitch in as well.

Captain Demetrius' troops found Queen Elise on the way to Dremald. She hadn't left the carriage and was half starved and quite mad. They brought her to the capital with them. The captain took command of Dremald's garrison and wrested control of the government. There wasn't much of a fight from the nobles. Their queen had gone crazy and the entire populous was against them.

Valtrek sat with the nobles and military leaders in negotiations while Locksher and Vannya delved into exposing Ewzad's crimes and discovering those who had conspired with him. In the end, the majority of the nobles were considered unfit for consideration and Captain Demetrius was given the temporary title of Lord Commander of Dremaldria. Valtrek stayed in the capital as the official Mage School representative until the proper line of succession could be decided.

It was three weeks before the funerals of the fallen were held at the Mage School. There was so much to do. The bodies of the dead were healed and maintained so that they could be viewed in the large procession. In the meantime, the grounds were repaired and the bodies of the enemies gathered and burned. The gelatinous remains of Ewzad monsters were a bit harder to get rid of. They didn't burn well and in the end the wizards were forced to open up a big pit and bury it.

Talks began on a new partnership between the school and academy, one that would provide a stronger academy presence within the Mage School as well as provide training for the warriors that could learn to use mage sight and spirit sight. In addition, a spot on the Academy Council would be opened up for a Mage School representative.

The Academy Council made a proclamation that all of the Training School students that still wanted to enter the academy were accepted without having to take the tests. In addition, a graduation ceremony was held for many of the academy students that had shown particular valor in the war;

Willum, Swen, Jhonate, Qenzic, and Poz were among them.

Sabre Vlad's position on the council was offered to Lyramoor. It was decided that the old rules forbidding certain non-humans from the academy would be abolished. In the end, however, Lyramoor declined, deciding he'd rather stay close to Qenzic. The position was filled by Bill the Fletch, head of the Archer Guild, instead.

Replacing the leadership was a much harder decision for the Mage School.

"What did you tell them, mother?" Justan asked. They were standing next to the moat when the funeral procession started pouring out of the Rune Tower gates.

Mourners and the veterans of the war lined the main road. The procession was set to travel out along the main road to the gates where the outer walls used to be and back. The academy's portion of the funeral was first and would be the longest.

Darlan glanced at him. "You look ridiculous, son. When Jhonate sees you, she's going to make you change."

He winced, hoping she wasn't right. He didn't have any true dress clothes, so he had chosen to wear a set of wizard's robes in blue and gold with his swords strapped on the outside. It would have been easier if he were able to wear his sheaths at his belt, but his swords were too long for that.

Darlan shook her head. "To answer your question, I couldn't say no to them this time. I agreed to accept a position on the High Council, but in the position of Official Wizard Representative to the Battle Academy. Whenever we get the academy rebuilt I'll be staying there."

"But what about me?" Fist asked, concern flooding the bond. The ogre wore his black robes with blue and gold trim and had his hair neatly combed. Squirrel sat on his shoulder wearing a tiny little jacket that Darlan had sewn for him for the occasion. The animal was quite proud of it, too.

"You're my apprentice still, Fist. That hasn't changed. You can come with me and I can continue to teach you. But you will have to return to the school to take the proper tests before you're raised to mage."

"Good," Fist said, but his smile faltered. "Do I have to become a mage?"

"Good question," Justan said. "What's the school's stance on that one?" His own contract with the school was up and there was no way they could force a named wizard to continue taking classes.

"It's still being debated. Since you're his bonding wizard, it has been argued that you should take over my role as his master. That way he'd never have to finish his studies as long as the two of you stayed together." She frowned. "But you know my position on the mage rule. It's why I left the school in the first place."

"Because of your last apprentice?" Fist asked.

"Look, Beth was at the point in her magic that she was fully capable of using it without being a danger to anyone," Darlan replied. "When they decided to quell her despite my objections, I couldn't take it anymore."

"She's done well for herself. It seems to me she turned out just fine," Justan said, looking over to where Hilt and Beth stood watching the procession. The two of them were planning on going back to Malaroo after the funeral was over. It had been a sad moment when Deathclaw had given her the Jharro whistle back the day before.

"Just fine?" Darlan snapped. "Justan, she can't have children. The quelling did that to her. Quelling is something that should be saved only as a punishment for severe crimes, not just for wanting to leave the school early." Darlan looked at Beth and Hilt and her glare faded. "I am glad to see that she's happy, though."

"Well, you're in a position to change things now, being back on the council," Justan said encouragingly.

"That's what I told Beehn I would do when he asked me to come back." She snorted. "He actually told me that was a good thing. 'The Mage School needs changes,' he said."

"Isn't that a good thing?" Justan asked.

"I didn't want to do it at all!" she said loud enough that a few of the mourners turned to look at her. Her face colored. "This just means I have to sit in a room full of old men and argue, leading them about by the ear all day."

"I think you'll enjoy that," Justan said. She shot him a withering glare and he left her side, looking for Jhonate. The last he had seen her, she had gone to put on her own formal attire. She had wanted to wear something traditional to her people and Beth had been helping her make it.

As he walked, he saw Deathclaw standing next to Charz and Alfred. One good thing that had come out of their long separation was that Deathclaw had become more comfortable being around other people. Justan moved over to them, intending to ask Alfred a question.

"You shouldn't have put away your sword all those years ago," Charz was saying. "I know what you were scared of, Alfred. But you're not like me."

"Oh, but I am," Alfred kept his eyes on the procession and didn't look back at the giant as he spoke. "All those years ago when you were on your rampage and Master Oslo and I were chasing after you and fighting off soldiers . . . I never had so much fun."

Charz chuckled. "Oslo was horrified, I remember. But loving to fight isn't your problem."

"Oh isn't it?" Alfred said.

"The difference between us is that I wanted to fight everyone," Charz said. "You wanted to fight the bad guys. You never would've done the things I did."

The gnome sighed. "I wasn't so sure of that. After Oslo died, fighting is all I wanted to do. Latva saved me from that."

"Naw," Charz replied, placing one large hand on the gnome's shoulder. "That was just you grieving."

Deathclaw moved over to Justan and nodded his head towards the procession. "Is this long?"

Each of the slain was laid out on a floating stone tablet pushed by one of his or her friends. The warriors were dressed in their armor, mended and polished, while an image of their face and reminders of their past deeds floated above them.

"There are a lot of them that died in this war," Justan explained. "We remember them all this way. It's a tribute to their sacrifice."

Deathclaw thought on it a moment. *This is . . . fitting for humans. Dead raptoids are left in the sands as a trap for the carrion feeders. In that way, the dead ones feed the pack for some time after they die.*

Justan didn't know how to respond to that. "Alfred, have you thought on where you're going after this?"

"I'm not sure." The gnome shook his head. "I'm afraid I'm losing my ability to concentrate already. All I've been interested in lately is battle."

"Grieving," Charz repeated.

"There are other wizards," Deathclaw said in an attempt to be helpful.

Justan winced, but Alfred didn't seem to be offended. "I just want it to be someone smart."

"Hey!" said Charz.

"I was wondering if you might consider coming to the academy," Justan suggested. "With Sabre Vlad gone, they need a new head of the swordsmanship guild. You could teach."

"I don't know. Gnome warriors don't make good teachers. I'll think on it, though." He sighed. "We'll see how stupid I get first."

"Hey!" said Charz again.

"Don't worry Charz. You get a say in this," Alfred patted the rock giant's arm. "We're in this together."

Charz smiled. "The academy could be fun. Lots of sparring. Lots of quests to fight monsters . . ."

Justan left them and continued on, looking for Jhonate. Where was she? He passed the central fountain and edged his way around the square.

"What're you doin' son?" Lenny and Bettie were standing with the rest of the dwarves. Lenny was wearing his polished plate armor, his helmet held under his arm. Bettie stood behind him, head and shoulders taller than the dwarf.

"I'm looking for Jhonate," Justan said. "Have you seen her?"

"Sure did," Lenny said. He leaned towards Justan, his eyes wide. "She was runnin' down the line wearin' a dag-gum dress!"

"Really?" Justan said, just as surprised as Lenny looked. He tried to imagine Jhonate in a dress, but he just couldn't.

Bettie slapped Lenny upside the head. "'Course she's wearing a dress, you corn-farmer! It's a funeral." Bettie's clothes were clean, but not fancy at all. She was wearing workman's clothes, leather pants with heavy boots, and a loose fitting tan shirt that still managed to bulge out under her belly.

"Never seen that woman wearin' nothin' but armor," Lenny grumped, raising a bushy eyebrow at her, but wisely not mentioning her lack of dress attire.

"Hey, Edge!" Bettie said suddenly. "Feel!" She grabbed his hand and yanked him over so she could place it on her belly. The baby kicked against his hand so hard he imagined he could feel its individual little toes.

"That's quite an impressive kick," Justan said with a nod.

"He's a Firegobbler," Lenny said proudly.

"It could be a she," Bettie said. A mage could have told them the gender of the child, but Bettie didn't want to know.

"I know what it's going to be," Justan teased.

"The hell you do," Betty growled.

"A little bird told me," he said. The baby was a boy. He'd asked around and Matron Guernfeldt had finally told him. He'd received a pinched rear for his trouble, but it had been worth it.

"A big-ol' handsy dag-burned bird's more likely," Lenny said with a knowing frown. "Best not say nothin' though. If'n you spoil the surprise, Bettie's liable to un-invite you to the weddin'."

"Did you decide when it's going to be?" Justan asked. Bettie had finally agreed to marry the dwarf after they'd come back from the battle with Mellinda. Justan wasn't sure what she'd been holding out for and Lenny wasn't saying. Fist seemed to think Squirrel had convinced her.

"We're gonna have it in Wobble after the baby's born," Bettie said.

"Yeah, we're leavin' here with Tolivar tomorrow to head to Coal's Keep. Bettie wants to have the baby there," Lenny said. "Then we'll head to Wobble'n make sure Chugk's got the gall-durn place set up right."

"I wouldn't miss it," Justan said with a smile. "Is that where you'll stay?"

Lenny sighed and Bettie spoke up for him. "Nope. Lenui here's gonna be the Wobble representative on the Academy Council."

"Really?" Justan said. "They roped you into it?"

"Temporarily," Lenny grumbled. "Till we got everthin' up'n runnin'. Then someone else can do it."

Bettie ignored him. "I'm gonna join the academy. Lenui don't like it but I already spoke to your dad and Harley and Oz. They say they'll need a new forgemaster once the academy's rebuilt."

"The academy ain't no place fer a dag-gum baby, much less a baby dwarf." Lenny grumbled, but it was evidently an argument he'd already lost because Bettie didn't shout back at him.

"She'll be raised with a hammer in her hands just like a Firegobbler should be," she declared firmly. "And she won't be a dwarf. She'll be half-dwarf."

"He'll be more dwarf than anythin' else, so that makes him a dwarf!" Lenny said.

Justan left them to argue and continued past the square where Willum and Samson stood. Swen the Feather stood on one side of Willum, his long face looking as if it were carved from wood, and Kathy the Plate stood on Willum's other side with her helmet tucked under one arm, one hand on Willum's shoulder. Justan had never seen Kathy with her helmet off before. Her blond hair was cut short and she had a pretty face, with a smattering of freckles across her nose.

"Hey, have you seen-." He began, but he shut his mouth when he saw who was coming up in the procession.

Justan stood solemnly with the rest of them as Zambon's body came along the center road pushed by his father. Tolivar's jaw was set, his eyes red-rimmed as he moved his son's floating tablet. An image of Zambon's smiling face hung in the air above him along with a list of his deeds and accomplishments that constantly rotated so they could all be read.

Zambon, son of Master Tolivar, graduate of the Dremaldrian Battle Academy. Served honorably as guard in the Dremald Palace and the Mage School. Assisted in the liberation of the prisoners of Vriil Keep. Assisted in the rescue of villagers in the Trafalgan Mountains. Assisted in the rescue of the Battle Academy and refugees of Reneul from Ewzad Vriil's goblinoid army. Veteran of the Battle of Sampo Road. Commander of Berserker forces in the Battle of Vriil's Folly.

Justan swallowed back the lump in his throat. Calling it the Battle of Vriil's Folly had been Willum's idea. He said Theodore had suggested it. Justan thought it was an appropriate name.

When Tolivar had passed by, Willum turned and gave him a sad smile. "Hello, Sir Edge."

"Just call me Edge, Willum." he said. "We're friends."

Willum nodded. "Did you hear we're leaving soon?"

"Bettie said you were going back to Coal's Keep tomorrow?" Justan said.

"Yeah. The Mage School kept Coal's body preserved. We're taking him home. Becca and Benjo don't know what happened yet. I'm not looking forward to that part."

"I'm so sorry," Justan said. "I wish I could go with you, but-."

"It's alright, Edge," Samson said. The centaur gave him a reassuring smile. "We know you have responsibilities here. We would like you to come back and visit, though. Everyone back at the farm would love to see you. Fist and Gwyrtha too, of course. I think Becca and Nala will be disappointed we didn't lug him back there with us."

"I will visit," Justan promised. "Fist would drag me there even if I didn't want to go. Is that where you're going to stay, Willum?"

"I'm not sure," Willum looked down at a sheet of parchment that was clutched in his hand. He handed it to Justan. "This came today."

Justan opened it up and as he read the flowing writing his eyes widened. "This is from Captain Demetrius." He read on and looked back to Willum in surprise.

"It's okay," Willum said, indicating Swen and Kathy. "They know."

"To Willum Odd Blade, Son of Nedney Pross and Jolie Vriil, Heir to House Vriil?" Justan frowned. "Who told him?"

"Father did," Willum said. "The day before you came to break the siege. He wanted Demetrius to know Dann Dowdy's crimes as well as Ewzad Vriil's part in my parent's death. I told him it was okay."

Justan continued to read. It was very dry and procedural.

"He . . . wants you to place your claim to the Vrill lands and fortune?"

"The Pross family says that the Vriil holdings should fall to their care since my father was a Pross," Willum sighed. "I'm inclined to let them. I've never wanted to be a noble. Besides, the Pross family is as good as any of the other noble families when it comes to the way they treat the people living in their lands."

"You would be better," Swen said. "The Pross family isn't cruel, but they still overtax their people. My parents live on Pross land."

"Yeah, well I wish they'd just erase the whole Vriil name!" Willum said.

"Your mother was a Vriil," Samson reminded. Willum chewed his lip and the centaur said, "They gave you until spring to decide. You have all fall and winter."

"You'll make the right decision," Kathy said, patting his shoulder. "But we'll miss you at the academy if you stay away."

Justan gave the letter back to Willum. "She's right. I'm sure you'll make the right decision."

"Yeah," Willum said and his brow was furrowed in thought.

"Have any of you seen Jhonate?" Justan asked.

"She was riding by on Gwyrtha a few minutes ago," Samson said.

"Her? Riding Gwyrtha?" Justan said incredulously. Jhonate would never admit it, but she was afraid to ride her. Gwyrtha begged her all the time and she always said no.

"And she was wearing a dress," said Kathy with an amused shake of her head. "I've never seen her outside of armor or traveling clothes."

Swen smiled at her. "You're one to talk."

Gwyrtha? Is Jhonate with you? Justan asked.

We ride! she said happily.

Can you bring her to me? Justan asked.

Yes! she replied. A few moments later he saw them coming, making a wide circuit around the center square, avoiding the crowds. Jhonate was riding high in the stirrups, leaning forward, her hands gripping Gwyrtha's mane. There was relief in her eyes when she saw him.

Justan's breath caught in his throat. She was wearing a long, flowing white dress that didn't seem to bunch up at the knees even though she was riding. Her hair was done up in a way Justan had not seen before. The braids that framed her face still hung long, but the rest of her hair was pulled up in an elaborate bun on the top.

Gwyrtha skidded to a stop at Justan's feet and Jhonate threw her arms around the rogue horse's neck, afraid she would be flung off. She grumbled as she swung her leg over, then sighed, grateful that she was back on the ground.

The dress was of a style new to him. White, embroidered with green thread in an intricate pattern, and tied with a wide green ribbon at her waist. She looked him up and down. "What are you wearing? You look ridiculous."

"You look . . . beautiful," Justan said, stunned.

"It is a dress the Roo use for formal occasions. Beth helped me with it," Jhonate said, looking down at the dress. "She is an excellent seamstress. I worked on the embroidery myself."

Ride, Justan? Gwyrtha said. *I can get big. Both of you could ride.*

Not now, sweetie, he said numbly, still taking Jhonate in. It was draped on her very well.

"Stop looking at me like that," Jhonate said, glancing away, her cheeks coloring, but there was a smile on her lips.

"I'm sorry I can't help it. You know I've never seen you in a dress before."

She rolled her eyes. "Everyone I have spoken to today has said that."

"I also can't believe you were riding Gwyrtha," he remarked.

She looked back at the rogue horse. "I decided that if we are going to spend the rest of our lives together, I should get used to the beast. I asked her to take me to you, but she's just been running me all over the grounds."

Gwyrtha! Justan knew she could have found him immediately. She was just taking advantage of the opportunity to carry Jhonate around.

She wanted to ride, the rogue horse said innocently.

Jhonate pulled her staff from the straps on the side of the

saddle. Her dress twirled as she turned back to face him and Justan couldn't handle it anymore. He grabbed Jhonate by the waist and pulled her in close.

"Do we really need to wait a year? Let's go tomorrow. I'm ready to allow myself to be beaten half to death by your father if that's what it takes."

"We have discussed this," Jhonate replied gently, reaching up to place one hand against his jaw. "I will finish out my contract. It is my duty."

"You could renegotiate," Justan teased. He let go of her waist and took her hand in his. "I happen to have connections with the head of the Academy Council. I'm pretty sure we can convince them to let you out of your contract early."

"I will have no more arguments. You know I want us to be married just as bad as you do." Her eyes smoldered. "Probably more. But I will not be tempted into backing out of my promises. Just remember I made a promise to you as well. I will marry you. A year of waiting is not going to change that."

Justan dropped her hands and let out a frustrated laugh. "All this waiting is going to be very hard on me. It will be difficult to be around you all the time, knowing I have to keep my distance."

"But you will not have to. Beth showed me something," she said. Jhonate grasped the end of her staff and gave it a slight twist. A small piece broke off in her hand. She concentrated and the gray wood formed a tiny circle. "You gave me a ring. Now I have one for you."

Justan's heart thumped as she placed it on his forefinger. He heard her voice in his mind.

I love you, Justan, she sent, her striking green eyes echoing all the emotion he felt coming through the ring.

I love you too, he replied and kissed her. At that moment he was sure it would all be worth it.

Trevor H. Cooley

Epilogue

"Just watch over her, Rufus, I'll be back shortly," John said.

The rogue horse nodded his gorilla-like head and sniffed at the basket. The infant inside gave a tiny sigh and Rufus smiled.

John patted the rogue horse's flank and headed through the trees towards the farm with the boy child in his arms. The one issue with using rogue horses for transportation is that one always had to keep them hidden. At least they were well behaved. Rufus would stay right by the child and protect it if attacked. Not that attack was a possibility in this place. John would have felt it.

Evening was falling, but he had no difficulty seeing in the dark. John came to the wooden fence at the forest's edge and leapt spryly over it. There were a few guard dogs. That was new from the last time he'd been here. But one sniff and they knew not to bother him. All creatures knew.

He stepped up to the front door and smiled. He could smell a roasted chicken along with some of that new honstule plant he had tried back at the Mage School. Children were talking animatedly inside. He raised his hand and knocked. He heard a chair creak as someone came to the door.

"I'll be right back and Jerrold, don't take your sister's potato, you know she likes to eat it last."

"Yes mother."

Footsteps approached and the door opened. A woman answered the door, pretty and in her forties with her hair tied back in a bun. Her eyes went wide when she recognized him.

"J-John!"

"Good evening, Nala," he said with a smile. "So good to see you."

"Why, would you come in?" she asked, opening the door wider. He saw the curious eyes of children peering at him from around the kitchen table.

"Sorry, I'm afraid not. I don't have much time, you see. I, uh . . . brought something for you." He held out the boy child.

She took one look at the infant and frowned. "John, that's a baby."

"Yes it is," he said. He placed it in her arms.

"Do you want me to watch it for you or something?" she asked suspiciously.

"I need you to mother it, Nala. This child needs you," he said, giving her the kindest smile he knew how.

"You're going to come knock on my door out of the blue when I haven't seen you in . . . well, since before David died and just give me a baby and say, 'Be its mother'?" she demanded, but she was already rocking it.

John swallowed. He had hoped this would go smoother. "His father was killed. He needs a strong woman and brothers and sisters . . . I immediately knew you were the mother he needed."

"You immediate-. Ugh!" She looked down at the infant. He hadn't even reacted to her outburst. He just blinked his little eyes and yawned. "You think just because you're the prophet I have to take this child. John! I am already raising these children alone! You can't just drop off another hungry mouth and he's . . . what? A week old?"

He raised his hands. "I know it is a lot to ask, but you won't be alone long."

The infant grimaced and she raised it to her shoulder and began patting his back. She gave John a scowl. "And what is that supposed to mean?"

"Well, your friends are returning. Samson and Bettie . . . they'll be back soon and they're bringing a man with them who will help you take care of your children," he assured her.

"What?" she shrieked.

The baby was startled and let out a short cry. One of the boys at the table stood. "Mom?"

"Sit down, Steffen!" she barked and the boy sat. She turned her glare on John as she comforted the child. "Now you say you've found me a new husband? What the hell, John? You can't just go around telling me what to do. I don't even know this man."

"I'm not saying you have to marry him," John said calmly. "You have your free will. You could say no when he asks you. I'm just saying that I've seen it and he does ask you and . . . you say yes." She opened her mouth to speak and he cut her off. "And one other tiny thing. You mustn't tell him that it was I who gave you the child."

That sparked another roar of outrage and it took another ten minutes of arguing before she finally bid him good night and shut the door. Thankfully she kept the baby inside. As he returned through the woods, he was glad that he hadn't followed his first instinct and brought her both babies. But as he had rode Rufus across the Wide River he had come to an understanding. It had been well known that Queen Elise had been pregnant with twins. He couldn't leave them both with the same mother. The Dark Prophet could eventually figure it out.

No, this was for the best. Besides, the two children's futures were linked. They would find each other eventually.

The rogue horse soon loomed into view. "Hello, Rufus. I trust everything went fine while I was gone?"

The rogue horse shuffled his feet and took a deep breath, then said one simple word. "Poop."

John lifted the basket and sighed. "Ah yes. She has."

He shook his head. Changing babies. Thousands of years with no children of his own and still he continued to find ways to end up changing babies. The Creator had such a sense of humor.

"Oh little one," he said as he cleaned up the child. "I am so sorry that I have to separate you from your brother. It is a necessity, you see. Don't worry though. I'll get you a good mother to raise you. I'll . . ." It came to him in a sudden vision as such things often did with the prophet. Yes, that would do nicely.

"I have just the right match for you," he said to her. He wrapped her back up and placed her in the basket. "I just happen to know of a certain named warrior whose wife can't have children of her own."

*   *   *

The rain had drenched Arcon by the time he saw the cabin. He limped towards it, grateful that he hadn't been mistaken. He hadn't been to this place in so long he had almost forgotten how to find it.

The door was boarded up, but he ripped the wood free with air magic and barged inside. He could use those boards for kindling later. The cabin was small, a single room, and the ceiling leaked in one spot, but he was just glad that no goblinoids or men had claimed it.

The last time he'd been inside, was the year before his awakening. His father had taken him hunting and they had stayed in the cabin for a week while they searched for elk. They had only brought down one, but the week had been full of good memories. That didn't matter now. His father was dead and this place had been abandoned for a long time.

The only furnishings were a chair and an old straw mattress, but at least it had a fireplace. Arcon started the fire quickly and stripped his wet robes and shirt from his body. He laid them in front of the fire and sat in the chair wearing just his damp trousers as he removed his boots.

He took the right boot off with a wince. The ankle was swollen and bruised, his toes purple. He had been such an idiot. His father had always taught him to pay attention to a horse. Pace it. Don't push it too hard. But he had been so eager to get away. He had ridden the poor horse to death. When it had finally keeled over, it had rolled onto his leg.

He probed the ankle with his magic. It wasn't broken but it was a bad sprain. He cried out and slammed his leg with his fist. He couldn't afford this injury. He had to keep going. Eventually someone would contact his mother and she would tell them about this place, he was sure of it. He needed to be long gone by then.

He glanced over at the satchel he had left at the door. The rings were inside. If he wore them he could heal himself. He shook his head and laughed. No. That would be stupidity. Ewzad had turned the rings' power inward and Arcon had seen what it had done to him.

Now Ewzad was dead. Arcon was sure of it. He had been mangled, with the enemy fighting nearby. Otherwise Arcon wouldn't have chanced taking the rings. The fool had fought Mellinda and died.

The funny thing is, he'd also freed Arcon in the process. When Ewzad had slapped the witch, Arcon had felt his connection with her die. He hadn't heard her voice since. Despite his fear and pain he hadn't felt so free in his life.

Arcon reached out with his magic and flared the fire until his robe steamed as the water in it evaporated. Arcon reached out with air and pulled the dusty straw mattress nearer the fire. He hopped over to the mattress, careful not to let his injured foot touch the ground, and rolled onto it, heedless of whatever vermin might infest it.

His thoughts wandered back to the rings. What should he do with them? He knew he couldn't just turn them in to the Mage School. That wouldn't earn him forgiveness even if Mellinda hadn't destroyed them. They would just take them from him and try him and quell him. They might even have him executed. He had killed so many people at Mellinda's orders, surely there was no forgiveness.

No, but perhaps he could sell the rings. Surely the dwarf smugglers would pay handsomely for them. If not, there had to be dark wizards, maybe in Alberri or Khalpany that would reward him. He laughed at himself derisively. The problem with dealing with dark wizards is they were just as likely to kill you as to pay you.

Besides, once Mellinda heard they'd been sold he would be running from her forever. He got a chill as he realized another possibility. She could already have sent Talon after him. Suddenly this room didn't seem so safe.

He sat up and used air to pull the satchel to him and opened it. He pulled out the rings, ten of them, each with a different precious stone and each linked with a golden chain. Perhaps he should put them on. If Talon did come, their power would be his only hope.

He laid back on the mattress and held them up in the light. No matter what he did, he was damned. Still, he smiled.

"At least I'm free of you, Mellinda!" he shouted. He felt the orange eye in his chest move.

This is the conclusion of the first Bowl of Souls series

Upcoming:

A new novel based in the world of the Bowl of Souls

TARAH WOODBLADE

Keep an eye on the Trevor H. Cooley Facebook page and trevorhcooley.com for more details.

CPSIA information can be obtained
at www.ICGtesting.com
Printed in the USA
LVOW13s1541020517

533000LV00009B/1114/P